THE DEVOURING

Billy Boyle
The First Wave
Blood Alone
Evil for Evil
Rag and Bone
A Mortal Terror
Death's Door
A Blind Goddess
The Rest Is Silence
The White Ghost
Blue Madonna

On Desperate Ground
Souvenir

THE DEVOURING

A Billy Boyle World War II Mystery

James R. Benn

Published by Soho Press, Inc.
853 Broadway
New York, NY 10003

Library of Congress Cataloging-in-Publication Data

Benn, James R.
The devouring / James R. Benn
Series: A Billy Boyle WWII mystery ; 12

ISBN 978-1-61695-773-5
eISBN 978-1-61695-774-2

1. Boyle, Billy (Fictitious character)—Fiction. 2. World War, 1939–1945—
Fiction. 3. Murder—Investigation—Fiction. I. Title

PS3602.E6644 D48 2017   813'.6—dc23   2017003759

Printed in the United States of America

10 9 8 7 6 5 4 3 2 1

In memory of Ranger
2002–2016

Faithful companion,
by my side for twelve Billy Boyle novels.

When gold speaks every tongue is silent.

—ITALIAN PROVERB

CHAPTER ONE

LIGHT IS FASTER than sound.

Strange, the things you think about when you're about to die. Even as tracers lit the night air, their silent silvery phosphorescence clawing at our small aircraft from the ground below, a tiny part of my brain mused on this practical demonstration of that scientific fact. The rest of my brain panicked madly, sending surges of adrenaline coursing through my body, urging me to get the hell out, *now*.

Which was not at all helpful, given that we were flying at five hundred feet, heading directly into heavy antiaircraft fire, making one hundred and eighty miles per hour.

Then came the sound. The chattering of ack-ack fire. Flak exploding in blinding flashes all around us. Shrapnel struck the aircraft, rending the metal, sounding like the devil's own hail storm on a sheet-metal roof.

"Hold tight!" shouted the pilot as he dove the Lysander and put it through twists and turns to evade the lead rising up against us. I looked below as he dipped the airplane and saw the twinkling of automatic fire from along the stretch of river we'd been following.

"They're on the road," I shouted to the pilot in the single front seat. It was a column of German vehicles, moving at night to avoid Allied aircraft, and we'd flown dead at them.

The pilot didn't waste breath answering. He banked left, violently, diving to treetop level at a right angle away from the river. Looking back, I saw tracer fire searching vainly for us, then fade as the Krauts gave up and continued on their way.

The Lysander jolted, loud *thumps* whacking against the aircraft frame.

"Sorry, chaps," the pilot muttered, pulling back on the yoke and gaining altitude. "Almost landed in the pines. She's a bit sluggish, might've caught some shrapnel in the rudder." He banked the Lysander, bringing us around to the river again, the only map to our destination.

"There may be other columns on the road," Kaz said, adjusting his steel-rimmed spectacles. Even after nearly being blown out of the sky and tossed around inside the cramped Lysander, he managed to sound nonchalant, his precise English leavened with the slightest of Polish accents.

"The Saône River is our only landmark," the pilot said. "Jerry's travel plans notwithstanding. If we veer off to the east, we run the risk of entering Swiss airspace. It'd be damned embarrassing to be shot down by the Swiss, after all."

"Why?" Kaz asked.

"You know the Swiss. Chocolate, watches, and sheep, that's what they're famous for. I'd never hear the end of it, if I lived to tell the tale."

"Personally, I'd choose death by chocolatier if I had any say in the matter," Kaz responded. Switzerland was our ultimate destination, and we weren't in the market for wristwatches.

"Don't worry about the Swiss or the Jerries," the pilot said. "I haven't lost a Joe yet, and I don't plan on starting tonight."

We were his Joes. It was what the Special Operations Executive pilots called the agents and commandoes they flew into occupied Europe. No names, nothing to reveal if captured and tortured, just an anonymous one-way ride to some grassy field in the countryside. In a few minutes we were back on course, flying low over dark hills and a glistening waterway, the bright half-moon at our backs providing a tempting target for alert Kraut gunners, the river our only guide.

"What's the next landmark?" I asked the nameless pilot.

"We'll bear left at the Rhône River in Lyon. There's a sharp bend in the river, it'll be easy to spot, even with only a half-moon. Then

Lake Gris, a narrow lake about twelve miles long. I set us down outside of Cessens, in a nice open field on a ridge overlooking the water. A bit tricky, but very secluded."

Tricky I didn't mind, if it meant no Krauts.

We flew on, no sign of movement below us, not a single light visible in the blacked-out countryside. The drone of the engine was mesmerizing, lulling us into a sense of security and safety, the sudden, surprising bright barrage of fire now behind us. The high, clear canopy gave us a majestic view of the sparkling heavens. The half-moon, the stars, and the faint glow from the instrument panel our only illuminations, guiding us as we traveled across a calm sea of inky black.

I almost relaxed.

"What is that?" Kaz asked, leaning forward and pointing at two o'clock. Searchlights flickered in the distance, an orange glow growing at the horizon.

"Bloody Bomber Command most likely," the pilot answered in a low growl. "Hitting the rail yards in Lyon. Or the airfield west of the city. Either way, they've stirred up a hornet's nest for us."

"Can we go around it?" I asked.

"No," he said. "I don't have the fuel. We're at the extreme range as it is. I topped off at a forward airstrip in Normandy, but I've barely enough to make it back."

"We must fly through that?" Kaz asked. As we drew closer, the night sky grew brighter with searchlights, explosions, and burning buildings.

"Unless you Joes want to abort the mission. Say the word and I'll turn around."

"Have you ever had to abort?" I asked.

"No. Thought I'd offer, that's all," he said, turning to smile at us. SOE pilot humor, I guess. "It's not as bad as it looks, mates. We're under their radar, and the Jerries are looking for high-altitude bombers, not our little Lysander."

"Don't fly under the bomber formation," Kaz said. "Being hit by an RAF bomb would be more embarrassing than being shot down by the Swiss."

"Right you are," the pilot said. "Now all we need to do is catch a glimpse of the Rhône River. It'll be even easier with the sky all lit up. Jerry's doing us a favor!"

That was one way of looking at it.

We drew closer to the city, the searchlights casting wide beams of white light, looking like columns holding up the night sky. Phosphorescent tracer bullets sought out the bombers, dancing against the darkness in graceful, deadly arcs. Bombs exploded in front of us, maybe a quarter of a mile away. The pilot banked the Lysander, moving away from the flames and smoke. The aircraft shook as shock waves from the explosions buffeted us, sending the plane into a sideways dive. The ground looked damned close.

"Hang on," the pilot told us, as if we hadn't already figured that one out. He pulled the small craft up, his voice a nervous quiver he couldn't quite hide. "That's the main rail yard. We should be fine now. Look, there's the river."

It was the Rhône, heading west from the burning city, shimmering with moonlight and mayhem, antiaircraft fire dying down as the bomber stream departed.

"Is the airplane damaged?" Kaz asked. There was a metallic rattle coming from the fuselage.

"She's banged up," the pilot said. "But I can hold her steady, don't worry. The good news is I can cut some time off our trip and make sure you chaps get to Cessens. The Rhône meanders a good bit, so I'll cut across the bends heading ninety degrees west. That'll bring us to Lake Gris all the quicker."

"What's the bad news?" I asked.

"It will bring us close to a Luftwaffe airfield. Sounds worse than it is, really. Any night fighters they have left will be airborne, going after the bombers. We'll scoot right by. You should be on the ground in thirty minutes."

"So the airfield poses no danger?" Kaz asked, his tone skeptical.

"Right. Long as one of the flak batteries doesn't open up on us. So, once again, hang on." He increased speed and lost altitude, skimming the treetops until we found ourselves over open fields. It felt as if he were going in for a landing at two hundred miles an hour. The rattle clanged even faster, the fuselage shuddering as we raced for the next bend in the river.

"Airfield coming up on the right," the pilot informed us through clenched teeth as he held the yoke firmly in his hands.

"There," Kaz said, pointing to black shapes that were probably hangers. The landscape zipped by underneath us, and we were nearly clear, about to leave the blacked-out airfield behind.

Then the sky lit up.

Searchlights, some only a few hundred yards away.

Bright explosions ripped into the blackness ahead, followed by a series of blasts falling across our path. I lifted my hands to shield my eyes as one of the beams caught us, sending blinding white light into the canopy. More explosions sounded as the pilot climbed, seeking to escape the clutches of the searchlight and the antiaircraft fire it would soon bring to bear.

Concussions from the bombs hit us, shaking the Lysander, dragging it through the sky as if it were a kite on a string. We'd guessed wrong. The bombers were targeting both the rail yards and the airfield. We'd flown straight into the second raid.

The light found us again, staying with the Lysander even as the pilot gave up on altitude and put the nose down, hoping to shake the flak. Tracers burned the night sky, hitting us in the wing, shearing metal, and sending us into a spin.

The searchlight lost us. I grabbed onto my seat and Kaz's arm, hoping the pilot could steady the aircraft. I braced for impact.

It didn't come. The sturdy Lysander managed to fly straight, so low we could've been hit by a well-thrown stone. I craned my neck to see behind us, the orange glow of flames and the white searchlights fading in the distance. Wind whistled through a bullet hole in the canopy, the clanging rattle of metal still sounding from within the fuselage.

"The aircraft is damaged," Kaz said, as calmly as he might observe that it may well rain.

"She'll get you there, don't you worry," the pilot said. "Although getting me back home is another thing altogether."

"You are welcome to join us, if you wish," Kaz said.

"Not in the cards, Joe. The Germans would love to get their hands on a Lysander. I'll stay with the plane until you're safely away and then put the torch to her. Maybe I'll get lucky and spend the rest of the war learning French from a farmer's daughter, if Jerry doesn't catch me."

"Sorry," I said. I felt bad for him, but at the same time I was glad he didn't take Kaz up on the invite. Things would be tough enough without an extra man along. If he was lucky, our Resistance contacts would leave somebody with him. But we had places to go, and fast.

"*C'est la guerre,*" he answered, the yoke vibrating violently in his hands.

A harsh knock came from the engine, followed by a metal-on-metal grating. The propeller stopped. Oil sprayed the windscreen.

"Oh shit," the pilot said.

The Lysander dropped from the sky.

CHAPTER TWO

"BILLY! WAKE UP!"

I felt someone push me. It was Kaz, bracing himself against my shoulder and grunting in between shouts for me to wake up. I tried to clear my head, but it hurt like blazes. I wanted nothing more than for him to shut up and get off me so I could go back to sleep.

Then I began to choke.

That got my attention. I tried to focus, wiping my eyes with the back of my hand. It came away wet and sticky with blood. Kaz was kicking at the canopy, using me to steady himself as he hammered away at the latch.

"It's stuck," he announced. Obviously, since otherwise why would we be inside a crashed aircraft filling with smoke?

"Let me," I said, twisting around in the seat to bring my legs up. I smashed both feet against the twisted metal frame, once, twice, and then again. The latch broke as I gasped for air, and Kaz shoved the shattered canopy back. The air drew smoke like a chimney, and my gasps turned to ragged coughs.

"The pilot," I managed to croak.

"Dead," was all Kaz said as he clambered down the ladder on the side of the fuselage. "Hurry!"

I leaned forward as I made for the opening. The pilot was slumped over the yoke, his bloodied head at a terribly wrong angle. Sparks flashed on his instrument panel, followed by the soft sound of gas fumes igniting. Flames drove me back, licking at my limbs as I made for the open canopy and jumped to the ground. I rolled into Kaz's arms and he dragged me away as fire spread from the engine, half-buried in the damp ground. It filled the rear compartment, roaring and swirling within the Perspex enclosure, the blaze an angry crimson column as it raced out the opening and into the air.

Then the fuel tank went up, a bright, searing fireball lifting the Lysander and slamming it back into the earth in a flurry of broken metal and black smoke. The heat scorched our faces as we scrambled backward, arms linked and eyes fixed on the conflagration.

"Are you badly injured?" Kaz asked.

I didn't know.

"I don't think so," I said, feeling my forehead. I winced as I found a gash on my scalp, hair matted in sticky blood. "We have to move."

"Right. We are not far beyond the airfield. This fire will be visible for miles, and the Germans are sure to investigate." Kaz helped me up, his eyes darting to the horizon. We were in the middle of a field, lush green grass that might have made good grazing for some farmer's herd of sheep. Our pilot picked the crash site well, if he'd had any say in the matter.

"Which way?" I asked. Kaz took a compass from his pocket and waited for the luminous hand to steady. The burning wreckage cast a flickering light against his face, the steel-rimmed glasses reflecting a shimmering yellow glow. His high cheekbones were marred on one side by a scar that split his face from eye to chin. The other side was darkness. Much like Kaz himself.

"East is that way," he said, snapping the compass shut and nodding toward the forested hillside ahead.

I brushed the dirt from my trousers and adjusted the strap of the small rucksack across my shoulder. We each had a few supplies. K rations, maps, matches, a flashlight, and extra cartridges, not to mention a wad of Swiss francs. We were both armed with a revolver, no real match for a swarm of Krauts looking for downed airmen.

Then it hit me.

The rear canopy was open. They'd know someone made it out, which meant they'd come looking. I stopped, watching the inferno burning itself out. But not fast enough. Kaz caught my eye, nodding his understanding.

We searched the ground for a stick or a branch, anything big enough to push the canopy closed without getting too close to the red-hot fuselage. I came up with a tree limb, probably snapped off by the crash. I tried to push against the canopy, but it was the wrong angle. The canopy opened to the rear, sliding on rails. With the aircraft nose down, it was too high to reach, and besides, the branch gave me nothing to grab on with.

"I could climb the ladder," Kaz said as I threw the useless wood aside. Lysanders had a metal ladder built into the side, to make for quick drop-offs and pickups. From the top, only a few steps up, the canopy would be within easy reach.

"The metal on the canopy is too hot," I said. "Not to mention the ladder itself. How could you grab hold?"

"Give me your overcoat," Kaz said. We were wearing civilian clothes, and I was taller by almost a head. He was going to use the longer sleeves as gloves.

"You sure?" I asked as I shed my wool overcoat.

"It's better than being chased by Germans," he said. He put my coat on over his, giving him more protection from the heat. I emptied my rucksack, putting the strap across his shoulder.

"Use this to snag the handle and pull it shut," I said. He tucked his hands as far inside the sleeves as they'd go and reached for the rung. The flames weren't as ferocious as before, but the fuel was still burning off. The stench of roasted flesh assailed us, and for a second, we both staggered back. I cupped my hands to give Kaz a boost. With one hand on my shoulder, the other grasping hot metal, he started up. I prayed the thick wool would protect him.

Two steps and he was close to the canopy. Still holding on with one hand, he leaned back and tossed the strap at the handle, tantalizingly close.

He missed.

Another toss, another miss. I checked the horizon in the direction of the airfield. Maybe they weren't coming.

Kaz made another throw, this time hitting the mark. He let go of the ladder, pulling on the rucksack with both hands. He grunted, leaning away from the fuselage. He yelled, cursing in Polish as he pulled as hard as he could.

The canopy slid forward. Kaz tumbled from the ladder, falling onto me. We both hit the ground hard.

"Are you okay?" I asked, checking his hand. The fabric was smoking.

"Yes, I think so." He shook his hand and winced. "A small burn, perhaps, but nothing too bad."

I could see a red line in his palm by the light of the fire. Another few seconds and it would have been much worse.

"But we must take care of that," he said, pointing to the canopy. The rucksack hung from the exterior handle. I looked around for the branch, which would now come in handy. As I did, I saw a faint light in the distance. Moving. Bouncing, as if going over a country road.

"Germans!" I whispered, even though I could have shouted without my voice carrying far enough to worry. On the run in civilian clothes behind enemy lines had that kind of effect. I grabbed the rucksack and gathered up the contents I'd emptied from it. The headlights were closer now, coming cross country and making for the burning wreckage. Kaz tossed me my coat and we hightailed it out of there, due east, up a gently rising knoll, until we were safely under cover in the pines.

"Give me your hand," I said, opening the first-aid kit. I squeezed burn ointment into his palm and wrapped it with gauze. Kaz whispered his thanks as we peered into the night, watching two trucks park near the Lysander, headlights illuminating the ground around it. Germans swarmed about the aircraft, dark smoke billowing from the engine as the fire lessened. I could make out shouted orders and saw soldiers fanning out in a methodical search. Nothing unusual about that. If they thought this was a planned landing gone bad, there might be members of the Resistance nearby. Not that any sane SOE pilot would voluntarily set down a few miles from a Luftwaffe airfield.

"We should go," Kaz said.

"Right," I said, stuffing the medical kit back into my rucksack. I rummaged through the contents, looking for the map, hoping it included our current area.

It wasn't there.

"Damn," I said with a hiss. "The map's gone. I thought I put it back."

"They might not find it," Kaz said. "Or they may think it came from the aircraft. The front canopy was fairly smashed." A dog barked. Sharp, mad dog growls.

"If he has a scent from the map—" I said.

"Run," Kaz said, grabbing me by the shoulder. I followed, working to keep Kaz in sight. Moonlight was sparse within the pine forest, the sound of Kaz's feet on the soft ground my best guide. We both took a few tumbles, tripping on roots and rocks invisible in the gloomy dark.

Soon the land began to slope downward, and we sped up, sliding and careening through stands of dead pine, many of the trees snapped in a windstorm like matchsticks.

"Careful," I panted, catching up to Kaz. "We don't need a broken leg."

"That would be inconvenient," he said, gasping for breath. "As would be a German shepherd at my throat." We took a quick rest, heaving in the crisp night air, listening for sounds of the chase. Barks echoed against the hillside, the dog excited at the prospect of a moon-light hunt.

"How fast can a dog run?" Kaz asked.

"Plenty fast," I said. "But his handler won't let him run free. He'll keep a tight leash until he has us in sight."

"And then?"

"Then they shoot us, or unleash the dog. Unless we give up, and then they shoot us later."

"The prospects are quite limited, Billy. Is there anything can we do?"

"Keep running, for one. There's a chance that dog is a plain old guard dog. He'd be dangerous if he saw us, but if he's not trained to follow a scent, all we need to do is stay ahead of him."

"Let's go," Kaz said. "Since we have no way of knowing, we should assume he is tracking us. Although it is *your* scent on the map, Billy."

Before I had a chance at a wiseacre comeback, the barking started up again. Too close for comfort, tracker or guard dog.

I wet my finger and held it up. The wind was coming from the east, the direction we were headed.

"We could start a fire," I said. "It's the only thing that could throw him off the scent."

"Burn all traces," Kaz said. "Good."

"The smoke will do most of the work. The wind will blow it right in their faces. Gather some wood."

We were surrounded by dead and weathered limbs, perfect for starting a forest fire. The trick was to get it going fast. They'd spot the fire in no time, so it had to be a blazing inferno with thick, choking smoke before they got too close. We stacked small branches against a fallen tree and I lit a match. The wind blew it out. I tried another, shielding it with my body. The flame took, climbing twigs and brush until it leaped onto larger sticks, the dry pine a tinderbox of roaring, dancing fire in no time. The wind fanned the sparks, sending glowing embers out over the fallen trees.

We had our inferno.

A rapid pace took us to the crest of the next hill, where we stopped to rest and check on our pursuers. Lines of yellow and red blurred by whirling smoke snaked down the slope, obscuring our visions. And theirs. No dog barked, no boots thumped against the ground.

"They've given up?" Kaz said.

"Or wised up," I said. "Why fight your way through smoke and fire when there are other Germans to the east? There have to be patrols along the Swiss border."

"We're not close enough for border patrols," Kaz said. "I prefer to think they've gone back to their warm beds. No reason for all of us to be miserable out here."

"You're a prince, Kaz," I said, slapping him on the shoulder as we leaned into the wind and continued our eastward journey.

"A mere baron, Billy, but thank you."

CHAPTER THREE

THE ESTEEMED BARON Piotr Augustus Kazimierz and I huddled in a shepherd's abandoned cottage. At least I hoped it was abandoned, since that would mean no one else had been forced to spend a night in this dump for years. It smelled like a barnyard and the wind howled through the one window, which held no more than a shard or two of glass. Moldy blankets littered a rough-hewn bed frame. We stretched out on the hard-packed dirt floor, which was the cleanest thing in sight.

Kaz—I called him that since his full name was a mouthful—was a lieutenant in the Polish Army in Exile. He and I worked for General Eisenhower, which probably had a lot to do with why we were in this ramshackle hut in southeastern France right now. Last night we'd had a rendezvous with an SOE Lysander. Special Operations Executive, that is. Lysanders are SOE's preferred means to ferry agents in and out of occupied France. We'd expected to be taken back to London after our last assignment, but someone had a better idea: send the two of us to the Swiss border, smuggle us across, and then have us make contact with the OSS, a different group of highly dangerous letters. The Office of Strategic Services was an American outfit, modeled after the SOE. Why they wanted us in neutral Switzerland, I had no clue, but I did have hopes it would be a rest cure in a peaceful nation. Some wags claimed OSS stood for "Oh So Social," since they drew a lot of personnel from Ivy League schools and the elites of industry,

Wall Street, and high-powered law offices. If it meant reservations at a nice hotel, I had no problems with their pedigrees.

But we were a long hike from the Swiss border. First we had to make it to Cessens and meet our French Resistance contact. Then a team of Jedburghs—SOE commando types—would get us across the border, evading both German patrols and Swiss border guards. After that, our orders were to meet with an OSS operative in Geneva, not too far from the border. Easy, right? That's what our pilot said when he'd briefed us at the pickup. Now he was a charred corpse.

It was supposed to have been so easy that we weren't prepared for an overland trek. We were dressed in suits and overcoats, with civilian IDs using our real names. The paperwork showed that we were attached to the American Legation as assistant economic *attachés* which would hold water for about ten minutes if anyone questioned us. Travel in or out of Switzerland was limited and strictly regulated. The Swiss government knew exactly how many diplomats were attached to each legation. Right now I would have happily traded my phony identification for a Thompson submachine gun and a grenade. All we had were the meager supplies in our rucksacks.

I was too worried to sleep. Kaz snored softly as I listened to the sounds of the forest, every rustle of leaves and gust of wind making me grip my .38 Police Special revolver even tighter.

"Billy, wake up," Kaz said, his low voice penetrating through the fog of sleep. Okay, so fatigue had trumped worry.

"What?" He pointed in the direction of the broken window. Outside, a man stood cradling a rifle. He was watching us, his face devoid of expression, the rising sun painting the clouds pink at his back.

"Bonjour," Kaz said, smiling as he slowly stood and pushed open the door. I followed suit, grinning at the prospect of better accommodations. The fellow didn't smile back, or do much of anything. He stared at each of us in turn, his rifle held lazily within the crook of his arm. He wore a black beret covering long, dark, curly hair. His corduroy pants were mud stained, and as dirty as his worn leather jacket and threadbare sweater. His boots, the bayonet in its leather scabbard, and his Kar 98k rifle were all German.

"Resistance?" I asked.

"Comment vouz appelles-vouz?" Kaz said, asking his name. He didn't respond, but moved toward us, taking Kaz's pack and searching through it. He studied the K ration packet, his brow furrowing as he contemplated the English description. Then he held up the box of bullets, his eyebrows raised.

Kaz understood. He slowly lifted his Webley revolver from his coat pocket, and then returned it. I did the same with my pistol. Our friend gave a quick nod, the closest we'd come to any kind of communication.

Kaz unfolded his map and held it open. *"Où sommes-nous?"* Yeah, it would be nice to know where we were. He studied the map, Kaz still gripping it. He smiled and pointed to a spot in the air, about a foot to the left of the sheet.

"I guess mine was the one we needed," I said as Kaz folded and stowed his map.

"Yes, this one shows more of Switzerland," Kaz said. *"Suisse?"* he asked, his finger tracing the Swiss border.

The swarthy fellow spat, his dark eyes narrowing at the mention of the nation. He crooked his finger and strode off. Kaz offered up a shrug and followed. We didn't have much choice, so why not? Any port in a storm, any Resistance fighter when you're lost in the forest. If that's who he really was.

He led us up another steep hill. The terrain was a series of folds in the landscape: a hill, a narrow valley, then an even higher hill. We trudged along, on paths and through meadows ripe with wildflowers. It was mid-June, and spring was in full bloom. Scant days ago, men had fought, struggled, and died to assault the beaches in Normandy. It felt strange to be walking amid such beauty, heading to neutral safety, as the battle to liberate France raged a few hundred miles to the north.

We neared the top. The trees were thinner here, and we moved with care along a rocky path, hunched over and heads down, watching the terrain ahead for any sign of movement. At the ridgeline, the view was stunning. Below, a wide valley glistened in the sunlight, a broad river cutting through lush green fields. In the far distance, snowcapped peaks floated in the haze.

"Switzerland," Kaz said. Our guide—or whatever he was—didn't respond.

"Cessens?" I asked, keeping things local. "Lake Gris?" At the mention of the lake, he faced me, his eyes quiet pools of dark light. He held my gaze for a long time, then glanced at my pack. I got the message. I broke open the K rations and gave him the can of diced eggs and ham. It went into his pocket, along with the small pack of Chesterfields. He sat, stretching out his legs on a flat rock. I handed around crackers and we all munched in silence, enjoying the view.

"*Américaine?*" His voice was gruff, nearly a growl, as if he didn't use it much. He pointed at me as he picked crumbs from his bushy mustache. I nodded.

"*Anglais?*" he asked Kaz, a sneer on his lips.

"*Polonais,*" Kaz said. That got something close to a smile, Poles obviously being in his favor more than the English.

"Cessens," he said, pointing with a sweep of his hand to the opposite side of the river, to the southeast. His hand moved to the right, pointing out a high ridge and waving as if jumping over it. "*Lac Gris.*"

"Is that the Rhône?" I asked Kaz.

"Yes. It's the last bend in the river before Cessens. It looks much wider than it did from the air, doesn't it?"

"Yeah. How do you say boat in French?"

"*Bateau. Avez-vous un bateau?*" Kaz leaned over to look the fellow in the eyes.

He shrugged. Maybe he knew where we could find a boat, or maybe he was bored.

"*Comment vous appelez-vous?*" Kaz said, trying again.

"Yeah, my name's Billy. What's yours?" This attempt didn't even warrant a shrug. Ignoring our questions, he rose and began walking down the slope. With no better choice, we followed.

Below us, a road paralleled the river. We were more furtive heading down, darting from the cover of trees and hiding behind boulders until we were sure the coast was clear. There wasn't much in the way of traffic, nothing but a few bicyclists and a farmer on a horse-drawn cart. Still, it didn't pay to take chances. Any of the innocent-looking French travelers could be an informer.

We halted in a grove of saplings, the last cover before open fields and the road ahead. With a finger to his lips, he gestured for us to be quiet as he peered out from behind the trees. Then, apparently satisfied with the silence, he beckoned us to follow. He sprinted across the field to the road, diving into a ditch on the opposite side. Thick grasses provided decent cover as we lay prone, waiting for who knows what. He waved behind us, his hand forming a pistol; then he aimed his rifle through the grass, right at a bend in the road.

"He wants us to watch the rear," I said, drawing my pistol. "What the hell is he up to?"

"He appears to be waiting for someone," Kaz said, his voice a whisper. "It seems he was not guiding us anywhere. He was simply heading here for this ambush."

"Why the hell won't he talk?" I said. Kaz gave me the finger-to-the-lips treatment, which was good advice in the ambush business, I had to admit.

We waited, scrunched down in the tall grass, the river on one side, an open field on the other, in the care of an unknown rifleman waiting to fix someone in his sights.

We heard the motor. A deep-throated growl, echoing off the hills. No, it was two engines, two distinct sounds. After checking the other direction—it was clear—I watched for the vehicles to round the bend.

First came a motorcycle, with a sidecar. The passenger held a Schmeisser submachine gun. Then a staff car followed about thirty yards behind. That had to be the target. One rifle against two Krauts on the motorcycle, a driver and maybe one or two officers in the car. Not the best odds, even with the two of us and our peashooters to watch his back.

The motorcycle drew closer.

A sharp *crack* sounded as he fired, metal flying from the hood of the car. He worked the bolt and fired again. The motorcycle wobbled, swerved, and crashed, the driver having taken a hit from his second shot.

A third shot, and the windshield on the staff car shattered. Steam gushed from the radiator, where his first bullet had been aimed to disable the vehicle. He fired a fourth round on general principle and stood, watching, as the staff car slowed and veered off the road, coming to rest in the ditch.

We followed, stealing glances to our rear as we approached the motorcycle. The Kraut in the sidecar struggled to get out, his Schmeisser still slung around his neck.

Kaz put a bullet between his eyes.

I glanced at the other German, who been thrown from the motorcycle. His chest was a red blossom where the bullet smashed through his sternum.

The staff car was tilted to the side, the doors on the right jammed against the ditch. The driver was dead, having taken a shot to the face. One officer stumbled out, fumbling with the pistol in his holster, a dazed look on his face. Our companion brought the Kraut to his knees with a rifle butt to the head.

His captive was a major. In the SS. He wore the runic symbols on the lapel of his gray uniform and the death's head insignia on his service cap, which lay on the road in front of him, an unspoken accusation.

Quite a prize, this major was. Red oozed from a cut on his temple, and he moaned as his hand came away thick with his own blood. He looked at us, his eyes wide in a silent plea for mercy. Much the same look as his captives must have given him when the tables had been turned.

Our man grabbed the Kraut from the back by his hair and drew his bayonet. Its sharpened edge shone bright in the morning light. He looked at the blade, admiring it, then to us.

"You wish to know my name? It is Anton Lasho, and I kill every German I see."

He twisted the handful of hair and pulled the SS major's head, laying the blade against his skin. He whispered in the German's ear as he drew the blade across his throat. He stepped back, watching blood spurt and gush as the major grasped his neck, fingers clutching the gaping wound in a futile attempt to stem the bubbling flow.

CHAPTER FOUR

LASHO DRAGGED THE four bodies into the middle of the road. He beamed when he saw how Kaz had drilled the motorcyclist, gracing Kaz with a maniacal grin.

"A Pole knows what to do with Germans, yes? Kill them," he said, "like the swine they are."

"I have ample reason not to disagree," Kaz said, his eyes downcast. He sure did, a whole family of reasons. I wasn't about to take Lasho to task for executing an SS officer, but it did make me wonder how unhinged he might be.

"There," Lasho said, admiring the arrangement of the bodies. He'd tossed the major's cap onto the toe of his boot, where it hung at a jaunty angle. "For all to see. Now come."

"Listen," I said as he walked down the road, "it's time for some answers."

"There are no answers," he said.

"What the hell does that mean?" I said to Kaz as we hurried to catch up. "He owes us an explanation, at least."

"I think our friend Anton is speaking at the metaphysical level," Kaz said.

"Yeah, that's where the major is, right?"

"Your grasp of philosophy is matchless, Billy," he said, as we watched Lasho veer off the road and into the thick grasses along the riverbank.

"Bateau!" he yelled, waving us over to where he stood, chest high in reeds. We ran through the muck and ooze, soaking our feet, and helped Lasho pull a small rowboat out from its hiding place. By the looks of the peeling paint, it could've been abandoned and left out in the weather for years. But there was caulking along the seams, and she looked like she might do well in a calm pond.

The river was maybe three hundred or so yards across, with a swift current. Given that the alternative was waiting for a pack of vengeful Germans to round the bend, I helped push as Lasho took up position at the oars. Kaz and I clambered in as soon as we were out of the weeds, with Kaz hanging over the bow and me knee to knee with Lasho. It was a small boat.

The oarlocks were wrapped in cloth to muffle the sound. Axle grease was smeared where the locks fit into the wood.

"Nice *bateau*," I said. "You usually use it at night?"

"Yes. But today was a special day." Lasho rowed on, watching the riverbank as we ventured out into the water. Deep creases lined his forehead and bags hung under his wary eyes. The hands on the oars were rough and calloused, his fingernails caked with dirt.

"It'll be a lot less special if the Germans catch us midstream," I said, craning my neck and listening for the sound of approaching engines.

"If they come now," Lasho said, straining at the oars as he gritted his teeth, "then we die." He gave a small shrug, as if it would be regrettable, but what can you expect? He had the manner of a man at ease with the thought of death. Moments before, he had been jubilant, with a frantic glint in his eyes, arranging the dead Germans just so. Now, the life had drained from his face, leaving nothing but sweat and strain as he heaved at the oars, finally breeching a thicket of reeds and drifting into the marsh, pulling in the oars, and ordering us over the side.

"No oars," Lasho said. "If the Germans see broken reeds, they know a boat came across the river. Push." Knee-deep in muck, we drove the small boat stern-first deeper into the thicket of stalks, tying it to a fallen tree that served as decent camouflage. Then we hoofed it to dry land, the rowboat invisible from the shore or the river.

"Now I eat," Lasho said, sitting on the lush green grass that grew along the riverbank. "Then we go."

"Where?" I asked.

"Cessens, where you wish to go. It is not far. But it is very steep. And there are Germans. So eat." He opened the can of diced eggs and ham and dug in, dirty fingers and all. Kaz and I did the same, using the remaining crackers to scrap out the congealed breakfast. After what we'd been through, it tasted pretty good. Lasho seemed to like it, but who knew when he'd last had a meal?

"Anton Lasho," Kaz said, rolling the name around as he spoke it. "You are not French, are you?"

"Then what am I?"

"Gypsy?" I guessed. He had the dark hair and looks of the few I'd encountered back home, and I remembered a lot of their names ended in the same letter.

"I am Sinti," he said. "Gypsy is what you *Gadje* call us."

"Romani," Kaz explained, downing the last of his cold eggs. "The Sinti are one of the major groups that emigrated to Europe centuries ago. We are *Gadje*; anyone who is not Romani."

"Are there other Sinti nearby?" I asked Lasho, who avoided my eyes.

"Now we go," he said, taking the ration cans and burying them under a rock. It was clear he wasn't going to tell us anything. And that he knew how to get us where we needed to be.

"Are you with the Resistance?" I asked, hustling to catch up with him as he stopped at a line of trees by a farmer's field. It was a simple question, but Lasho focused on the open space before us instead, lifting his face to smell the air, searching out the smell of German sweat, cigarettes, and leather.

"You must save your breath," he finally said, pointing to the far side of the field. A steep forest faced us, wind gusting through the pines, their boughs waves of undulating green. He took off at a run on the hard-packed path along the line of trees dividing the fields, leaving no footprints. We followed, into the woods, and from there up, bounding over logs and boulders, ducking dead branches, and trying to keep up with the silent Sinti.

It had been good advice; I needed every breath and gasp of air I had to stay with Lasho.

After an hour of hard climbing, we left the thickly wooded slope and came to a meadow, flat and soft, covered with thick green growth. It looked familiar, like a lot of Lysander landing spots in occupied France probably did. Isolated, with plentiful grasses, where sheep might have grazed until the Germans had come along and confiscated everything with four legs. It had even terrain, wide enough for the small aircraft to set down, make a turn, and take off again.

"Cessens?" Kaz asked, his hands on his knees as he caught his breath. Lasho held up his hand as he scanned the field and the tree line beyond. He trotted around the perimeter, swiveling his head as he searched the undergrowth. About two-thirds of the way around, he halted, sniffing the air, his nose held high like a dog searching out a scent.

He knelt, his hand combing through the long grass. He came up with a cigarette butt, crushed indifferently into the ground. The word *Privat* was visible on the paper. It was a cheap brand issued to German soldiers. Somebody had been watching the place. Maybe a Kraut, maybe a guy who'd taken the smokes from a Kraut he'd killed. Hard to know, but one thing was clear: he'd waited a long time, long enough to get bored and risk lighting up.

Lasho said, "This is where the English land. Now you are here."

"But too late, and we're not the only ones who have been here," I said. "Can you take us to the Resistance?"

"No," Lasho said. "But I will take you to the abbey. It is safer."

"Thanks for your concern, but I think we'll be safe enough with the Resistance," I said.

"You? Yes. Me? No. So we go to the abbey. The black robes will help you. Come." He strode across the field, not bothering to see if we followed. We did.

"So Lasho doesn't like the Germans or the Resistance," I said to Kaz, keeping my voice low as we trailed behind him.

"Not exactly, Billy. He hates the Germans but wishes to avoid the Resistance. Some sort of personal dispute, perhaps?"

"He said he wouldn't be safe, not that he had a beef with some Frenchman," I said. "Something's wrong with him. Maybe he's off his rocker."

"Perhaps the locals do not like the Sinti. It could be as simple as that," Kaz said, his halfhearted tone telling me he didn't believe it either.

"I don't think Anton Lasho is a man given to simple solutions," I said. "Even if the folks around here didn't like Gypsies before the war, the Resistance wouldn't mind one who could pull off the kind of ambush he did. There's something he's not telling us, and we've got enough problems without adding his to the mix."

"So far, Lasho has been our only source of assistance," Kaz said, holding back a branch as we threaded our way through the thicket.

Far as I was concerned, if our only ace in the hole was Lasho, our mission was FUBAR, which was GI slang for something that was worse than SNAFU—"situation normal, all fucked up."

FUBAR? That meant "fucked up beyond all recognition," which pretty much fit.

We came to a trail that switchbacked down the hillside. Lasho crouched and waited, listening for the sound of boots. The air was filled with chirping birds and the soft rustling of green leaves, but no clomping feet. He signaled us to follow, and we crossed the trail, bushwhacking our way down, avoiding the obvious, and easy, route. I had to admit, Lasho exhibited a healthy sense of self-preservation. Crazy like a fox, maybe.

He stopped at a rock outcropping above the curving trail and waited for us. "*Lac Gris,*" he said. Below us, a long lake glistened in the sunlight, nestled between two hills. Afternoon shadows were already beginning to reach into the valley, and I felt the chill of night even as the sun was on my face.

"The abbey?" I asked. Lasho didn't deign to answer. We followed. Situation normal.

An hour later the abbey came into view, on a hunk of land that jutted out into the lake. From our perch, we could see gray slate roofs, granite walls, a courtyard, a steeple, and cultivated fields outside the main building. Little figures in black scurried across the landscape, tending crops and doing whatever monks did to fill their time between prayers.

We filtered down through the forest, Lasho even more alert as we neared the abbey. We came close enough to make out the monk's faces as they worked their hoes in the garden beds. Lasho settled in behind the trunk of a massive tree, the rifle cradled in his lap and his eyes on the abbey walls.

"What now?" I whispered.

"Wait," Lasho said.

"For?"

"A light. See the windows on the top, to the left?" He pointed to a row of narrow windows on the third floor. "Stained glass. One is very red, one is bright blue. When the sun sets, we wait for a candle. If it lights the blue window, we go inside. If it lights the red window, we run, back up the mountain."

"What if there is no candle?" Kaz asked.

"Run faster."

CHAPTER FIVE

WE WAITED. MY shoes and socks were still damp from the river, and the cold was beginning to creep up my bones. I shivered as Kaz shared the last of the food; dried fruit bars wrapped in cellophane. Lasho shot a dark glance my way as I fumbled with the wrapper, the crinkling sound not much to his liking. He produced a pocket knife, neatly slit open his package, removed the fruit bar, and stowed the wrapper in Kaz's bag. Silently.

We waited some more. The monks gathered their tools and went into the abbey. The sun set. Lasho turned his head twice, listening to distant sounds. Once we heard an engine, far away, fading as it drove off in another direction. A dirt lane led to the abbey, winding along the shore of the lake, faintly visible in the moonlight. I kept my eyes on the road while Lasho watched the windows. No one except the Germans or the Resistance would be out after curfew, which began at sunset. We didn't want either of them for company.

The last light disappeared at the horizon, and the stars began to twinkle. I wondered how long before candles would be lit, if at all, and where we'd be right now if everything had gone according to plan. Across the border sipping hot chocolate in front of a fire? But that was a wasted thought. Nothing goes according to plan. Our pilot knew that. The Krauts who had been barreling down the road, masters of their piece of France a few short hours ago, knew it as well. If the dead realized anything.

Soft lights began to flicker at a few windows. I watched as a glow made its way room by room, closing in on the top floor. It settled in at the blue window, the stained glass the color of the sky.

Lasho rose, his dark face streaked with ghostly moonlight. The grimness and strength he'd carried all day had vanished, his gaze hesitant and his mouth slack-jawed. He stumbled off, looking more like a tired old man than a stalking killer. I felt the way he looked, but then I'd felt that way since I woke up in that shepherd's shack.

We worked our way around the abbey walls to the rear until the lake lapped against the shore only yards away, the gray granite looming over us. Lasho picked his way through a jumble of rocks that hid a well-trodden path to a small wooden door. The wood was shiny and worn, held by iron hinges that looked centuries old. No latch, only a knotted piece of rope that hung from above. No access from the outside, no noisy knocker to attract attention. Tailor-made for those on the run and seeking sanctuary.

Lasho pulled on the rope twice, deliberately. Soon the door swung open, the ancient ironwork smooth and quiet. A hooded, dark form emerged and took Lasho's rifle, then pulled him inside. Others reached out for me and Kaz, and before we could blink we were inside, the door closed and locked behind us, as we were disarmed, searched, and pushed down a dimly lit corridor by more men in dark cowls.

Two of them escorted Lasho down one corridor while three others moved Kaz and me down a set of ill-lit stairs to the musty basement, reminding me of dank prison cells and how this whole mission was definitely not going according to plan.

Things looked up as we were brought into a well-lit, warm kitchen. A large cast-iron stove took up one wall, with a square table and chairs of plain, rough wood at the center. The hooded men were quickly revealed to be monks in black robes, as Lasho had described. Chairs were held out for us and soup ladled from a pot simmering on the stove. Wine was poured from an earthen jug, and when they were done serving, the monks stepped back, one of them leaving the room. Kaz spoke in rapid-fire French. I didn't understand much, basically because

I was too busy slurping soup to pay attention. The monks stood in silence, no response offered.

No wonder Lasho liked it here.

"I think they are Benedictines," Kaz said, as he tasted the wine. One eyebrow went up, which I took to mean he was pleasantly surprised. "The black cloaks and the silence."

"How are we going to communicate then?" I asked. "Sign language?" I took a gulp of wine. Not bad. Not that I'd know good.

"Benedictines practice periods of silence, but they are not a silent order. And they are released from silence when necessary."

"Where do you think they took Lasho?" I said. "Why separate us?"

"They obviously know him, if that means anything," Kaz said, blowing on a spoonful of soup. "They took his weapons immediately and brooked no argument from him."

"Ours too, for that matter. But I can understand monks not wanting armed men wandering the abbey." The door opened, and the two monks moved to make room, giving a slight bow as they stood aside. The fellow who entered wore the same black getup, but he was obviously high up in the holy pecking order. He tossed back his cowl and smiled pleasantly.

"Welcome, gentlemen," he said. "You are the answer to our prayers." He spoke in a clipped, precise manner, his French accent barely discernable.

"Thank you, Father," I said, getting to my feet, not sure what you called a monk. Nuns were sisters, so were they brothers? I should have paid better attention in parochial school back in Boston. "I have to wonder what you've been praying for. My name is Billy Boyle and this is—"

"No names, please," he said, waving his hand apologetically. "It is better for all concerned. Please, sit and eat." He pulled up a chair next to Kaz and took his time studying our faces. His was well-lined, peaceful, and calm. Stands to reason, it was a pretty peaceful life here by a beautiful lake, with crops in the field and jugs of wine at hand. Except for guys like Lasho dropping by, that is.

"A wise precaution," Kaz said. "If names are not known, they cannot be spoken."

"Exactly," our host said. "Even an alias, if the Germans hear it repeatedly, can cost lives."

"I thought you were in the business of saving souls, not lives, Father." I figured since he hadn't corrected me, that title would do.

"We are shut away from the world, my son, but we are still of the world. We do what we can to ease suffering, something that should not be as dangerous as it is today. But that is the world God has given us, so what else can we do?"

"Well, you've eased our hunger, and for that we're grateful," I said, raising my glass in his direction. He smiled and bowed his head in acknowledgment. "But you may not want us here for much longer."

"Are the Germans searching for you?" he asked.

"Our aircraft crash-landed some distance from here. They may have given up the chase for us by now, but our friend may have stirred up a hornet's nest."

"Hornets?" he asked, taking a second to figure out what I'd meant. "Oh yes, *le frelon*. And there's no need to avoid *his* name. Everyone knows Anton Lasho, especially the Germans."

"Why?" I asked.

"That is a long and sad story. And it has to do with what we've been praying for. But first, please, eat and drink. Then the brothers will take your garments to be washed and show you to your quarters. Soon I will explain everything."

"Thank you," Kaz said. "It will be a relief to have these muddy clothes clean again."

"Of course," he said. "You will have to look your best in Switzerland, won't you?" With that, he departed, leaving us to wonder how he knew about Switzerland. We'd mentioned it to Lasho when we'd tried to get a fix on our location, but we hadn't said it was our destination.

Bread, soup, and wine distracted me from any further thoughts on the matter. When we were done, our monk escorts brought us to a small room upstairs, lit by a single candle. There were two beds, a few chairs, and a small table with a jug of water and wooden cups. The monks took all of our clothes and shoes, in exchange for a couple woolen nightgowns. Itchy woolen nightgowns, but I told myself not to complain.

"What do you think the good Father has in mind?" Kaz asked as he sat on the straw mattress. "He seems the decent type."

"That's what worries me," I said. "The decent types are ones who want you to risk your neck to do the decent thing. As they see it, anyway."

"You are too young to be such a cynic, Billy."

"Hey, I'm still alive. Made it to the quarter-century mark, so I must be doing something right."

"Pure luck," Kaz said, smiling as he stretched out on the bed.

"Let's hope that luck holds, and the Father will know how to contact the Jedburgh team, or at least the local Resistance." Knuckles rapped on the door, and speak of the devil—if that isn't too sacrilegious—the black-robed monk himself stepped into the room.

He took a seat and gestured for us to do the same. I felt a bit ridiculous in my nightgown, but maybe that was the idea. Sure, he was basically wearing the same sort of thing, but on him it looked good.

"Father, I don't know how involved you are with the Resistance, but I have to ask if you've seen any Allied soldiers in the area."

"You mean the Jedburghs?" he said. "The Frenchman, the Englishman, and the American."

"Yes! Can you put us in touch with them?"

"They are dead, I am sorry to say. As well as a good number of *maquis*." The Resistance fighters who lived in the hills. "Yours was to be the last Lysander landing at that location; it was too well known and had become dangerous."

"Father, how do you know so much about our mission?"

"There is no reason for me to tell you exactly how I know. Suffice it to say I am in communication with those who do know." He meant a radio. He also meant that if we were captured, we'd talk. Sooner or later, with the right application of pain. Smart guy. "I am aware the Jedburghs were to guide you to the Swiss border and make contact with someone who could get you across. But all that has changed. They were caught up in an antipartisan sweep and killed. Luckily for them, since it was quick, at least in relation to what the Germans would have done. God bless their souls."

"I'm sorry to hear that," I said. "But do you have a way to get us to that contact?"

"It would be difficult, but not impossible," he said. "It is a journey of eighty kilometers. I've sent a courier to ask the Resistance chief to provide a guide for you."

"They will take us, surely?" Kaz said.

"It is not so simple," the monk said, as if struggling with how to deliver the bad news. I tried to figure the angles, to understand what he wanted, to put together the bits and pieces of what I knew about the situation.

Lasho hated the Germans and had a problem with the Resistance.

The Jedburghs and the *maquis* had gotten caught up in a sweep. Who were the Germans hunting in their sweep?

Lasho was a killer.

No more Lysander flights were scheduled for Cessens because it was too dangerous.

Why?

Because Anton Lasho was running amok, killing every German he could find, not caring about the consequences, life, or death. The Father cared about all three. Presto, the answer presented itself.

"You want us to take Lasho with us. All the way to Switzerland."

"Yes," he said. "And the Resistance will not help. They will likely kill him if they find him. They have their own rules. Harsh rules, but sensible."

"Like no indiscriminate killing," I said.

"To a degree, yes. An attack has to be worthwhile, in terms of reprisals. Anton does not follow any such rule."

"Why?" I asked. "And why do you care so much about him?"

"I care for his soul. But I also care for his sanity. Anton has suffered greatly, and I fear the burden may break him." He rubbed his eyes.

"There is terrible suffering all around us," I said. "What's so special about Anton's?" I knew there had to be guilt at work in this monk's desire to help Lasho. It's a great motivator, especially for a decent guy.

"We helped Anton some time ago. He and his family. You must understand, we can only do so much for refugees. The Germans search the abbey often. We can do little but provide food and shelter for one night and send people on to the Swiss border."

"Plus you have a radio, and you can't risk that being discovered," I said.

"If the Germans find anything here, we face certain death. Then we could help no one," he said, his voice quivering in anger at my insinuation, at the intolerable truth of it. His glistening eyes looked beyond us, searching for forgiveness, or perhaps simply dreaming of a simpler time. "A radio, a single refugee, an escaped prisoner, or a rifle. It does not matter to the Germans. Any contraband at all is enough for an arrest. Which means torture, and secrets ultimately forced out, followed by a bullet to the head."

"What happened to Lasho's family?" Kaz asked, placing his hand on the monk's arm, a comforting, coaxing gesture.

He began the story.

Anton Lasho was born in Germany, but as a Sinti, he and his clan were never welcome. His parents died when he was a child, and he ended up in England, brought up by an aunt and uncle. They lived the itinerant life, traveling throughout Great Britain and making occasional journeys to France, where Anton met and fell in love with Soraya, a Sinti from southern France. They married and had two children, Livia and Damian. When war broke out in 1939, Anton and his family—Livia was five years old and Damian eight—were in France. Travel to England was difficult, and Anton made plans with other families to head to Spain, hoping to avoid being caught up in the conflict.

Soraya wanted to stay in France for a few more months, to celebrate the festival of Saint Sarah, at Saintes-Maries-de-la-Mer on the coast of southern France. Sarah was the patron saint of all Roma, and many made the annual pilgrimage to the festival. Anton agreed, so in May 1940, his family and a caravan of other Sinti were camped out on the Mediterranean coast, awaiting the day when they would all walk into the warm waters and reenact the arrival of Sarah in France.

The Germans beat them to it.

The invasion of France came in early May. The surrender of France followed in late June.

By July, the government of Vichy France had begun to arrest Jews, Sinti, Roma, and antifascists, corralling them into internment camps. Vichy was a slice of southern France, a bone the Germans had thrown to Marshal Pétain to provide the illusion that the French still governed themselves. Pétain and his fascist militia gnawed that bone hard, giving the Nazis a run for their money when it came to tracking down Jews, Gypsies, and anyone else who didn't fit the new European order.

Anton's Sinti caravan scattered. Some were picked up right away, while others went on the run, splitting up and hoping for the best. Anton and Soraya were lucky. They found refuge with a farmer who'd hired them for seasonal work the year before. He took their horse and cart, along with what little cash they possessed, but he gave them a small room and shared what food he had. They all worked the farm, even little Livia and Damian pitching in at harvest time.

It was two years before the Germans came to the farm. They weren't hunting Jews or anyone else. They were after food. They took the farmer's two pigs and a dozen sheep. They took most of his grain, his apples, and even the jams Soraya had preserved from the wild strawberries she'd picked. The officer in charge gave the farmer a receipt. It didn't matter. He couldn't read, and the paper was worthless anyway.

One of the soldiers—maybe he was a farm boy and felt guilty—whispered to the farmer, telling him in schoolboy French to get his identity papers in order. With a knowing glance in Anton's direction, he warned him of security troops checking papers and arresting anyone without proper identification.

Anton and his family left the next morning. They began walking east, to the Swiss border. Wary of patrols, they kept to the forest, coming out only to beg for food at small village churches. They were turned away often, fed occasionally, sheltered and comforted twice.

One priest put them in touch with the Resistance. They said Anton could join them, but Soraya and the children would have to make their way alone. Anton refused, and they left the Resistance camp with the name of another priest twenty kilometers distant who might help.

It was that priest who brought them to the abbey. The children were sick, their clothes filthy and ragged. Anton and Soraya were pale and thin, most of their food having gone to Livia and Damian. The monks nursed them back to health, hiding them whenever the Vichy militia came to call.

THE FATHER LEANED back in his chair and took a long drink of water, shaking his head as if to clear away the memories.

"It sounds as if you provided the Lasho family with everything they needed," Kaz said. "What went wrong?" It had to be plenty for the Father to put so much time into setting the stage.

"Everything," he said, taking another drink and setting the cup down, hard.

IT HAD BEEN relatively easy for the abbey to give shelter and solace to the Lasho family. At that time, the province of Haute-Savoie was occupied by Germany's Italian allies. The Haute-Savoie was the only French province on the Swiss border that was not occupied by German troops. For the most part, the Italians did not share the German enthusiasm for rounding up Jews and other refugees on the run. Many a blind eye was turned, especially at border crossings. The Swiss, however, preferred the Nazi approach, since it kept the influx of unwanted refugees to a minimum.

The Lasho family stayed at the abbey for months, hiding in plain sight, making themselves useful or scarce as the situation demanded. Plans were made for them to get to the border, eighty kilometers away. A guide was arranged to take them across, evading both the Italian and Swiss border guards.

Then everything changed. The Italians got rid of Mussolini and switched sides. The Italian occupation troops left for home, and the

Germans took over, sealing the Swiss border completely. No guide wanted to risk the journey, at least not for what they'd charged before. And the Swiss had closed the border to all but deserters, escaped POWs, and political refugees. Jews and Romani were defined as non-political, a convenient strategy for the Swiss to keep unwanted minorities out. But they did make some hardship exceptions. Parents with children younger than six years old were allowed, if they survived the crossing. Anyone sick, pregnant, or over the age of sixty-five would also be granted asylum. Not that the sick or elderly would stand a chance of evading the Gestapo and the border guards. Children traveling alone under the age of sixteen were also allowed in under the hardship rules.

Which meant that Anton and Soraya had only one chance for Livia, age ten, and Damian, age twelve. Send them across the border alone.

Pressure mounted at the abbey for them to leave. The Gestapo paid a courteous visit to the abbot, counseling him to refuse help to the Resistance, report any strangers in the area, and mind his own business. Then came the first raid. It was only the dust cloud from the approaching convoy that gave any warning. The Lashos were spirited out of the abbey and hidden in the woods as the Germans tore through the abbey, thankfully finding nothing. It was decided. It was too dangerous for Anton and his family to stay any longer.

The Lashos left in the morning, leaving their sanctuary behind.

The monks had done what they could, making arrangements to get them to the border. They walked to a nearby village and hopped a freight car that slowed, even more so than usual, at the bend in the tracks where they waited. When the train braked to pull into Annemasse, they leaped off and were met by a priest who led them on back roads to a small chapel. They rested and spent what they hoped would be their last night in France, sleeping by the altar.

They left at dusk the next day, staying in the shadows, the priest in the lead. As soon as the sun set, they could be shot on sight for being outside after curfew. He took them through fields planted with beans, the ripe tendrils wound around tall stakes. It was good cover. Beyond the bean field, the land sloped down to the river. The priest told them it was shallow, barely up to their knees. They had to cross it, continue straight on, and cross again, where the river meandered back on itself. Then they'd be in Switzerland. But they had to be quiet; there was a customs post two hundred meters away, manned by Swiss and Germans who spent the day staring at each other, when they weren't hunting desperate refugees.

Anton and Soraya led the children across the river. The priest waved, then disappeared. They were alone. The water was cold. Livia stumbled, falling in up to her neck, but Damian caught her and held his sister's hand. Up on the sand bank, and back into the river, they made the final crossing.

The ground felt the same as it had on the other side of the river. It was Switzerland, but they were still in danger. They had to get the children away from the border, far enough away that the Swiss authorities wouldn't be tempted to chase them back across the river.

In the darkness, they crept beside a road, keeping to the ditch, ready to hide at the first sign of alarm. It was the same roadway that led to the customs stop at the border.

That route was a mistake.

A truck came rumbling down the lane, its taped headlights illuminating the ditch as the road curved to the right. Soldiers stood in the open bed, pointing at the four of them as the driver braked.

Anton told the children to run. They hesitated, fearful and confused. Soraya grabbed them by the hands and sprinted away, a sorrowful glance all she could spare for Anton. He understood. She'd get them away and then leave them to be found. He'd distract the guards. Maybe he'd get away, maybe not.

He jumped up, waving his arms, stepping between the lights and his fleeing family. Two soldiers grabbed him, while the others ran past, not distracted at all, intent on their quarry. Anton raged against the men holding him, tearing loose from their grip, knocking one to the ground with a ferocious blow, and speeding off after the other guards. He heard a shot and kept running, certain that the remaining soldier wouldn't fire in the direction of his comrades. Then another shot, and it felt like he'd been struck in the side by a red-hot iron. He stumbled, fell, got up again, and ran on.

Into the darkness.

He awoke in the woods, his side sticky with blood. Broken ribs and a bloody gash. He had no idea where he was. It was daylight, just past dawn. He kept to the woods, hoping to find Soraya and the children, hiding, excited to see him. Then they'd make another plan, get the children to safety, and take their own chances.

Lasho knew he'd run out of chances when he came to the forest edge, which looked down on the customs station. He could see the river where they'd crossed, the double bend and the shallow water. He stared at the river, watching the icy Alpine waters flow freely across the land, past the customs station they'd so carefully avoided the night before.

Something was wrong.

The gates were raised. German and Swiss soldiers mingled in the roadway, smoking and laughing. Lasho knew what the raised gates at the customs station meant. He knew what the truck waiting on the French side with its swastika markings was for. He knew what the approaching Swiss police sedan meant as well.

It squealed to a halt dead on the border. The Swiss were taking no chances with a mother and her two children. They'd been caught together, and since the children weren't alone, they weren't a hardship case. Lasho watched as the Swiss border guards opened the doors and escorted Soraya, Livia, and Damian to the waiting Germans. Soraya turned her head, perhaps looking for him, perhaps looking away from her captors.

It was over in seconds. The truck drove away, the sedan backed up and left, the gates came down.

Lasho's family was gone.

CHAPTER SIX

"THAT IS THE story Anton told to me," the Father said. "We traced Soraya and the children to an internment camp outside Orleans. Then to a work camp inside Germany. Slave labor, I should say."

"A death sentence," Kaz said.

"Yes. Which is why Anton has declared his own war on the Germans," the Father said, with a great sigh. "For the past several months he has roamed the Haute-Savoie, hunting Germans. As you said, he has brought out the hornets."

"Making it difficult for the Resistance to operate," I said.

"Indeed. Since he is only one man, he can vanish into the hills with ease and evade the patrols that hunt him. But the *maquis* and our couriers cannot hide as he can; they must risk capture in order to carry on their work. We have lost too many brave souls to the *Boche* already. This cannot continue."

"How does he survive?" Kaz asked. "He must need supplies and shelter."

"I know he steals food. As for shelter, he cares little for comfort. I imagine some people help him, thinking he is part of the Resistance."

"Yesterday, it was obvious he knew to expect an SS officer at a certain time and place. How did he get that information if he's not with the Resistance?" I said.

"He takes prisoners when it suits him. I believe he tortures them for information. And his own pleasure, if it can be called that."

"You want us to take him off your hands," I said.

"You must," the Father said.

"We have a mission," I said, not happy about having to drag Lasho along while convincing him to stop killing Germans, which was pretty much the whole point of this war.

"Of course. And I shall be happy to assist you in crossing the border into Switzerland. If you take Anton with you."

"And if we don't?"

"Then, sadly, I would decline to assist you. I will be much too busy dealing with the crisis he has forced upon us to oblige," the Father said.

"Father," Kaz said, his voice nearly a whisper, "you've told us Lasho has caused much trouble for you. Why not simply lock him up? Or turn him over to the Resistance?"

"They will dispense their own rough justice. A bullet and an unmarked grave," he said. "Anton deserves more. He came to us for succor, his wife and small children in hand. I welcomed them in, and it was I who made the decision that they must leave. I must make things right, for Anton's spirit and his soul. And for my very own, I confess. I am sorry to stoop to coercion, but it the only tool I have at hand. You look to be competent and decent men; I trust you will keep your word if you agree."

"We have little choice, Father," Kaz said. I nodded. Decent men seldom do. The Father left us, and Kaz blew out the candle. Blackness shrouded us, the smoky odor of tallow lingering in the air.

"So," Kaz said, "our Swiss contact probably thinks we are dead. The pilot who flew us in is dead. The Jedburghs are dead. Lasho's family are all dead. Do you sense a common theme?"

"I hope you're dead wrong, pal."

I heard Kaz chuckle, and felt sleep overcome me like the slumber of the dead.

In the morning, the monks brought us our duds. The clothes were clean, or clean enough. They felt rough and smelled of wood smoke, probably from being dried in front of a fire all night. We gathered in the kitchen and were served ersatz coffee and bread fresh from the oven. One of the monks said Father Rochet would be with us shortly, which earned a sharp look from the black robe tending the stove. He'd forgotten the no-name rule.

Father Rochet—who I figured for the abbot himself, but knew enough not to ask—came in with Lasho and sat him down with a smile and a pat on the shoulder.

"Anton will be going with you," he announced, as if the idea had just occurred to the both of them. "You have no objections to traveling with him?" Yeah, he was the head man all right.

"None at all," I said, noticing a monk standing behind the abbot and holding our bags. Which contained our identity papers and weapons, and probably would have been kept if we hadn't agreed.

"Good," the Father said, flicking his finger for the monk to come forward. He handed over our revolvers, ammo, and identity papers. We stuffed everything into our coat pockets as the empty rucksacks went into the oven. Probably not too smart to carry bags in the open with US ARMY stenciled on the side.

"What is the plan, Father?" Kaz asked, as he finished off a piece of warm bread. I watched Lasho, who drank and ate mechanically, as docile this morning as he was mad and ferocious yesterday.

"Through the forest today, to a village fifteen kilometers from Cessens. After dark you will board a train when it stops to take on water for the boiler," he said.

"Is the train guarded?" I asked.

"Not unless it carries military goods, which it does not today, although the Gestapo may conduct identity checks at any time. It is a small provincial line and terminates at Annemasse, near the border. We have contacts among the railway workers, all good Frenchmen."

"What if they do check?" I asked.

"Trust God and your pistols," he said. "Do not be taken alive."

I was wondering if the church had a special blessing for pistols when shouts echoed from the hallway. Someone was giving the alarm.

Boche! Gestapo!

"Go!" the Father shouted, grabbing Lasho by the collar and

pushing him toward the door. We scrambled for our coats, making for
the rear exit in hopes of getting into the trees before the Krauts saw
us. We burst out into the open and ran along the side of the abbey,
stopping to check the road for Germans. Nothing.

"Trucks," Lasho said, catching the noise before we did. "Come."

We ran, hard on his heels. The monks must have kept a lookout
in the church steeple, which gave us enough of a head start to get clear
of the abbey and halfway up the hill before we heard the noises.

Shouts. Brakes skidding on gravel. Boots hitting the ground. This
wasn't a social call.

Higher up the hill, we stopped and looked back, catching our
breath. Two trucks and a staff car had pulled up. About a dozen Krauts
fanned out around the abbey, blocking the exits. Another dozen
stormed inside, followed by a couple of officers and a guy in a brown
leather coat. The Gestapo boys liked their leather.

"They might be searching everywhere after the shooting yesterday,"
Kaz said.

"Father Rochet sent a courier. To ask for a guide," I said.

"The *maquis* will not help," Lasho said. "He should have known
that. If the courier was caught, he may have talked. It was not worth
the risk."

"Father Rochet wishes to help you," Kaz said. Given the situation,
I guess it didn't matter much if we knew his name. "He feels responsible."

"I know," Lasho said. "As do I."

Gunshots came from the courtyard. The *pop-pop-pop* of pistol
shots echoing off granite.

"The courier," Lasho said. "He talked."

Pop-pop-pop.

We couldn't see into the courtyard, but it was easy to guess what
was happening. They'd shoot monks until Father Rochet gave up the
radio and surrendered us. Since we were gone, and the shots kept up,
it didn't seem like good news for the monks of Abbey de Hautecombe.

Lasho ran off, heading farther uphill, stopping a few times as if
getting his bearings. We stayed with him, wondering if he'd finally

gone off the deepest end. He stopped at the foot of a pine tree and climbed up the bottom branches. I saw him untie and lower a canvas bag from the upper limbs, all of which was camouflaged by the thick covering of green boughs.

It was a rifle, wrapped in oilskin. Lasho grabbed it and pushed past us, going back downhill.

"No!" I hissed, not wanting to risk a shout. "Lasho, no, it's not worth it."

"Lasho, stop," Kaz pleaded, slipping and sliding through the undergrowth. "There are too many of them."

I knew we should let him go his own way. He'd get himself killed soon enough, and the good people of the Haute-Savoie would have one less terror to worry about. But we'd promised Father Rochet, after a fashion, so we careened down the slope, hoping to restrain Lasho before he put another notch in his gun.

He halted behind a boulder jutting out from the hillside. By the time we got there he was lining up a shot, waiting for the Germans to come outside. My money was on the brown leather coat.

"Lasho, it will only make things worse if you pull that trigger," I said. "They'll kill anyone who's left."

"You don't know the Germans," he said, tucking his cheek snug against the stock. "Things are already worse."

Soldiers began to return from the perimeter, standing around the trucks, smoking and chatting. Others came out of the abbey, prodding ten or so monks with their bayonets, loading them into the vehicles. I didn't see the Father.

Two more shots sounded from the courtyard, a deadly afterthought. Maybe those were for him.

No. Father Rochet was pushed out the door, his black robe ripped and hanging off his back. Even from this distance I could see he'd been beaten, the blood bright red on his chin.

The Gestapo man in the brown leather jacket followed him, shouting orders at his men.

"Lasho, don't do it. There'll be plenty of other Germans—"

He pulled the trigger.

The shot took Father Rochet dead center in the chest. He folded at the knees and fell, as if in prayer, coming to rest on his side.

Lasho left the rifle in the cleft of the rock and calmly walked back into the deep, dark woods. We kept up with him, not saying a word, matching his deliberate pace to the east.

It had been the only decent thing to do.

CHAPTER SEVEN

WE DEBATED TRYING for the train. If the courier gave up information about Father Rochet under torture, that was at least understandable. But why would he volunteer the train rendezvous?

"Because he wanted to live," Lasho said. "It is a great failing of many people."

"So he gave them more than they asked for?" I said.

"Yes," Lasho said with a quick nod. "And then they killed him. Even the Germans would not trust such a man."

God help me, I understood his logic.

"No train then?" Kaz said. "Eighty kilometers is a long way without food, not to mention evading German patrols."

"Yes, we take the train. But not where they expect us," Lasho said.

We double-timed it through the forest, reaching our original rendezvous point midday. The plan had been to board a boxcar when the steam locomotive pulled in for a water stop that night. We were early, but so were the Germans. From our vantage point we watched as a truck rumbled down the road and crossed the tracks, screeching to a halt. An officer jumped from the cab and directed his men to various positions, well-concealed and covering the approach to the water tower.

We eased back into the woods and kept walking. They'd have a long, boring night waiting for us.

"Twelve kilometers," Lasho said. "There is another water stop."

"That's more than seven miles," I said, my feet already sore from the day's march.

"But there will be no Germans," Lasho said.

"That's worth the shoe leather," I said. "But how can you be sure they won't be there too? Or onboard the train?"

"I use the train," Lasho said. "I know the signs. A rag tied to the latch of a boxcar means no Germans on board at the start of the trip, and that the car has room to hide."

"At the start," I said. "What if they board later?"

"The railroad men are brave, but not stupid. It would be too obvious to remove the rag if the Gestapo boards, yes?"

I had to agree. Brave and stupid was a deadly combination. The hanging rag was not an ironclad guarantee. "You're sure of the railroad workers?"

"Very sure. Brave men, to risk death from the Germans if they are found out, and death from your bombs as well. If we see the rag, we get close to the border."

"Then what? We don't have a guide."

"I have been to Switzerland," Lasho said. "The Father told you?"

"Yes," Kaz said. "He told us. Is that route still open?"

"No. The Germans put up wire along the river. And mines. I know another way. No more talking. Walk faster."

We did both. Maybe Lasho didn't want to talk about his last trip over the border, or maybe he wanted us to save our strength. Or both.

After a couple of hours hoofing it uphill, we saw the next water tower in the distance. The tracks ran along a good-sized stream, with a mill and a couple of buildings clustered around the tower and an open field on the far side of the tracks. If there were Germans, they'd be hidden in the buildings.

"Let's take a look," I said. "We have another hour or so of daylight."

"I do not think the Germans are there," Lasho said. "They are very predictable. If the courier told them about the rendezvous, that is where they go, nowhere else. But we should look."

"There may be food," Kaz said. That sounded good; breakfast had long since worn off.

"No. No one lives there. The mill has not been used in a year. The Germans took all the grain, so people stopped bringing it. The farmer's son was killed in 1940, and the father died last winter. He was a kind man. He gave me shelter and asked me to shoot a German in his son's name. Come."

We crept up on the buildings, listening for the sounds of soldiers who didn't expect company for hours. No whispering or canteens clattering against leather belts. No cigarette smoke.

The buildings were empty.

We took up watch on the second floor of the mill, which afforded a good view of the road in both directions. Lasho slumped to the floor. I moved a chair close to the window, keeping my face in the shadows. Kaz pulled a chair to the side of the window, watching the road in the direction we'd come from. The evening was silent.

"I'm sorry," I said. "About your family."

"Yes," Lasho said, his voice soft with weariness. "I sometimes dream about them. Not so much anymore."

"Father Rochet wanted you to go to Switzerland," Kaz said. "To stop killing."

"I see little reason to do either thing," Lasho said. "But he was a wise man. It is my fault he is dead, so I will do what he wished."

"Lasho, you saved him from horrible suffering at the hands of the Gestapo. Those brutes call their torture chambers kitchens, after all," Kaz said.

"I do not mean he is dead because I shot him. He is dead because he helped me. If I had never gone back, none of this would have happened."

"He was helping us as well," I said.

"Yes. You are to blame also," Lasho said. "No more talking."

That pretty much shut down the conversation. We waited, which usually I didn't mind. I'd gotten used to it in the army. Waiting generally meant no one was trying to kill me, and I'd learned to treasure those moments. But hiking all day with no food I did mind.

It was a relief when the whistle on the steam locomotive sounded in the distance.

"Maybe there is food in the boxcar," Kaz said.

"Quiet," Lasho said as he gazed out into the darkness. Wind rustled the leaves, and the noise of the engine began to fill the night air. He nodded for us to follow and slipped down the stairs in silence.

We took up position about thirty yards from the water tower. The engine would stop there to fill the boiler, which was ancient and constantly in need of filling. Or so the railway men claimed to the Germans, according to Lasho. There were generally two passenger cars and then as many boxcars as needed. But never more than six. We'd be able to spot the signal easily enough.

The train pulled in, steam escaping as the engineer applied the brakes. The passenger cars were blacked out, but there were no guards visible. If any Germans were on board, they might be nothing more than passengers.

The boxcars pulled into view. They looked tiny compared to American trains, due to the narrow-gauge rails. Forty and eights, my dad used to call them, having ridden in one to the front during the last war. He said they'd gotten the name since they could carry forty doughboys or eight horses. Tonight, we only needed room for three.

There were four cars, and sure enough, an oily rag was knotted around the latch on the last boxcar. We waited until the cars came to a full stop, the last one clanking against the steel bumpers. Lasho held up his hand, peering down the track, waiting for the engineer to swing the giant spigot around and yank the chain to let loose the water. The second the water flowed, we darted to the last car. I grabbed the latch and slid the door open, Kaz going in first and then Lasho. I hoisted myself up and closed the door, my eyes adjusting to the dim light.

Kaz and Lasho stood still in front of me, crowded by crates and canvas bags on one side. I pushed between them, wondering what was holding things up.

I was looking straight into the eyes of a German soldier. Holding a submachine gun aimed at my stomach.

"*Langsam*," Kaz said, using his most soothing voice to tell the Kraut to take it easy.

I gave Lasho a quick glance, having a hard time taking my eyes off the barrel of the MP 40. He was as still as stone, his hands at his sides. Kaz's were raised, but in a placating gesture, not surrender. The German stepped back, stumbling on the boxes at his feet. I winced, hoping Lasho wouldn't go for his throat. One pull on the trigger and we'd be sprayed with a dozen rounds.

Lasho didn't move, which gave me time to look at the Kraut.

First thing: he was wearing his backpack. Second thing: no helmet, only his wool field cap. Third thing: he was a kid, dressed for travel, not battle. Fourth thing: he'd been sitting on the box he tripped over. Hiding.

Fifth thing: we were still alive.

The train lurched forward, the boiler evidently filled. The German lost his footing for a second, but it was long enough for Lasho to snatch the MP 40, giving him a kick in the stomach that doubled him over. He sat on the box, clutching his midsection, gasping for air. Lasho held the gun to his head. The locomotive chugged forward, the steam whistling, the steel wheels rolling on the rails. No one would hear the shot.

Lasho smacked the German on the head, sending his cap flying. He grabbed him by his sandy brown hair and pushed the barrel against his cheek, which was covered in tears.

"*Wie alt bist du?*" Kaz asked.

The kid didn't answer, likely distracted by the gun barrel pressed under his eye. Lasho lowered the submachine gun, smoothing the hair that he had gripped so savagely. Then he handed the weapon to me.

"*Achtzehn,*" the kid answered, wiping his cheeks dry. Eighteen, said with enough conviction to tell me he was probably a couple of months short.

"A deserter, yes?" Lasho said.

"*Deserteur, ja,*" he said, glancing between us to see what we'd do. Lasho sat on the box, head in his hands. I searched the kid while Kaz grilled him. He carried a wirecutter in one pocket and a bunch of letters and photos in the other.

"His name is Hans Amsel," Kaz reported. "He was conscripted three months ago and sent to France right after the invasion. A few days ago he got the news that his parents were killed in a bombing raid. His older brother was already dead in Russia. He decided to desert because he has no family left for the Nazis to retaliate against." I looked at the photographs. Smiling parents posing proudly with their two boys on the steps of a house that had probably been blown to bits by now.

"Let me guess," I said, handing the papers back to Hans. "He wants to go to Switzerland."

"Who doesn't?" Kaz said. We both studied the kid, who sat with his arms crossed against the evening chill. Enough moonlight filtered through the slats to see his eyes widen as he stared at Lasho.

"*Sind Sie der Zigeuner?*" Hans whispered, his voice trembling with fear.

"What?" I asked.

"He's asking if Lasho is the Gypsy," Kaz said, and spoke to Hans for a while. "He says they have all heard stories. A tall, dark Gypsy with cold black eyes and a big mustache. He kills and vanishes like a ghost."

"Tell the lad I am a deserter as well," Lasho said. "*Der Zigeuner* is done with the war."

"The boy says he is sorry," Kaz said, after a brief conversation. "He said he knows the Nazis do terrible things. Which is why he deserted."

"Tell him I wish him no harm," Lasho said, squeezing his eyes shut and banging his head against the wall. "Tell him he's a good boy."

CHAPTER EIGHT

WE LEFT THE train before dawn, as it slowed for the station at Ville-la-Grand. Lasho knew a spot where the engineer always slowed going into a curve, even more than necessary, since the embankment sloped away gently, the ground softened by thick grass.

We gave Hans the MP 40 back. Unloaded, since trust only goes so far between recent enemies. But if we ran into trouble, perhaps he could bluff his way out. We set off, Lasho in the lead, hunched over and running low along stone walls bisecting pastures and fields.

Luckily for us, Hans' pack was filled with food he'd swiped from his unit. Black bread and hard sausage, which tasted like heaven. Lasho had stayed quiet, which was his normal approach, even when we asked how we were getting over the border. Hans had no plan himself, simply hoping to find some place to cut through the barbed wire and slip across.

I figured Lasho didn't see the percentage in telling us, since anyone could get captured. We didn't need to know until we got there.

Morning came, and we had to move more carefully, keeping out of sight and close to cover. Once a light aircraft flew low, the black cross and swastika visible as it dipped one wing to give the observer a better view of the ground. Routine, or were they looking for us?

Finally, we halted, going prone at the top of a small hill, warily looking ahead as Lasho pointed out our destination. Across a weedy, untended field, a small church sat surrounded by white stucco buildings, their clay roof tiles drenched in sunlight. A low wall surrounded the compound, except on one side where it was ten feet tall.

"The other side of that wall is Switzerland," Lasho said. "*Schweiz,*" he added for Hans' benefit, who nodded enthusiastically.

"Look," Kaz said, lowering his head to point where the road ran in front of the buildings. An open truck, packed with German soldiers, drove slowly by. I watched Hans, in case he got cold feet with his pals so close. His hands were shaking. Good sign.

"They are a regular patrol," Lasho said. "At ten o'clock the guard changes, a few kilometers down the road. We must go now."

We ran hunched over through the field, making for the closest stone wall. It was about four feet high, and we vaulted over easily, catching our breath as we crouched against the cool rock. The church, with its thin, tall steeple, stood at one end of the courtyard. Two buildings, each three stories high, were to our front and left. One of the structures backed up to the high wall, which was topped with barbed wire. The open ground in front of us had once been a garden, the rows of mounded earth now strewn with weeds.

"What is this place?" I asked.

"It was the Juvénat School, a seminary, until the Germans shut it down," Lasho said. "The priests were smuggling people over the wall. Resistance, escaped prisoners, Jews. Many Jewish children, especially."

"They were discovered?" Kaz asked.

"Yes. Too many people learned of it. The Germans arrested four priests and sent the rest away. All dead by now." Without another word, Lasho sprinted to a shed, rummaged around until he came up with a crowbar, and beckoned us to follow him inside the seminary.

"If the Germans know about it, isn't it too dangerous to use?" I said.

"Exactly! Who would be stupid enough, yes? So the Germans expect nothing. Father Rochet had the idea. Good, eh?"

He popped the locked door with the crowbar, wincing at the loud noise. I carefully closed it up behind us and we climbed the stairs, our shoes echoing in the empty space. The top floor was chaos. Clothes, open suitcases, books, papers, and other debris littered the floor. It looked as if the Krauts had closed the place in a hurry and sent the inhabitants where they'd have no need for a change of clothing. I hoped no refugees had been here when it happened, captured only a wall's width from freedom.

"Here," Lasho said, kicking aside a pile of clothing and opening a hallway door. Inside the narrow space was a single boarded-up window. He applied the crowbar to the planks, working quietly, prying off the wood piece by piece. "It is the only window on this side."

Kaz and Hans were gathering bedsheets and knotting them together. "We'll loop these lengths around the radiator. That way we can pull it down after us and not leave a sign for the Swiss border guards," Kaz said.

"I'll go last and shut the window as best I can," I said.

Lasho had one more board to go. While Kaz finished knotting the sheets, Hans dashed off into another room, leaving the submachine gun and his pack on the floor.

"What is he doing?" Lasho grunted, pulling at the wood plank.

"Getting civilian clothes," Kaz said. "He doesn't want to be put in a camp with other soldiers, or worse yet, sent back to Germany."

"Smart boy," Lasho said. "He trusts no one, not even the Swiss." With that, the last board flew off. Outside the window, it was a free country.

Hans returned wearing corduroy pants, a cloth cap, and a baggy sweater. With his backpack and boots, he looked like a high school kid off on a hiking trip. Not so far from the truth.

Kaz gathered up the knotted sheets, looping them once around a radiator pipe. "Remember to grip both lengths," he said. "Otherwise it will be a fast drop." He confirmed with Hans that he understood, then nodded to Lasho to open the window.

The dry wood creaked and groaned as Lasho pushed against it. He waited a few seconds, then tentatively stuck his head out, scanning the ground ahead. There was a clear strip of land, about ten feet wide, beyond the wall. Then rows of grape vines, thick trunks sprouting green shoots and leaves, strung up on wires. Mountains in the distance. It looked peaceful.

Lasho jerked his head back in.

"Swiss border patrol," he said. "Two men."

I gave a quick glance outside. They sauntered along the barbed-wire fence, rifles slung over their shoulders. It looked like a routine patrol, two bored soldiers, hardly on high alert. I checked my watch: almost ten. The Kraut patrol would be headed back this way.

"Lasho," I said, my voice a whisper. "Do the Swiss and German patrols talk to each other?"

"Yes, all the time. Sometimes it seems they are passing the time of day; other times it sounds official, as if they are exchanging information."

"If the truck stops to chat with these guys, the Germans might decide to stretch their legs and search the seminary," I said.

"They might see the door," Kaz said. "We need to hurry these men along."

"*Was ist los?*" Hans said. Kaz filled him in on the problem. They went back and forth in German for a minute.

"Hans offered to go out and surrender to them," Kaz said. "He's willing to risk an internment camp if it will help us."

"Tell him thanks, but that could attract too much attention to his route over the border. The Swiss might ask the Germans to check the building," I said. Still, I liked the idea of a diversion. Kaz and Hans spoke, and I could see they'd hatched a plan. Hans stripped off his civvies and donned his uniform again, snatching up the MP 40.

"He's going to warn the guards of an attempted crossing, a kilometer down the border, away from the German patrol," Kaz said. Hans pulled his field cap on tight and adjusted the MP 40's leather strap across his shoulder.

"Give him bullets," Lasho said.

"What?" I said, not believing Anton Lasho wanted to give any German a loaded weapon.

"If things go wrong, he will need them. Things always go wrong," Lasho said, looking Hans straight in the eye. I looked at Kaz, who nodded. I released the empty clip and gave Hans one that was fully loaded. Kaz explained, and Hans's eyes went wide.

"*Mach schnell, Hans*," Lasho said, his voice low and gruff. The kid nodded and sped off.

"I hope you're right about this," I said.

"I am," Lasho said. "He could have killed us in the train. He is more afraid of his own people than any of us, yes?"

"Doesn't say much about his people," I said.

"Which makes a decent German all the more important," Kaz said.

Decent again. I hoped decency and luck went hand in hand.

A couple of minutes later, we heard Hans shouting outside, his voice echoing against the stone wall. He used his best Kraut voice, authoritative, loud, harsh, and demanding.

"He's telling them about a group of refugees, probably Jews, that his squad has been tracking. Two women and three small children. They found the wire cut a kilometer back," Kaz said.

"Smart," Lasho said. "No need for the Swiss to call for reinforcements."

"There they go," Kaz said, craning his neck out the window. "They are falling over themselves to be first on the scene."

"Let's go," I said, gathering up the knotted sheets. Lasho opened the window, checking to be sure the Swiss soldiers were out of sight. I tossed the sheets out, grabbing hold of both lengths to stabilize them. Hans burst into the room, laughing, proud of the best prank he'd ever pulled. Lasho grinned and went out the window. I held on, his weight heavy on the sheets. It was three stories down, and it took some time.

Hans was still changing back into the civilian clothes, so Kaz went next. Lasho stood below, gripping both ends, ready and waiting.

An engine growled outside. The truck. The changing of the guard. Fresh troops. Would they be more inquisitive? "Go," I told Kaz. Hans tossed his uniform and weapon aside as he pulled on the corduroys. Kaz climbed out the window and went down hand over hand, as fast as he could.

Shouts from outside. The engine cut out. Had they spotted the smashed door frame?

"Come on," I said to Hans, gesturing with my free hand. I checked on Kaz; he was on the ground.

Boots thumped on the stairs. They were coming up. Hans grabbed the MP 40 and pointed toward the window.

"*Moment,*" he said. Then pointed to himself, the stairs, then the window. I got it. He'd fire to make them take cover, then come back and scale down to join us.

"Okay," I said. "*Mach schnell!*" I went down the sheets as two bursts of submachine gun fire echoed from within the seminary. I imagined the Krauts fanning out throughout the building, ducking and taking cover, the gunfire unexpected and damned unnerving. If it bought us a minute, it was worth it.

There wasn't time to explain. I held tight to the sheets along with Lasho, as Kaz stood ready with his Webley. The shooting was bound to bring the Swiss back, but we'd have a good head start on them.

Hans practically flew out the window, his hands grasping the knots and his feet flailing. He jumped the last couple of yards, hit the ground with a grin on his face, and I tugged the sheets loose, tossing them under a bush. We took off, running along the rows of grape vines, our feet digging into the chalky soil of Switzerland.

A shot rang out. I heard the *thrumm* of the bullet in the air. Had the Swiss guards gotten back so fast? I turned, zigging and zagging as best I could in the narrow rows of grapes, hemmed in by the staked vines. I saw a rifle at the window. Some pissed-off Kraut, not caring about an international incident.

I saw the muzzle flash and dove for the ground. In the next row, Hans did the same.

I watched the window slam shut, imagining some noncom giving his men hell for firing into neutral territory. I got up.

Hans didn't. His cheek was buried in the dirt, his eyes open, and a terrible red stain spreading below his shoulder blade. Lasho ran back, turned him over, checked for a pulse. He shook his head, slowly at first, grinding knuckles into his eyes as he gritted his teeth.

He leaped up, screaming, a deep-throated cry of anguish, horror, curses, and disbelief. His fists shook at his side, his face red and stained with tears. Kaz and I each took an arm, guiding him away from Hans and the demarcation between war and peace, not that a line on the map had made any difference at all.

CHAPTER NINE

WE HAD TO hide. The border guards were sure to investigate the shots and find Hans in the vineyard. Then there'd be more soldiers, along with police, government officials, and maybe even a German from the Nazi embassy to claim the body and apologize for the understandable enthusiasm of his countrymen in stopping a common deserter.

Maybe he wouldn't want to claim the body. Which might be a good thing. Hans didn't deserve to be buried under the swastika flag that he'd tried to leave behind. Maybe the Swiss would give him his own plot of free ground.

Right now, we had our own problems above ground. I doubted the German patrol would stick around to take responsibility for firing into neutral ground, so at least we didn't have to worry about them ratting us out. But we'd left footprints in the loose soil between the rows of grape vines. Unless the guards got all excited and ran to the road to call for help, it would be obvious there were more than one of us. Once they put two and two together, they'd start searching.

The only good news was that they'd probably assume we were all deserters. Fortunately, we were attired in coats, jackets, and ties, and we had a substantial stash of cash. Unfortunately, we looked like well-dressed bums who'd been sleeping rough. That's one reason we needed to hide, at least until nightfall, when we might pass for good Swiss citizens out for a stroll.

The other reason was Lasho. He looked shell-shocked. Even under the cover of darkness, he'd draw unwanted attention. Seeing Hans killed had done something to him. Odd, after he'd killed so many Germans, but maybe that was the trouble. He'd let go of his hatred and saw this kid as what he was: another person trying to do the right thing in the worst of circumstances. I think it made him feel good, maybe restored a bit of his faith in humanity. Hans taking a slug in the back destroyed all that.

Or maybe Hans had reminded him of his own son; Damian would have been only a few years younger.

Whatever the reason, we needed to hide and figure out our next move. We filtered through the vineyard, skirting buildings that were sure to be searched. A wailing siren came closer, the first of many vehicles we could expect to converge on the scene.

"We've got to get beyond the perimeter," I said, guiding Lasho into a grove of apple trees.

"How far is that?" Kaz asked.

"See that road ahead? It looks like it encloses this orchard, maybe the vineyard too. They'll search this whole area up to the road. After that, they might figure we hopped a ride."

I didn't like being in the orchard. The neat rows of trees made concealment difficult. But time wasn't on our side, so we ran straight for the road, hustling Lasho between us. He didn't complain or resist, but he didn't exactly break any records for the hundred-yard dash either.

I think he didn't much care.

We made it to the end of the row, crouching at a rusted barbed-wire fence a few feet high, the kind of fence meant to keep out animals and apple-hunting children. I watched the road, still hearing the siren. It sounded like it was behind us, pulling into the vineyards. No vehicles were in sight, so we stepped over the fence and darted across.

We began walking west, as far as I could tell. Geneva was thataway, maybe ten or twelve miles. We hugged the edge of the road, ready to dive for cover if a vehicle approached. We were still in farm country, nothing near us but a herd of grazing sheep. At a bend in the road, I

moved off into the shrubbery with Lasho while Kaz trotted ahead to check things out.

"A garage," Kaz said, after running back and joining us. "There are a lot of vehicles. Automobiles, farm machinery, and trucks."

"Maybe we could steal one," I said.

"Or at least hide," Kaz said. "There seem to be a number of abandoned vehicles in the back."

We worked our way to the rear, staying off the road so they wouldn't see us coming. It was a big, squat building, with an old gas pump out front. It looked like any shop in the States, only with different model automobiles. Rusted wrecks in the back, a scattering of newer cars in the front. Metal clanged from inside, and an engine fired up. One fellow strolled outside, his blue coveralls stained and dirty. He lit up a smoke and stretched. Hard work, keeping vehicles in repair during wartime.

He turned, shouting and pointing at someone inside.

"What's he saying?" I asked Kaz.

"Basically, 'I don't pay you to talk, I pay you to work.'"

"So he's the boss?"

"Yes. Does that help us?"

"Maybe," I said. "It means he's a businessman. Maybe instead of hiding, we could make a deal."

"What kind of deal?"

"A cash deal," I said. "We've got a lot of Swiss francs."

"We could easily buy a brand-new automobile for each of us," Kaz said. "I will go and speak to him. One stranger is less intimidating than three."

"Lasho, how does that sound? We'll ride into town," I said, trying to sound cheery and hoping for a lucid response.

He looked at me and sighed, with a slight nod. At least he heard the question.

"Watch the garage," Kaz said. "There's a chance he could be pro-German. If he attempts to restrain me, you may need to come to my rescue."

"Shout out if you need me," I said.

I watched as Kaz strolled in and began chatting with the owner. It didn't take long before they went inside. I wanted to get closer, but we were well hidden, and I didn't want to risk being seen. I waited, giving Lasho a reassuring pat on the shoulder. He didn't look especially reassured.

Five minutes passed. How long did it take to work a deal?

I glanced at my watch. Another three minutes gone. If he wasn't out in two more, I'd drag Lasho along and go in with my pistol drawn. Why not add larceny and armed robbery to our Swiss crime spree?

Then I heard an engine start. A black Peugeot sedan backed out of the garage, and Kaz waved for us to come forward, a smile on his face.

"Billy, shake hands with Monsieur Andreau," Kaz said, as the mechanic stepped forward to open the door for me. "He has family in France." He gave me an energetic shake and did the same with Lasho, who took refuge in the backseat.

"*Au revoir*," Monsieur Andreau said, waving and looking quite happy with himself.

"What about the other mechanics?" I asked.

"His nephew and son," Kaz said. "They were happy to help, knowing the conditions their relatives live under in France, not to mention the easy money. And look, food as well." A cloth bag held a loaf of bread, a good-sized chunk of cheese, and a bottle of wine, half full. "We had to toast the deal, of course."

"Of course," I said. "Nice car."

"Monsieur Andreau said he would report it stolen. Tomorrow. He asked if we would be good enough to leave the key in the glove box."

"Least we can do," I said, tearing off a chunk of bread and slicing cheese with my pocket knife. I handed the food to Lasho, who held it in his hand as if it were a strange and foreign object. I passed back the bottle of wine. That, he had no problem with.

We drove into Geneva, passing two police cars, an ambulance, and a truck full of Swiss soldiers going the other way. Kaz whistled a tune as we motored along, three guys out for a ride in a Peugeot 402 sedan, one of the most common automobiles in France, and in Switzerland, as far as I could tell.

"What was the name of the street again?" I asked Kaz.

"Rue Montbrilliant, number two. The Hotel Le Montbrillant. We go through the center of town, cross the river, and it is near the train station, about half a mile from the lakefront."

"We need to talk with Lasho," I said.

"Yes. Once we cross the bridge, we'll find a place to leave the car and walk to the hotel. We'll talk then."

"About what?" Lasho said from the backseat. His voice had a tremor, a deep quivering bass note of fear.

"About what you wish to do next," I said, tapping Kaz on the arm and motioning for him to pull over. We parked in front of a row of buildings, offices and stores mainly, with a park across the street. It was busy, green, and populated with people who weren't looking over their shoulders every two seconds.

It looked a lot like peacetime, except for crops being grown in the open spaces. Being land-locked by Germany and Italy, food production was likely a priority.

"What should I do?" Lasho asked, distracting me from pacific thoughts.

"We can give you money," I said.

"What will I do with money? If the Swiss discover I have no identity papers, they will turn me over to the Nazis. Jews and Sinti are not allowed, yes?"

"That's right, especially men. Do you have any relations in this country?"

"No. The Sinti never came here. The Swiss do not like us."

"What kind of work can you do?" Kaz asked.

"Farm work, and I can fix some things. You know what I am good at: killing Germans. But now I do not want to go back to that. Tell me, what work are you here to do?"

"It's top secret," I said.

"We really don't know yet," Kaz said, a bit more honestly.

"It is for the war, yes? You help defeat the Germans with what you do?"

"I hope so," I said. "We're detectives, really. For the Allies."

"Detectives? Like Maigret?" This seemed to impress him.

"More like Dick Tracy," I said, which only confused him.

"Please, Lasho," Kaz said, "never mind all that. We must find a place for you. Somewhere safe."

"There is nowhere safe. And I have a place. I stay with you. Together, we will do something good, yes?"

"Lasho, we don't need any help," I said.

"You needed help the first moment I saw you, yes? I took you with me and helped you. Now, you take me with you. It is only fair."

"Kaz?" I said, holding back on commenting that it was the only decent thing to do.

"Yes, I think. Welcome, Lasho. You now work for General Eisenhower." Ike was far away, so who's to say he'd disagree?

"Good. Now drive away. A policeman is coming," Lasho said, already pulling his weight.

Kaz eased the sedan out into the road as the cop strolled along the sidewalk, his eyes moving, assessing his surroundings. It was a familiar look. We eased into traffic as his gaze settled on us for a split second, then moved on as another driver honked his horn. A typical cop, walking his beat.

"I guess we can use an extra pair of eyes, Lasho," I said.

"The Swiss police are not looking for three men," Lasho said. "Yet."

We crossed a bridge over the river, flowing into the wide expanse of Lake Geneva on our right. We drove along the waterfront and parked on the road near a promenade along the water. Kaz stashed the key as Monsieur Andreau had requested, and we hoofed it across the railroad tracks until we found the Hotel Le Montbrillant.

It was easy to spot. Not a huge place, it was set snug between two streets that converged on an open square with a view of the lake, partially obstructed by the rail yard and train station beyond. A convenient spot for travelers. Four stories, bright white paint job, blue shutters and trim, with matching blue and white umbrellas displayed along an outdoor café on the terrace.

"I hope our contact enjoyed the accommodations well enough to stay a few extra days," I said.

"If not, we shall have to get ourselves to Bern on our own," Kaz said. Bern, located in the center of Switzerland, was our ultimate destination. That was as much as we knew, except to meet our contact at this hotel.

We dusted ourselves off, adjusted our ties, and took a minute to check our surroundings. No obvious police presence, uniformed or plainclothes. At one table, three men in business suits, too well-tailored for cops, were drinking wine. A few couples leaned into each other at their tables, oblivious to the world. A woman had her nose in a newspaper, her back to us. It looked safe.

"Maybe you should go alone," I said to Kaz. He spoke French perfectly, which was the preferred lingo in this part of Switzerland. And somehow he managed to look downright spiffy, even after all we'd been through.

"I will walk around the hotel first," Lasho said. "If there is a police car parked in the back, then they are waiting for us inside."

"Smart guy," I said, watching Lasho melt into the pedestrian traffic.

"He seems to have gotten over the shock," Kaz said. "It may help him to have a purpose."

"As long as he doesn't get in the way of our doing our job," I said. Not that I had a clue what that job might be. We waited as Lasho circumvented the block, appearing at the far end of the hotel, near what looked like a delivery entrance. He gave a thumbs-up, and Kaz sauntered into the lobby to ask if room 608 was available. Since there were only four floors, it was obvious this was a code, and the hotel staff had been briefed to expect the question.

Lasho rejoined me, his eyes darting up and down the street. We were surrounded by war, but it was hard to tell from the Swiss citizens in this busy city. Not many uniforms were in sight, and there were more guys my age in civvies than I'd seen since I left Boston. They may have been growing cabbages in the park, but no one looked too inconvenienced.

"I have never been in a hotel," Lasho said, nudging me, his voice low as if this were a terrible secret.

"Really?"

"I washed dishes in a hotel kitchen. Birmingham, I think. But I have not been in a real hotel room."

"How long did you work there?"

"Two weeks. Then someone stole from a guest. So they fire me because I am Sinti. We are all thieves, they say. Will they let me stay in this hotel?"

"I'd guess there are fancy hotels in this burg that would turn us all away as tramps," I said. "But I think our money will be good here."

"Because you are American?" he asked.

"No. Because we have a lot of it. Tell me, Lasho, how are you? Are you holding up okay?"

"Holding up?" he said, as if thinking about what that meant. "I feel strange. Everything before, everything I did, it was simple, yes? I hunt Germans; I kill them. Now nothing is simple. So I stay with you."

"To keep things simple?" I wasn't sure how we'd do that.

"If I help you, I will not want to go back. I have other rifles hidden in the forest, and I wish to leave them to rust." We stood in silence, leaning against a wall as sunlight warmed the stone. No sign of Kaz. Lasho sighed, quietly, as he might have done hiding in the forests of the Haute-Savoie.

"If you hadn't shot Father Rochet, he'd have suffered greatly," I said.

"He would have been tortured, yes. But his greatest suffering would have come if he gave in to those *bâtards*. He had a great heart, but no man can say what he will do to make the pain stop. He might have betrayed a dozen people, and cursed his own soul."

"Until they put a bullet in his head," I said.

"No. He believed deeply in the soul. There, in his soul, he would remember."

He sighed again, louder this time.

Kaz whistled from across the street and waved us over. I wondered about Lasho's thoughts on the human soul, since he'd dispatched so many to the afterlife, then decided some questions are best not asked.

CHAPTER TEN

"WHO THE HELL is this?" the woman sitting alone on the terrace wanted to know. She snapped her head in Lasho's direction, then focused her dark eyes back on Kaz. She wore a two-piece suit and a matching hat, with the brim down to her eyebrows. It was greenish-gray, close to the same color as a German uniform, but on her the look was much preferable.

I looked at Kaz, waiting for him to reply. Since he'd been the one to make contact, I was glad to let him handle what sounded like an interrogation.

"Sit down," she snapped. "You're drawing attention. Just the two of you. Tell your friend to take a walk."

We settled in at her table as Lasho retreated across the street, back to the sunlit wall.

"*Gdzie można studiować na uniwersytecie?*" she said to Kaz, taking out a small compact and applying lipstick. Or checking in the mirror for spies, it was hard to tell.

"Oxford, of course," Kaz said, crossing his legs and shaking out the crease in his mud-stained trousers.

"What about you, hotshot?" I was going to ask how she knew, but the query was laced with enough sarcasm that I didn't want to tempt a rejoinder.

"Well, I've been to Cambridge a few times," I said. "But it was the one outside of Boston, and I wasn't going to school there."

"All right, now that we've established your bona fides, tell me who your traveling companion is and what does he know?"

"Hang on, sister," I said, going for the same brusque approach she'd dished out to us. "Who are you, and why should we tell you a thing?"

"Not bad, William," she said, leaning back in her chair and letting the smallest of smiles crack her mouth. She was somewhere in her thirties, or maybe even forty. Expensive clothes, nice makeup, and the dough to afford both tended to soften the lines of age. She was good-looking in a square-jawed sort of way, but what made her most attractive was the sharp intelligence that danced in her eyes. Not counting the pot of coffee by her arm.

"Billy," I said. "And this is Kaz. I'm sure you know all about the baron part."

"Baron Piotr Augustus Kazimierz," she said, her eyes tilted upward as she recited from memory. "The Swiss love barons, counts, all that noble claptrap. No offense intended, Baron."

"None taken, Miss—?" Kaz raised an eyebrow, after a quick glance at her left hand. Our gal was single.

"Conaty," she said. "Maureen Conaty. Now that we've introduced ourselves, let's go back to tall, dark, and ill-shaven over there. As I already asked, who the hell is he?"

"Maureen, first we need to order more coffee and food. Then we need to call Lasho over to help us drink and eat it."

"Gypsy?" Maureen asked, raising a finger to summon a waiter as she studied Lasho, who stared back at her from across the road.

"Sinti, to be precise," Kaz answered, waving him over. "Without Anton Lasho, we would be dead by now." Maureen ordered more joe and pastries. As soon as the waiter scurried off, Kaz introduced Lasho, who took Maureen's hand as if she were a duchess.

"You don't happen to know the Gypsy who is terrorizing the Germans, Mr. Lasho?" Maureen said as she gestured for him to take a seat. "*Der Zigeuner.*"

"Why do you ask?" Lasho said, glancing at us with questioning eyes. He sighed as he sat, the weariness we all felt evident on his face.

"I'd like to pin a medal on him," she said. "And then tell him to stop. Killing Germans is a worthwhile occupation, but he's starting to interfere with intelligence operations. We can't get any information from the Resistance with the Germans hunting for him all along the border."

"I will tell him, if you like," Lasho said. "But I am sure he has stopped. For the time being."

"Good," Maureen said, a smile playing on her lips as she drummed her fingers on the table, assessing the situation. She knew damn well *der Zigeuner* was sitting right next to her. "I hope he finds a more peaceful occupation. What are your plans, Mr. Lasho?"

The waiter arrived with a fresh pot of coffee and a basket of warm brioche and croissants, giving us time to think about a good answer, not that I could focus much with the aroma of real steaming coffee assailing my nostrils.

"I work for General Eisenhower," Lasho said, and grabbed a croissant. It was gone in seconds.

"He is helping us," Kaz said, looking around to see if anyone had overheard Lasho's zealous statement.

"And you two work for Ike," Maureen said. "I know all about SHAEF's Office of Special Investigations. You're the general's troubleshooters, and you mix it up pretty well when you need to. Not what I anticipated, Billy, when I first heard you were Ike's nephew. I expected a feather merchant."

"Feathers?" Lasho asked, dumping sugar into his coffee. I hadn't seen this much sugar the whole time I'd been in France.

"A feather merchant is slang for a soldier with an easy assignment," Kaz explained. "A fellow who gets by with as little effort as possible." He smiled, enjoying my discomfort at Maureen's description.

"Yeah, sort of like a baron," I said. Lasho caught the looks on our faces and hesitated a moment before he laughed. "Actually, the general and I are distant cousins on my mother's side. He needed a trained detective, and I'd made the grade in Boston when the war broke out. I guess he likes having a family member to depend on, but he doesn't cut me any slack on account of that."

What I left out was that we hadn't known Uncle Ike—he was

older, so cousin twice-removed or not, uncle it was—had been tapped to head to England in early 1942. My family, no slouches when it came to calling in favors from Boston politicians, had schemed to get me appointed to his staff when he was still an unknown colonel in the War Plans Department down in DC. You see, we're all good Irishmen, which means we don't give a damn for the British Empire and its boot heel on a free Ireland. Dad and Uncle Dan lost their older brother Frank in the First World War, and they didn't plan on sacrificing another Boyle lad to keep the Brits afloat. So, I headed to Washington, DC, finding nothing in the sentiment of survival to argue with. But then Uncle Ike was made a general and sent to England to head up all US Army forces, with me tagging along, a freshly minted second louie. Now he was the supreme commander, and I was a captain, taking on top-secret investigations, solving low crimes in high places. Which is how I found myself sitting in a nice Swiss café. Strange war.

"No, it doesn't seem that he's given you any breaks, based on your file," Maureen said. "I'm amazed you're still alive."

"I'm a careful man," I said. "Kaz and I watch each other's backs. And now we have Lasho. He's proven his worth."

"You two still have your identity papers?" Maureen said. I nodded and reached into my pocket. "No, not here. There's no reason why you'd show your papers to a woman in a café. You have to watch yourself very carefully. I trust your papers will pass inspection, but if anyone checks with the authorities, they will quickly see you're not on any diplomatic list."

"What would happen then?" Kaz asked, tearing off a bit of croissant. Half-starved, his manners were still impeccable.

"An internment camp at best," she said. "Perhaps prison. Or expulsion."

"Unpleasant," Kaz said, watching Lasho, who set his cup down hard, spilling coffee into the saucer.

"Quite," Maureen said, her eyes steady on Lasho. "Do you have papers, Mr. Lasho?"

"I have nothing."

"Well, then I need to get to work," she said. "Finish up, boys. I'll take you to our next stop."

"We're not staying here?" I asked. Clean sheets and a soft bed seemed so close.

"No. Everyone knows this is where OSS people hang their hats when they come to Geneva. No one with forged papers stays here."

"Why not?" I asked.

"Because we bribe the staff to take messages and pass them on to us, like asking for room six-oh-eight."

"So?" I asked, still not getting the problem.

"If a man can be bribed," Lasho said, "he can be bribed." Once again, he proved to be a quick learner.

"Exactly," Maureen said. "The bartender probably sells gossip to Swiss military intelligence and the *Abwehr* as well. So finish your coffee and we'll take a stroll."

"Then you'll tell us what we're doing here?" I said.

"All in good time, cowboy. The first order of business will be to get you all new clothes. And a bath. The Swiss are fixated on cleanliness, and the three of you need a good scrubbing." She wrinkled her nose and drew in a sharp breath. Can't say I blamed her.

I turned up the collar of my overcoat as we followed Maureen's clicking heels down a side street, away from the fancy waterfront neighborhood and into a warren of narrow winding streets and buildings festooned with colorful shutters. We entered a wide alley and Maureen halted, raising a finger to her lips, motioning for us to stay put. She doubled back, and we listened as her steps receded and then returned.

"No tail," she said.

"How long have you been doing this spy stuff?" I asked. I didn't want to burst her bubble, but a professional wouldn't fall for the doubling-back routine. He'd melt into a doorway or double back himself.

"Ever since I was a reporter in the city," she said. "Be a gentleman, will ya, and don't ask how long ago. Come on."

"What city?" Kaz asked as we trailed her. Lasho took up the rear, checking our six as Maureen forged on.

"When a Yank says that, it usually means they're from New York. Anyone else would be nice enough to mention the name of their hometown," I said.

"Bostonians are jealous of a real city with skyscrapers and a great baseball team," she said, taking a ring of keys from her handbag and unlocking a stout wooden door as we gathered on the stone steps. She gave me a wink to say it was all in good fun. I smiled and glanced at the open bag. Nestled inside was a .25 caliber automatic. Maybe that's why she wasn't so worried about a tail.

The stairway was dark, the walls showing long cracks in the plaster. Two flights up, Maureen opened an apartment door and ushered us in. A dismal hallway led into a large room with high ceilings and the lingering scent of rotten food. Two mismatched couches ready for the rubbish heap, or perhaps rescued from it, sat in the center of the room. They faced away from the kitchen, which was their best feature.

"It ain't much, fellows, but this address doesn't attract much attention," Maureen said, pointing out two bedrooms off the main room. "Right now, you fit in nicely. Soon as we get you spruced up, we'll take the train to Bern and set you up in better digs."

"The forest was cleaner than this," Lasho said. His face was impassive, but I decided to believe he'd cracked a joke, and laughed. He nearly smiled.

"How about some information first," I said. "Tell us what was important enough to bring us here from occupied France."

"Gold. Lots and lots of gold."

That was all she said before heading out to round up duds for Lasho. There were already clothes waiting for me and Kaz, suits and a couple of suitcases neatly packed. A tan trench coat was mine, slightly used, with a brown felt fedora rolled up in the pocket. Kaz scored a nice new gray coat along with a snappy black fedora. The sizes were right and the new coat was perfect for Kaz, who was a bit of a clothes-horse. Which told me that the OSS knew a lot of details about us, besides having a good tailor on the payroll.

Before Maureen left, there'd been a knock at the door. Two short raps and then a third hard one. She seemed to expect a visitor, but palmed her pistol all the same. Turned out it was a barber, and as soon as he saw Lasho, he knew why he was there. He didn't speak, just got to work, no questions asked. Scissors snipped as hair littered the kitchen floor. By the time Lasho's mustache was trimmed and he had a shave, he was nearly handsome, in a scowling sort of way.

Kaz and I had a shave as well. Not bad, fighting the war Swiss style.

The barber packed up his gear, and I gave him some Swiss francs at the door, since my dad had taught me always to tip the guy who holds a razor to your throat. After a while Kaz emerged from the bathroom—sparkling clean compared to the rest of the joint—a towel draped over his shoulders.

"You look like a new man, Lasho," Kaz said.

"I think I will have to be," he said. "This is not a country for Sinti or for hunting Germans."

"It may be a different kind of hunting," I said, taking a seat on the lumpy couch.

"If we hunt for gold, there will be others in the hunt as well," Lasho said, walking into the bathroom and examining himself in the mirror. He rested his hands on the sink as he stared at his reflection. Kaz shut the door, leaving Lasho alone with himself and whatever memories were at work behind those hooded, dark eyes.

"He's right," Kaz said. "I wonder how much gold."

My feet were already up on the couch. The next thing I knew, I was dreaming of gold coins and croissants.

CHAPTER ELEVEN

IN THE MORNING, we followed Maureen at a distance, keeping her blue coat and matching wide-brim hat in sight. It was easy to follow from a block away, and it hid her face nicely. I didn't know who might be watching, but if we were walking around with pistols stuffed in the pockets of our snazzy new jackets, then it stood to reason there might be Germans doing the same.

Maureen had brought food for us last night, along with clothing for Lasho. We had a lot of questions, but she begged off, saying she had a rendezvous with a contact and that there'd be plenty of time on the train for a briefing. She left us with ample sausage, olives, cheese, and wine, so we didn't mind.

She'd come up with a second-hand black wool coat for Lasho. He trailed behind us, looking a bit like a butler attending to his baron. Me, I still felt like a cop, wearing my trench coat and slapping shoe leather on pavement. Like old times. We were cleaned up, rested, and looking the part of three travelers, clutching our suitcases and walking down the Rue Voltaire on our way to catch a train, enjoying the spring sunshine.

Maureen's blue hat slowed, then halted a block ahead. The foot traffic kept going around her, some people heading to the station entrance, others continuing on.

"What's wrong?" Kaz asked. I set my suitcase down and put my foot up to tie my shoe, buying time. Lasho craned his neck to see ahead.

"There are people at the station entrance," he said. "Waiting in line."

"So why isn't she moving?" I asked. It could be anything. But she'd given us our tickets and told us what train to board; she'd be waiting in our first-class compartment. It was her idea not to be seen with us in case anyone was watching the station. She was never entirely clear on who *anyone* was. The Germans? Swiss intelligence? MI6 or some other allied competitor? A jealous boyfriend?

"We are attracting attention," Kaz said, as people stepped around us on the sidewalk, some of them staring as they heard English spoken.

"*Avec moi*," Lasho said, tapping me on the shoulder. A police car drove slowly by, an officer gazing out the passenger window. I followed, as Lasho pulled the brim of his cloth cap lower. A few steps ahead, I could see why Maureen had stopped.

She was talking with a man. He wore the gray uniform and kepi of the Swiss army. It didn't look like an interrogation. He leaned close, his head angled down close to her face, hidden by her dark blue hat. He laughed, throwing his head back. She placed a hand on his arm, an intimate but restrained gesture. Then she turned and walked toward us, the officer vanishing into the crowd.

Maureen wasn't laughing.

"You didn't tell me about the deserter," she said, the words coming out of clenched lips as she stood with one hand on her hip.

"Hans," Lasho said.

"I don't care what his name is. You should have told me. The border patrol is in a frenzy, and the Germans are demanding the other three deserters who escaped with him," she said.

"But Hans was the only deserter," I said, the light dawning as soon as I spoke. "They must know Lasho was with us. They want the Gypsy."

"Yes. And they're demanding the Swiss turn all of you over. The Swiss are protesting the shooting into their territory, the Germans are protesting the sheltering of deserters, and everyone looks bad. Do you know what that means?"

"Yes. They need a fall guy, someone to take the heat off everyone," I said.

"Right. Any one of you will do nicely right now, according to my contact," Maureen said.

"That officer?" I said. "Can you trust him?"

"More than I can trust you three, when it comes to the truth," she said, casting a quick glance back at the line forming outside the station entrance.

"You didn't have much time to spare for us, sister, so don't blow a gasket," I said.

"What do we do now?" Kaz said, not unreasonably.

"Should I give myself up?" Lasho whispered.

"Forget it," Maureen said. "I paid too much for that coat to send it to the Germans. Give Anton cash. A lot." Kaz drew a wad of Swiss francs from his pocket and handed it over. "Listen, Anton, we need to get to Bern. You'll never make it through an identity check without papers. Get yourself there however you can. Steal a car, hitchhike, pay a truck driver, but don't get caught. Then go to Herrengasse 23. Got that? It's in the old city, along the river."

"Herrengasse 23," he repeated, pocketing the cash as he watched the road.

"Do you want a pistol?" Kaz asked in a hushed voice.

"No. The temptation would be too great," Lasho muttered as he vanished into the crowd. I didn't take that to refer to using it on others.

"The good news is that they're searching for German deserters, not a couple of attachés," Maureen said, her eyes trying to follow Lasho. "You two go together, I'll be right behind you."

"Famous last words," I said to Kaz as soon as we were out of ear-shot. "You trust her?"

"She lives in a constant state of lies, deceit, and deception. It may not be wise to trust her motives entirely. She's a tough cookie, isn't she?" Kaz loved trotting out American slang when he could, rolling it around his Oxford-educated accent like the student of languages he was.

"Nah. A tough cookie would have thrown Lasho to the wolves. She talks a good game, like a lot of reporters, but she's probably got a soft spot for down-and-outers."

"Her current employer, you mean?" Kaz said, not wanting to trot out those three initials, OSS.

"No, pal, I mean a big-city newsroom. If Maureen didn't get her lunch handed to her at whatever Gotham rag put her on the payroll, then she knows how to put on a good front."

Like any obedient civilians waiting in line, we shuffled along, suitcase in tow, with our worn leather wallets in hand. They were stuffed with Swiss francs, our identity cards from the American embassy, and the usual flotsam that ended up in any guy's wallet. Ticket stubs, a photo of a girl, a business card, the kind of thing that projected a sense of normalcy.

Passing muster with phony papers was all about showing a combination of boredom and frustration. Bored because you'd done this a hundred times before. Frustrated because you had to catch a train. Nervous, well, that was the mark of a guy who had something more than a missed connection to worry about. Nerves you kept to yourself.

"*Bonjour*," Kaz said, handing over his ID when it was our turn. There were soldiers in their gray uniforms and plainclothes guys who were probably cops. Or intelligence, since the hunt was for three deserters, perhaps armed. The soldiers checked papers while the plainclothes men kept their eyes on the crowd, watching for furtive glances and grimy clothing.

Kaz complained to me about the wait, checking his watch, muttering and shaking his head as the soldier with his papers handed them back and moved him along, irritated at his chatter. I offered my papers, which he took a quick look at and waved me through, not wanting to take a chance on another cantankerous American. Or Polish American, in Kaz's case.

"I wonder what Lasho will do," Kaz said as we made our way to the platform. "Or if we ever will see him again."

"Let's hope so," I said, realizing that our Sinti friend had grown on me. "He's survived alone in the forests of France. Switzerland should be a breeze."

On board the train we settled into our compartment and waited for Maureen. We watched as people hurried along the platform, delayed by the security check. Soldiers patrolled in twos, their rifles slung over their shoulders and their eyes dancing over the flow of travelers.

"There is quite a difference being hunted by the Swiss rather than the Germans. While I have no wish to be apprehended, the thought is not accompanied by the same terror, is it? I imagine the Swiss police can be brutal at times, but it is nothing compared to the Gestapo kitchens," Kaz said.

"Yeah. It's more like a game here. What's the worst that could happen to us?"

"An internment camp. Humiliation and boredom, I expect," Kaz said.

I spotted Maureen outside and rapped on the window. She pretended she didn't notice. Probably something they taught her in spy school.

"No problems, fellas?" she asked as took a seat next to Kaz.

"It was a breeze, doll," Kaz said, using his best American accent.

"Well listen to you, Kaz. You'd fit right in on Forty-second Street," she said, stowing the small bag she'd brought aboard. It looked expensive. Italian leather, maybe.

"No luggage? Weren't you waiting days for us?" She looked sharp in a blue tailored jacket and skirt, not to mention that hat. If she dressed like a million bucks every day, she'd need a steamer trunk.

"I had the hotel ship it to Bern last night," she said, pulling out a compact and checking her lipstick.

"Late night meeting with your contact?" I asked.

"Oh, Billy, tell me you're not one of the banned-in-Boston crowd. Are you a prude, dear boy?"

"Sorry," I said. "No offense. I just wonder about things. Occupational hazard for a cop. Like I wonder how that Swiss officer met up with you just in time to warn you this morning."

"Because I asked him to last night," she said. "And he was glad to oblige. I figured there might be a search on, and I wanted to know what to expect. I needn't have bothered if you told me about the German deserter. I would have sent Lasho to Bern by a more secure route."

"His name was Hans," Kaz said.

"I would have been more interested in his name if you told me yesterday. Now he's only a sad story."

"Okay, we should have told you. Sorry if you wasted time with your contact," I said.

"Oh, it wasn't wasted, Billy." She smiled conspiratorially at Kaz, and I felt my face redden. Maybe she was a real tough cookie, and I did have a touch of the prude.

"Let's move on," I said, trying to cover my obvious embarrassment. "Now would be a good time to brief us on our mission."

"Right," she said, as the train lurched forward and pulled out of the station. "Some bright lights at the treasury department came up with a scheme to prevent the Nazis from salting away money in neutral nations for use after the war. SS bigwigs and a lot of Hitler's cronies are already hedging their bets and making private deposits in Swiss banks. Uncle Sam wants to be sure they can't afford to start up a Fourth Reich a decade or so after we finish off the Third. Plus, we don't want banks in neutral nations funding getaways for Hitler or Himmler once we get to Berlin."

"That sounds swell, but why treasury? What do we have to do with a bunch of bean-counters in Washington?" I said.

"Treasury came up with the idea. Money is their business, after all. They call it Operation Safehaven. Once the treasury boys got over here, they realized Safehaven depended on gathering intelligence about where the Germans were squirreling away their dough. So the OSS was brought on board. We're supposed to identify where German funds are hidden, here and anywhere else in the world, and let treasury negotiate with the neutral governments to keep the money out of the hands of the Nazis and use it to rebuild Europe after the war."

"An exemplary idea," Kaz said. "What do you need us for?"

"Two things. The first is to keep the Gestapo at bay while we do our work. There are a number of Gestapo agents active in Switzerland. As you can imagine, they can come and go as they please. The Germans don't know about Safehaven yet, but as soon as they think their hidden wealth is in danger, there'll be hell to pay."

"At bay? What does that mean?" I said.

"Make sure they don't discover what we're up to. Without creating an international incident. Can you handle that?"

"We'll try not to leave a trail of bodies in the street," I said. I was kidding, but she nodded approvingly anyway.

"What's the second thing?" Kaz asked.

"Look into any irregularities our finance people uncover. Bribes, anything that can be used to pry information from the Swiss banking establishment."

"You mentioned gold," I said. "How much are we talking about?"

"No one knows for certain. That's what we need to find out. But hundreds of millions, certainly."

"That's a lotta dough. One Swiss franc is about two bits, isn't it?" I said.

"I meant dollars, Billy. Hundreds of millions of *dollars*." I whistled. "When we get to Bern, Allen will fill you in on the details. Banks bore me, and Safehaven is all about banks. Except for the Nazis, who do tend to keep me focused."

"Which banks?" Kaz said, his eyes steady on Maureen.

"Ah, Baron, you're beginning to see the light, aren't you?"

"What do you mean?" I asked, sensing that Kaz was a few steps ahead of me on this one. Me, I wanted to know who Allen was.

"The baron has legitimate interest in several of the major Swiss banks. The family fortune and all that," Maureen said, giving us that coy smile of hers.

"How do you know? Isn't privacy the whole point of Swiss banks?" I was getting steamed and it wasn't even my dough.

"Yes, and that's part of the challenge. Suffice it to say we have influence with certain banks in London," she said, leaning back in her seat and gazing out the window. I wondered how Lasho was getting on out there. Not that it mattered, since he probably didn't have a bank account.

"And my London bank kindly gave you information about fund transfers from Switzerland," Kaz said, his mouth set in a grim line.

"Well, not *me*, Baron. Someone very British and very stuffy, I'd guess. All part of selecting the right men for the job. You can walk into the Swiss National Bank, Credit Suisse, Swiss Bank Corporation, and any others we may not know about and chat with senior bankers."

"One bank isn't enough, Kaz?" I knew he was rich. Really rich, actually. But why so many banks?

"As you are obviously aware, Miss Conaty," Kaz said, displeasure edging out the veneer of politeness he normally cultivated, "my father had sufficient foresight concerning the inevitable Nazi threat to Poland to convert his holdings into cash and transfer those funds to Switzerland." The Kazimierz clan was some sort of minor Polish nobility, and their patriarch had substantial land holdings as well as industrial investments in Warsaw and Kraków. He was a smart guy to sell all that off in the late 1930s. The guy who bought them, not so smart.

"He was one of the few who did," Maureen said.

"He fought in the Polish-Soviet War in 1920. Before that, he'd watched the armies of the Great War roll across Poland, creating massive devastation. He knew what a modern war would do, especially one between two madmen."

Kaz told Maureen the basics, but I think he was too angry about the snooping into his private affairs to give away much. I knew the real story: about how his parents had visited Kaz when he was attending Oxford and told him of their plans. There were still some details to work out, so they returned to finalize the sale of property in Kraków and organize passage for the extended family. Brothers, sisters, cousins, aunts, and uncles. It would be only a matter of months before the entire family relocated and joined Kaz in England.

That was the summer of 1939.

Germany attacked Poland on the first of September. By the end of the month, it was all over. Stalin and Hitler divided up Poland between them, and then the real killing began. Kaz's family was wiped out, part of the German plan to eliminate the intelligentsia and reduce what had once been Poland to a slave state.

Kaz was the last Kazimierz, a lonely Polish baron with nothing left to lose. Except, apparently, for a whole lot of cash.

"I am sorry, Baron, about both your family and this intrusion into your private affairs. But, I assure you, it was in the best of causes. There are few Swiss bankers sympathetic to the Allies; any advantage we have will have to be used to the utmost."

"If they're unfriendly, what can we do about it?" I asked. "I mean, Kaz is an important client, but so are the Krauts, and they make deposits in gold."

"True," Maureen said, "but if we can gain the trust of the right banker, he can tell us if the Swiss are lying about the amount of Nazi gold they're holding. We'd also like evidence of looted wealth in private accounts held by any top Nazis. The greatest service you could provide would be to find a sympathetic banker where you have an account and cultivate that relationship."

"You mentioned the Gestapo," I said. "Are we bound to run into them?"

"Watch out they don't run into you. There are all sorts of German agents in Bern, often working at cross-purposes. The Gestapo, the Abwehr, the SS Economics Office, the German Foreign Service, and probably a few more I don't know about. But there is one Gestapo man in particular you should keep an eye on. Georg Hannes. He's a sophisticated brute. He specializes in ferreting out Swiss bank accounts owned by people in Germany or the occupied countries. It's illegal for anyone under the thumb of the Third Reich to have private accounts outside the country. The rule doesn't apply to the top boys, of course."

"How does he do it?" Kaz said.

"Bribery and flattery go a long way. It helps that he's got an unlimited expense account. He wines and dines the bankers and is quite good at getting them to reveal account numbers of illegal German depositors. A lot of these bankers are pro-Nazi to begin with, so he knows who he can approach. If the account holder is Jewish, and still alive, they can easily be persuaded to withdraw their funds and turn them over to the Nazis, in exchange for their freedom. Which is occasionally granted."

"If they're not Jewish, a visit from the Gestapo is probably enough to get them to sign their fortune away," I said.

"Right. I've watched Hannes drag account owners into the bank with him. Whatever the Swiss think, they have to turn over funds to the owner, even if he looks frightened to death."

"My god, I hope they never knew of my father's accounts," Kaz said. "I'd hate to think of him being tortured."

"If you have your money, then he didn't talk. I mean, they never found out, obviously," Maureen said, trying to backpedal on the notion of Kaz's father being tortured to death.

"Hannes sounds like a worthless excuse for a human being, but why do we need to watch out for him?" I asked.

"He's smart, and we can't risk him alerting the Nazis to this investigation. Obviously, he's got contacts throughout the Swiss banking community, so he's bound to learn of it eventually. Let's make sure it's later. Much later. That's also a big part of your job."

"Makes sense. But what should we do if we run into Hannes?" I asked, figuring Kaz would have a few suggestions.

"If the opportunity presents itself, he should be killed," Maureen said calmly. "If Lasho makes it to Bern, he'd be the one to do it."

"Why Lasho?" Kaz said. "I have no problem putting a Gestapo agent in the ground."

"Because you two have a mission, and that's paramount," she said. "Hannes should be eliminated on general principles. The world would be a better place without him. Plus the Germans would lose a valuable agent right when they need his nose to the ground. This isn't an order, you understand. It's just something I'd like to see done."

And by Anton Lasho, the Gypsy killer. A patsy if there ever was one.

I had to admit it. Maureen Conaty was indeed one tough cookie.

CHAPTER TWELVE

BERN LOOKED LIKE a nice old burg, and not only because no one was dropping bombs on it or shooting its citizens in the street. In the medieval heart of the city, around which the River Aare ran in an oxbow curve, orange-tiled buildings stood above narrow streets decorated with overflowing window boxes, fountains, and statues. Maureen led us on a short walk from the train station to the Golden Eagle Hotel, where rooms had been booked for two junior economic attachés from the consular office in Zürich. We dropped off our luggage and followed her back down the street, along sidewalks protected from the weather by elegant vaulted archways.

"Allen's office is close by," she said, as we weaved our way through the flow of pedestrians.

"Allen who?" I asked.

"Dulles. He has some fancy title, special assistant to the American ambassador, something like that. But he works out of his apartment. More hush-hush," she said, whispering the last part. "He's a brilliant man." There was real admiration in her voice. I had to agree. A guy who got himself a job working out of his own home in neutral Switzerland while war ravaged the rest of Europe had to be pretty damn sharp.

Maureen pointed out the landmarks so we could find our way back to the hotel. We turned at a cathedral, its spire rising above all the other buildings. From there, we crossed the Herrengasse, the street where Dulles had his place. But instead of taking the sidewalk, she took us down a path that led along the river, through a small vineyard set on the sloping ground. In any other city cultivated grapes would have been an odd sight, but in Bern's quaint old town neighborhood, they looked right at home.

"The rear entrance is more convenient," Maureen said, leading us up stone steps to a recessed doorway, completely shielded from view.

"As well as discreet," Kaz said while she worked the key.

"This is a city of spies. Nazis, Allied, Swiss, not to mention the freelance types of all nationalities. Everyone watches everyone else," Maureen said. "That's where you come in. More eyes on the Swiss bankers and Georg Hannes." We followed her up the wide basement steps to the main floor of the four-story building, entering a hallway that ran the length of the apartment.

"Maureen," a voice called out from the end of the hallway, echoing against the marble floor. A man in a striped three-piece suit stepped out of a room, his hand still on the door. He was in his fifties, his white hair and mustache neatly groomed. Not yet grandfatherly or gone to seed, he stood up straight, adjusted his rimless spectacles, and eyed Kaz and me. "These the fellows you've been waiting for? Good, bring them into the office."

As we passed through the double doors, I glanced into the room he'd come out of. It was a bedroom, unremarkable except for the rumpled sheets and a woman applying lipstick in front of the mirror. Dark-haired, perhaps the same age as Maureen, and a looker. Allen Dulles was a busy man. Maureen caught my eye and raised an eyebrow, a business-as-usual gesture, which told me the woman was someone other than Mrs. Dulles.

In Dulles's office, Maureen handled the introductions after we'd hung up our coats. Dulles sat behind an oak desk, a large map of Europe on the wall at his back while he fiddled with his pipe, leafing through a file of papers. About us, evidently. We took seats in front of his desk and Maureen landed on a couch near the windows. She glanced outside, checking for guys in trench coats with fedoras pulled down over their faces. Guys like us, but with German accents.

"Baron, it will be quite useful if you can gain the confidence of your bankers," Dulles began. "It's fortunate you have your funds spread out over several institutions. Smart, as well."

"That was entirely my father's doing," Kaz said. "He was an astute businessman."

"Excellent. I can tell you from my time on Wall Street, you want to keep bankers hungry. If they have all your money they tend to take you for granted," Dulles said, firing up his pipe and turning his attention to me. "Are you really Eisenhower's nephew, Captain Boyle?"

"We're distant cousins on my mother's side," I said. "But since he's older, it's always been Uncle Ike." He nodded, puffing away, and I could see him file that tidbit away for later use, if needed. "Is there anything else you can tell us about our assignment, Mr. Dulles? It's hard to believe meeting bankers is going to help win the war."

He sighed, as if preparing himself to explain the obvious to a dullard schoolboy. "There's still a lot of war to be fought, but now that we're on the Continent, and the Russians are approaching East Prussia, the defeat of Germany is certain. When that happens, we don't want Hitler and his cronies taking off for parts unknown," Dulles said. "Our analysts doubt Hitler would, actually. He's more likely to fight until the end. But Goering, Himmler, and the rest of the top Nazis are another story. Tell these fellows about von Ribbentrop, Maureen."

"First, you have to understand that Swiss society is very insular. They're not big on outsiders, and conversely, they tend to place a great deal of trust in each other," she said.

"It is a small nation, surrounded by larger ones," Kaz said. "That makes sense."

"One of the ways that plays out is that their diplomatic service doesn't use official couriers. They entrust diplomatic pouches to private individuals traveling on business. Which makes it easier for us to intercept and inspect the pouches," she said, with a pleased smile. "We recently found one Swiss diplomatic pouch stuffed with half a million American dollars, earmarked for the private account of Nazi foreign minister Joachim von Ribbentrop in a Buenos Aires bank."

"Rats jumping a sinking ship," I said.

"Preparing to," Dulles said. "That was just one deposit we happened upon. You can bet there are plenty of others for the SS, Gestapo, and Nazi Party leaders. We need to hold these men responsible, and not allow them to escape the hangman with stolen riches."

"Safehaven will do that?" I asked.

"If the Germans don't get wind of it," Dulles said. "That's why we need new faces talking to the bankers, and watching German agents like Georg Hannes."

"What about the Swiss? If they're helping von Ribbentrop smuggle dough out of the country, won't they tip off their Nazi pals?" I asked.

"Such smuggling is unofficial, handled by conservative bankers and government officials who are sympathetic to the Nazi ideology," Dulles said, waving his hand in the air as if dismissing the foolishness of such men. "We need the Safehaven negotiations to proceed quietly, so as to not arouse their suspicions. Once we have an agreement in place to seize Nazi assets when the war is over, the Germans will have a hard time moving their funds to any other neutral country."

"If Switzerland agrees to Safehaven," Kaz said, "others will see the handwriting on the wall."

"Exactly, Baron. I'm not saying it will be easy, but the longer we keep the Nazis ignorant, the better our chances are," Dulles said, as a knock sounded at the office door. "Ah, that must be Hyde."

"Victor," Maureen said, rising from the couch as the door opened. "Come meet our new friends." She took Hyde by the arm, introducing me and Kaz. Victor Hyde was a snappy dresser, outfitted in a black overcoat and a charcoal gray suit. His shirt was gleaming white, his tie burgundy, with matching wine-colored cuff links. His hairline was receding, which made him look a little older than he probably was. Maybe twenty-five or so. Dark eyes, broad cheekbones, and thin pink lips filled out the picture.

"Victor is a financial specialist, on loan from the embassy," Dulles said. "He's our contact with the banking community here for Safehaven. Those who are sympathetic, that is."

"It's our job to provide Victor with intelligence on what the Germans and their Swiss bankers are up to," Maureen said. "He puts it all together in secret files that will form the basis for the Safehaven protocols we'll establish with the Swiss. Have I got that right, darling?" Maureen said, patting the couch for him to sit next to her.

"Nail on the head, as usual," Victor said, giving Maureen a bright smile and a brush of his hand on her arm. "But now I need to take the baron and Captain Boyle away from you. There's been a development in that Credit Suisse situation. Could you call Emil Escher, Allen, and tell him we'll be at police headquarters?"

"A positive development?" Dulles said, reaching for the telephone.

"Ask him to meet us at the morgue," Victor said, by way of an answer. Dulles frowned as he dialed.

"What's going on?" I asked as we stood to leave.

"I'll explain on the way," Victor said, waiting as Dulles spoke a few quick sentences into the phone before he hung up.

"He'll be there in ten minutes," Dulles said, setting aside his pipe and opening a file. We were dismissed, Maureen ushering us out and closing the door. We pulled on our coats and made for the back hall, Victor telling us that it was a short walk to the police morgue. Kaz donned his hat, and I realized I'd left my fedora in Dulles's office.

"Hang on," I said, heading back. I opened the office door and took a quick step to the hat rack in the corner, not wanting to distract Dulles.

But it was Maureen who was distracting him. Seated on his desk, her legs crossed provocatively, she leaned in, whispering, close enough for her breath to warm his cheek. She turned and eyed me. Dulles didn't take his eyes off her, a pen in one hand still poised over a file on his desk, the other on her thigh. When did this guy get any work done? I slammed the hat on my head and pulled the brim down to keep from gawking as I made my retreat.

Kaz shot me a glance as we descended the stairs, making for the back door. I guess I still had a surprised look on my face, and tried to lose it. If Victor thought he and Maureen were an item, there was no reason to tell tales out of school. It wasn't that I cared so much about hurt feelings; it was that I didn't want a jealous spat to get in the way of our job.

We worked our way through the vineyard path and took a series of steep steps leading down to a walkway along the river. The Aare was in full current, the spring melt waters from the Alps churning along the riverbank as it took a sharp turn around the old city. Victor checked the other pedestrians, apparently satisfied that we weren't under surveillance. It was a sunny day, but the breeze was lifting a chill from the rushing water, and everyone was moving at a good clip, hands stuffed in pockets.

"We had word that Georg Hannes was bringing in a Jew from Germany to withdraw a large amount from an account at Credit Suisse. You've been told about him?" Victor said.

"Maureen told us he's a Gestapo man who's good at getting people to hand over their money in exchange for their lives," I said.

"And in getting bankers to reveal information," Kaz said. "I thought the Swiss were thought to be paragons of secrecy."

"When it benefits them," Victor said. "But it works both ways, on occasion. I had word from a junior bank officer that Hannes was testing the waters at Credit Suisse, trying to locate an account."

"Testing how?" I asked.

"He'd been making the rounds at several banks, trying to deposit ten thousand Swiss francs in an account belonging to Werner Lowenberg."

"Deposit, you said?" Kaz asked.

"Yes. He's done this before," Victor said, pointing the way up another stone stairway. "His story is that he's making a deposit for a friend who cannot leave the country. A reasonable story these days. If a teller accommodates his request, then he has confirmed the presence of an account outside Germany, which is illegal, and in exactly which bank the account was created. That is enough to convince anyone to cooperate, if they have had any reservations."

"Hannes confirmed the account at Credit Suisse?" Kaz asked.

"He did, yesterday. Usually, Hannes goes back to Germany and escorts the account holder here, where he has him withdraw all his funds in exchange for his freedom. He releases him dead broke to an internment camp. A marked improvement from what he could expect in Germany."

"Why does he bother to keep his word?" I asked, huffing a bit as we climbed the steep stairs. "The Gestapo isn't known for such niceties."

"He takes a picture of the fellow in Swiss custody and has him write letters confirming he's been freed. It helps convince others to give up their wealth. We've learned this from talking to those who have been let loose here. Not all of them are Jews or other enemies of the state, so he likes to have a reputation for keeping his word. It's good for business."

"But Werner Lowenberg is dead?" Kaz said as we reached the top and headed down a quaint street with steep medieval roofs overlooking the river.

"Yes. And two million Swiss francs withdrawn from his account," Victor said. "Unusual that it happened so quickly. Hannes must have had him close by."

"And unusual that Lowenberg was killed?" Kaz said.

"Yes. It's messy, and Hannes is anything but messy."

"Maybe there's no one left to extort," I said.

"I talked with a German Jew last week," Victor said. "He'd been hiding for years in Munich, but the Nazis found him and matched his name to a list Hannes had put together. Good news for him, since he's alive, but it cost him over a million dollars—all the gold and currencies he had stashed with the Swiss National Bank. There's still money to be made for the Third Reich, and they need it, believe me."

"Money doesn't mean much if you're dead," I said, as we walked into a large, open square, dominated by a massive white granite building overlooking the river, its copper roof towering above the skyline.

"Some of these poor souls were hoping their children would survive and make their way here after the war," Victor said. "But Hannes broke them down. Fear, intimidation, and the sudden hope of life, these are his tools."

"What is this place?" Kaz asked Victor as we walked across the plaza. The story he was telling was too close to home for Kaz, and I knew he was changing the subject. "So we can get our bearings."

"It's the Bundesplatz, the government plaza. That's the parliament building," Victor said, indicating the large granite showpiece that overlooked the river. "And see the smaller building tucked up on its left, with the brown roof? That's the Swiss National Bank. Money and power are never far apart in Switzerland. Unlike justice. That's police headquarters, at the end of the Waisenhausplatz." He pointed to the far end of the wide thoroughfare, where a squat building sat alone behind a wrought-iron fence.

Inside police headquarters, Victor asked the desk sergeant for *Inspektor* Emil Escher. At least I figured he was a sergeant, since every stationhouse I've ever been in put a sergeant out front. His uniform was gray, and it fit his attitude. He lifted a receiver and spoke into the telephone as if he were doing us a big favor. I wondered if he didn't much like Victor Hyde, or Americans in general. Or maybe the inspector.

After we spent a few minutes staring at wanted posters in German, French, and Italian, the door behind the surly sergeant opened and another cop escorted us downstairs to the basement. Sparkling clean tile floors, painted brickwork, and large glass windows marked this as the morgue, hidden away at the rear of the building. A man in plain clothes waited in the hallway. Behind him, two uniformed policemen leaned against the wall, puffing away, a lungful of cigarette smoke always welcome after viewing an autopsy. The plainclothes guy was about thirty, with dirty blond hair brushed back and receding on either side of his wide forehead. He had striking blue eyes and rounded, high cheekbones, all sitting above a narrow chin and a mouth turned down in displeasure.

"I do not work for *Herr* Dulles, Victor. And officially, neither do you, since you are part of Ambassador Harrison's staff." I knew Leland Harrison was the American ambassador, and of course we were supposed to be on the legation staff. I hoped Inspector Escher wasn't about to look into our credentials.

"Certainly not, Emil," Victor said. "I simply asked Allen to make a call so we could arrive as quickly as possible. I didn't want to waste your valuable time."

"If you have any information about this case, it will be worth my time. If not, you've used your last favor. Who are these gentlemen?"

"Mr. Boyle and Mr. Kazimierz, also from the legation. This is Inspector Escher, of the *Kantonspolizei* Bern. Boyle was a police detective before the war and offered his assistance."

"Inspector, I never liked telephone calls from politicians either," I said, shaking his hand.

"Oh, is that what *Herr* Dulles is today?" Escher said, giving me half a smile. "Come. Our good doctor is almost done." He opened the door to the autopsy room. The usual scents assailed me. The intense chemical smell of formaldehyde, the sour, acidic stench of bile, the muddy earthen aromas arising from viscera. I was glad we hadn't eaten in a while.

Four stainless-steel tables were arrayed in the center of the room, with sinks and counters behind them. One of the tables held the stitched-up body we'd come to see. Enamel bowls on the counter held organs, the brain easily recognizable. The rest looked like mush, not that I lingered over the display. A tall, thin man with graying hair and stooped shoulders was washing his hands at one of the sinks. His rubber apron was splattered with gore.

"*Inspektor, wer sind diese Leute?*" he asked as he dried his hands. He looked us over, a bit irritated, a bit more curious.

"*Herr Doktor* Frenkel," Escher said. "These men are from the American legation. They are interested in what you've found out about the victim."

"Do not rush to judgment, young man," Doctor Frenkel said in excellent English. "Victim implies a perpetrator. This Jew drowned, likely a suicide."

"How do you know his religion, doctor?" Kaz asked, his brow furrowed as he studied the body.

"One can tell. But in this case, he had a passport in his jacket pocket." Doctor Frenkel pointed to a pile of sodden clothing laid out on the counter. A German passport lay open, a large red *J* marking the holder as Jewish. The pages were soaked and stuck together, but the passport picture matched the man on the table. Werner Lowenberg. Or as the passport said, Werner Israel Lowenberg.

"The middle names are always Israel, for a man, or Sara for a woman," Escher said, studying the picture. "As required by the German racial laws."

"An intelligent approach. It is good to know the kind of people you must associate with," Doctor Frenkel said.

"I would have thought the big *J* would be a clue," I said, studying the body. Lowenberg wasn't in the best shape before he went into the water. Thin and gaunt, but not starvation thin. Maybe he'd been ill, or perhaps he'd always been a skinny guy.

"No, I mean for my own country," Doctor Frenkel said. "We are overrun with Jews, and what are we to do with them? They are nothing like us. Completely alien to *schweizerisch* culture." He waved his hand over the corpse as if swatting a fly. Victor stood silently, his hands held behind his back, looking like he was trying to avoid an international incident.

"Here," Kaz said, turning the left forearm, laid close to the torso. It was a tattoo. A170603.

"What is that?" Escher asked.

"It means this man came from a place in Poland. Auschwitz," Kaz said, laying the arm back down gently. We both knew what that meant. It was an extermination camp. For Jews, Gypsies, political opponents, all the groups that didn't fit into the glorious future the Third Reich had in mind for Europe.

"He is not Polish," Escher said, checking the passport. "This was issued in Berlin, less than two weeks ago."

"No, he's not Polish," Kaz said. We exchanged glances, both of us holding back what we knew. This wasn't the time or place, and it would serve no purpose. We'd read the report from a Polish soldier who'd escaped the death camp. We understood what went on there. It wasn't a slave labor or a punishment facility. It existed purely to massacre people on an industrial scale. It was too horrific to imagine, and most people couldn't manage it. There was no reason to draw attention to ourselves by trying to convince these two guys, especially Frenkel, given his attitude.

"I wonder what the tattoo means," Escher said. It made sense that he wouldn't have seen one. Some of Hannes's victims may have had the tattoo, but it wasn't the kind of thing they would have rolled up their sleeves to show off.

"It is a numbering system to keep track of Jews," Doctor Frenkel said. "I heard about it in Russia."

"What?" I think all three of us said it at the same time.

"I was part of a Swiss medical mission on the Eastern Front in 1942. A ghastly winter," he said, standing over Lowenberg's body and giving a slight shiver at the memory. "We saw the Germans relocating whole villages of Jews. An officer I treated told me they'd all be tattooed. It was simpler than paperwork, you know. It's a huge job to move them to safe areas and put them to proper work. All for their own good, of course."

"Of course," Kaz said. He remained calm in the face of this drivel, the only clue to the rage I knew was beneath the surface was a small tic at the corner of his eye. "I wasn't aware the Swiss sent medical units to combat areas."

"I have a reserve commission in the army. It was an excellent opportunity to observe the fight against Bolshevism. And, of course, there is nothing like warfare to spur advances in medicine. Some of our junior doctors gained valuable experience."

"Has Switzerland sent medical missions to other nations?" I asked.

"Other nations? No, of course not," Frenkel said, spitting a short, sharp laugh. "Now, what else can I do for you?"

"This is interesting," Escher said, wisely ignoring the conversation. He was holding up the tie Lowenberg had been wearing. In the other hand, he held the passport. The tie in the photo was the same. It was harder to tell with the jacket, but the material looked the same as well.

"He evidently liked the tie," Frenkel said, with a sigh of boredom.

"You said he died from drowning," I said. "Water in the lungs?"

"Yes. He was found tangled in a tree branch downstream from the Dalmazibrücke, a pedestrian bridge over the Aare," Frenkel said. "There is an iron railing he easily could have gone over."

"Or been pushed," Inspector Escher said. "Why do you say it was suicide?"

"No wallet, no watch or other personal effects, except for that passport. He may have found the promised land not to his liking." Frenkel grinned at his pathetic joke. I looked more closely at the body. Lowenberg's hands were small, almost delicate. Except for traces of dirt still caked under his fingernails, they belonged to a man who worked indoors. Which made sense, if he'd accumulated enough money to open a Swiss bank account.

"Would you say he suffered from starvation or any abuse?" I asked.

"Not starvation, based on the condition of his organs," the doctor said. "There is no evidence of liver damage or muscle wasting, which would be evident after even a few days without adequate food. His musculature indicates a sedentary life, which would account for his thinness. He'd eaten a meal of sausage and potatoes recently."

"Any wounds or marks?" Escher asked.

"On his back, a cut likely made by the branch his coat caught on. Nothing that would have caused any permanent damage. Here, on the back of the skull, there is a contusion." He lifted the head and turned it. The torn skin was surrounded by a red lump.

"He could have been struck from behind and dumped over the railing," Kaz said.

"Or hit his head against the rocks along the riverbank," Frenkel said. "Perhaps, Inspector Escher, you should look for reports of an altercation on or near the bridge. Failing any evidence to the contrary, I see no reason to consider this other than a suicide. A poor wretch, alone in a strange country, penniless and despondent, takes his own life. Sad. But really, where could he go? When the war is won, Germany will not take them back. We Swiss cannot continue to feed thousands in the internment camps. The future must have seemed bleak to him."

"Won?" Kaz asked. "By Germany?"

"Of course. Look at all the National Socialists have accomplished. They certainly cannot allow the Communists to win. Once they defeat your forces in France, they will turn their attention back to Russia. So you see, Switzerland cannot be a land of refuge for Jews forever. Now excuse me, it has been a long day. An attendant will see to the body."

"Thank you for your valuable time, doctor," Victor said, holding the door open for him. Frenkel grunted, discarded his gloves and apron, and left us alone with the corpse.

"Hardly a neutral attitude," Kaz said as soon as the door slammed shut.

"You cannot complain about Doctor Frenkel and in the same breath ask for my help," Escher said. "If I practiced neutrality, you would not be here now."

"No offense meant, Inspector," I said. "The doctor has a right to his opinions." I shot Kaz a look, trying to smooth things over. A friendly cop was an asset to be cultivated. Kaz nodded and kept quiet.

"He is an ass," Escher said, the epithet hissing between his teeth. "He's active in the SVV, the *Schweizerischer Vaterländischer Verband.* They're Nazi sympathizers with a good number of senior army officers among their membership, including General Henri Guisan."

"Guisan?" Kaz said, wrinkling his brow in disbelief. "Isn't he the armed forces commander?"

"Yes," Escher said with a smile. "Welcome to neutral Switzerland. I am sorry for my display of petulance in the hallway. With others watching, I did not wish to be seen as overly sympathetic. You know, Victor, I will do whatever I can to help."

"I understand," Victor said, clapping Escher on the arm. "Are we done here, gentlemen?"

"I have one question," I said, gazing down at the mortal remains of Werner Lowenberg. "If he was alone and penniless, who fed him sausages and potatoes?"

CHAPTER THIRTEEN

"Hurry," Victor said as we left the police station. "We've got five minutes to get to the Café Fédéral, in the Bundesplatz."

"Do we have a reservation?" Kaz asked, quickening his step to keep up with Victor's strides.

"No, but we need to get there before they close off the streets. Otherwise you'll miss the show."

"What show?" I asked, curious, but mostly hungry. Autopsies had that effect on me. They were nauseating to watch, but once I got back into the fresh air, I always felt an overwhelming joy at being alive, along with a desire for food and drink, as if I'd escaped the coroner's slab myself.

"The *Reichsbank* convoy is due any moment," Victor said. "It's quite a sight."

We made it with time to spare. The Café Fédéral sat at one corner of the plaza, facing the parliament building with the Swiss National Bank to the left. Victor made his way to an outside table with a perfect view of the *Bundesplatz*, occupied by a dapper gent in a pin-striped suit who raised his glass in greeting.

"Henri, these are the men I told you about," Victor said. "Baron Kazimierz and Billy Boyle, this is Henri Moret. A good friend."

"Victor is always kind when I pay for drinks," Moret said. "Allow me." He filled our glasses with a red wine, and I caught Kaz checking the label. He arched one eyebrow, which meant he was quite impressed.

"To what lies beneath," Victor said as we clinked glasses. I asked what he meant, but Henri spoke before he could answer.

"There and there," he said, pointing to two side streets that led off of the plaza. Police cars had pulled across the lanes, blocking access. Uniformed cops began to filter in, standing at street corners, watching as the last vehicles left by the one remaining route. It was after five o'clock, and like most government towns, the place emptied pretty quickly. "Soon, they will arrive."

Henri Moret was a good-looking guy, a hair south of forty. He had dark hair that was beginning to expose his widow's peak, and a strong, dimpled chin that gave his face character without spoiling it. His eyes were lively and his suit well-tailored. As a matter of fact, Switzerland was full of well-tailored suits, unlike England or France.

"They?" Kaz asked.

"The gold convoy from Germany," Victor said. "A delivery direct from the *Reichsbank* in Berlin."

"How do you know all this?" I asked, tasting the wine. I didn't know a lot about wine, but I knew this was the good stuff.

"Because I work there," Henri said, nodding in the direction of the Swiss National Bank. "I handled the paperwork myself. Of course, the more senior bank officers will greet the *Reichsbank* officials, and the more junior staff will do the actual unloading and accounting. I am middle-level management, so I may leave work on time to sit and drink wine with you gentlemen. Much preferable, don't you think?"

Henri spoke with a light French accent, his English as flawless as his cheery manners. He smiled as he opened a cigarette case, silver, with his initials engraved, and offered them around. Victor was the only taker, and Henri produced a gold lighter to get their smokes going.

"It's only gold plate," Henri said, catching me staring at the lighter. "I haven't figured out a way to take my work home with me. Not yet."

"Sorry," I said. "The thought hadn't crossed my mind. Not yet."

"Good one, Billy," Victor said, giving Henri a friendly jab to the arm. "Henri's a real kidder. Hard to know when to take him seriously."

"Do you two work together?" Kaz asked, swiveling his head to see who might be listening.

"Henri is a valued contact within the banking community here in Bern," Victor said. "We are hoping that he'll be involved in the Safehaven negotiations soon. Meanwhile, he provides what information he can."

"Such as this little parade," Henri said, as the roar of motorcycles sounded in the distance. "It should demonstrate the scale of the issue."

"But why are you helping us?" I asked. "You work for the Swiss National Bank, after all."

"I have my reasons," Henri said, tapping ashes from his cigarette as the noise grew louder. "Now enjoy the procession."

The roar of revving engines echoed off the stone buildings, announcing their arrival before we could see them. Six police motorcycles finally came into view, turning a corner into the wide thoroughfare leading to the plaza. They proceeded slowly, two abreast, the riders keeping a perfect formation. A Swiss army open staff car came next, officers in their kepi hats in the backseat, soldiers with submachine guns standing on the running boards.

Then came the main event. Five Mercedes-Benz heavy trucks, all with the German eagle and swastika insignia stenciled on the door. The canvas flaps were tied down, giving no hint of the cargo inside. But their slow pace and sagging truck beds were dead giveaways. One last truck was filled with Swiss soldiers, rifles at the ready. The convoy crossed the empty Bundesplatz, the Swiss escort peeling off, vanishing down a side street. The Germans drove to the Swiss National Bank, taking a road along the left side of the building and slowly turning right as massive wooden doors opened to greet them. With a great grinding of gears, the large trucks made the turn, moving into the interior of the block. The wooden doors shut with a great *thud*, followed by silence.

"How much gold just passed us by?" I asked.

"Each truck carries four thousand pounds of gold. Less than their capacity, in case one breaks down. Gold is going for thirty-six dollars an ounce, which is, let's see," Victor said, taking out a pen and doing the math on a napkin.

"In American dollars, five hundred seventy-six dollars per pound.

That's a little over two point three million per truck. Eleven and a half million and change," Henri said.

"Only a banker would consider twenty thousand bucks loose change," Victor said, finishing his calculations.

"The bank takes a cut," Henri said. "A fraction of one percent for unloading, registering the deposit, that sort of thing. And then there's the personal deposits for the Nazi leaders who suddenly see the wisdom of keeping a secret account. In addition to the gold bars, there are briefcases stuffed with cash, jewelry, and securities, all destined for personal accounts."

"Accounts that are illegal for Germans to hold," Kaz said. "Won't Georg Hannes be interested?"

"The Nazi bosses are above all that. There is no legality in the Third Reich," Henri said, the gracious smile gone from his face. "There is only what the Nazi leaders want. Hannes is undoubtedly following their example and salting away his own stolen funds." A waiter hovered nearby, but Henri waved him off.

"Is this sort of convoy commonplace?" I asked.

"Less than it used to be," Victor said. "One of the goals of Safehaven is to expose the illegal gold transactions coming out of Germany. The Nazis don't care about legalities, but the rest of the financial world does."

"I'm sorry, I don't understand high finance," I said, draining my glass. "Can you give me the simple version?"

"Of course," Henri said, filling my glass and signaling to the waiter for another bottle. I didn't argue. "There are international treaties going back to before the last war, which say that a conquering nation may expropriate public property, but not private property. Most banks, even if they function as a national bank, are private."

"But the Nazis make no such distinction," Kaz said.

"Precisely," Henri said. "But other nations do and will not overtly do business with an offending nation."

"It's a matter of public record that Germany began the war with less than a hundred million dollars in gold reserves," Victor said, leaning in and keeping his voice low. "They spent that much in gold buying Swiss francs last year alone. All told, they've sold about three hundred million in gold to Switzerland and nearly that much to other nations since the start of the war."

"Looted gold," Kaz said.

"Yes," Henri answered. "Over two hundred and twenty tons from Belgium's banks, and thirty-nine tons of gold confiscated from Dutch citizens, as two examples."

"Do you know about gold from the concentration camps?" Kaz asked.

"Yes, although at times I wish I did not," Henri said. "Gold fillings, wedding rings, jewelry, all melted down into gold bars. A good bit of that goes into the private accounts for the SS."

"Okay, so there's a law against using that gold. If that's the case, why are the Germans sending so much of it here?" I asked.

"Oh, because Swiss banks can be very obliging," Henri said. The wine came, and he poured himself a large glass. "Especially my own. The SNB accepted the Belgian gold after the Nazis melted it down and gave each bar a predated stamp. The bank knew and turned a blind eye."

"Do they know about the gold from the concentration camps?" I asked.

"They do not wish to know," Henri said with a heavy sigh.

"But I still don't understand," I said. "If other nations won't accept the gold, what good does it do the Germans stored here in Bern?"

"Well, it's not so much that governments don't want the gold," Henri said, sitting back and taking a drag on his cigarette. "It's that they don't want to be seen taking it."

"Here's an example," Victor said. "Germany needs tungsten. Portugal has plenty, but doesn't want to be a pariah in the world community, so they won't take looted gold. They're also not fools, so they don't accept cash from the Germans. Reichsmarks won't be worth a penny when the war is over."

"But they will take Swiss francs," Henri said. "And right now, across the plaza, Nazi purchasing agents are selling that shipment of gold to the Swiss National Bank for Swiss francs."

"Which the Germans will then use to pay the Portuguese for tungsten," Kaz said, putting it all together. "Who will then sell the Swiss francs back to the bank for gold bullion."

"Manganese from Spain, chromium from Turkey, it's all the same. Everyone wants gold, no matter where it comes from, as long as the paperwork is in order," Victor said.

"Gold stolen from banks, homes, and ripped from the jaws of the dead," Henri said. "We Swiss take a small percentage, a handling charge, and everyone gets rich. While Europe burns."

"And the gold never moves from the SNB vaults," Victor added, glancing toward the bank, where the wooden doors opened as engines roared to life. The five vehicles filed out, rumbling across the plaza and passing us by, their canvas flaps loose, their truck beds empty.

"You mentioned what lies beneath when we toasted," I said. "The vaults?"

"Yes," Henri said, gulping the last of his wine. "The SNB vaults are deep underground beneath this beautiful plaza. The gold of defeated nations, murdered Jews, and all the other unfortunate victims of the Nazis lies buried safely there, deep in the bosom of Switzerland's most sacred space, our national bank." His face was clouded with anger, and he turned away to stare at the bank. Or to avoid meeting our eyes.

"You are doing all you can to help, Henri," Victor said. "It can't be easy, keeping such a secret."

"It is hardly enough," he said.

"Your sympathies are not known?" Kaz asked.

"I do my job, and try not to reveal my true feelings," Henri said. "It is best for my family that way. They think of Switzerland as a bastion of freedom and a democratic, neutral state. A moral center amid a depraved Europe, as my father says. I don't know which would devastate him more—knowing the truth of what we've done, or finding that I've worked with Victor, an American, to end it. Neither fits their picture of the true Switzerland."

"It was Henri who tipped us to Hannes asking about Lowenberg," Victor said.

"A newly hired teller gave Hannes the information," Henri said.

"He came to me the next day because he sensed something was not right. Before we could do anything, Hannes had returned with Lowenberg, who closed out his account. As Victor probably told you, Hannes never worked that quickly before."

"Would you lose your job if the bank discovered you were passing on this sort of information?" I asked.

"Most likely. My superiors view me as a bit of a dilettante, so they excuse my friendship with Victor and other foreigners. We Swiss are really very insular and mistrust nations that claim to be great powers. We prefer things on a smaller scale, as befits our geography. Except for gold, which we prefer in large quantities. But enough of that. Let us eat, gentlemen. It is a beautiful evening, the air is warm, and we have riches at our feet."

Henri passed around the menus, smiling as Victor and Kaz laughed. He was the kind of guy who was full of words, which made him seem full of life, but there was something that lay beneath the surface, and it wasn't gold. It was a darker secret that he masked with a playboy's nonchalance.

"What do you recommend?" I asked, perusing the menu, which wasn't in English.

"What are you in the mood for?" Victor asked.

"Sausages and potatoes."

CHAPTER FOURTEEN

WE ALL ORDERED sausage with potatoes and toasted the memory of Werner Lowenberg. Henri chose a bottle of Swiss chardonnay, declining the waiter's suggestion of a German Moselle. After dinner we strolled down to the Dalmazibrücke, the pedestrian bridge over the Aare River, to see if Doctor Frenkel's theory of suicide made any sense. Victor filled Henri in on our visit to the morgue as we walked. The sun had set, but it was a clear night, easy enough to find our way even in the blackout.

"A suicide?" Henri said as we crossed the bridge. "I think the police need a new coroner."

He had a point. The bridge was low, only fifteen feet or so from the river. The railing was only chest high, so jumping wouldn't have been a problem. But the height wasn't enough to do more than give you a good soaking.

"Perhaps he could not swim," Kaz suggested. "The current is quite swift."

"What about that bridge?" I said, pointing to the dark form of a larger and higher span upstream.

"The motorway bridge has a high fence," Victor said. "Not very likely."

"But it would be easy enough to whack a guy on the back of the head and heave the body over this railing," I said. "You'd only have to stun him, so the wound looks like a contusion from being rolled around in the water."

"Especially if the coroner is a Nazi sympathizer," Victor said.

"Do you think Frenkel is deliberately covering up a murder? That's much worse than official indifference because Lowenberg was a fugitive Jew," Kaz said.

"Frenkel is active in the SVV. You heard his opinion of Jews. An approach by the Gestapo would not be inconceivable," Victor said. "The Swiss government at all levels often works closely with the Nazis. Do you know how the red *J* came to be stamped on passports held by German Jews?"

"I had assumed the Nazis instituted the practice," Kaz said. "To mark the bearer as Jewish."

"They had no need to. Passports are for travel outside the borders, not within Germany. It was the Swiss government that came up with the idea. To make it easier to identify refugees attempting to cross the border as Jews," Victor said.

"And turn them away, back to certain death," Henri said, his voice trailing off as we all leaned on the railing, gazing into the cold water, wondering at Lowenberg's fate and that of so many others who had been denied sanctuary. Henri was at my shoulder as he lit a cigarette and snapped his lighter shut.

"Henri, back at the restaurant you said you had your reasons for helping Victor with Safehaven," I said. "If you don't mind my asking, what are they?"

"Uncle Rudolf. It was he who gave me this cigarette case when I graduated from university," he began, looking at the silver case with a smile before stowing it away. "He was always kind and patient with me. Unlike my father, who believes his duty is to be stern and set a proper example. Perhaps that is because he's the oldest brother, and Rudolf the youngest, I don't know. Whatever the reason, Rudolf has always been good to me. He is a doctor and has a reserve commission in the army, which is not at all unusual."

"Like Doctor Frenkel?" Kaz asked.

"Yes, but other than that, the two men are quite different. Uncle Rudolf did participate on the medical mission to the Eastern Front with Frenkel. He wanted to see the war firsthand, and thought he might find new medical techniques. But he learned more than he bargained for and came back a changed man. For Frenkel and his SVV friends, it was a chance to stand with the Nazis and aid them in their struggle against Bolshevism. Or Jewish Bolshevism, as they often call it. They came back even more fanatic than before."

"Frenkel talked about the Germans relocating Jews on the Russian front," I said.

"Relocating them to shallow graves, more likely," Henri said. "Uncle Rudolf saw Jews being shot by the dozens outside Smolensk. He saw the Lodz ghetto and the horrible conditions there. Bodies in the streets, little food, and primitive medical facilities. Frenkel and the others saw the same sights, but kept quiet about it, telling everyone a sanitized story of how humanely the Germans were handling the Jewish problem in the East."

"Your uncle did not remain quiet?" Kaz asked.

"No. He spoke out against the Nazis and their crimes. He told his story to the newspapers and spoke at public meetings to describe what he saw. People were incensed at first."

"At first?" I said. "What happened?"

"The government charged him with violating Swiss neutrality. His case was brought before parliament, right up there on the Bundes-platz," he said, arching his head to the nearby government building. "The army revoked his commission. Senior government ministers spread the story that he was suffering from nervous fatigue and his memory was not dependable. Soon, he began to lose patients, some because they disagreed with his politics, others because they feared the rumors about his health and mental stability. Today, he still sees a few faithful patients, but he is a ruined man. He thought he knew the Swiss character, that people would believe him and rally against such crimes against humanity. Instead, he's become an outcast in his own land. That is why I will act against the Nazis and the Swiss who help them. It may be only a few pieces of paper now and then, but they are the only weapons at hand."

"They're powerful weapons, my friend," Victor said, reaching out to clasp Henri on the shoulder.

"I may have the most damning piece of paper yet," Henri said. "Soon, I promise you."

"What is it?" Victor asked.

"An invoice. You all must report to Dulles, so it is better if I say nothing else until I have proof. No one must have a warning of what I am after."

"We wouldn't say anything," Victor said. "You must know I won't."

"It's for your own protection, my friend. Dulles is a very important man, and what he knows he passes on to other important men. I cannot risk anyone finding out about this. I am sorry, Baron, and Billy, I don't mean to offend you. You seem trustworthy, but I think it best to be cautious."

"Standing on a bridge where a man was likely murdered, that's hard to argue with," I said. "Good luck, and let us know if we can help when the time is right."

We made arrangements to meet Victor at Dulles's place in the morning, then parted ways, Victor and Henri heading off to their apartments while Kaz and I walked along the river, taking the route through the vineyards to our hotel.

"Billy, do you think there is any hope of the police investigating the death of Lowenberg?" Kaz asked as we sauntered along the river, lit by the half-moon.

"No, not if the coroner brings in a report of suicide," I said.

"Then perhaps Maureen had the right idea," he said. "Hannes should be stopped, but the politics here seem impenetrable."

"You mean by Lasho?"

"I don't really care who," Kaz said. "I'd be happy to put a bullet in Hannes's brain and toss him off that very bridge. Wouldn't you?"

"Yes," I said, after no more than a moment's thought. The more this war taught me about my fellow man, the less time I needed to consider weighty moral implications. I followed Kaz up the steps leading from the river, pausing near the entrance to the cathedral to look back at the river below. The city was dark, the reflected moonlight rippling in the river's current.

"You know, I've become so used to blackouts that I never thought to question why they have them in Switzerland. It's not like anyone's trying to attack them. They don't need to hide their cities from night bombers," I said. There had been a few accidental bombings by off-course aircraft, but that hardly compared to the wholesale destruction of German cities. "As a matter of fact, keeping the lights burning would protect them. A well-lit city would obviously be in Swiss territory."

"Interesting," Kaz said, standing with his hands in his pockets, rocking back on his heels, letting his brain work as he studied the panorama below us. "Let us consider who the blackout benefits. The Swiss? As you point out, they may have more to gain by lighting their cities. The Allies? The blackout only makes navigation more difficult and increases the chances of accidental intrusions over Swiss territory. The Germans? They have the most to lose if Switzerland turned on the lights. There's Basel, Schaffhausen, and Zürich, all large cities on the northern border with Germany. Illuminated, they would be excellent navigational aids for British and American bombers. If General Henri Guisan, commander of the Swiss Army, is an SVV member, who knows how far the pro-Nazi sympathies reach?"

"Before today, I would have said you were off your rocker. But right now, you're making a whole lot of sense," I said.

"Perhaps it is the wine," Kaz said with a smile as we walked to our hotel, the open arches of the enclosed sidewalks casting eerie shadows into the street. It had been quaint in the daylight. Now, it was faintly sinister. Or maybe that was the wine as well.

CHAPTER FIFTEEN

IN THE MORNING we entered Dulles's apartment by the front door, just for a change of pace. Victor arrived at the same time and we went in together, finding Maureen and Dulles speaking with a familiar figure.

"Glad you made it, Lasho," I said. "Any problems?"

"It was simple. I went back to where we left the car. I drove it to Lausanne and took a train here. It was far enough from the border that no one checked for identification papers," Lasho said. "I bought a ticket to Zürich, in case anyone asked about me, but got off here in Bern."

"You'd make an excellent agent," Victor said, with a knowing glance at Maureen. He leaned against a wall, watching Lasho in his seat by Dulles's desk.

"Would you like to work for us?" Dulles said. "Unofficially, of course."

"What do you think?" Lasho asked Kaz. "You are not American, but you work for them."

"I work for a free Poland," Kaz said. "I am glad to work with anyone if that is a common goal."

"What should I work for then?" Lasho asked, looking at the large map of Europe behind Dulles. "What country? What freedom?"

"We've had some reports from the Resistance in France," Dulles said. "Your people who fight with them have a name for what the Nazis are doing with the Roma. They call it the *Baro Porrajmos*. What does that mean, Mr. Lasho?" Dulles said it in a calculated manner like the lawyer he was. Whatever the answer, he already knew it and was certain it would work to his benefit.

"The great devouring," Lasho said, his voice a whisper.

"We will help you as best we can," Dulles said. "I don't know what we can offer that has any value, except for a chance at revenge."

"Don't listen to him, Lasho," I said. "They'll use you and then toss you aside. What they want is too dangerous."

Dulles gave me a stare that probably worked well on underlings who cared what he thought of them. Lasho smiled and nodded.

"Thank you, Billy," he said. "You are a good friend. But what can I do except take revenge? I have no family, no nation, and no hope. I will let them use me, and see what comes of it. After all, men are like fish; the great ones devour the small."

"So you need a big fish on your side," I said, with an amused glance at Dulles.

"This is obvious. Mister Dulles, tell me what you want," Lasho said.

Dulles looked at Maureen, who withdrew a photograph from a file. He then turned his glare on me, and I have to admit, I felt it.

"We want you to follow this man," Maureen said. "Georg Hannes, a Gestapo agent. Here's a list of the locations where he's likely to be seen. We don't know where he lives, but these are his favorite restaurants in Bern, and several banks, as well as the address of the German consulate. Keep your distance from the consulate."

"Follow him. Is that all?" Lasho said.

"For now," Maureen said. "Be careful. The Germans are bound to notice anyone loitering around their consulate, so don't be obvious. See if you can find where he stays. Then we'll decide what to do."

"He is Gestapo?" Lasho asked, studying the photograph. "Then I will kill him when you tell me to. Maybe before. You won't mind?" Lasho smiled, watching Dulles pretend he hadn't heard the question.

"Here's some more money," Maureen said, following Dulles's lead. She handed Lasho an envelope stuffed with Swiss francs. "Buy some clothes and whatever you need. We have a room set up for you in the attic. Use the rear entrance and don't draw attention to yourself."

"I will need identity papers," Lasho said. "The police may stop me no matter how careful I am. Then I will go to prison or be turned over to the Nazis. Either way, you will not get what you want. To find out where this man lives, I mean. And the police will want to know why I am in Bern. It would put me in a difficult position." Lasho managed to couch his blackmail in the most diplomatic terms. No papers, no dead Gestapo agent. And if they waited too long and he was picked up, he'd sing like a canary. I had to admire his moxie.

"We'll see what we can do," Maureen said. "First, bring us some information."

Lasho ignored her and kept his eyes on Dulles, who began to fidget, perhaps remembering this man had been *der Zigeuner,* the unstoppable scourge of Germans in occupied France.

"Very well," Dulles said. "But first, come back with a useful report."

"I will," Lasho said, rising quickly. "In the dark of night, at your back door."

He left, leaving a sense of menace lingering in the air.

"Looks like he has some ideas of his own," I said to Maureen. "Not exactly a chump, is he?"

"Listen here, Boyle, you keep your mouth zipped about this, got it?" Dulles said, clenching his pipe between his teeth. "I don't have time for sentimentality. Don't you have something to do? Somewhere else?"

"Yes, we do, Allen," Victor said, pushing off from his post at the wall and stepping between us. "I'm going to take the baron around to some banks, and then later we have that reception at Huber's place."

"Right. I'll see you all there tonight. Now get out."

We obliged. Maureen followed us into the hall, telling Kaz and me that she was having tuxedos sent to our hotel today. This reception was a fancy-dress shindig, and we had to fit in with the swells. She gave Victor a peck on the cheek, then went back into Dulles's office. I guess the order to get out didn't apply to a dame who sat on your desk and showed you her garter belt.

"You're staying at the Golden Eagle, I hear? They have a decent jazz band playing on weekends. I'll have to join you fellows for a drink. I've been trying to convert Henri to jazz, but his tastes are more classical," Victor said as we walked down the hall.

"A Swiss jazz band, that'd be worth seeing. Now what's this about a reception?" I asked Victor once we were outside.

"Max Huber is the president of the International Committee of the Red Cross," Victor said. "He's quite renowned in Switzerland, as a lawyer, judge, and businessman, but mainly as the head of the Red Cross. He's hosting a gathering of influential Swiss businessmen and bankers, which means he's going to twist their arms for donations. Diplomats are invited as well, for background color, I suppose. And so the wealthy Swiss can show off their good works."

"Cynical," I said, as we stopped beneath the grape vines. It was a warm day, the sky a clear, vivid blue, and the air carried the fragrance of spring.

"I work in finance, Billy. Probably second only to police work when it comes to seeing the underside of humanity. In any case, this reception will be a good chance to meet and mingle with Bern's upper crust. Now, which bank should we visit, Baron?"

"I actually have business at Credit Suisse," Kaz said. "It was the last account my father set up, and I never received the papers confirming my access."

"Good. They're on the Bundesplatz, near the SNB. I have to see Henri and pick up our invitations, so we can meet afterward."

"Huber knows our names?" I asked as we walked by the river.

"Huber's people, not the man himself. Henri arranged for the invites," Victor said. "Since his bank does a lot of business with *Alusuisse*—Huber's firm—he was able to arrange it. It's going to be quite the swanky affair. You'll be rubbing elbows with a few Germans, so be prepared."

"Hannes among them?" Kaz asked, his voice a whisper as we passed a man leaning against the railing, reading a newspaper.

"No, although the man he reports to is likely to show. The reception is in Kirchenfeld, a high-class neighborhood across the river. Lots of embassies over there, so the ambassadors and their ladies will be out in force. Not to mention spies and informers, so be on your toes."

At the Bundesplatz, we went our separate ways, Kaz and I making for the Credit Suisse bank headquarters. It was a massive granite structure, six stories high, decorated with overhanging archways on the ground floor and window boxes filled with geraniums. Inside was gleaming marble and polished wood, and people speaking in hushed tones, as if it were a museum. Kaz gave his name and asked to see someone about his account. In seconds we were whisked upstairs, where the décor was even fancier, as of course it would be for those with numbered accounts. We cooled our heels outside an office for about two minutes, until a young guy with hair so blond it almost matched his starched white shirt showed up with a folder. He rapped on the office door, entered, and was back in seconds, telling us to go right in.

"Baron Kazimierz, I am *Herr* Becker. Shall we speak English? My Polish is quite poor." Becker was a little gnome of a guy, white-haired and short, with reading glasses perched on the end of his nose. "And your companion?"

I gave a slight shake of the head, wondering how Becker would react to a silent partner at the proceedings. He took it in stride.

"English will be fine, *Herr* Becker," Kaz said, taking an offered seat in front of a large desk with little on it except for the folder. I sat on a sofa along the wall, watching them both, figuring that's how Georg Hannes would play it.

"How can I help you?" Becker asked, giving nothing away.

"I have an account number," Kaz said. "And a code word."

"Please," Becker said, sliding paper and pen toward Kaz, who wrote out a string of numbers and letters. Becker left with the paper and returned a few minutes later with an expandable file folder tied with red string. He opened it and read through about half a dozen pages of mumbo jumbo before putting it all back.

"You are Piotr Augustus Kazimierz, correct?" Becker asked, checking the form Kaz had filled out downstairs.

"Yes, as I told the person in the lobby. I have identification if you'd like to see it," Kaz said.

"That is not at all necessary. Because if you are not Rajmund Kanimir Kazimierz, there is nothing I can do," Becker said.

"That is my father," Kaz said. "He gave me the account number and the code word. He was to have sent a form to my bank in London adding me to this account."

"Well, he has not. I cannot even officially confirm the existence of an account, even to a relative," Becker said. "Perhaps you could contact him?"

"In Poland? Even if he were alive, you know that would be impossible."

"My condolences, Baron. If you were to present a death certificate, then perhaps we could help. As it stands, we must protect the privacy of the account holder."

"A death certificate? From the Nazis? They murdered my entire family! Do you think they bothered to fill out death certificates?"

"Baron, please understand," Becker said, steepling his fingers, as if he were explaining rules to a young child. "Credit Suisse is bound by Swiss banking laws. We are obligated to maintain a sphere of secrecy around our relationship with clients."

"If my name was on the account, or if I produced a death certificate from my pocket, you would then give me access to the funds?" Kaz said.

"If there were such an account, and either of those two requirements were met, then yes, of course," Becker said, settling back into his seat, happy that Kaz finally understood.

"*Herr* Becker, who is that man?" Kaz said, pointing at me.

"I have no idea. You brought him with you, so that is your affair. Now, I must ask you to leave. You've taken enough of my time," Becker said, closing the folder and tying the red string in a tight knot. He didn't look up as we left.

"So much for the sphere of secrecy. You could have been Gestapo for all he cared," Kaz said as he stormed out of the bank.

"Yep. Makes you wonder how much dough they'll keep in their vaults after the war. I don't know much about numbered accounts, but I always thought just knowing the number would be enough," I said.

"That's probably what a lot of people thought," Kaz said, stopping to look around the Bundesplatz for Victor. For a second, I thought he spotted him. Instead, he nudged me. "Billy, see the fellow in the black trench coat to our left? Leaning on the façade, reading a newspaper?"

"Yeah," I said, giving a quick glance. His head was down, his face covered by a wide-brimmed fedora. "We passed by him, down by the river."

"Is it Hannes?" Kaz said. We were both trying hard not to look at him so he wouldn't know we made him.

"Can't tell," I said, thinking back to the photograph Maureen had shown us, and risking a fast glance at newspaper man. "Big heavy shoes. Cop, spy, or Gestapo. Not banker's shoes, I'll tell you that."

"Let's lead him on," Kaz said. "The Union Bank is next on my list. If he follows us there, perhaps we can arrange a quiet word."

"Let's go," I said, not wanting to wait around for Victor and spook our tail. We walked across the plaza and past the restaurant where we'd eaten last night. It was a busy tree-lined street with shops open for business and plenty of pedestrians. I stopped at a bakery, trying not to get distracted by the pastries as I checked the reflection for our shadow. No dice. In a couple of blocks I spotted a barber shop. Kaz and I decided we could do with a trim to look our best tonight, which would also put our tail out in the open where we could spot him. Or maybe he was a guy who liked his morning newspaper and he'd be long gone.

Kaz chatted with the barber and was the first in the chair, which gave me a chance to take a seat and watch the approach to the shop as I leafed through a copy of *Signal*, the German army propaganda magazine distributed all over Europe. Maybe the barber was pro-Nazi, or maybe he liked free reading material. At least it had a lot of pictures.

Soon as Kaz had his ears lowered, we switched chairs. The barber blabbered on the way barbers do, the scissors snipping as I ignored him and checked the view out the window. Soon he whisked the hairs from my neck, Kaz paid up, and we donned our coats while scanning the street for a familiar face. The day was growing warmer, and I made a note to find a shoulder holster somewhere. The only reason I was wearing a coat over my suit jacket was to have a place to stuff my Police Special revolver.

"No sign of him," Kaz said as we pushed open the door. "Let's keep walking." The road led to a small park with a promenade overlooking the river. It was too wide open. If he were still following us, it wouldn't give him enough cover and he might give up. We walked away from the river and took a street alongside a church, heading for a busy intersection. A row of attached houses ran on one side, with parked cars and leafy trees out front. The other side of the street was fancier, with larger houses, most of them with brass plaques at the door. Lawyers and doctors, maybe. A ritzy neighborhood, judging by the architecture and the automobiles.

I knelt to tie my shoe next to a Mercedes-Benz, glancing into the rearview mirror. An obvious ploy, I know, but that was the point. I caught a glimpse of newspaper man ducking behind a car down the block. He'd just turned the corner and was now squatting behind a Hispano-Suiza, the low-slung roadster with its elegant lines barely high enough to hide him.

I stood and found Kaz mounting the steps to the next building. Three stories of gleaming white stone topped by a gray slate roof, it had a Red Cross sign above the door.

"It's the headquarters of the Swiss Red Cross, Billy," Kaz said. "Perhaps we could spot our pursuer from inside."

"And then go out a back door and tail him," I said. "Can you bluff your way through?"

"I'll say I'm looking for a relative, a possible refugee," he said. "It should be no problem." We took the last step and I grasped the door handle.

The *crack* of a pistol shot sounded from behind us as chips of granite flew past my ear. We both ducked as a second shot sounded, this one hitting the step beneath us and ricocheting off. There was no cover except for a low hedge under the windows, not counting the inside of the building, but bringing a gunfight to the Red Cross was probably not the best way to maintain a low profile.

"Around," I said to Kaz, who scurried behind the building as I jumped behind the hedge, hearing another shot smack into the wall behind me. Running low, I made for the back of the building but then darted behind the next one, seeing Kaz do the same on his side. He'd understood. If the shooter wasn't already hightailing it for home, we'd have him between us.

Or he'd have one of us in his sights as we came out into the street.

I dashed out to the Hispano-Suiza, hunched over, and almost felt bad about this fine vehicle taking a couple of bullets for me. Kaz came out from behind his building, taking cover as I did. Sirens drifted in from far away, the high-note-low-note distinctive European variety that meant cops were on the way. In this neighborhood, gunfire was certainly looked down upon. We had about two minutes to find this guy and get the hell out before Swiss cops put us in handcuffs or the morgue.

I doubted our man was waiting around. I signaled Kaz to stand as I began to inch up, figuring that if he was, he'd reveal himself and one of us could get a shot off.

I was wrong. He was there, shielded from Kaz as he laid his arm over the hood of an automobile, pistol aimed straight at me. I ducked as two bullets smashed through the windows of the Hispano-Suiza, pretty much ruining its nice lines. I heard Kaz fire and ran across the street, sliding in front of a sedan and readying my pistol as I took a careful look down the sidewalk.

"He's running!" Kaz shouted as he sprinted across the road, going parallel to the row of attached dwellings. I ran to catch up, glad to leave the scene before the guys in kepis showed up.

At the last row house, steps led down to a side street with a small park, and I followed Kaz as he made his way to the corner, kneeling behind a low concrete wall. Pistol fire rang out, one round hitting the wall and sending up a spray of concrete dust while the other slammed into the building behind us.

"He's going to get lucky sooner or later," I said, my head pressed against the gritty concrete.

"Or we will," Kaz said. "Watch for him." With that, Kaz ran down the steps, vaulting over hedges and disappearing into the greenery. I had my pistol up and caught a quick movement as a dark figure slipped behind a tree. The little park was lit by sunlight filtering through dappled shade, and I couldn't be sure if it was our man or some civilian taking cover. I vaulted the wall and zigzagged down the street, looking to get an angle on him. He fired, but not in my direction, and took off at a fast clip. The street curved left, going up and joining the main thoroughfare again. I stayed on his heels, my pistol low and to my side, as he weaved in and out of pedestrians. More than I wanted between us. I had no idea where Kaz was, but I had to keep up or he'd get away. I ran by his black fedora on the ground, either tossed away in an attempt to be less noticeable or lost as he ran.

There he was. On a street corner, standing sideways, presenting the smallest target he could, his pistol leveled at me as I careened forward. People scattered and dove out of the line of fire, screaming as this madman calmly aimed at his target. Me.

The shot was deafening at this close range, echoing off the building and drowning out the shrieks of those prone on the sidewalk.

A plume of blood burst from the side of the shooter's head and he crumpled, his ruined skull thumping against the wall. Kaz strode closer, his smoking Webley held on the man, a wise but unnecessary precaution.

"Check his papers," I said, gasping for breath as I knelt by the body. "And thanks."

"You are quite welcome," Kaz said, his hands busy rummaging through the man's pockets as a small crowd gathered. Hearing the sirens, some dusted themselves off and moved on, perhaps anticipating another gun battle. A group of older men clustered around us, whispering to each other.

"He is Wilhelm Hochler," Kaz said, opening a wallet. "Or should I say, *Kriminalinspektor* Hochler of the *Geheime Staatspolizei*, better known as the Gestapo."

"Gestapo!" muttered one of the men watching us. Kaz pulled at Hochler's tie and grabbed his identity disc. It had *Geheime Staatspolizei* stamped on it, along with his number, 5324. That's all the Gestapo needed to be a law unto themselves, in German territory, at least.

"Why did he try to kill us?" Kaz said, cocking his head in my direction. The sirens were close now, only a street away, probably following the pointed fingers of outraged Swiss citizenry.

"*Komm mit uns*," one of the men said, and I noticed that they'd moved into a protective cordon, shielding us from view. One of them opened a door as the others pulled us inside. It was only when I saw the writing on the lintel above the door that I understood.

It was Hebrew. We'd chased a Gestapo agent down and Kaz blew his brains out on the street below a giant Star of David, which I now saw in its stained-glass setting from inside the synagogue.

"Thank you," I said as we followed half a dozen men down the aisle. "Kaz, tell them they might get in trouble."

"Young man, we would be in trouble with the Almighty if we did not help you," a man with a graying beard said before Kaz could translate. The others ran back to the door as he led us down a staircase to a rear entrance. "We were engaged in Torah study, discussing the *din rodef*, the law of the pursuer." He opened a door and took a quick look, then closed it.

"Thank you, Rabbi," Kaz said.

"No, thank you. I do not know who you are, but Torah teaches us that we must save those who are being pursued with evil intent, as you certainly were. Then to see that man was of the Gestapo, the message could not have been clearer. He was a *rodef*, and his killing was justified, if you have any doubts yourself."

"I am Polish, Rabbi. I have no doubts," Kaz said. "I wish I did."

"Shalom, my friends. If you need help, you will find it here." He eased the door open again and gave us the all-clear. We scooted out, working our way down a narrow courtyard and emerging through an alleyway onto a busy street.

"Shalom. Peace," I said. "It'll be a while."

"Thank God for them they are Swiss," Kaz said. "That may be the only way for Jews to survive in Europe these days."

"Even if they turn away refugees at the border, at least they don't turn on their own people," I said, thinking of the French Jews who'd been rounded up by the Vichy police. We turned a corner, trying to look like two guys out for a stroll and wondering what was going on like everyone else. As we did, the first thing I saw was a big American flag flying from a building surrounded by an iron fence.

"Jesus, it's the American embassy," I said, spotting the sentries at the front entrance. I grabbed Kaz and pulled him across the street, putting space between us and the stars and stripes. I couldn't say much for our choice of a neighborhood for a gunfight, other than at least it was some distance from the police station.

"We should split up, in case they are looking for two men," Kaz whispered.

"Yeah. Meet you back at the hotel," I said, keeping my voice clipped and low. Kaz kept walking and I sauntered toward a newsstand, looking over the papers and picking the *Neue Berner Zeitung* because it had a picture of American troops pouring ashore at Normandy. I dropped a one franc coin on the counter, figuring that would cover it. I was about to leave when I realized that nothing leaves an impression like an overtipper, so I waited for my change like any normal person. I pulled my brim down as the proprietor thumbed a bunch of small coins onto a little tray. I scooped them up and strolled out, finding a bench down the street that gave me a view of the embassy.

I opened the paper, lowering it so I could see the flag and the front entrance. If an official-looking automobile showed up driven by angry Swiss cops, then they knew a Yank was involved. What that meant for me, I had no idea. I thought about ditching my pistol, but then remembered the sound of bullets buzzing my ear and gave up on that notion.

Why had a Gestapo *Kriminalinspektor* tried to kill us? It wasn't as if he were hot on the trail of anything. Hochler was tailing us as soon as we'd left Dulles's apartment. Or at least I'd first noticed him along the river. No surprise that the people who came and went from the Dulles abode were under surveillance, by the Germans, Swiss, or even freelancers. But why start a shooting war in neutral Bern? All we'd done was visit a bank, leaving with nothing for our troubles.

It made no sense.

Which was why I sat there for an hour, idly flipping the pages, waiting for someone to show up. If the Swiss police were on to us, it might make some sense of all this, put some structure to it so I could understand what was happening. But no one showed. It was business as usual.

Not so with the war news, as far as I could figure from the pictures. More men and tons of supplies were landing in Normandy. Among the men was General de Gaulle, who'd been cheered in the streets of Bayeux by throngs of liberated French, many of whom had likely cheered General Pétain when he'd taken over nearly four years ago to the day and declared de Gaulle a renegade. It looked like Hitler had finally trotted out one of the wonder weapons he'd been going on about. Rockets called *Vergeltungswaffen* if I was understanding the caption. The picture was a grainy shot of a pilotless rocket with stubby wings, apparently called the V-1 for short. They were falling on London and killing people.

That was all interesting, not to mention deadly, but I had more pressing concerns. Like figuring out why the Gestapo had marked Kaz and me for death. I left the newspaper on the bench and hoofed it back to the hotel.

Kaz was waiting for me in the lobby. We went into the bar for food and a drink.

"Any ideas why Hochler was after us?" I asked after Kaz had given our order.

"I can see no reason," Kaz said, lifting his glasses and rubbing the bridge of his nose. "Unless it has something to do with Lasho."

"How could it?"

"I have no idea, Billy. But it is the only thing we've done—bringing *der Zigeuner* into Switzerland—that could possibly engender such a deadly response. Really, what else have we done? Looked at a corpse. Had dinner. Visited a bank."

"Maybe Hochler thought we'd uncovered evidence connecting Hannes to Lowenberg's death," I said.

"If we had, it would be a matter for the police, not us. Anyway, all Hannes need do if he felt he were in jeopardy is to leave Switzerland. There are other Gestapo agents who could take his place."

Our drinks came. Two large glasses of foamy beer.

"Here's to one less," I said, raising my glass.

We had a hearty meal, digging in with the enthusiasm of men who'd dodged death and left a *rodef* with a ventilated skull flat on the pavement. In our room, we found the tuxedos hung in the closet, along with shiny black shoes, cuff links, and all the other folderol that goes with fancy dress.

Deciding it would be best to stay out of any more trouble, we took a nap.

CHAPTER SIXTEEN

WE ENTERED DULLES'S office and found him at his desk, reading a file. He held a fountain pen, jotting down the occasional note. He ignored us. We waited.

He finally closed the file, capped the pen, and set it down neatly on top of the file. Only then did he look up and acknowledge us.

"What the hell on God's green earth have you two been up to?" Dulles bellowed. "Your first full day in Bern and you assassinate a Gestapo officer on the steps of a synagogue? Are you trying to broadcast your presence here?"

"We didn't assassinate anyone," I said.

"I shot him in the head," Kaz said, standing with one hand in his pocket, as if discussing a triviality. "To prevent him from shooting Billy in the chest. Although I must say, he was a terrible marksman. He might have missed altogether."

"And around the corner from the American embassy, for God's sake," Dulles said, invoking the deity once again, as if our actions had disgraced him in the eyes of the Lord.

"I admit it was an unfortunate neighborhood in which to save Billy's life," Kaz said, in that calm, deliberative, soft voice of his, half Oxford and half Continental Europe. Maureen was sitting on the couch, her eyebrows raised.

"How did you hear about it?" I asked, trying to distract Dulles from Kaz's sarcasm. I hoped Dulles might say how snazzy we looked in our monkey suits, but he was too busy bawling us out to appreciate our sartorial elegance.

"All of Bern's heard about it, at least all of Bern that cares about who's shooting whom. Inspector Escher was kind enough to call and give me a description of the two men involved," Dulles said.

"Does he suspect us?" I asked.

"Suspect? No. He knows it was you. Who the hell else would it be? And on the steps of a synagogue, of all places." He was so steamed he was repeating himself. "And that pious rabbi, saying he didn't see or hear a thing. Is that how you got away?"

"Never mind the rabbi," I said. "He had nothing to do with this. Escher's not going to arrest us?"

"That's not how things work in Bern," Dulles said. "We prefer the civilized approach."

"I am sorry, Mr. Dulles," Kaz said. "We have perhaps been too long where the uncivilized approach is what keeps one alive."

Dulles didn't know what to say, which may have been the objective. It was a barbed comment, aimed at Dulles's safe Swiss sinecure, but it also possessed a good deal of truth. The kind of truth that made men shut up and think.

"Sit down," Dulles muttered, pointing with his smoldering pipe at the chairs in front of his desk. "You'd do well to remember we are guests in a neutral nation. Any violence could result in our expulsion."

"It was *Kriminalinspektor* Hochler who started shooting," Kaz said. He tossed Hochler's identity card on Dulles's desk as he took his seat. "Although we cannot think why."

"He tailed us from here when we left with Victor," I said. "I spotted him along the river and then as we left Credit Suisse. We tried to shake him so we could turn the tables and follow him. At that point, we had no idea who he was."

"When did he start shooting?" Maureen asked.

"We started up the steps to the Swiss Red Cross, on Rainmatt-strasse," Kaz said. "That's when he first fired."

"My God, the Red Cross too? You didn't leave anyone out of the line of fire, did you?" Dulles said.

"What happened at the bank?" Maureen asked, more to the point.

"Nothing much. Kaz knows his father opened an account there, but they wouldn't verify it. Or let Kaz have access, even though he has the account number," I explained.

"Unless I produce a death certificate," Kaz said. "Which is, for the bank, conveniently impossible."

"Remind me to look into that after the dust settles from your escapades today. Maybe I can help," Dulles said. He asked Kaz to write out his father's full name and address, then tucked it under his blotter. "You didn't spot Hannes during this gun battle?"

"We never saw him," I said. "The only thing we can come up with is that they know we came across the border with Lasho, and they're out to get him. He's killed a lot of Nazis."

"But if it was Lasho they were after, surely they'd grab you for questioning, not kill you. What would that get them?" Maureen asked.

"Unfortunately, all we have are theories and questions, no answers," I said.

"All right, it's over and done with," Dulles said, studying the identity card. "Maybe Hochler went off the deep end. Perhaps there's no logical explanation."

"What, from the stress of duty in neutral Switzerland? The guy's probably hunted Jews and Gypsies all across Europe, and tortured Resistance fighters before putting bullets in their brains. You think he went nuts from too much Swiss chocolate?" I said. "There's something going on that we don't understand."

"Be careful," Dulles said. "I think you may be right." Which for him, was quite a statement, since it implied he'd been wrong.

"We'll see you at the reception, Allen," Maureen said, rising from the couch. She wore a long black coat of thin, delicate velvet with a fur collar. "I have a car waiting for us."

"You aren't armed, are you?" Dulles asked her, giving me a hard stare.

"Why, Allen, wherever would I hide a gun?" Maureen said, opening her coat to reveal a slinky black dress cut very low, finished off with black lace gloves above the elbows. She didn't have room for a single bullet, much less a pistol. "Come on, boys, let's not be late to the party." She gave me a wink as Dulles stared, her curves driving out any thoughts about our armament.

"We'll meet Victor there," she said, ushering us out to a waiting car. A nice Opel Kapitän, which reminded me of the expensive cars shot up this morning. "He'll point out all the important banking people so you can get to know them."

"Thrilling," Kaz said as he held the door open for her. There was plenty of room in the back, and I got in on the other side, leaning in to check the driver, who looked straight ahead.

It was Lasho.

"What better way for him to learn the city streets?" Maureen said.

"It is a fine automobile," Lasho said. "I hear you killed a Gestapo man today. Very good."

"Don't encourage them, Anton," Maureen said as he drove away from the curb. "If you see Hannes tonight, leave the keys and follow him."

"And kill him?"

"No, Anton. We mustn't kill two Germans on the same day. Very untidy, and our Swiss hosts are very clean, organized people," she said.

"Your automobile?" I asked.

"No, borrowed from a friend for the evening. Cars are difficult to come by these days. Everyone's building tanks and trucks."

"We put a few out of commission this morning," I said. "It probably keeps a lot of mechanics busy these days, keeping prewar cars running."

"If you can find a mechanic around here. Opel's hiring bunches of them for their repair facility outside Basel," she said.

"Repairing cars?" Kaz asked.

"Silly boy. No, German army trucks. They bring them down on flatbeds and do the repair work here. Saves them from being bombed, obviously. Funny thing, Opel is owned by General Motors in the good old USA. They're making a bundle off this enterprise."

"It's a damned bizarre war," I said.

"Wait. Tonight should be positively surreal," she said.

"Dulles is attending?" Kaz asked.

"Oh yes, Allen will make his entrance fashionably late. Victor and I will bring him up to speed about who's there, and then he'll start chatting with diplomats, bankers, fascists, lawyers, and even more sordid types."

"Who are they?" I said.

"Journalists, those who can be trusted to stay off the record," she said with a lilting laugh. "And probably a few evadees."

"I thought Switzerland put all military personnel in internment camps," I said.

"Those are internees," Maureen said. "Now pay attention, see if you can follow the bouncing ball. If you're shot down and parachute onto Swiss soil, you become an internee. If your parachute lands elsewhere or if you escape from a German POW camp and make it into Switzerland while evading capture, you're an evadee. Evadees get to stay in cushy ski hotels, which are mostly empty, given the shortage of tourists these days. They can travel with the proper permissions. Don't ask me to defend the logic, but it's how the Swiss do things."

The car pulled up in front of a palatial house, the kind of joint that had a fountain out front, wide steps leading up to a giant front door, and a wrought-iron fence around the grounds to keep out the commoners. Big windows and smiling, sleek people in fine clothes. Gravel crunched under the tires as Lasho drove the Opel around the fountain and let us out.

"I will be nearby," he said, his eyes moving constantly, checking each person as they came close. "It is tempting."

"What is?" Kaz asked.

"To prove what they say about Sinti. That we are all thieves. There will be much to steal in such a grand house."

"Resist the impulse, Anton. I'd much prefer you to find Hannes than the family silver," Maureen said. "Now move, boys, before all the canapés are gone."

We followed Maureen's clicking heels up the steps. She gave our names to a big guy at the door. He looked like a pro. Hooded eyes scanning the arriving guests, short haircut, and a well-cut tux that couldn't hide the bulge of his holster. A slightly smaller guy with a clip-board stood off to his side and checked off our names. He nodded us through, his look lingering on me for a fraction of a second. Maybe he made me for a cop, or maybe I looked like I didn't belong. Kaz fit right in with this crowd, and Maureen was a known quantity, so I was deserving of a second glance, which I got, and no more. Which would not have been the case if we'd come packing with telltale bulges like the doorman's. Maureen told us she'd gotten our measurements from her tailor in Geneva and arranged for the tuxedos to be altered. I had a double-breasted job, and it fit like I glove. I looked like a million bucks. An unarmed million bucks, which isn't necessarily the best combination.

We moved through the foyer into what formerly was a grand ballroom, like you see in the movies, where once upon a time ladies in big hooped skirts waltzed around the dance floor with men in frock coats. A waiter carrying a tray of drinks slowed down enough for us to snag glasses of champagne, and we flowed through the crowd in Maureen's wake as she cheek-kissed her way to one corner of the room.

"Now to see who's here, who's talking, and who's stalking," Maureen said, delicately picking up a smoked salmon canapé from a roving waiter.

"Stalking who?" I said, stuffing salmon on a tiny piece of rye bread into my mouth.

"This is a gathering of rich industrialists, government officials, movers and shakers in Swiss high society," she said. "Someone always wants something. It's instructive to watch and see who is circling for the kill and who tries to slip away. Now don't bother trying to remember all the names, dear boy. Simply soak up the decadent ambiance."

Maureen downed her champagne and grabbed another glass, taking three steps up a staircase to a wide landing. The curving stairs led to a mezzanine along one side of the room, decorated with paint-ings of stern-faced Swiss through the ages. The height advantage gave us a perfect view of the crowd. Jewels draped around graceful necks sparkled as women in brightly colored gowns linked arms with men in their black-and-white uniforms. Smiles and laughter lit faces untroubled by war and destruction. They all had the pampered skin of the rich, soft and creamy, marred by nothing more than ruddy cheeks from the ski slopes.

"There are Germans, here, of course," Kaz said, his champagne untouched.

"Oodles of them, darling," Maureen said. "Behave yourself."

"Do not be concerned. I left my revolver at the hotel," Kaz said.

"Well, I wouldn't come unarmed," she said, lowering her voice to a conspiratorial whisper. "I've got a .25 caliber Browning in my clutch. Haven't had to use it yet, but I'll admit, I could put the six rounds to good use in this crowd. See those two men standing near the window, a third of the way across the room?"

"The guy with the thick lips and long face? Next to the dour older fellow?" I said.

"Yes. The thick-lipped gent is Emil Bührle, owner of Oerlikon industries. You've perhaps heard of his guns?"

"The twenty-millimeter Oerlikon cannon?" Kaz said. "They are used by every major power."

"And produced under license to Oerlikon in all those nations, which makes Emil a very rich man. Perhaps the richest in Switzerland. Of course, all the weapons manufactured here in Switzerland are sold directly to the Nazis."

"Hardly seems like a neutral act," I said.

"Oh, Emil would sell to anyone. And he will, once the Allies reach the Swiss border. Now the man he's talking with, that's Kurt von Schroder. Heinrich Himmler's favorite banker. He does all the important transactions for the SS."

"This is pretty one-sided, all these Nazis doing business openly," I said, tossing back my drink and looking for another. "So much for neutrality."

"It's not only the Swiss and the Germans, dear Billy," Maureen said. "One of von Schroder's jobs is to take cash payments from IT&T and pass them onto Himmler. Our very own International Telephone and Telegraph has serious business interests in Nazi Germany through their subsidiaries. It's von Schroder's job to look out for them, and bribing Himmler is one way IT&T makes certain those subsidiaries keep paying dividends."

"What do you mean?" I said, having a hard time believing any American company would do that.

"They own twenty-five percent of Focke-Wulf, which produces the best fighter plane the Germans have. It brings them a tidy profit and they keep the wheels of commerce greased with payments to Himmler and his bunch," Maureen said. "Sad to say, it's the truth."

"A truth I doubt we will read in the newspapers," Kaz said. "What do those two men have in common?"

"Emil is a big art collector. Von Schroder has put him in touch with Hermann Goring, who sells him artwork at cut rates. You know, stuff they stole from Jews. Emil likes Impressionists and Postimpressionists, especially. I hear there's a Cézanne he's after. Maybe that's what they're chatting about."

"I'm glad you said I don't have to remember their names. Are there any nice people here?" I asked.

"Bless your sweet soul, Billy, I doubt it. Oh, wait, goodness prevails," Maureen said, waving at two men who were making their way to her. She explained one was a Swiss lawyer and the other a German diplomat, but we shouldn't hold it against either of them.

"*Herr Doktor* Veit Wyler, and Vice Consul Hans Bernd Gisevius," she said, after giving them our names and supposed occupation. "Dear friends, this is a group that bears no deep scrutiny. Billy asked if there were any decent sorts in the room and I almost gave up hope until I spotted you two. Have a nice chat while I go powder my nose."

"Dr. Wyler, is it your clients who bear no scrutiny?" Kaz asked as he cast a wary eye toward Gisevius, German diplomats not being high on his list for party chitchat.

"You must not take Miss Conaty very seriously," Wyler said. "She is a delightful person, but prone to exaggeration." Wyler had a round face and a pleasant smile. Only the bags under his eyes hinted at the secrets he held.

"I agree on both counts," Gisevius said. "But in this case, she hardly exaggerates. Veit is famous in certain circles, infamous in others."

Gisevius clapped Wyler on the shoulder, grinning broadly. He was slightly older, tall, with graying blond hair and intelligent eyes behind tortoise-shell glasses.

"How so?" I asked.

"He is a legal genius," Gisevius said. "He's helped a number of Jewish refugees make it across the border. Veit found an obscure paragraph in an old law volume, which said that no person crossing the border into Switzerland wearing any part of a Swiss army uniform could be turned away. Probably something dating from the Napoleonic Wars. So he gathered up as many old uniforms as he could and distributed them at the more well-known crossing points. Brilliant!"

"I would not think your government would consider it so brilliant," Kaz said, his mouth turned down in disdain.

"No, but things are not always as they seem, are they, gentlemen? Now, please excuse me, there is someone I must speak with." Gisevius gave a little bow. I expected him to click his heels, but he didn't oblige.

"Is that true?" I asked.

"Yes," Wyler said. "I expect it is why I was invited by the Red Cross. Although, with the number of government officials here, I wondered if I'd be arrested instead." He smiled, to show it was a joke. The kind of joke that's only funny because it might be true.

"Then I am surprised to see you in company with a Nazi," Kaz said.

"And me being a Jew," Wyler said. "I should be shocked myself." He raised his glass to us as a farewell and wandered off.

"There is much about this place I do not understand," Kaz said. "I almost prefer the battlefield."

"Almost," I said. "But there's a lot to be said for champagne and no shrapnel on the side." We nibbled on pâté canapés while waiting for Maureen to return, wary of being surrounded by Nazi bankers. Boston bankers were bad enough. Too many people I knew had lost their homes during the Depression for me to feel any kindness toward the business class. Especially ones wearing little swastikas on their lapels.

"You two look lost," Henri Moret said, one of the few decent banker gents I'd met. He carried a small black briefcase, no drink or food in hand.

"It's not my usual crowd," I said. "You working?"

"I have some papers to deliver to Mr. Huber. Bank business. Have you seen him?"

"Wouldn't know him," I said. "Maureen's been giving us the low-down on the nefarious characters in the room, but then she took off."

"You were talking with Wyler, I saw," Henri said. "A good man. You heard about his uniform trick?"

"Yes," Kaz said. "And we also met a very strange German. Hans Bernd Gisevius."

"Best not to ask too many questions about Hans," Henri said. "Ah, here's Victor."

"Sorry I'm late. I was looking for a friend I expected to see here," Victor said. "Vadim Fournier, who works in Huber's finance office."

"Too bad, Vadim's always the life of the party," Henri said. "Not the staid banker type at all."

"Anyway, you fellows should have waited for me this morning," Victor said, patting his pockets. Henri seemed to recognize the routine and withdrew his silver cigarette case, opening it and offering Victor one of the Parisienne cigarettes lined up neatly inside, before taking one for himself. As he flicked his gold lighter, his eyes moved to the side, spotting someone on the mezzanine. "Did you hear about the shooting, Henri?"

"No, but tell me later. There's Huber, and I need to get this to him. I'll be back."

We watched Henri take the steps up to the mezzanine and work his way to Huber, who was surrounded by a semicircle of friends, admirers, or lackeys. It was hard to tell the difference.

"It must be damned important," Victor said. "Henri always likes to hear the latest news and gossip from the streets."

"He had papers from the bank for Huber to sign," I said. "I guess banker's hours don't apply to the wealthier clients."

"It's a foolish banker who ignores a man with Max's holdings," a voice from behind me said. "Hello, Victor. What are you up to these days?"

"Thomas McKittrick," Victor said, as I stepped aside to make room in our little circle. "I don't think you've met my colleagues." Victor gave our names and little else about us. "Mr. McKittrick runs the Bank for International Settlements."

"I thought I knew most of the consular staff," McKittrick said, as he gave us the once-over. He had a large, wide forehead made even more pronounced by a thatch of receding white hair.

"They don't let us out of the office very often," I said. "What's an American doing running a Swiss bank?"

"Swiss? Hardly," McKittrick said with a laugh. "I guess you don't work on the financial side with Victor." I gave a noncommittal nod.

"BIS was created after the last war, to help transfer reparations from Germany to other nations," Victor explained. "Today it serves as an international central bank for other central banks."

"So it's not the kind of bank where I can deposit my pennies," I said.

"Not quite," McKittrick said, with a condescending smile, his eyes already searching out company more equal to his stature.

"Perhaps you will be back in the reparations business soon enough," Kaz said.

"I hope not. Last time around, the victors were too harsh on Germany. If Germany loses this war, I hope wiser heads prevail," McKittrick said.

"If?" I said. "I'd say it's only a matter of time."

"A German defeat could mean a Soviet army in the heart of Europe," McKittrick said. "That would be a disaster." He seemed stunningly unaware of the disasters wrought by the Third Reich already. Or uncaring.

"We will not allow it," another voice said in a gruff German accent. Our circle widened to include a stocky gray-haired man with heavy jowls and a Nazi Party pin on his lapel. "The Bolsheviks have no place in modern Europe."

"*Herr* Hermann Schmitz," McKittrick said, laying a friendly hand on the shoulder of the new arrival. "He serves on the board of the BIS. This is Mr. Boyle and Mr. Kazimierz of the American consular staff. You know Victor Hyde, I believe."

"*Ja*, Victor, we know each other. But these gentlemen I have not met." He leaned forward and squinted his eyes, like a guy who needed glasses but didn't want to admit it.

"Please excuse me," Kaz said, his voice like ice. He turned away, finding Dr. Wyler nearby and joining him in conversation.

"Quite rude," McKittrick said, guiding Schmitz away. He glanced at Kaz and Wyler, then leaned in close to speak to Schmitz. "Another Jew, probably," I heard him say.

"Admirable restraint on your friend's part," Victor said. "An incident here would do us no good."

"We're more used to killing Nazis than making small talk with them," I said. "McKittrick seems to have no trouble with it, though."

"No. His bank has helped launder a good deal of stolen gold. Twenty-three tons from Czechoslovakia, for instance."

"Jesus, how do you tell the good guys from the bad guys around here?" I asked.

"That's easy," Victor said. "The good guys are the ones who wonder about that very question. The bad guys don't even understand it."

"Like McKittrick?" I asked.

"He likes gold, whatever the source. He has certified Nazis on his board of directors. He doesn't care for Jews very much, not to mention our Soviet allies. Does that answer your question?"

Kaz rejoined us at the same moment as did Henri, a glass of champagne in hand.

"Do you know who that man was?" Kaz asked, his mouth set in a grim line of anger.

"Schmitz? Besides being on the board of BIS, he's chairman of the board at IG Farben. Why?" Victor asked.

"Do they make fighter planes as well?" I asked.

"Billy, you should spend more time actually reading the intelligence reports the fine people at SHAEF put together for us. IG Farben is a major Nazi arms manufacturer and uses vast numbers of slave laborers. One of their products is a gas called Zyklon B."

"What's that?" Henri asked. I'd heard of Zyklon B, and felt a shudder at the thought of a fellow American's hand on the shoulder of the Nazi businessman whose company produced it.

"It is a poison gas. Very fast acting. It is used to murder vast numbers of Jews and others in the extermination camps," Kaz said. "That man is the worst kind of mass murderer. He profits from it."

A waiter passed by, halting at the edge of our circle with a platter of cheeses and smoked ham. No one was interested. At this point, hiding out in the hills of occupied France and living on stale bread seemed preferable to another moment in this gathering of the evil, the elite, and the greedy.

"Look who I found, boys," Maureen said, making her way through the crowd with Dulles in tow, her arm linked with his. "What's to report?"

"Nazis, bankers, industrialists, the usual crowd," Victor said. Then his gaze lifted to the mezzanine. "But there's a threesome we haven't seen before."

McKittrick was introducing Schmitz to Max Huber. The two of them were shaking hands while McKittrick grinned like a Boston banker foreclosing on the O'Hara widow.

"What's the head honcho at IG Farben got in common with the president of the Red Cross?" I asked.

"Money?" Henri said.

"Or maybe they're working a deal," Victor suggested. "Something that would make Schmitz look good after the war. Releasing slave laborers or something like that."

"Why would McKittrick care?" Dulles asked. "It's hardly a BIS matter."

"Maybe he wants to look good after the war as well," I said.

"He's too rich and connected to worry about that," Maureen said. "Let's go our separate ways and see if there's anything else."

"Billy, one moment," Henri said as the group split up. He pulled me aside until we weren't surrounded by partygoers and lowered his voice. "Do you see that bar up on the mezzanine?"

He nodded to the far end of the room, opposite where he'd disappeared with Huber on their way to his office. There were bottles of booze and bubbly set up on a table manned by two busy bartenders.

"Sure," I said, uncertain what he was after.

"In ten minutes, exactly, could you manage to knock one of those bottles over? Preferably to the floor below, so it will be very loud."

"I could hurt somebody," I said, eyeing the setup. It wouldn't be hard to manage, but there was quite a crowd below.

"Then choose your target well. Or make some sort of scene. I need a distraction."

"For what?"

"Will you do it, Billy? It's quite important." I remembered what Henri had told us yesterday: that he was about to come up with something big, something that would help with Safehaven.

"Why not? I usually have no trouble being clumsy," I said.

"Thank you," Henri said, gripping my arm and slipping away. I checked my watch and headed to the bar. I caught Kaz's eye and motioned him to follow. I filled him in on the plan, such as it was. We checked our watches, agreeing on the exact time for the maneuver. Kaz's job was to stay below and move any bystanders before I sent the glassware tumbling.

"Oh, I'm glad I found you two," Maureen said, appearing from a gaggle of brightly colored gowns and French chatter. "See old Kurt von Schroder over there?"

"Yeah. Himmler's banker and the bag man for IT&T, right?"

"Go to the head of the class. Now the charming man he's talking to is Siegfried Krauch. He's a senior man in the Gestapo. Lower than all these old party men, of course. But Krauch is Georg Hannes's boss. If we're lucky, he could lead us to Hannes."

"You want me to tail him when he leaves?"

"You read my mind, darling. You on foot, and Anton in the car. That way we can stay with him no matter how he travels. I had Anton get a look at Krauch's face when I brought him to the kitchen for something to eat. Oh, look, there's dreary Dr. Frenkel and his SVV friends. You know, the Swiss fascists." Maureen sipped champagne, staring at Frenkel and two beefy blond boys who looked like storm-troopers. Bodyguards? Why did Frenkel bring muscle with him to this swanky joint? Maybe he was showing off for the high-rollers in attendance.

"I've had the pleasure of attending one of his autopsies," I said, watching as one of the bully boys pushed past Dr. Wyler, elbowing him hard enough for Wyler to spill his drink. Frenkel smirked as he wound his way through the crowd.

Maureen fluttered off. I checked my watch and began to climb the stairs. I stopped, taking another look at Krauch. A tall fellow, six foot easy, with dark hair slicked back. He looked athletic, broad at the shoulders and thick-necked. Not an easy guy to take down if he spotted me, so I planned to stay a fair distance behind him. He was well-dressed, at ease in his tux, and I wondered if the OSS and the Gestapo used the same tailor.

But I had other business to attend to, and not much time to get into position. I reached the top of the staircase and glanced discreetly at my watch, not wanting to look too obvious about it. As I looked up, I was surprised to see a US Army Air Force officer headed straight for me. A captain in his pink and greens, which for some reason is what the army called the brown uniform jacket and khaki dress pants.

"Hey, you're a Yank, right? Walt Bowman, glad to meet you," he said, extending his right hand while gripping a drink in the other. "I heard you talking to that Swiss fellow and thought I'd say hello. Don't get to see too many new faces these days. American faces, that is."

"Billy Boyle," I said, trying to work my way past him. I didn't want to be rude, but I was on a deadline.

"Come on, Billy, I'll buy you a drink. You with the embassy?" Bowman wore a big grin under a Clark Gable mustache that he probably cultivated to look older. He had light brown hair and dark eyes, which darted across the room as if he were watching for enemy fighters. Maybe he'd tangled with some of IT&T's Focke-Wulfs.

"Yes," I said, realizing I might not have time to ditch Bowman. "You a fighter pilot?"

"I am," he said, puffing out his chest a bit. "Three kills and one probable. Before flak got my Mustang over Stuttgart. I bailed out close to the Swiss border and managed to get across."

"Evadee status, then?" I moved with Bowman closer to the bar.

"Yeah. Pretty lucky. They put me up in a hotel and let me out on furlough now and then. The Red Cross got me an invite to this party, but it's pretty dull, isn't it?"

"It's about to get rowdy, Walt. Tell me, are you willing to take a risk?"

"I'm a fighter pilot, Billy. A bored fighter pilot. What do you need?"

"I need you to not ask any questions. Walk over to that bar and when I give you the go-ahead, slug me. Hard enough to make it look like we have a beef, but don't break my jaw, okay?"

"That's it? All right, but how will I know when to hit you?"

"You'll know," I said, risking another glance at my watch. Sixty seconds. We joined the line at the bar where one bartender was mixing cocktails while the other poured champagne. I counted down silently and edged closer to the champagne table where a new bottle had just come off the ice. I saw Kaz below and nodded. Ten seconds. I turned to speak to Bowman, my back to the chilled bottle.

"Captain, is it true what they say about Mustang pilots running for home whenever they run into a Focke-Wulf?"

Two seconds.

"You bastard!" Bowman yelled, and connected with a punch that grazed my cheekbone. I went flying backward like it was a roundhouse hit from Sugar Ray Robinson. I crashed into the table, making sure that I flung my arm back far enough to guide the bottle over the railing, hoping Kaz was directing traffic below.

I'd never seen a champagne bottle hit a tile floor from a height before. I didn't actually see the impact, but I sure heard it. And so did everyone else in the joint. A loud, shattering crash and crack of glass was followed by a *pop* as the cork exploded and sent a spray of champagne into the crowd as Kaz pushed people back, taking the brunt of the bubbly. I hustled Bowman downstairs, watching as some in the crowd began to laugh while others sputtered in indignation. Waiters scurried around with towels and apologies, a few of them pointing out Bowman and whispering among themselves.

Kaz came forward, quietly slipping Swiss franc notes to the waiters, who busied themselves wiping down Kaz's tux, and apparently forgetting all about who started the rumpus in the first place.

"What the hell was that all about?" Victor demanded as Bowman and I tried to make ourselves inconspicuous. Dulles and Maureen trailed him, and I noticed Dulles's trousers had taken a soaking. I figured it wasn't the best time to admit it was intentional.

"We were kidding around, and I bumped into the table, that's all," I said. "This is Captain Bowman, an evadee out for a night on the town."

"Bowman?" Dulles said, looking to Maureen. "I don't think we've debriefed him, have we?"

"No, he's been on my list," Maureen said. "We'd love to hear how and where you made it across the border, Captain Bowman. Especially since you're in town. It saves me a long drive." Maureen smiled and studied the young pilot. "It gives us so much more time together, darling boy. Where are you staying?"

"At the *Schweizerhof*. Exactly who are you people?" Bowman asked. "You don't act like diplomats."

"Thanks for the compliment, Bowman," Dulles said. "You're in good hands with Miss Conaty, I assure you. Boyle, keep your eyes on Krauch. That's your assignment for tonight. Baron Kazimierz, you stay with Mr. Lasho in the car. There's a chance Krauch may lead one of you to Hannes."

With those instructions, Dulles left and intercepted Gisevius, guiding the German diplomat by the arm and whispering whatever secrets passed between enemies on neutral ground.

"Okay, Billy," Victor said, "what's going on?"

"I too would like to know," Kaz said, "since my tuxedo was a near casualty of this action."

"Ask him," I said, noticing Henri across the room, talking with McKittrick and Schmitz like they were old pals. Of course, he probably knew them from the banking world, but it was still disconcerting. I'd known some killers in my time, but they were all innocent babes compared to the man who sold Zyklon B for a living. Henri broke away and headed in our direction, after chatting with Dulles and Gisevius for a few seconds.

"Henri," Victor said, his brow creased in worry, "what have you done?"

"Nothing at all," Henri said. "Simply wandering around the place. There are some fine seventeenth-century paintings upstairs. I heard a lot of noise and came down. What did I miss?"

"A slight mishap with a champagne bottle," Kaz said. "Which was carried off admirably by Billy with the assistance of Captain Bowman."

"An evadee, I take it? Glad to meet you, Bowman," Henri said, introducing himself. "Where were you shot down?" Bowman recounted his story, he and Henri moving on to talk of the ski slopes at Zermatt without missing a beat.

"If Henri doesn't want to give you a straight answer, it's hopeless," Victor said, shaking his head as his friend ignored us and promised Bowman a skiing holiday on his next furlough, handing him his business card.

"Well, are we done here?" Henri asked, coming back into our circle.

"The captain and I will adjourn to the bar at the Hotel *Schweizerhof*," Maureen said. "They make divine martinis. We can begin the debriefing there." Maureen gave us a little wave of her hand and took Bowman's arm, guiding him away for interrogation. I think I definitely livened up the party for him.

"Well, good for her," Henri said, watching the couple depart. "I'm glad someone's having a good time. These soirees become dull very quickly, after the best food has been consumed. I was going to ask for a ride, but Dulles mentioned he'd detailed you to follow a Gestapo man named Krauch."

"You're not going to tell us?" Victor asked, ignoring Henri's patter. Henri simply smiled. "Well, in that case, give me another of your Parisiennes, will you?"

"Sorry, Victor, all out. You'll have to buy your own," Henri said. "Billy, is *Herr* Krauch the broad-shouldered Teutonic type with too much pomade in his hair?"

"Sounds like him," I said.

"Well, there he goes, heading for the door," Henri said. "Shouldn't you follow him?"

CHAPTER SEVENTEEN

HENRI AND VICTOR both decided to call it a night and walked out with us, which helped Kaz and me to blend in with the departing crowd. Even with banker's hours, a lot of these folks had to wake up early and get to work in the morning, so there was a decent number of Bern's elite milling around on the sidewalk, waiting for automobiles or doing some last-minute buttonholing.

Krauch was among them. He looked like he was delivering a lecture to a guy in a grubby raincoat. Obviously not a partygoer.

"I think that's Hannes," Victor said. I took a few steps to get a better angle. He was right. Now we had two guys to follow.

"Can we help?" Henri said.

"No, but thanks. Tailing a Gestapo officer takes some experience," I said. "And luck."

I watched as Henri and Victor departed, keeping an eye on Krauch and his subordinate. Krauch was obviously angry, but it was impossible to know about what. Hannes had the look of an underling who knew he had to wait out the storm until it blew over. Resigned, but not worried is what I guessed.

Our car pulled up. Krauch gave it a glance, probably thinking it was his ride. He gave no sign of recognition when Lasho got out, and went back to jabbing Hannes in the chest with his finger.

"You see?" Lasho said as he joined us, nodding his head slightly in Hannes's direction. I filled him in on Maureen's instructions.

"Krauch has led us to Hannes quite easily," Kaz said. "Should we all tail him?"

"He'll spot us," I said. "Lasho, if Krauch leaves in a car, you follow and see where he goes. Kaz and I will split up and follow Hannes on foot if he walks. If not, we all pile in the car and go after him. Okay?"

"Yes," Lasho said. "He must be an important Gestapo man. Should I kill him?"

"If he goes down a dark alley, be my guest. But otherwise, don't make a scene. Our main objective is to find out where Hannes hangs his hat without being spotted. Strictly reconnaissance."

A sleek limousine pulled to the curb, just the thing for ferrying a top Gestapo man around. Without missing a beat, Krauch halted his diatribe and opened the rear door as Kurt von Schroder—Himmler's banker, if I remembered the cast of nefarious characters correctly—stomped down the stairs and heaved himself inside. Krauch followed, leaving Hannes alone on the sidewalk, the sigh he released visible in the rise and fall of his shoulders.

Lasho went to his car and eased into the flow of traffic, close to Krauch and von Schroder. Kaz and I walked slowly down the stairs as Hannes stuck his hands in his pockets and sauntered away. We trailed him, staying together as we mingled with the other guests strolling in the cool night air. In a few blocks, the pedestrians thinned out, and I told Kaz to cross the street and drop back. Basically, his job now was to tail me as I tailed Hannes. In theory, our quarry wouldn't spot me, but Kaz would watch my back in case Hannes, or a confederate, doubled back on me.

Theory holds little sway on a dark night in a strange city, following a man schooled in the ways of terror and torture. I followed footsteps, trusting my ears to recognize Hannes's gumshoe gait.

I didn't have much going for me. Hannes was in the business of surveillance, and likely to be aware of what was going on around him even without thinking about it. I'd tailed plenty of guys, but never in a tuxedo. It had worked for me as we left the party. Now, if Hannes scanned the darkened sidewalk behind him, I would hardly blend in.

He strolled on, seemingly unconcerned, down a residential street lined with parked automobiles. I darted into the street, keeping him in view with the vehicles between us. Up ahead, he turned right, and I jogged ahead, trying not to slap my shoe leather too loudly on the pavement. At the intersection, I pressed my body against the corner of a building and peered around it, my line of sight blocked by scaffolding and a pile of bricks. I scurried forward, taking advantage of the cover the construction material gave, and saw Hannes crossing the road, pausing for a break in the traffic.

Kirchenfeldstrasse, I saw on the street sign, making a mental note of where Hannes was leading us. I looked back and spotted Kaz, waved him forward, then took my chances crossing the street. There wasn't a lot of traffic, but with the blackout, it was still a dangerous undertaking. Hannes made it, weaving between oncoming traffic, leaving me stranded on the center median. He must have spotted me. I watched him take the closest side street, probably hoping I'd hurry to catch up.

And walk into his trap. My bet was that he'd be waiting around the corner. With a knife at the ready, or brass knuckles if he were in a peaceful mood. I took a street down the block instead, circling around behind him, trusting that Kaz was keeping up.

I spotted Hannes in a doorway when he edged out to look in the other direction. I glanced around for some sort of weapon, which was hard to come by in a ritzy city neighborhood. I figured the odds were against sneaking up on him, given that I had no cover and he'd hear my steps on the empty street. So I found my own doorway and stepped into it, hoping to turn the tables when he got tired of waiting.

Then I heard the scream.

It sounded like Kaz calling my name from the direction of Kirchenfeldstrasse. I burst out of the doorway, running as fast as I could past Hannes and his hiding place, hoping the element of surprise would keep him from blocking me as I headed for the shouts echoing off the stone building ahead.

I skidded around the corner, trying to keep my balance and spotted Kaz in the darkness. I saw forms scuffling on the sidewalk, their movements all blurred shadows and angry grunts. I sprinted toward them, wondering if Hannes was at my back and if Kaz could hold off his assailants.

Then I saw two things. The first was that a man was down, writhing on the ground, clutching his knee. The second was the swing of an iron bar, coming in low to the ribs as another man took a wild swing at Kaz, his fist finding only air.

I heard the crack of bones and saw a big guy go to his knees, gasping in pain. Kaz raised the iron bar and gave him a smack in the face, just enough to break his nose. Breathing was going to come hard to this guy, but he'd go on doing it.

"Billy, are you all right?" Kaz asked, winded after his exertions. He held the bar like a walking stick, looking like a dandy out for a late-night stroll.

"Fine," I said, looking behind me. No trace of Hannes. "I think we lost Hannes, though. Who are these guys?"

"Hansel and Gretel, don't you recognize them?" It was the two SVV heavyweights from the party. Like many before them, they'd underestimated Kaz, and paid the price. They were both moaning, trying to crawl away from Kaz and not having a lot of luck. "I heard them following me and took the opportunity to arm myself from those construction materials." Now I saw the iron bar was from the scaffolding.

"What did they want?" I asked.

"They said they were going to search me and teach me a lesson. They accomplished neither of their objectives. Shall we ask them what they were after?"

"Make it snappy. We still might be able to find Hannes," I said. Kaz tamped the sidewalk with the iron bar and spoke to the two blondies in rapid-fire German. Between groans, they shook their heads. Kaz swung the bar in a high arc and brought it down next to the remaining good knee of the goon who could still breathe. It clanged and bounced off the pavement, recoiling into the perfect position for Kaz to take another, more precise swing.

Gretel decided to tell Kaz everything. As a matter of fact, we couldn't get him to shut up.

There had been a big hubbub at the party after the champagne bottle distraction. Frenkel huddled with von Schroder and Huber, then told them to assist the Gestapo in whatever they wanted. Krauch ordered them to follow Kaz and me, and search us for papers. That's all he knew; any paperwork they found on us was to be delivered to Krauch. There was a lot of *bitte, bitte,* after that, and we left the two hardcases to find a hospital on their own.

"Papers?" I said, checking the street where Hannes had been lying in wait. Alpenstrasse. He was gone.

"Nothing more specific," Kaz said. "You haven't had a chance to tell me, what was that stunt with the champagne all about?"

"Henri wanted a distraction," I said. "He wouldn't let on a thing afterward."

"He did tell us he was on the trail of—what did he call it?—a damning piece of evidence."

"That's right," I said, remembering the details of what he'd said at the restaurant yesterday. "He mentioned an invoice. A piece of paper."

"What invoice would be so important as to have the SVV and the Gestapo following us?" Kaz said.

"Well, Hannes wasn't following us; we were trailing him," I said as we carefully worked our way down the street. It grew darker as we walked under leafy branches swaying in the breeze. I was glad Kaz still had his trusty club.

"Perhaps his role was to lead us astray," Kaz said. "If so, he may have decided to retreat, or he might try and ambush us."

"If he saw how those two fared against one of us, he might have second thoughts," I said. We walked slowly, watching alleyways and alcoves for any sign of Hannes.

Kaz swung the iron bar casually, and I marveled at the change I'd seen in him since we first met back in '42. He'd been thin as a rail and suffering from a heart defect that should have kept him out of uniform. Along the way he decided to toughen himself up and see the war through, whatever his heart decided to do. He wrangled his way out of a safe office job and began to exercise, lift weights, and go for quick-paced long walks in Hyde Park when we were lucky enough to be in London. He was still an egghead with steel-rimmed spectacles, and certainly the smartest guy I ever knew, but now he had stamina and muscle too. I hoped his heart could keep up with the rest of him.

His was a heart that had been broken, and it had almost killed him. When I first arrived in London back in '42, my first friends were Kaz and Daphne Seaton. Two lovers made for each other. They were happy. Then Daphne was murdered, and Kaz fell into darkness. He became careless with his own life, toying with death again and again. Then, somewhere along the line, he decided to live. Perhaps it was because it's what Daphne would have wanted.

Perhaps it was because so many Nazis needed killing.

"Do we have any hope of finding him?" Kaz asked, stopping to survey the street ahead. Tall four-story structures lined both sides of the street, apartment houses with large windows and small balconies, all with shutters closed against the blackout.

A muffled conversation floated out into the street from one of the buildings, one of the voices holding a hint of menace. Wide steps led to the main door, with access beneath them to the basement area, probably where the concierge holed up. Lots of places to hide. We stood still, watching for any sign of who was gabbing. Is this where Hannes was headed, or was it simply an argument between neighbors?

A door opened and shut, the noise sudden and jarring in the quiet night. Kaz nudged me and I saw him. A figure rose from beneath the steps across the street, the familiar form of Hannes in his raincoat. We slowly knelt behind the fender of a car, watching as he looked up and down the empty roadway. He buttoned his coat and walked to the apartment house across the street. He took a few steps down the basement stairs, and leaned against the wall. Waiting.

For what? For who?

I tapped Kaz on the arm and we eased back a few paces, taking up a post at the rear fender of a Citroen Avant.

"He's got that placed staked out," I said.

"Yes, I would guess he talked with the concierge," Kaz said, keeping his voice low. "Perhaps he bribed him. Or tried to gain entry to an apartment."

"I don't see what good we can do here," I said. "Hannes hasn't led us to his place, and he might wait for hours. If he's got surveillance duty, it could be all night."

"We could come back in the morning and speak with the concierge," Kaz suggested. "Or we could wait in the gutter until dawn."

We decided to wait an hour. The hardest part was inhaling the odor of stale champagne from Kaz's tuxedo, still damp from my clever diversion. Hannes didn't move. No one came or went in the apartment building. A long hour passed, and we decided to give it ten minutes more. That's when Hannes moved out from his hiding place. He stretched, his hands going to his back, like any guy who'd been standing on pavement too long. He walked away from us, to the corner. Seconds later, an automobile pulled to the curb on the next street. Hannes trotted over and got in, and it sped off, our quarry gone. Apparently he'd come up as empty-handed as us.

We stretched ourselves and left, figuring we'd come back to question the concierge at 20 Alpenstrasse in the morning. Then we'd see Henri and find out what he'd been up to at the reception and if that was what the SVV and Gestapo boys were buzzing about. It was enough for one night.

CHAPTER EIGHTEEN

THE NEXT MORNING Kaz and I were drinking coffee in Dulles's office, reporting on our late-night stroll. No one else had showed up yet, and I was wishing we'd slept in a bit longer ourselves. The telephone rang and Dulles took the call, speaking in French. I watched as his eyes widened and he worked to recover from whatever surprise had been sprung on him.

"Henri Moret is dead," Dulles said, replacing the receiver. "Murdered."

"Henri?" I said. Even though I was a detective, I wasn't immune to asking the same inane questions everyone asked when stunned at the news of murder. "Where?"

"He was found in his apartment early this morning," Dulles said. "That was Inspector Escher. He's on the scene and will let you look around. Be discreet and see if this looks like it's connected to Safehaven in any way." He scribbled an address on a piece of paper and handed it to me.

"Elfenstrasse, in Kirchenfeld, where we were last night," I said. "At least it's not where Hannes was standing watch."

"Not that it did Moret any good," Dulles said. "Find out what you can and report back. I'll get Maureen and Victor in here. God knows when Lasho will decide to turn up. Go!" He was on the telephone before we were halfway out the door.

"I wish we knew what Henri was up to at the reception," Kaz said as we got into a taxicab. "Or if it got him killed." Kaz gave our driver the address, and he nodded in the rearview mirror, tipping his cloth cap in what seemed like an old-fashioned gesture.

"I wonder if some other SVV thugs followed him home," I said.

"Or the Gestapo," Kaz said.

"They don't mind murder," I said as our driver crossed the river. "But there'd have to be a damn good reason in a neutral capital. Otherwise it would just bring down the heat."

"But the SVV might see it as more of a local matter," Kaz said, gazing out the window. "Henri was certainly outspoken. It may have earned him enemies."

"Or maybe it was a burglary gone bad," I said, not believing it for one second.

"I am even more interested in the occupant of the building at 20 Alpenstrasse now," Kaz said, as the taxi slowed and turned onto our street.

"And I'll be relieved once we know Victor and Maureen are safe. There's no telling who else was followed last night, and for what reason."

"If we want to find Maureen, we may need to stop at the Hotel *Schweizerhof*, where Captain Bowman is staying. I have a feeling the interrogation may have continued into the night," Kaz said.

He paid the driver and we got out, stepping into a familiar scene. Police cars, a hearse, uniformed cops, and a crowd of onlookers. Everything was different: the uniforms, how *police* was spelled, and the language spoken by the gawkers. But it was also the same, the sad, standard routine of a crime scene, from the bored faces of the cops standing at the door to the gasps and whispers of the neighbors.

Kaz gave our name to one of the gray uniforms and he opened the door, pointing upstairs. We went up to the landing, where Inspector Escher met us. He looked tired, the kind of tired that comes from working a corpse in the early dawn hours.

"Henri Moret was a good man, which is why I took the step of informing *Herr* Dulles," he said. "If his death had anything to do with his consultations with your people, I want to know about it."

"Of course," I said, wondering who else Escher might be reporting to. Besides his regular boss, that is. Or who his boss might get on the telephone. This was kid-glove territory. "What happened?"

"A struggle," Escher said, leading us into the apartment. "Do not touch anything."

The door and lock were intact. It wasn't a forced entry. First was a foyer, with a hat rack and a closet. A marble floor in a black-and-white pattern led into a large sitting room, the tall windows looking out over trees planted along the sidewalk. A pleasant view, the greenery blocking out the sidewalk and much of the street.

Henri was on the floor. He wore a robe, more of a dressing gown, in a rich burgundy color, with a silk lining. Nothing underneath. A thick carpet covered much of the marble floor, but Henri lay at the edge, his head on the bare marble. His eyes were wide open, staring at the ceiling. Or, more accurately, at where the person choking him had been.

"You see the marks?" Escher said. I did. Bruises around his throat showed where his assailant had throttled him. It looked like it had been a one-handed attack. Right handed, judging by the largest discoloration, where a thumb would have dug into the flesh.

"Is that what killed him?" Kaz asked, on his knees and studying Henri's neck.

"Perhaps not," Escher said. "He struck his head on the floor. It could have happened when his assailant grabbed him by the throat. They struggled, and Moret fell, striking his head. It may not have been an intentional killing."

"Or he was pushed to the floor, and the other guy grabbed him by the neck and pounded his skull against the marble. Intentionally," I said. A few feet away, a chair was knocked over and a side table had been upended. A glass and some magazines were strewn across the plush carpet. It wouldn't have made a lot of noise. "I don't suppose anyone heard anything?"

"No," Escher said. "A neighbor coming downstairs found the door open and looked inside. They called the police a little after six o'clock."

"Whoever did this was in a hurry to get out," Kaz said. "Or didn't want to risk the sound of a door closing."

"Or wanted the body found," Escher said. "We can't find anything that was stolen. His wallet, watch, and other valuables are all here. Do you have any information that could help us?"

"We were at a reception with Henri last night," I said, avoiding a direct lie. "We left about the same time. All I noticed was that a couple of Gestapo types were up in arms about something. On our way home, we were waylaid by two SVV boys who'd been at the reception with your friend Dr. Frenkel."

"Colleague, please," Escher said. "I choose my friends with care. Do you know why they came after you?"

"No idea," I said, leaving out the part about us tailing Hannes, which may or may not have been connected. "But ask them. Two big blond fellows. One of them is probably in traction and the other has a broken nose."

"And ribs," Kaz said. "Not that we admit to causing any bodily injuries. But they should not be hard to find in any hospital in the Kirchenfeld neighborhood."

"We are in Kirchenfeld," Escher said, shifting his gaze between Kaz and me. "Are you sure there is nothing else you wish to tell me?"

"If you find out what Frenkel's stooges were after, you'll have more information than we do," I said.

"Stooges?" Escher asked, his brow crinkling as he tried out the new word.

"Goons. Thugs. Gunsels," Kaz said, showing off his American gangster slang.

"Ah, yes," Escher said. "Yes, many of the SVV are stooges, as you say. But you must not withhold any information from me. I am *polizei*, not SVV."

"I know, Inspector Escher. I swear, nothing we did had any bearing on this, as far as I know. If we find anything out, we will inform you," I said, gazing at the inert form of Henri Moret. "For his sake, if no other."

"Forgive me for asking, Inspector," Kaz said, "but are your superiors as clear as you are about the distinction between the police and the SVV?"

"My immediate superior, yes," Escher said, lowering his voice, which told me he wasn't as sure about the uniformed *polizei* stomping through the apartment. "If there is information of a delicate nature, I will do my best to keep it out of any written report. But I cannot promise."

"Okay," I said, stepping away from Henri's body and moving away from the other investigators. "We were following Georg Hannes. He showed up outside the reception, and we tailed him. The two SVV men followed us and jumped Kaz. Their mistake."

"First, be careful. Failure does not sit well with those people. Second, did this have anything to do with the reception?" Escher asked.

"No way to tell," I said, leaving Henri's brief absence out of it. I trusted Escher, but we needed to control who knew what until we'd figured this thing out. "Can we look around the apartment?"

"Yes, but do not touch or remove anything. We will check for fingerprints, but neighbors have told us a cleaning lady was in yesterday. She does two other apartments as well."

"A lazy cleaning lady is the detective's friend," I said.

"Billy, this is Switzerland. Everything will be spotless," Escher said with a grin.

We started in the kitchen. Scrubbed and sparkling. A corkscrew and a cork sat on the counter next to the sink. Several of the drawers were open and showed signs of being searched. We checked the dining room, which held a waxed table and hutch with glassware. Not a speck of dust, but the glass doors were open, as if someone had quickly checked the contents. The bedroom was different. Henri's tuxedo was tossed on an armchair, the pockets turned inside out. A circular table by the window held a silver plate, with his watch, cuff links, cigarette lighter, and wallet, along with small change. Dresser drawers were pulled open, clothes dumped out, evidence of a thorough search.

Bedsheets were strewn over the mattress. Matching pillows held the impression of the last heads to rest against them. A half-empty bottle of wine was on the dresser, and wine glasses had fallen on the floor near each nightstand, their contents spilled on the rug.

"Henri wasn't alone last night," I said.

"No, and this is an excellent vintage," Kaz said, taking in the label. "He may have been celebrating. Or he kept nothing but the best."

"He looked pretty pleased with himself last night, but he didn't spill the beans to anyone. If he told his guest in a moment of weakness, she might be in danger herself. Maybe she saw the whole thing."

"And ran out after the assailant left, leaving the door open in her panic," Kaz said. "It could have happened that way, if she had somewhere to hide. We should ask Victor who the likely candidates are."

"Ask Escher to see the wine," I said. "You'll be a better judge of that. It feels like it might be important."

Kaz went to find the inspector, and I stood still, studying the room, trying to get a read on what had happened here. Henri was the one who wanted to leave the reception first. Now it was evident why. Maybe his date was already here, waiting. They drink some wine, do some cavorting, and then what? Sleep? Or does she go home? I couldn't really find a decent hiding place, not one that would have stood up to the concerted search that had gone on here.

Or maybe the dame was part of the setup. She gets Henri sloshed, then lets in the intruder. He comes out in his robe, and things go south.

But no. This wasn't a robbery. Henri's wallet, watch, and gold cigarette lighter were left in plain sight. What was wrong with this picture?

"Henri was well stocked with wines," Kaz said, entering the room. "But this open bottle was one of his best."

"Something you'd have for a special celebration?"

"Yes, it was definitely not an everyday wine, even for a man of Henri's refined palate," Kaz said.

"So Henri leaves the reception," I said, pacing back and forth in the bedroom, stepping around clothes scattered on the floor.

"No, start with his request for a diversion," Kaz said. "He must have had a reason for that."

"Right. He gave me ten minutes to get into place. You moved in to make sure nobody got hit in the head. I went upstairs and bumped into Bowman, who wanted to chat with another Yank."

"Did you see where Henri went off to?" Kaz asked.

"No, he melted into the crowd. So I enlist Bowman, who's up for a prank, and we send the champagne flying," I said, tapping my finger against my mouth.

"Drenching me with the stuff," Kaz said. "Then we all gather downstairs, and Henri strolls in, looking smug, I'd say."

"And then he decides to leave early," I said. "Maureen takes off with Bowman in tow, after Henri and Bowman talk about going skiing somewhere."

"Zermatt," Kaz said. "A beautiful spot. Then what?"

"Wait a minute!" I snapped my fingers, remembering a detail of what happened next. "Earlier in the evening, Victor had asked Henri for a smoke. He gave him one from a silver case full of Parisienne cigarettes. But then after Maureen and Bowman left, Victor asked again, and Henri said he was all out."

"You're right. He wouldn't have had time to smoke all of them."

"And the only thing that's missing here is that silver cigarette case," I said. "It's not with his lighter and his other valuables."

"Why would his killer take it?" Kaz said.

"I don't think he did. Otherwise the place wouldn't be torn apart. The whole apartment was thoroughly ransacked for a reason. The killer was looking for something he didn't find."

"Why the cigarette case?"

"Because it contained something valuable. The invoices Henri was talking about, maybe. He brought those papers for Huber, and we saw them head to Huber's office. Then later, Henri had me create a distraction. I'll bet he snuck back there, stole the paperwork, and hid it in his cigarette case."

"Billy, what would the Red Cross acquire that would be so controversial? What secret purchase would be worth a life?"

"I don't know," I said, moving the curtains and looking out to the street below. The crowd had dispersed. Move on, folks, nothing to see here. "But it's the only thing that makes sense. It's why Henri didn't give Victor a smoke. It's why the place was tossed. It's why someone roughed Henri up and smashed his skull against the marble floor. Perhaps it was intentional, or perhaps the assailant simply went too far. The question is, where is the case now?"

"Perhaps Henri gave it to his companion for the evening," Kaz said. "She leaves at some point, and the killer arrives later, thinking he can simply take what he wants."

"With a little rough stuff, yeah. After all, it's stolen goods. Henri couldn't exactly call the police and report a theft," I said. It looked like Henri's plan had backfired. He'd hidden the cigarette case, and paid with his life. "It's likely he didn't give up the dame's name. Otherwise he'd probably still be alive."

"Are you finished in here?" Escher asked, standing in the doorway. He was writing in his notebook, barely sparing a glance in our direction. I was sure he hadn't overheard anything.

"Yes, Inspector. Thank you for the courtesy, but I don't see anything here except a well-searched room," I said. "Do you have any ideas?"

"If the victim were a woman, I'd consider a lover's quarrel that got out of hand," Escher said. "I doubt a woman could have grabbed Moret by the throat and pushed him down on the floor. But it does fit with the search. Looking for love letters or some such thing."

"Can't say I haven't seen it before," I said. "Good luck."

"Stay in touch and out of my way," Escher said. "Or else after the war I will come to Boston and bother you while you conduct a murder investigation." He said it with a smile, but it was a friendly warning. No cop wants somebody else muddying the waters while they're doing their job.

I understood. But as we passed Henri's body, I knew what we had to do.

Find his killer.

Stop him before he killed again.

CHAPTER NINETEEN

"SHALL WE GO to Alpenstrasse and speak with the concierge?" Kaz asked as we stepped outside. "It is not far."

"Let's work this through first," I said. Across the street was a park that ran the entire length of the road. We decided it was in the right direction for Alpenstrasse and that it would be a good place to talk without being overheard.

And if we had to shoot, there were fewer bystanders to worry about.

"Are you sure we shouldn't tell Escher about the cigarette case?" Kaz said.

"Yes," I said. "Whoever has it is in danger. Even people who don't have it are in danger. No matter how trustworthy he is, word could leak out. It's better for us if the opposition thinks we haven't figured out what Henri was up to."

"The opposition must include the SVV," Kaz said as we entered the park, taking a wide gravel path that ran through well-tended gardens, full of spring flowers. "Undoubtedly they wanted to search us for the case last night."

"And Hannes was probably waiting for another candidate at Alpenstrasse," I said. "So who else is in their crosshairs?"

"When Henri returned, there was Dulles, Maureen, you and I, Captain Bowman, and Victor. In our immediate circle, at least. I can't think of anyone else," Kaz said.

"On his way to us, I saw him talking with McKittrick, the guy from the BIS bank, and Schmitz, from IG Farben. Then he spoke with Gisevius for a few seconds."

"For all we know, he could have handed it off to Dulles," Kaz said. A pair of bicyclists passed us on the left. We both scooted to the right to make room for another pair coming up behind us. "He is a man of secrets. He may not have seen any reason to tell us."

"It could have been Gisevius, for that matter," I said. "Henri seemed like a decent guy, but we have to consider he might have been working both sides of the fence."

"In theory, yes," Kaz said. "Although I think we can discount Schmitz and McKittrick, unless we become desperate for clues. They are too grotesque to consider Henri being in league with them. He seemed a cultured man, after all."

"Gisevius also seems cultured, for a Nazi diplomat," I said. Kaz stopped, his brow furrowed. "What?"

"Henri spoke with Dulles and Gisevius before joining us," Kaz said, resuming our stroll. "He said Dulles told him we'd been ordered to follow Krauch, correct?"

"Right. Which was an odd slip to make in front of Gisevius. And Dulles doesn't seem like a man who makes mistakes like that," I said.

"Which means that he trusts Gisevius," Kaz said. "Is Gisevius working for Dulles? And if so, does it have anything to do with Henri's murder?"

"Okay, first we have to ask Dulles if he has the invoices and see where that leads," I said, looking back as the sound of gravel under cyclists' wheels drew closer. Two men were bent over their handlebars, making the best time they could.

One of them, the guy closest to us, reached into his jacket pocket.

I did the same, gripping my revolver. I tapped Kaz's arm with my other hand, and he followed my gaze, digging into his pocket a second later.

There were people on the trail, but no one close. Kids kicked a football around in a field to our left, where the cyclist would be in a

second. I withdrew my pistol, ready to fire, turning to get an angle
away from the kids.

The cyclist's hand came out of his pocket.

It held a handkerchief. He shook it out and blew his nose.

I jammed the weapon back into my coat pocket.

"Seeing the corpse of a friend who suffered a violent death makes
one wary," Kaz said. "With good reason."

"We've got a lot of bases to cover," I said. "Maureen and Victor
after Dulles. Then Bowman, although I don't think Henri would have
entrusted the invoices to a man he'd just met."

"Perhaps, but an American fighter pilot in uniform would seem
to be a safe bet if Henri felt he was in danger of discovery. We can also
ask Victor if he knows any of Henri's lady friends," Kaz said. "Maureen
may have an idea as well. She seems to have her fair share of relation-
ships, so she may be more aware of those others have."

"Yeah, women are often more observant about that sort of thing,"
I said, thinking of Diana and wishing she were here. She'd probably
pick up on any number of things I was missing. "All right, let's put
Alpenstrasse on the list, but after Dulles. He may be able to clear
things up."

The path split up ahead, one lane going deeper into the park, and
the other in the direction of the main road, where we planned to grab
a taxi. A few more cyclists came down the path in the opposite direction, and I had to laugh at myself, nearly plugging a guy for blowing
his schnoz.

"What's funny?" Kaz asked. I told him, and he chuckled, turning
to glance at another gaggle of bicyclists behind us in the left lane.

Kaz stopped in his tracks, drawing his revolver without hesitation,
aiming it at the lead cyclist, a guy in a cloth cap and baggy jacket. He
looked familiar, but the suddenness of Kaz's move caught me off guard.
He took a step closer to the oncoming group, standing in their path
with his arm outstretched and his Webley tracking the progress of the
cloth cap.

The rest of the cyclists panicked, for damn good reason, and went
off the path in every direction, some of them crashing into each other

while others managed to turn and flee the scene. Which is exactly what the guy in the cloth cap did, glancing over his shoulder as he put distance between the Webley and himself.

"I hope our taxicab driver is not merely a cycling enthusiast," Kaz said as he pocketed the revolver. "If so, I owe him an apology. But I doubt it, don't you?"

"I thought he looked familiar," I said. "I think you just saved our lives."

"And his, too," Kaz said. "I decided we didn't need another shooting to complicate our day. It is enough to know we are on the right track."

"That we are. But I'd like to know where the track leads," I said.

We hotfooted it out of there, shouts in German and French echoing through the park, along with cries for the *polizei*.

We took a streetcar back across the river, deciding we'd had enough of taxi cabs for a while. I should have been suspicious of any taxi passing by Dulles's office. All sorts of reprehensible types might be interested in information they could glean from people who had met with America's top spy in Switzerland. Whether our driver was SVV, Gestapo, or freelance didn't matter. What mattered was that we were marked men, even though it didn't seem like we knew enough right now to be that much of a danger to anyone.

But we were a danger to anyone else we'd mentioned during the cab ride.

"Kaz," I whispered, leaning in close among the passengers on the crowded streetcar. "Didn't we talk about Bowman and Maureen in the taxi?"

"Yes. And the name of the hotel," he said, shaking his head. "We were idiots!"

The streetcar rattled across the bridge spanning the River Aare, where Lowenberg had drowned a few days ago. Georg Hannes was a ruthless man, a murderer, but this seemed bigger than one Gestapo agent. Resources were being pulled in from the local talent, and there had to be someone high up on the food chain coordinating it all. Krauch, maybe. Or von Schroder, if you wanted to think big. But why was Himmler's banker involved?

We got off the streetcar and hoofed it to the Hotel *Schweizerhof* after Kaz asked for directions. He was careful to ask a nice old lady, who didn't look like a Nazi in disguise, but you never know. The hotel was a fancy joint, taking up a good portion of the block, its ornate cornices and baroque design lending a sedate elegance to the street.

Which was somewhat marred by the police cars and a group of cops and soldiers standing out front. We edged closer, staying behind a gathering crowd of pedestrians, curious to see what the ruckus was about. I thought it might be us.

I was wrong. The hotel doors swung open and two Swiss soldiers dragged Bowman out, followed by more cops.

"Hey!" I shouted, pushing my way through the onlookers. "Where are you taking him?"

The only answer I got was three burly *polizei* stepping forward, the stern looks on their faces telling me they were ready to use their truncheons first and ask questions later. Or never.

"Billy!" Bowman yelled as they stuffed him into the backseat of one of the automobiles, slamming the door.

Kaz held out his hands in a placating manner, speaking first in German, and then French. The soldiers ignored him, getting into the car that held Bowman and speeding off, leaving the *polizei* to deal with us. Finally one of the cops spoke to Kaz, and they went back and forth in French for a while.

"He says Captain Bowman was arrested for assault," Kaz said. "The army took over since he violated the terms of his furlough, and they have jurisdiction over evadees."

"Who did he supposedly assault?" I asked. "We saw him go off with Maureen, on their way here."

"This officer told me their names, which meant nothing. But he did describe the injuries Bowman is charged with inflicting on them. A broken kneecap among them."

"Hansel and Gretel," I said.

"Yes. The SVV and the Gestapo used their injuries to frame Bowman."

"Then someone searched the room," I said. "Or they're at it right now. Ask him if there was anyone unusual involved."

"He said the army officer did a thorough search of Bowman and went through the contents of the room. He wondered what they were looking for, and asked, but was told it was an army matter," Kaz translated. "They seemed angry that they found nothing."

"Does he know where they're taking him?"

"Yes. He says to a punishment camp in Wauwilermoos, outside Lucerne. A bad place, he claims, and says he is sorry; he only did what the law required. He says if Captain Bowman is a friend of ours, we should send him a food parcel."

I studied the cop. He had the look of a guy who wasn't happy doing the army's dirty work but who knew his duty. A sadness around the eyes, a mouth set in grim determination, the shoulders a little slumped. I wanted to buy him a drink, but we had business elsewhere.

"*Merci,*" I said, and we left before his thoughts of duty outweighed his sympathy and he asked to see some identification.

We walked two blocks and hailed a taxi, keeping our lips zipped and getting out a block from our destination. We went in through the vineyard and found Maureen with Dulles. Both of them looked worried.

"They've taken Bowman," I said.

"And Victor is missing," Dulles said. This wasn't a good start.

"Who took Captain Bowman?" Maureen asked. "The police?"

"On a trumped-up charge of assault," I said. I was too much of a gentleman to ask when she'd left him, at least not in front of Dulles. "The two goons who jumped Kaz last night swore out a complaint saying Bowman attacked them. The police grabbed him at the *Schweizerhof,* but it was the Swiss army that took him away. To what they call a punishment camp, at Wauwilermoos."

"That's not good," Dulles said. "It's where they house men who try to escape from internment camps, or evadees like Bowman who try to get across the border. Some have made it through Italy to our lines. The Swiss don't like it much. They put a pro-German commandant in charge and it's a hellhole."

"What did you find out at Henri's?" Maureen asked.

"The place was thoroughly searched," I said, hanging up my coat and flopping down on the couch. "Someone roughed Henri up, but his death may have been unintended. His head hit the floor with some force."

"Horrible," Maureen said, her hand going to her mouth.

"Quite," Kaz said, sitting across from Dulles, who puffed on his pipe. "We need to ask, Mr. Dulles, did Henri give you anything at the reception?"

"What? No, he didn't," Dulles said, with what looked like real surprise. "What do you mean?"

"Do you have any idea what Henri was up to?" I asked. "Outside of his usual work with Safehaven."

"This may sound cold, gentlemen, but Henri Moret was an asset. A valuable asset. He provided inside information on who was doing business with the Germans within the banking community. But his primary usefulness would have come once we begin negotiations with the Swiss government. We have not gotten to that point. Moret did nothing more for us than provide data. Victor Hyde may be able to say more, but he's nowhere to be found." Dulles sucked on his pipe, but it had gone out. He looked disappointed it had stopped working, sort of like his attitude toward Henri's death. An irritant.

"Henri mentioned something about invoices," I said. "He said it was important. A damning piece of evidence, he called it."

"Regarding Safehaven?" Maureen asked.

"That was the impression," Kaz said. "But I think he said invoice, the singular. And it came up in connection with his uncle. A doctor who went on one of the medical missions to the Russian Front. Evidently he spoke out about what he saw."

"Yes. Rudolf Moret," Dulles said, leaning back in his chair. "The Swiss government did not like him revealing the mass executions he saw. Jews and Russian POWs alike. It put the Swiss in a bad light, assisting the Nazis."

"One invoice," Maureen said. "You think Henri passed it to someone at the reception?"

"That's the theory," I said. "Which is why we were followed, why Bowman was arrested after they searched his room, and why Henri was killed."

"Wait a minute," Dulles said. "Where did he get this invoice?"

"Henri came to the reception with papers from his bank for Max Huber. He could have lifted it at the bank, but I bet he lifted it from Huber's office. Otherwise he wouldn't have needed the distraction."

"You mean that clumsy move with the champagne bottle?" Dulles said.

"Not so clumsy," Maureen said. "Everyone looked to see what it was all about. If Henri wanted to slip away, that was the perfect time. And as Billy says, he and Huber had bank business to conduct, probably in Huber's office."

"When Henri returned, no one the wiser, apparently," Kaz said. "But not for long. The document was found to be missing, and the Gestapo came up with a plan on the spot. They dragooned the SVV men into following us and went after the rest of the group that had gathered around Henri."

"They haven't come after me," Dulles said. I couldn't tell if he was relieved or peeved at being left out.

"Not yet. But watch yourself," I said. "Kaz stopped one of them from pulling a gun on us today. It was the taxi cab driver who picked us up here this morning. He dropped us off at Henri's place and then tried to waylay us in the park."

"Don't tell me you shot another man?" Dulles said, as if defending yourself in public was in poor taste.

"I convinced him to leave us alone without pulling the trigger. Unfortunately, Billy and I discussed Major Bowman during the cab ride. That is how they got to him at the hotel," Kaz said.

"We don't know exactly who we're up against," I said. "Swiss fascists and the Gestapo are enough to worry about. I hope whoever is behind Henri's murder, as well as Lowenberg's, doesn't have the entire Swiss government working for them."

"I doubt that very much, but as you've learned, there are factions at work. Unfortunately, the pro-German groups are very strong," Dulles said.

"But surely that will change as the war goes against the Germans?" Kaz said.

"Don't count on it," Maureen said. "Some of the SVV types are true believers. Others are simply making a mint off the war, whether through banking or arms manufacturing. Those people will be sad to see the war end, but only because it means an end to their profits. They are not at all worried about being held accountable. That's the beauty of Swiss neutrality."

"I wonder if what Henri took threatened all that," I said, remembering something he'd told me when we'd first met. "The cigarette case was a gift from his Uncle Rudolf."

"So?" Dulles said.

"He didn't have to use that case. He could have put the papers in his pocket, or stuffed in an envelope. Maybe he did it deliberately, as a symbol of the revenge," I said. The case was handy, to be sure, but I couldn't see Henri handing it off unless it was important to the whole scheme, if only in his mind.

"It may be worth a talk with *Herr Doktor* Moret," Kaz said. "Henri may have confided in him."

"They were very close," Maureen said. "Someone needs to tell him, and it would be better than a telephone call from the police."

"But what about Victor? For all we know the Gestapo has him, along with the document," I said.

"Victor doesn't have it," Maureen said.

"How do you know?" I asked.

"I was with him last night," she said, looking away from Dulles. It was the first time I'd seen her so shy and demure, almost embarrassed. "He dropped by the hotel while Bowman and I were having drinks. We left and went to his place. He never mentioned a thing."

"You're sure he didn't have the cigarette case?" I asked.

"As sure as I can be. I hung up his tuxedo for him, and I would have noticed it. There wasn't any place else he could've hidden it," she said, delivering that line with a smile that was more in character.

"You and Victor?" Dulles said. "I never would have guessed." He sounded more surprised than jealous. I guess their flirting and whatever followed wasn't an exclusive arrangement.

"It's nothing serious, darling," Maureen said, digging around in her purse for a cigarette. I could see she still had her little automatic pistol.

"No one's approached you either?" I asked Maureen.

"Not a soul," she said. "But poor Lasho took a few lumps last night. It seems Krauch turned the tables on him and led him into a trap. He and another man dragged him out of the car and searched him. Went through the car as well."

"Is he okay?" I asked.

"Yes, he's resting upstairs. A few bruises, that's all. I'd say Krauch had no idea he had his hands on *der Zigeuner* himself. He probably lost all interest after discovering Lasho didn't have the papers."

"That's right. You brought him inside to lay eyes on Krauch, right?" I said.

"Yes. Krauch must have spotted him with me. These damn Germans are thorough, I'll give them that," Maureen said.

"You two need to watch your back," I said. "Do you have any security? Bodyguards?"

"I'll call the embassy," Dulles said. "They'll send some people. They're already out looking for Victor."

"When was the last time you saw him, Maureen?" I asked.

"Oh, late. Or early this morning, if you prefer," she said. "He called a taxi for me. I'm not one for lingering over breakfast. The morning light is far too revealing."

"He mentioned nothing about Henri and the reception?" Kaz asked.

"Only to comment on how oddly he'd behaved, but that was Henri. Always secretive and distracting you with a joke," she said, blowing smoke toward the ceiling.

"They must have grabbed him on his way out this morning," Dulles said.

"Or he found out about Henri and went into hiding," I said. "He has good relations with the police, or at least with Escher. Maybe someone tipped him off."

"Then he is a smarter man than all of us," Lasho said from the doorway. He sported a shiner and sat on the couch with a grimace.

"You're looking better, Anton," Maureen said, flashing her most dazzling smile. If this was better, then he must have been a mess last night.

"I do not like giving in to the Germans," he said, his voice a snarling growl. "There were too many to fight, so I let them hit me. Some days you get the bear, somedays the bear gets you."

"Quite intelligent, Lasho," Kaz said.

"I can be so intelligent only once. Next time, I will kill the man who struck me. Krauch. He will not like how I do it."

"Can you drive, Lasho?" Dulles asked. It seemed as if the man saw little except for how useful people could be. He was a smart guy, and obviously well-connected. He probably served his country well, but there was something about him that made me feel like a replaceable cog in his spy machine.

"Yes. Where do you want to go?"

"Not me. Take these two to this address. Moret's uncle. He lives in a small town about an hour away," Dulles said, consulting a thick address book and scribbling the directions. "Then tomorrow, I want you three to go to Wauwilermoos. It's on the outskirts of Lucerne."

"That's where they have Bowman," I said.

"Right. Conditions at that camp are intolerable. We recently received an order from SHAEF to assess the potential for organizing a mass breakout once the Allied lines in Italy get closer," Dulles said. "They have about one hundred of our men there, mixed in with common criminals."

"It's an unpleasant place," Maureen said. "We haven't had time to get anyone up there yet, but this is good timing. We'll put together a demand for Bowman's release. I doubt it will do any good, but it should get you inside the camp."

"The policeman who arrested Bowman said we should bring him food," Kaz said. "He seemed genuinely concerned."

"He should be, if he's a decent sort," Dulles said. "We'll pack up some food, but it will probably go into the commandant's larder. It's that kind of camp."

"Shouldn't we help search for Victor?" I asked.

"The embassy has people doing that," Dulles said. "They know his usual haunts. They're even driving out to see his parents, up in the mountains. If you're right about a connection with Moret's uncle, that's a good place to start."

"Okay," I said. "We'll grab our stuff at the hotel before we go. We might be on the road a few days."

"Call in with any news," Maureen said. "You fellows need anything? You're all packing, I assume?"

Lasho looked at her, his brow furrowed as he tried to understand what she meant. I slapped my jacket pocket, and he smiled, nodding his head.

"Can you get us shoulder holsters?" I asked. "It's clumsy carrying these six-shooters around in a coat pocket."

"Already done," Maureen said, pointing to a box on the table by the door. Lasho opened his black leather jacket to show off his own.

"Watch yourselves out there," Dulles said. "If you're on the trail of this document, the opposition will follow you to see what you know. Maybe you can get the drop on them. I wouldn't mind a few persuasive words with one of these Nazis. Right, Lasho?"

"I will do the persuading, and you do the talking, Mr. Dulles," Lasho said. "It is what we both do best."

CHAPTER TWENTY

I COULD STILL hear Maureen's stifled laugh as we adjusted the shoulder holsters and put on our jackets. It felt better not having the revolver bulging out of my pocket, and safer not getting the hammer snagged on fabric. We exited the office and made for the automobile, a Citroen Rosalie, parked in an alley off Herrengasse. Lasho was right: he had a lot of experience persuading Germans, mainly to die, while Dulles spoke with the assured authority that comes from generations of government service and family privilege. I'd heard his granddaddy had been secretary of state under Benjamin Harrison, and that's going back a ways.

But Dulles was also canny. The trip to see Henri's uncle made sense. He might actually have something useful to tell us; I could see Henri telling him of his plans to strike back at the Swiss government for all that was done to disgrace Doctor Moret for simply speaking the truth.

But to drive all the way to Wauwilermoos was different. It sounded like a hellhole, and I'd be glad to help out Bowman and our other guys imprisoned there, but I didn't buy the story Dulles had spun. Maybe SHAEF did want to organize an escape, but there were plenty of legitimate embassy personnel who could conduct that reconnaissance.

At least he'd given us a warning. We were bait, and he was hoping we'd get the best of whoever came after us. But if not, it would be easy to write off a Sinti and two outsiders to a traffic accident or some other concocted story. I carried a carton of canned goods and other foodstuffs out to the car, the letter to the camp commandant safely secured in my pocket. Most important, Kaz still had a good supply of Swiss francs. I figured a decent bribe would be far more effective than a piece of paper, even one signed by Allen Foster Dulles.

"We should stop at Alpenstrasse first," Kaz said as Lasho started the engine. "With everything that went on this morning, we forgot to mention Hannes watching it last night."

"Right, we'll check in with the concierge. He might need some persuading." In the rearview mirror, I could see Lasho crack a grin. First, we drove to the hotel and grabbed our meager belongings. Everything except the tuxedos.

We headed back across the bridge, watching the traffic behind us. Lasho made a few quick turns down narrow residential streets, and I couldn't spot another vehicle on our tail. Then we circled the block around Alpenstrasse, watching for the watchers, and coming up empty. Of course, if they really wanted to keep an eye on the place, another apartment across the street would be ideal. The fact that Hannes had been sent over to stand outside meant that it hadn't been an organized surveillance—at least not as of last night.

Lasho parked a few doors down from number twenty. He and Kaz went in. We'd decided that Kaz's knowledge of French and German, along with Lasho's menacing presence, was all that was needed. We all do what we're best at, as Lasho had observed.

Which meant I stayed outside, wandering up and down the street, watching for trouble. I kept my eye on windows, watching for curtains drawn back, and was rewarded with a glimpse of a gray-haired lady eyeballing me. Every neighborhood has one. I walked to the corner, out of her line of sight, and leaned against the wall, with the entrance to number twenty in view. No suspicious types lurking in the shadows. I walked back to the car, figuring it wouldn't be long before Kaz and Lasho finished with their questions.

I saw Kaz standing in the doorway. He motioned me inside.

"Victor Hyde lives here," Kaz said. "His apartment has been searched."

"So that's why Hannes was watching the place. Any sign of violence?" I asked, following Kaz up the steep steps. Lasho kept a lookout at the door.

"No, other than the disarray," he said. "The concierge was quite obliging, once I gave him sufficient cash. He said men from the American embassy came looking for Victor this morning, and when they showed identification, he let them in. He claims the apartment had not been searched, and that he locked up after they left."

"Great, so they were followed," I said. "The obliging doorman probably let them in too."

"Doubtless," Kaz said, opening the door to Victor's place. It had small rooms and high ceilings, the building probably having been subdivided into apartments after its grander days had passed. We walked through the sitting room, where comfortable furniture was clustered around a radio and phonograph player. Books had been thrown from shelves and lay scattered across the room. Drawers had been emptied, even in the kitchen. It was the same in every room. The concierge had to have heard something.

"There is nothing to learn here," Kaz said. "As with Henri's apartment, they searched thoroughly."

"Which probably means they didn't find what they were after," I said, giving the place a final walk-through. I've tossed plenty of joints myself, and I can't remember ever finding what I was looking for at the tail end of a search. When every square inch of a place has been gone through, it's a sure sign of failure.

We stopped downstairs at the concierge's basement apartment. Kaz rapped on the door and spoke roughly to the guy, then slipped him a few more Swiss francs, pointing to where Lasho stood. I couldn't pick up on the French, but I got the message. Lasho would be back if he didn't do what Kaz told him.

"We were never here, right?" I said.

"Yes. I told him to stop helping the Nazis, and he swore up and down he would never do such a thing. He admitted to giving information to Hannes, who asked about Victor and his routine, although he claims he had no idea he was Gestapo."

"I do not think he cares who pays him," Lasho said as he held open the door.

"What did he tell Hannes about Victor?" I asked as we took the steps down to the sidewalk. Clouds parted and the sun shone through, the warmth welcome on my face.

"That he works long hours and is often out late, or all night," Kaz said. "Nothing unusual for a young man in a large city."

"You saw no one following us?" Lasho asked, casting his gaze up and down the street.

"No. Nothing but an old lady across the street, peeking through her curtains."

Of course. I'd been stupid, and now here we were, three sitting ducks. Kaz and Lasho both caught the look of dawning knowledge on my face.

"The best surveillance," Kaz said. "A lonely woman with time on her hands, and a telephone."

"Okay, I have an idea," I said, telling them my plan.

Lasho drove past her apartment as slowly as possible, giving her plenty of time to see our black-and-white Citroen Rosalie, and even take down the license plate number. With its snazzy two-tone paint job, it didn't exactly blend into the flow of traffic, but the Rosalie was originally built as a race car, which might come in handy on the open road.

We went around the block again, stopping a few buildings back from Victor's place, where a narrow alley provided just enough room for Lasho to back the Rosalie in. We split up, Lasho staying with the car. Kaz and I each took one side of the street, me on the same side as the snoopy old lady, to stay out of her line of vision.

Collars up, hat brims down, we sauntered down the sidewalk. About one building away from Victor's place, we eased into doorways to wait. I hoped I hadn't been wrong.

I wasn't. A black Peugeot took the corner too fast and almost fishtailed into a parked car. The driver slammed on the brakes in front of number twenty and two men raced out from the backseat, eager to question the concierge. The Peugeot was double-parked, so they left the driver. Not that they would have needed three guys to get anything out of their informant. A thin roll of worn Swiss francs would take care of that, and have him promising that, of course, he would never help the Americans.

Kaz walked back toward the car, tipping his hat to Lasho, the signal to get ready. Then he moved toward the Peugeot, its engine idling roughly. Cigarette smoke wafted up from the driver's side. He had the window open and his arm draped on the frame. Oblivious to the oncoming threat.

Until Kaz darted to the Peugeot, squeezing between the cars, and stuck his Webley into the driver's face. I ran to the passenger's door and yanked it open as Lasho braked right behind me. I reached in, grabbing the driver by the collar and dragging him out into the street, jamming the revolver into the back of his neck. Kaz opened the rear door of our Citroen and I shoved our captive in. By the time Kaz jumped into the front seat, I'd frisked our captive and tossed his wallet to Kaz. He wasn't armed.

The cigarette was still between his fingers. I threw it out the window.

His mouth was wide open, a gaping oval of shock and fear. He was in his early twenties, sandy brown hair, small eyes, and grease under the fingernails. He wore a corduroy jacket, well-worn, over a shirt frayed at the collar. A mechanic, maybe, pressed into service as a driver.

"Are they following us?" I asked Lasho, not wanting to take my eyes off our reluctant passenger, who'd managed to close his mouth and sit up straight.

"I think not," Kaz said, holding up a set of keys. He rolled down the window and drew his hand back to toss them out.

"*Nein, bitte!*" The guy looked more worried about losing the keys than the revolver I had jammed into his gut.

"Very well," Kaz said, dropping the keys on the seat. "For now. Do you speak English?"

"A little, yes. The automobile belongs to *mein Chef*. The man I work for. Please, I must return it."

"Your boss's car?" Kaz asked, looking through the mook's wallet.

"Yes, boss. There will be trouble. I will my job lose, I think."

"Our friend's name is Oskar Wendig, a member of the *Schweizerischer Vaterländischer Verband*," Kaz said, holding up his membership card with his photograph and SVV emblazoned across the top. He flipped it out the window. "That, you can do without, Oskar."

"What do you want?" Oskar asked, his gaze flickering between my pistol and Kaz, nervous at what damage each might do.

"Oskar, we don't want you to lose your job, understand?" I said, in the most soothing tone possible. "Or die."

"*Sterben*," Kaz translated, just to be sure.

"No, please, I only drive. When they tell me," Oskar said. "I do nothing bad."

"Where do you work, Oskar?" I asked as we crossed one of the many bridges over the River Aare, this one downstream from Bern. The road was narrow, with little traffic. We hadn't been driving long, but the view was already turning bucolic. Whitewashed houses with steep roofs and the ever-present flowerboxes dotted the hillsides. Heidi country. "A garage?"

"My boss sells automobiles. I fix," Oskar said.

"Your boss is not in the SVV? He doesn't know you took the car?" I asked.

"No. He does not think about politics. He will be mad if I lose the Peugeot, very mad."

"Billy, do you think Inspector Escher would be interested in a case involving a stolen vehicle?" Kaz asked, turning in the front seat to face Oskar.

"Grand theft auto, we call it in the States," I said. "You will go to prison, Oskar. For years. You will be an old man when you get out."

"No, please, it was only for one hour, they said. Please, give me the keys," Oskar said, his voice cracking. Tears would come soon. Right where we wanted him.

"Lasho, pull over," I said. He eased the Citroen onto the verge, sheep in the field by the side of the road paying us no mind. Oskar's eyes widened, not knowing what was coming next. Today had probably started like any other day, and then he got the call. A quick trip around the city, no big deal. Maybe he'd been nervous, or proud at being chosen by the SVV. Then we'd grabbed him at gunpoint and his world had turned upside down. Prison, betrayal, death, none of those had seemed likely a few short hours ago. Now, here we were, holding pistols and the promise of freedom. Which would it be?

"Oskar, we want to know everything. Who the men with you were, what you know about them, what they are after. Every little thing. Do you understand?" I said.

"Yes. But I should say nothing. I made a vow to the *Verband*," he said, summoning up a sudden reserve of courage.

"Oskar, look out the window. Tell me what you see," I said.

"The grass. It is green. The blue sky, the sheep," he said, as if reciting vocabulary words he'd learned in school.

"Sheep, grass, sky. If you keep that vow, they will be the last things you ever see," I said. "Stay loyal to the SVV, and I will put a bullet in your brain and leave you on the side of the road. Look, that's where your body will lay, near those wildflowers. A nice spot, isn't it?"

"No, you would not," Oskar said. After all, this was neutral Switzerland, he was probably thinking.

"We have killed many Nazis between us," I said. "One SVV man means nothing. Now get out, and make this easy."

"No, please," Oskar cried, grabbing onto the seat cushion. "I will tell you. Everything."

"Good, Oskar. Very smart," I said. "After all, where is the SVV now? They left you all alone. You don't owe them anything. We are the men who will save you from prison and from losing your job. You have to trust us, and tell us the truth. Go ahead, tell my friend, in your own language. *Sprechen Deutsch, ja?*"

He nodded and wiped his eyes, clearing away the tears that built up as he considered his final resting place. I holstered my revolver. It was time to make nice.

"Tell us, and we can make things right for you," I said. Kaz held up the keys, jangling them just out of Oskar's reach. I patted his arm, like an old pal.

He took a deep breath and started off in German, slowly at first, then building up a head of steam once he got used to the notions of betrayal and survival. Kaz snapped questions while Lasho stared him down with his dark eyes. Kaz's words and Lasho's persuasive gaze, a one-two punch.

"He says he does errands for the SVV," Kaz said, after Oskar wound down his story and sat staring out the window. "His father is a member and admires the Nazis. Oskar says he does what his father tells him to do. He is worried about his father being angry at his failure."

"Did you get anything except a sob story?" I asked.

"Yes. The Bern SVV party chapter has been put on alert to assist the Gestapo in their search for Victor Hyde. Oskar was told to borrow a vehicle from his garage and assigned to drive two of the Germans this morning, since he knows the city and they had arrived from Zurich only last night."

"Does he know why the Krauts want Victor?" I asked.

"No. But he heard that Victor was not to be killed under any circumstances," Kaz said. "He had driven the two Germans out to Alpenstrasse earlier in the morning, and they'd searched the apartment. Oskar says they found nothing and were very upset. He asked what they were looking for, but they wouldn't say."

"Was the old lady one of them?" I asked.

"Yes. The SVV set up observers at several locations where Victor might show up. His apartment, his office, the embassy, and so on. They got a call from the woman across the street and went to find out what we had said to the concierge and if he'd learned where we were going next."

"Where were they when the call came?" I asked, wanting to know if there was an SVV headquarters we might want to visit.

"At a warehouse on the north side of Bern, just outside the city," Kaz said.

"What kind of warehouse?" I asked. Kaz shrugged and looked at Oskar.

"There were big trucks," he said. "They had a lot of telephones and a radio. For shipping and transport, yes? *Aluminium.* I think it must be where one of the SVV leaders works. There was a big fence so no one could see. There were many Germans, some in uniform."

"Warehouses and trucks shipping aluminum?" I said, turning to Oskar. "What was the name?"

"I am sorry. I was more interested in the trucks. Very big trucks, and I work on engines, yes, so I looked at them and not the signs. But I could tell you where. And how to get there," Oskar said, eager to help. I'd seen it before: when you get a guy to turn on his pals, you then become his best friend, and he'll do anything to please you, since you're all he's got. It's pathetic, and I began to feel bad for the kid.

Kaz found a pencil and paper in the glove box and gave it to Oskar, who licked the lead and got to work. When he was done, he handed it to me. An address and a rough map, showing a route across the Aare River, ending at a place marked *Zentweg*.

"What's that?" I asked.

"The name of the street. It is close to the railroad, see?" He pointed to hatch marks along the road, which were supposed to be tracks. "It is a small road, and the warehouse is at the end. It is easy to find. I will show you. Then you will let me go, yes?"

"How far from here?" I asked, not answering his question.

"Ten, twelve kilometers, perhaps," Oskar said. "I show you, then you give me *der Schlüssel*, yes?"

"The key," Kaz said, with a quick nod.

"It will still leave us time to visit the doctor," Lasho said, wisely avoiding mention of his name and location. Which set the wheels turning.

"Right," I said. "Oskar, you have a deal. We'll take you back now."

"Now?" Oskar asked, surprised. "*Jetzt?*"

"*Ja, jetzt,*" Kaz said, tossing him the keys. "Now. Right Billy?"

"Sure. Not all the way. Close enough so Oskar can get to a telephone. I don't want him to get into trouble over that Peugeot, not after he's been so helpful," I said as Lasho turned our car around and headed back to town.

"Thank you," Oskar said, clasping the keys in his hands as if in prayer.

"No problem," I said. "The warehouse should be easy to find, and we can't get there until tomorrow anyway. We have to deliver a package to Geneva before nightfall. I'm sorry if you're going to have trouble over this, Oskar."

"If I get the Peugeot back, I do not think I will lose my job. My boss, he does not like the SVV, but he knows my father. He understands I must follow my father's orders," Oskar said, turning his face toward the window. He didn't seem happy, which was what I counted on.

"I meant trouble with your father, Oskar. You can always get another job, but you're stuck with your old man."

"*Ja,*" was all he said. "He will be angry. He says I am weak."

"Would you like us to help with that?" I asked.

"How?"

"Answer the question, Oskar," I said. "Even if it causes you pain, would you like us to help fix things with your father?"

"If you could, yes. Please." I eyed the road ahead as Kaz gave me a quizzical look. Not the first one he'd ever given me. He tossed Oskar his wallet, followed by a nod, which told me he'd follow my lead.

"Pull over ahead," I said, tapping Lasho on the shoulder. "Near that big oak tree."

Now Lasho shot me the same quizzical look in the rearview mirror. Oskar had the same expression, except his had a good deal of fear mixed in.

"You will let me go here?" Oskar asked.

"Yes. There are houses and shops down the road. You should be able to find a telephone. Now get out. You too," I said, tapping Lasho again as I exited the backseat.

"But you told me you would help," Oskar said, watching Lasho as he loomed over him.

"I will. Are you right-handed?"

"What? Yes, I am."

I grabbed Oskar by his right arm and dragged him over to the tree. It was a hundred years old at least, its bark rough and gnarled. With a two-handed grip, I drew back Oskar's hand and drove it against the tree trunk.

He took it well. Or he was too shocked at the sudden violence to complain. I studied the effects. Raw bloodied knuckles. Excellent.

"Why did you do that?" Oskar wailed, clutching his hand.

"That's not the worst of it, kid," I said. "You got that fighting us when you made your escape. But not before you got clobbered, good." I nodded to Lasho. "Black eye or a decent bruise, no lasting damage, please."

"No," Oskar said. Not that he was in control of the situation.

"Do not worry, young man," Lasho said, placing a fatherly hand on Oskar's shoulder. Then he hit him, and Oskar fell to the ground. "I am more used to long-lasting damage, but you will live to tell many lies about this fight."

Then he helped Oskar up, whose eye was already swollen.

"Oskar, can you hear me? Are you okay?" I asked. He nodded, cupping his good hand over his bad eye. "We can't drive you any closer; we have to catch a train. Now go and call your father. Tell him you escaped. He'll be proud of you."

"Thank you," Oskar said, and stumbled off down the road, trailing thank-yous, his scraped hand stuck in his pocket.

"Now what do we do?" Lasho asked as we got back into the car.

"Watch the warehouse?" Kaz guessed.

"Yep. Oskar is going to be redeemed in his father's eyes. He fought, he escaped, and he came back with information."

"The package," Kaz said. "They will think we have the silver cigarette case."

"Yes, and if I'm right, it won't be long before every goon left in the warehouse heads for the train station or Geneva to intercept us," I said.

"Very smart," Kaz said. "And poor Oskar earns praise from his stern Swiss father. Nicely done, Billy."

"Until the old man realizes we've tricked Oskar," Lasho said, taking a turn for the area north of Bern. "Then I almost pity the young fascist."

"Well, maybe he won't know," I said. Maybe we'd get into the warehouse and out again without anyone noticing. The SVV might think they missed us in Geneva, and maybe they'd lay off, thinking we had the documents, whatever they were. Maybe Oskar wouldn't snitch on us to his old man, but I doubted it. I served up the idea on a silver platter, and I knew that he was worried about disappointing his father. I knew I always was, and I have a great dad. With an SVV bastard for a father, a guy would have only so many options.

Oskar would be a fool to not betray us. Too bad for him.

CHAPTER TWENTY-ONE

USING OSKAR'S MAP we found Zentweg easily enough. It paralleled the railroad tracks that crossed the Aare River, a stretch of road populated by small factories, a lumberyard, and a string of brick warehouses, all of them close to a siding where materials could be easily loaded or unloaded from boxcars.

Zentweg intersected with a road that crossed the tracks, and that's where we found the warehouse. Not that we could see it, with a six-foot cinderblock wall surrounding the property. Strands of barbed wire were strung along the top, in case anyone didn't get the message. Lasho slowed as we passed the entrance, which featured two gates that swung inward, wide open and revealing half a dozen automobiles and trucks in front of the warehouse. We only had time for a quick glance, but it looked like the vehicles were parked in front of an office. Beyond them, lined up along the side of the warehouse, were larger trucks, probably ready to carry aluminum or whatever Oskar had mentioned they stored here.

Faded paint on the wall declared the business to be *Aluminium Industrie Aktien*. A newer sign, brightly painted blue, gave *Alusuisse* as the firm's name.

"Where have I heard that name before?" I asked as Lasho turned the corner.

"I think Victor may have mentioned it," Kaz said, craning his neck to check the wall encircling the property. "It looks like the barbed wire does not extend to the rear. We may be able to get over the wall there." He pointed to a spot where a row of pine trees gave some cover from the road.

"Okay," I said. "Let's swing around and find a spot to watch from." Lasho made the turn and we crossed the railroad tracks, parking on the side of the road. We had a good angle on the main gate and settled in to watch for what I hoped would happen.

"*Alusuisse*," Kaz said. "I am certain Victor mentioned it at the reception."

"I think he said Max Huber owned it, didn't he?" I said, watching as two flatbed trucks loaded down with lumber drove past the ware-house.

"I do not recall," Kaz said. "I remember the name, since it combined the words aluminum and Switzerland. It would be quite the coincidence if indeed Huber controlled the company providing the headquarters for a joint Nazi and SVV operation."

"Well, as my dad always says—"

"'Coincidence is the word people use when they cannot see who is pulling the strings,'" Kaz jumped in to say.

"So I've mentioned that before?"

"On a few occasions, yes," Kaz said. "Repetition has not made it any less true."

"Huber is the fellow who owns that fine mansion?" Lasho asked. Kaz nodded. "Then we should speak to him. Kaz and I, you under-stand?"

"He's a very important man, Lasho. Head of the International Red Cross," I said.

"Then he is the one pulling the strings. You do not think the men driving around looking for us are in charge, do you?"

"No, of course not. We want the man who killed Henri Moret. And Lowenberg, for that matter. I don't think Max Huber is going around Bern murdering people," I said.

"Although he was quite friendly with Hermann Schmitz of IG Farben," Kaz said. "Who has quite a lot of blood on his hands, meta-phorically speaking."

"Maybe he's selling aluminum to the Germans," I said.

"Of course he is," Kaz said. "Switzerland sells to any country with hard cash. Or gold. That's the beauty of neutrality. But it's not much of a secret. Nothing to kill for, of that I am sure."

"Where was it when the Gestapo inspector shot at you?" Lasho asked.

"Outside the Red Cross office," I said.

"Then you go to a reception at Huber's mansion, and Henri Moret meets with him. Later that night he is killed. Today we are sitting outside one of Huber's warehouses," Lasho said. "And still, you wonder who is making the puppets dance?"

"It wasn't the International Red Cross office," I said. "It was the Swiss Red Cross. Part and parcel, I admit, but it could be, um, well, you know."

"Not a coincidence?" Kaz said, his eyes glued to the *Alusuisse* gate. Even so, from the backseat I could see his grin.

I was saved from the necessity of a reply by the revving of engines, echoing from inside the enclosure. Within seconds, cars sped out into the road, spitting gravel as they headed away from us. Trucks rumbled behind them, men perched on the running boards. I couldn't spot any uniforms, but there were a few trademark leather coats, making this a joint SVV and Gestapo operation.

"Bless you, Oskar, and your mean old man," I said. "I hope he gave you a pat on the back."

"Should we wait longer?" Kaz asked.

"No. This looks like all hands on deck. Maybe they even dragooned the guys who actually work here. After all, they have to check the Bern train station and send a bunch of guys to Geneva before the next train arrives. Not to mention checking points in between." I was talking myself into thinking this would be easy. Then I saw that it might be. "Look, the gate's still open."

"If everyone left, wouldn't they lock it?" Kaz asked, sensibly.

"Maybe. Or maybe they left all hell for leather and didn't give it a thought," I said.

"Hell for what?" Lasho asked as he started the engine and drove right through the gate. He parked by the office door at the front of the warehouse. I saw a few guys in blue coveralls walking around the big trucks backed up to the loading docks. Workers. They ignored us, probably figuring us for more muscle.

"Lasho, stay here and keep an eye peeled, okay?" I said.

"Do what? Speak English, please."

"Keep watch," Kaz said. "Honk the horn once if there's trouble."

"I will. Thank you for translating," Lasho said, adjusting the rear-view mirror for a good view of the road.

"I didn't realize Lasho was such a funny guy," I said, as we approached the door.

"He is unique," Kaz said. "We need to be sure Maureen gets identity papers for him. He's in danger, especially traveling with us."

"We're about to add breaking and entering to the list," I said. "Unless—" I turned the door handle. It was unlocked. "We're in luck."

We entered, shutting the door quietly behind us and stepping up to a counter strewn with newspapers and coffee cups. I glanced at the papers. *Das Schwarzer Korps*, the *Volkischer Beobachter*, and other Nazi rags. We walked around the counter into the main office. Four desks were pushed together, piles of paper stacked everywhere. From what I could tell, they looked like bills of lading. Shipping information. Purchase orders. I pushed the piles around. Everything was coated in grime, from carbon paper, oil, and years of cigarette smoke. Your typical warehouse shipping office. The place was silent. A wisp of steam rose from one of the coffee cups, abandoned scant minutes ago.

There were two doors on the far wall. Kaz made for the one on the right and opened it, revealing a small office, cleaner and brighter than the main area. A bottle of schnapps sat on the desk, along with a stack of papers and an overflowing ashtray. Kaz sorted through the contents, and I headed to a second matching door next to the one Kaz had opened. I glanced out the window, catching sight of two workers loading a flatbed truck with sheets of rolled aluminum. Other than that, it was quiet.

Then I heard the second door open.

"Haben Sie nicht mit den anderen verlassen?"

I spun around to see a stocky figure emerge. He was busy adjusting his tie and smoothing down his hair. Behind him, I saw a couch with a blanket bunched up on it. I guess this guy rated a nap while everyone else went on the wild-goose chase.

I gave a little shrug, trying to cover my surprise and avoid a conversation. I picked up one of the newspapers and leaned against the counter, hoping to convey nonchalance, which was tough with my heart hammering inside my chest.

"Komm, lass uns gehen," Kaz said in a sharp tone as he exited the office. He snapped his fingers at me, sparing a nod for the Gestapo man, who yawned and returned to his couch. I tossed aside the paper and followed Kaz, who chattered at me in German until we were safely outside.

"Let's go," I said as I climbed into the backseat. "We seemed to have awoken the dullest Gestapo man in Switzerland." Lasho eased the automobile out of the parking lot, taking his time and not attracting any notice, the mark of a good getaway man.

"Did you kill him?" Lasho asked as we drove back the way we'd come.

"No," Kaz said. "We let him go back to sleep. He wanted to know why we hadn't gone with the others, and we left as if we were late to the party."

"Well, all right," Lasho said, forgiving us for not leaving a corpse behind.

"But it was not a wasted visit," Kaz said, taking a piece of paper from his pocket and unfolding it. "This mentions Georg Hannes." He held it up for me to see, but with all the German script and swastika stamps on it, I couldn't figure out what it was all about. Hannes's name was inscribed at the head of the document, along with his rank. Other than that, I had no clue.

"What am I looking at?" I asked.

"An arrest warrant," Kaz said. "Ordering the apprehension and immediate arrest of Georg Hannes, for crimes against the state. Financial crimes, it says."

"Good. Now if we don't kill him, the Gestapo will," Lasho said.

"Always look on the bright side, that's the ticket," I said.

"Neither the Swiss nor the Germans seem to care he most likely murdered Lowenberg," Kaz said. "But if he violated banking laws, then they come for him."

"Hey, they got Al Capone on income tax evasion, so don't complain," I said. "Anything else in the arrest warrant?"

"Nothing specific," Kaz said. "He is to be returned to the Gestapo headquarters in Munich for theft and misuse of funds belonging to the Reich while on duty in Switzerland."

"The bank accounts," I said. "That's why he killed Lowenberg. It probably wasn't a sanctioned operation."

"It did seem hurried, compared to his usual routine," Kaz said. "At least, as far as Victor described it."

"We've got to find him," I said. "That's good news about Hannes, but it doesn't get us any closer to who killed Henri. We need that cigarette case."

"Let us hope Henri's uncle can help," Kaz said, unfolding a map from the glove box. "Oberburg. It looks to be an hour away, perhaps longer on the mountain roads."

"It will be dark soon," Lasho said, glancing at his watch. *Wehrmacht* issue, of course. "Should we wait until the morning?"

"No, let's see him today. He might not know what's happened. We owe it to Henri to tell him," I said. Not to mention, any clue he might be able to provide would be useful. If Uncle Rudolf knew anything at all, it was worth the trip.

I soon had second thoughts about that as the sun began to set beneath the mountains. The road to Oberburg was dark, narrow, and winding, following the course of a river through forests of towering pines. Finally, we drove into the small town, nestled beside a lake, a shimmering darkness in the fading light of day. We passed a railroad station and church, the largest buildings in sight. The houses all sported long sloping roofs, testament to the winter snowfall in the Swiss Alps. We found Doctor Moret's place easily, just outside the town center. The second-floor balcony was hung with flower boxes heavy with geraniums, a wood-shingle roof jutting out over it. The ground floor looked to house his office, going by the shiny brass plaque at the door. A sliver of soft light shone between curtains in the office windows. As we got out of the car, one of them was pulled aside for a moment. Then the lights went out.

"Not very welcoming," I said as we approached the door. Kaz lifted the knocker and called out for Doctor Moret in German. No response except for the sound of a door slamming shut inside the office. Lasho darted around the back as Kaz kept up his yammering, as if we hadn't noticed the doctor had decided to take a powder. I backed up, watching the windows above us. The nearest house was a good twenty yards away, and no one was taking much notice. Nice thing about a blackout: you have plenty of privacy.

I walked around one side of the house. Firewood was stacked neatly against the wall beneath the overhanging roof. Lasho turned the corner, his hand firmly gripping the arm of an older gentleman.

"*Lass mich los*," the fellow snapped, trying to pull his arm away. He carried a small suitcase in his free hand and held a doctor's bag in the other. His Vandyke beard was gray and his expression a good deal darker.

"Kaz, please explain we do not mean him harm," Lasho said.

"Then let go of my arm, you *verdammter Dummkopf*!" He wrenched free of Lasho's grip and turned his eyes on me. "I demand to know who you are and what you want." His accent was more English than German, although his tone was definitely Teutonic.

"Doctor Moret? We're friends of Henri's. I am sorry to be the bearer of bad news," I said.

"Yes, yes, I know. Henri is dead," he said, straightening his shoulders as if trying to stand tall in the face of death and strangers at his door. "I still do not know who you are, and what you intend with me."

"A few minutes of your time, please," I said. I introduced myself, Lasho, and Kaz, giving Kaz's title, which usually mollified, or at least distracted, most people.

"Come inside, if you must," he said. "If you meant to do me harm, I expect you would have already." Lasho took his suitcase, gently, so as not to startle him. Moret led us to the rear door, unlocked it, and we followed him upstairs. He turned on the lights and checked the shades, gesturing for us to sit.

It was a pleasant room, with a tall, narrow, wood-burning cast iron stove in the corner. A low-timbered ceiling, a well-worn leather couch, and a couple of easy chairs completed the picture. A collection of pipes sat on the end table, next to a stack of medical journals. The room was comfortable, but none too tidy. Odds were Moret lived alone.

He doffed his hat and opened the stove, tossing in a few chunks of wood. Kaz and Lasho took the couch, and I eased myself into a chair, leaving the one closest to the stove for Moret.

"Now," he said, turning and reaching into a coat pocket. "Tell me who you really are."

He had a revolver in his hand. It was pointed at my chest.

"Captain Billy Boyle, US Army," I said, adding my rank and branch of service to what little I'd told him before. Looking down the barrel of that gun, I had a sudden urge to be honest with this guy. He moved the pistol to Kaz.

"Lieutenant Piotr Kazimierz, Polish Army in Exile," Kaz said. "And baron of the Augustus clan."

"And you?" he said, moving the pistol Lasho's way.

"I am Anton Lasho. I am Sinti. I work for General Eisenhower. As do these men. I hate the Nazis. I do not like the Swiss very much, either." Lasho was also being honest, a little too much so, I thought, given the situation.

"That is the first intelligent thing I have heard from any of you. Not that I believe you are acquainted with General Eisenhower," Moret said.

"Doctor Moret, we worked with Henri," I said. "On certain banking matters. Did he speak with you about such things?"

"Never mind that," he snapped. "Why are you here? Who sent you?"

"Allen Dulles. Do you recognize the name?"

"I may. What do you want?"

"For you to put that pistol away, for one," I said. "We met Henri only a few days ago, but he struck me as a decent and honorable man. I'd like to find out who killed him."

"Very well," Moret said, stuffing the revolver back into his coat pocket. He sat down heavily, casting out a sigh and rubbing his eyes. "Tell me what you know."

I glanced at Kaz, uncertain how much of the story to give the doctor. He gave a slight nod in Moret's direction, a signal to tell as much as necessary. So I did. If he and Henri had been close, he deserved to know the whole truth. I started with Henri's first mysterious comments about an invoice, went on to the reception and his actions there, the Gestapo and SVV men on the streets, and how his body was found.

"So you think he placed the document in his cigarette case and passed it on to someone?" Moret said, tapping his finger on his chin.

"Yes. You know Victor Hyde, Henri's friend?" Moret nodded and I continued. "He's disappeared, and his apartment has been searched. We think the Gestapo is searching for him as well, along with the woman Henri spent the night with. I'm sorry to bring that up, sir." I wasn't sure if he was the type to disapprove of even the mention of an evening's dalliance.

"What young men in the city do with their nights is of no concern to me," Moret said. "You work with Victor also?"

"Yes, we do. He's part of Dulles's team. Had Henri ever mentioned Safehaven?"

"He had. He was quite impassioned on the subject of Swiss banks and their collusion with the Nazis. I think some of that came naturally to Henri, but certainly some of his strong convictions came from the way I was treated. Over the medical mission to the Russian Front, which I'm sure you heard about."

"You were not silent about what you saw," Lasho said.

"No, and it cost me dearly. My commission, my reputation, most of my business," Doctor Moret said.

"But you have your honor," Lasho said. "Riches enough for any man."

"Perhaps," Moret said. "Although at times I do wish honor and ruin were of a less intimate acquaintance. What I saw in Russia was a disgrace. For all of humanity, not to mention Switzerland's role."

"Surely medical assistance, even for the Germans, was humanitarian," Kaz said.

"My own government forbade us from helping the Russian wounded," Moret said. "Not that many survived to be brought in to the aid station. But when they did, we were forced to watch them suffer and die. Swiss neutrality apparently does not extend to Russians. As for the Jews we saw massacred, most in our medical mission were content with silence. I was not."

"Silence is for the weak," Lasho said, his voice tinged with bitterness.

"Tell me, my Sinti friend, how did you come to Switzerland? I understand the borders are closed to Jews and Romani," Moret said.

"I tried to bring my family in. They were sent back and taken to a camp, which means death. Then I started killing every German I could find. That went on for a very long time. Too long. Now, I help these men."

"We actually do work for General Eisenhower," I said. "Lasho helped us get out of France and across the border."

"I am sorry for what happened to your family, Mr. Lasho," Moret said. "My nation has not been as welcoming, or as brave, as I wish it to be. And as for your mission, gentlemen, I do know of it. Victor told me earlier today."

"Where is he?" I asked, surprised to hear we'd been that close to finding Victor.

"One question first," Moret said, holding up a finger. "When you dined with Henri and Victor on the Bundesplatz, what did you order?"

"Sausage and potatoes," I said, smiling in approval of Victor's prudence. "All of us."

"Good. I doubt even the Gestapo or the SVV would have taken note of that detail," Moret said. "Forgive my caution, gentlemen, but it is necessary given the times we live in. Henri was engaged in a project that threatened powerful people, and now he is dead. Victor is in fear for his life as well. It would be wise of you also to take care."

"Do you know what Henri was after?" I asked.

"No, he only said it would show how corrupt and hypocritical Swiss society was. At the highest levels, he claimed. Henri told me it was too dangerous to say any more until he acquired the document he was after," Moret said.

"Does Victor have it?" I asked.

"I did not ask him," Moret said, shaking his head and rubbing his eyes. "He came to tell me of Henri's death, which was the greatest concern for both of us. Henri and I were very close, more so in the years since his father grew more distant from him."

"Henri told us. He was very proud of what you did," I said. "He showed me the cigarette case. It meant a lot to him, and I'm not surprised he used it to hide the document."

"Yes, that fits Henri perfectly. He would enjoy the irony," Moret said, a weary smile on his face. "His father would not. A stern man, he would be aghast at the notion of theft, however noble the cause. But still, he must be shattered at the news. I was about to leave for the train station when you arrived. However different we are, we are still brothers."

"Will you be safe?" Kaz asked.

"I should hope so. My brother is a police sergeant in his village. He has never been political, and I trust him."

"We need to find Victor," I said, leaning forward and locking onto Moret's eyes. "To protect him, and to find out what he knows. Are you sure he didn't tell you anything about the document?"

"Very sure. He left quickly, spending only a few minutes here. He was afraid he might have been followed. He said a Gestapo agent named Hannes was after him," Moret said.

"Hannes in particular?" Kaz asked.

"Yes. A disreputable character apparently, even for the Gestapo, according to Victor," Moret said.

"Where was Victor going?" I asked. "If he spent only a few minutes here, he must have been headed somewhere in this direction."

"He was," Moret said, rising from his chair with a sigh. He took a map from a side table and unfolded it. "I have a mountain chalet in

Alpthal, a small village east of here. Victor and Henri skied and hiked there often. He thought it would be a safe place to hide." He tapped on the map, east of Lake Lucerne.

"Would you write out the address?" I asked.

"No. Nothing in writing. Take the map if you wish. South of Alpthal is a road, Haupweg, leading off into the mountains. At the very end you will find the chalet, built of pine timbers with bright red shutters. It sits high in a field overlooking the valley. I would advise you not to approach at night. I gave Victor my rifle," Moret said, with a rueful smile. "Now I must go if I am to catch the next train. My brother expects me."

"We'll drive you to the station," I said, glancing at my watch. "It's the least we can do. Is there a hotel or inn in town? It's too late to keep driving at this point."

"I've already trusted you with Victor's life, I may as well trust you with my home. Please, spend the night here. That way, no one in the village can speak of strangers in case the SVV comes searching for you," Moret said. "It is a short walk to the station. I can manage on my own."

"I will drive you," Lasho said. "To be sure you do not shoot anyone. Come."

Moret gave in without a fuss; Lasho was not an easy man to say no to. He told us to help ourselves to food and drink, and to get the man who'd murdered his nephew. Both were high on my list.

Kaz and I studied the map as we waited for Lasho to return. We'd be driving within a few miles of Wauwilermoos on our way to Alpthal. We decided to make a stop there in the morning. I wanted to check on Bowman and bring him the food. I still felt guilty about getting him involved, and from what everyone said, that prison camp was no picnic.

Then we raided the kitchen. Cold ham, pickles, cheeses, and a fresh loaf from the breadbox made for a fine spread. When Lasho returned, we opened bottles of Eichhof beer and dug in. We went over the map and told him our plan for the morning.

"You can go," he said. "I will wait outside the gate."

"Why?" Kaz asked as he cut slices off the ham.

"The best way for a Sinti to stay out of prison," he answered, "is to stay out of prison."

CHAPTER TWENTY-TWO

LASHO'S WORDS OF wisdom stayed with me as I tried to fall asleep on Moret's couch. The Germans and the SVV were on our heels, and we were about to voluntarily enter a prison camp run by a pro-Nazi commandant, who was probably on the SVV membership rolls. The good news was that they'd never guess we'd do something that dumb, so the chances of their being alerted to detain us was low.

But not nonexistent.

Then if we made it out, we'd head to Victor's hideout, hopefully arriving before nightfall, where Victor might shoot first and eliminate the need to ask questions. Simple. All we had to do was avoid imprisonment and long-range rifle fire. All in a day's work.

The fire in the wood stove was beginning to die out. Moret liked his place toasty, but the evening was mild and the quilt I'd grabbed from the bedroom was thick and warm. Kaz was in a guest room and Lasho was stretched out on the doctor's own bed, his snores already rattling the rafters.

The stove began to send out *tick, tick, pings* as the metal cooled and settled down. As I was about to fall asleep, Lasho's snoring died down, which only made the metallic noise seem louder.

Tick, tick. Ping. Click.

Click?

I threw off the quilt, my stocking feet hitting the floor. I listened, reaching for my pistol in the shoulder holster on the floor by my side. I eased off the couch, back to the wall, searching for the sound, hoping it was the house settling or any of a hundred random night-time noises.

A door opened, the creak of hinges as unmistakable as it was subtle. I felt a breath of cold air waft through the room. A wide hallway led up a flight of stairs from the rear door. Maybe Kaz had gone out to the car, parked behind the house, out of sight? I waited, hoping to get a clear glimpse of who it was, not wanting to move closer in case someone else tried the front door.

I calmed my breathing so the pounding in my chest wouldn't drown out sounds from the intruder. Nothing. Soft-soled shoes prob-ably, creeping up the stairs, slowly, trying to avoid the creak of a warped floorboard. Headed for the bedroom. Odds were, they'd come for Moret, either knowing or hoping that Victor had been here and left the cigarette case.

I decided not to worry about the front entrance. Chances were, he—or they—wouldn't risk being seen, even late at night. No reason to. And that their first priority would be the bedroom, to silence Moret so they could interrogate him and search the house.

Which was good, since that meant they wouldn't kill him right off.

Which was bad, since finding Lasho would startle them, and who knew what they'd do?

I went low and made it to the wall near the entrance to the hallway. I flattened myself, ready to swing into the opening with my revolver aimed at the first guy I saw. Which was a problem, since if there were two, the guy behind him would have cover. If the guy in front of him was a pal, it might stop him from shooting. If it was some nameless SVV yokel driving an experienced Gestapo man around, then I'd plug the yokel and buy some lead from the Kraut.

Not a good situation.

I decided on a defensive move. After all, maybe it was a neighbor with a key checking up on Moret's place after he left. Doubtful, but the last thing I needed was a dead civilian at the bottom of the stairs. Moret's standing in town was low enough already.

I walked into the hallway, not looking down, and headed to

Moret's bedroom. I counted on the element of surprise, since they wouldn't expect anyone from that direction. I hoped.

I made it into the bedroom and turned, pistol at the ready, counting on Lasho to wake up quickly and take in what was happening. I chanced a glance at the bed.

It was empty.

The window was open.

I was tempted to jump out.

Now I had Kaz to worry about, asleep in the room down the hall. I gambled that the intruders—if there were more than one—were nearing the top of the stairs. And *gamble* was the operative word, since my next move was straight out of a neighborhood pickup football game. Chin tucked in, shoulder down, ramming speed out the door.

I connected with a body in the darkened hallway. He was two steps from the top. I knocked him down and kept on going, my forearm catching another guy behind him square in the neck and sending him reeling backward. He went down hard, with me on top of him, his head thumping against the wooden steps as I rode his body down the steep stairs like a toboggan.

We came to rest at the foot of the stairs and I rolled off, aiming my pistol up the stairs. A body was sprawled midway, with Kaz—dressed in not much more than his Webley revolver—standing over it. Lasho appeared from outside, outfitted in long johns and grasping a knife. I checked the guy beneath me. His head lolled at a strange angle. He'd taken a hard hit to the throat and a lot of punishment going down. Dead.

"Check his pockets," I said to Lasho, who got to work.

"No one else outside," he said, grabbing the dead man's Luger pistol. "No vehicle in sight."

I followed Lasho upstairs, where Kaz had divested the other guy of his weapon, a more modern Walther P38. My money was on him being Gestapo. He moaned and moved stiffly, trying to get up. His eyes opened, and then closed again, as if he hoped the scene might play out differently next time.

"Come on, Fritz," I said, pinning an arm behind his back and dragging him into the sitting room. "*Sprechen Sie Englisch?*" He shook his head, either saying no or loosening the cobwebs in his addled brain. I held my pistol under his chin as I patted him down and took his wallet.

"*Ihr Freund is tot,*" Kaz said a minute later, having taken the time to don a robe. I knew *tot* meant dead, and I watched for a reaction as I shoved the guy into the chair by the stove. The other fellow apparently wasn't a pal, since he gave a slight shrug, the corners of his mouth turned down. No big deal. Definitely Gestapo. Square-jawed, gray-flecked black hair cut short, and in need of a shave. Dark bags under his eyes and little red broken blood vessels on his nose and cheeks. A tired-out heavy drinker.

Lasho stood in the doorway, the Luger aimed at our guest. Kaz rummaged around in a closet and came up with a length of rope, which he used to tie his hands and feet.

"Kaz, throw some more wood on the fire, will you? We may need it before we're done." He opened the stove and threw on some small pieces as I watched for another reaction. Maybe he really didn't speak English. I flipped through his wallet, coming up with his identity card.

"*Kriminalkommissar* Ernst Wielen, Gestapo," I read. "From Dijon. They're certainly pulling them in from everywhere."

"Bruno Blocher," Lasho said, checking the other wallet. "From Lucerne. Swiss, probably his local SVV partner."

"Ask him why he's here," I said, eyeing Wielen. Kaz spat German out at him, but Wielen remained impassive.

"*Kriminalkommissar* isn't a high rank, is it? Pretty low for an older guy," I said. He took notice at the mention of his rank.

"Correct," Kaz said, throwing another log onto the now blazing fire. "Equivalent to a lieutenant. There are a number of Gestapo ranks above his, and not many below."

"Ask him if he wants a drink," I said. I had a feeling Ernst liked his booze. Probably needed it to sleep at night after a busy day torturing French kids.

He did want a drink, no surprise. Lasho found cognac and tipped a glass down Ernst's hatch. Then another. He didn't object. Not to a third, either. I signaled for Lasho to stop, and our graying *Kriminal-kommissar* looked downright disappointed.

I took a poker from beside the wood stove and opened the door, adding another log and stirring the embers. I left the door open and stuck the poker into the glowing coals.

Lasho smiled.

"Ask him if he knows who the Gypsy is," I said.

"*Wissen Sie, wer der Zigeuner ist?*" Kaz said.

"*Ja,*" Ernst croaked, his gaze focused on Lasho, who jammed the poker farther into the flames.

"Tell him he can have the bottle, and that *der Zigeuner* will not harm him," I said. "But he has to tell us everything. No one will ever know."

Kaz spoke to him soothingly, like a mother to a frightened child, telling her kid everything will be all right as long as he tells the truth. I'd never believed that line as a kid myself, but all I cared about was Ernst believing it. They talked for a while, Kaz stopping to give him a drink when his gaze strayed to the bottle of cognac.

"They came to search for a document," Kaz said. "They were told Victor Hyde had been here and might have hidden it. I asked him how they would recognize it. All he knows, apparently, is that it will refer in some way to *Alusuisse* Industries. They were to secure any paperwork mentioning that name and return to Bern. Failing that, they were to learn from Doctor Moret where Victor had gone. By any means, they were told, but he was not happy about killing a Swiss doctor in his own home."

"What does he know about Georg Hannes?" At the mention of that name, Ernst looked eager to talk. And thirsty. I poured him another drink, but held it back while he and Kaz spoke. I wondered what *Alusuisse* had to do with this, but I was more interested at the moment to keep tabs on Hannes.

"Hannes is a traitor," Kaz reported. "There is a lot of ill will against Hannes within the Gestapo for profiting from his post here in Switzerland. This is a plum assignment, obviously, and Hannes took full advantage to deal in illegal financial transactions and blackmail."

"Who is he blackmailing?" I said.

"I asked, but Ernst says he does not know. I believe him," Kaz said. "He asked if you were going to kill him."

"No," I said. "We may want to let our new friend go. Tell him we are after the same thing he is. We questioned Doctor Moret and found out nothing. Say Victor had been here but left before we arrived, and Moret has gone to Bern to claim his nephew's body. Tell him Dulles is after Victor, same as Krauch. Describe Victor as a renegade, threatening to sell the documents back to *Alusuisse*. Or whoever is the highest bidder." I had no idea if the aluminum firm cared one way or the other, but I was pretty sure this thug didn't either.

"I told him we have a common purpose," Kaz said after he finished. "As distasteful as that was. What else?"

"Tell him Moret told us where Victor is hiding. In Lugano, and we are heading there in the morning to take Victor back to Dulles in two days. We will spare his life if he doesn't mention any of this to his boss." Kaz gave Ernst the lowdown.

"He wants to know when you will let him go, and what he should say about the dead SVV chap," Kaz said. "And he thanks you for sparing his life. He says he was a regular policeman before the SS took over, and he is not a Nazi."

"Maybe, maybe not. Tell him we'll release him in the morning," I said. "As for his Swiss partner, he tripped and fell down the stairs. Not so far from the truth."

"Why?" Lasho said, as Kaz pulled up a chair and chatted amiably with Ernst, the Webley an afterthought. "Why let him live?"

"Because we need to find someone who knows what this is all about. I'm tired of these low-level goons," I said. "I'm hoping this will draw out Krauch. He's the one who must know what this is all about."

"Then have him tell you about Krauch," Lasho said. "There may be something useful, yes?"

"Yeah," I said, giving Kaz a go-ahead nod. "Good idea." I took the poker out of the fireplace, raising it up and blowing ash from the red-hot tip. Ernst sort of lost his train of thought, then regained it as I set the poker back in its rack. Nothing like a little reminder of what might be in store for an uncooperative guest.

That was the stick. Now it was time for the carrot.

I untied his hands from behind the chair, then tied one down tight to the armrest. I poured cognac for all of us, and I gave Ernst his. He gulped it and smiled, nodding his head and saying *danke, danke*. I poured him another.

"*Polizei*," I said, tapping my chest, going for the common bond between cops of all nations.

"*Polizei, ja*," Ernst said, his words beginning to slur. "*Kriminalpolizei. Kripo, nicht Gestapo.*"

"He was originally a homicide detective," Kaz said, after listening to a rambling story. I knew *Kripo* was slang for the criminal police in Germany, all of which had been brought under the command of the SS. "In Freiburg, near the French border. He speaks some French, which was why he was sent to Dijon. He claims he never joined the Nazi Party."

"Ask him if Siefried Krauch is *Kripo*," I said. If Ernst really was a washed-up, alcoholic police detective, then maybe he'd spill the beans on Krauch, especially if he was a no-nonsense Nazi.

"He says Krauch kisses Nazi ass," Kaz reported, a sharp laugh escaping his lips. "He married a party official's daughter and used that connection to get into the Gestapo. Krauch couldn't solve a real murder case on his own, which is not really a problem because these days it's the Gestapo doing the killing, not everyday criminals and drunks like in the old days, and why are you being so stingy with the bottle?"

"Christ, he *is* a cop," I said. "One more question. Where does Krauch do his drinking?"

"Krauch brought the new men to a place on the Postgasse, in the old quarter, when they first arrived. The Altes Keller, it was called. The staff knew Krauch, and he believes it is owned by a member of SVV," Kaz added. Then Ernst spoke to Kaz, but with his eyes fixed on mine. "He says he doesn't mind helping a fellow policeman, especially one with a gun and a bottle. But please do not mention to anyone that he talked with us. He has a wife and a daughter in

Freiburg, and it would not go well for them. He also has a son, missing somewhere in Russia."

"You believe him?" I asked Kaz.

"I think so," he answered, pouring us all another round of drinks.

"Billy Boyle," I said, extending my hand.

"Ernst Wielen," he said, taking my hand and meeting my eyes. We were both working on trusting each other, and if he was telling the truth about his family, then his was the greater risk.

"It is never a good thing to get to know your enemy," Lasho said. "Now I would have a hard time killing him."

"Don't worry," I said. "He's doing that all by himself, the slow, hard way."

CHAPTER TWENTY-THREE

THE NEXT MORNING, I'd expected Ernst to have a hangover and a case of the regrets. Instead, he was almost chipper, asking for a glass of water and if there was any coffee in the kitchen. I didn't entirely trust him, but brewing up a pot of joe for an enemy prisoner and fellow policeman didn't seem out of line. We got the coffee going, polished off the bread and cheese, and made a departure plan. Ernst sat at the table with us, his legs tied to the chair, cutlery safely out of reach. Just in case.

Kaz and I quizzed him some more, asking if he'd been told our names. The answer was yes, we'd been tagged as working for Dulles, OSS men. But no, there was not an order to shoot us on sight. Nice to know, but perplexing. He knew about how Hannes worked, identifying folks who had opened Swiss accounts and shaking them down, all for the good of the German Reich, at least until lately. He'd heard rumors about Hannes killing Lowenberg, but obviously that wasn't what angered the Gestapo bigwigs. It was his theft of bank accounts that the Nazis thought belonged to them.

What it really came down to was that Krauch and his bosses desperately wanted the document Henri had swiped. He hadn't heard that it was an invoice, and had no idea what it might be. Which was fine by Ernst, since the less they told him, the less he had to drink to forget what they'd told him.

It made sense to me, sad to say.

We'd laid out the body of the SVV guy last night, so he'd be easier to handle when rigor mortis set in. Ernst explained to Kaz that he'd been paired with him since he knew the local SVV contact in town: the owner of the inn where they'd stayed, and the guy who'd spotted Victor. Which meant that they'd put out an all-points bulletin on Victor. If the SVV's reach made it to this little burg, Victor might not even be safe in the remote mountain village of Alpthal.

We dressed and washed up. I let Ernst borrow Moret's straight razor for a shave. He laughed when I stood in the bathroom door with my Police Special aimed at his back. An approving laugh, delivered with a wink and a nod.

"*Sehr gut, Billy,*" he said. "*Es ist klug, vorsichtig zu sein.*"

"It is clever of you to be careful," Kaz said, passing by with his gear packed up. Lasho had already left to pick up the Renault Ernst had left at the inn, and we were ready to pack in the SVV corpse. Then we'd drive Ernst a few miles out of town and let him out to hike back. It's clever to be careful.

"Yes, Ernst," I said, thinking how clever this man must be, and if it was enough to get him through the war with his family intact, not to mention his dignity. The burst blood vessels decorating his cheeks might have been a map of the deceit, appeasement, and self-loathing it took to be a halfway decent cop in the Third Reich.

First time I ever felt sorry for a *Kripo* man.

We piled into our Peugeot once the stiff was crammed into the small Renault, where I left Ernst's Walther in the glove box. Lasho insisted on keeping the Luger. Smart guy. Plenty of GIs would pay top dollar for that particular souvenir. It was a sunny morning, with a slight chill in the air, just right for a walk down a country road. After about two miles, we pulled over, and Ernst shook hands with each one of us. Formally, as if it meant something. I gave him the keys to the Renault, and then he stuffed his hands in his coat pockets and walked off, shoulders hunched, head bowed, making his way as best he could.

"This is a strange war," Lasho said, before I could. "In a strange country."

"I miss the deprivations of London," Kaz said, glancing back at Ernst as Lasho drove off. "Rationing, the odd bomb now and then, too many Americans throwing money around in the clubs. Right now I'd gladly trade the ambiguity of this neutral ground for the absolute clarity of wartime England."

"I wouldn't mind a meal and nice bottle of wine at the Dorchester myself," I said. Kaz kept a suite at the Dorchester Hotel, where he let me bunk in with him. It was the last place he'd seen his family, when they visited before the war broke out. It was the same suite they'd occupied, and I think he kept it because he couldn't bear to break that last connection with them. With all the dough his father had stashed away, money was no object, so why not?

"I have heard of the Dorchester Hotel," Lasho said, as he turned onto a main road and followed it north toward Wauwilermoos. "Too precious for a Sinti, I think. When we get to London, I will stay somewhere else. A small room is all I need."

"We need to get your identity papers from Dulles," I said. "Then we'll figure out London."

"Actually, no one has spoken about a plan to get us out of Switzerland," Kaz observed. "We are surrounded by enemy territory."

"Hey, we got in, we'll get out," I said, with far more conviction than I felt.

First we had to find the POW camp, deal with Henri's killer, find Victor and the mysterious invoice, and then figure out what the hell that had to do with Safehaven. Maybe nothing, but I doubted it. The only thing that nagged me was why our Gestapo tail had taken potshots at us. If I knew why we'd posed a threat, I might be able to figure out what the big secret was.

I sat back and tried to stop worrying about it. My father always told me the best way to figure out a puzzler was to let your subconscious do the heavy lifting. He's a homicide detective back in Boston, and a damn good one. He taught me everything I know. Truth be told, he tried to teach me a lot more, but I was a know-it-all kid, a rookie who didn't always listen to everything his dad had to say, so there was a lot I missed. But that bit of advice stuck with me, since it was a good excuse for a nap now and then. So as the terrain turned to green rolling hills and we left the chilly mountain air behind, I shut my eyes in the backseat and gave my subconscious full throttle.

All I got was a stiff neck.

"We are close," Kaz said from the front seat as he studied a map. "We just passed through the village of Iberswil, so it should be ahead."

"Lasho, you want to wait in the village?" I said, not knowing how long we'd be.

"No, I will wait where I can watch the main gate. And where they cannot see me," he said.

"That might be tough," I said, scanning the open, flat fields. The ground looked wet and soggy, fields marked off by low stone walls, the dark soil sprouting rows of budding plants.

"There," Kaz said, as we came upon a sign for *Straflager Wauwilermoos*.

"What does that mean anyway?" I asked as Lasho turned and slowed to survey the terrain. Trees lined the road, a break in the monotony of the flat wetlands.

"Literally, the prison camp at the swamp of Wauwil, which is the next village," Kaz said.

"Ernst would say I am clever to stay outside," Lasho said. He slowed near the drive leading into the camp. The trees gave him some cover and he had a clear line of sight to the main gate. "Good luck."

"And the same to you if we don't come out," Kaz said. I got into the driver's seat and Lasho vanished into the greenery.

"That's not very encouraging," I said, as we jolted down the muddy dirt path, slowing for the guards at the gate.

"Neither is this," Kaz said as I hit the brakes. Helmeted Swiss soldiers advanced, one on each side of the car, while two others blocked the entrance, fixed bayonets pointed at us. I rolled down the window, keeping my hands in view, and let Kaz do the talking.

He handed the letter Dulles had given us to the guard, who then demanded our *Ausweispapiere*, which I knew meant identity papers. I opened my jacket to take mine out, and I saw the guard on Kaz's side eyeing me.

"*Pistole!*" he yelled, catching a glimpse of the revolver in my shoulder holster. Things were not getting off to a good start at the prison camp in the swamp of Wauwil.

We were hauled out of the vehicle and spread-eagled over the fender, feet kicked apart and faces pressed against the hood, relieved of guns, wallets, and probably some loose change I'd forgotten about. These guys were no novices at conducting a search. It was over quickly, done with enough roughness to show they meant business.

I kept my mouth shut. We'd brought two pistols and a letter. They had four rifles with bayonets; the odds were on their side. Prodded by rifle butts, we made our way into the camp. The ground was soggy, water squishing up under foot. The sun was out, but it was impossible to shake the damp chill that rose from the ground. Hard to blame the guards for being in a bad mood.

The place wasn't much to look at. Wooden shacks in rows faced each other across muddy tracks, surrounded by barbed wire. I could see guards, their rifles slung, patrolling outside the fence with dogs barking and straining at their leashes. Prisoners in nondescript filthy clothing looked away as we approached a row of wooden buildings with fresh paint and wood plank sidewalks built over the marshy ground. Officer country.

Our guards pushed us up steps leading into the largest of the buildings, slapping our legs with the flat side of their bayonets, and having a good laugh over it. Suddenly they were at attention, grins vanquished, rifle butts slammed on the ground, eyes forward. What got their attention, and mine, was an officer on horseback, coming down the lane at a canter, mud flying as the horse's hooves churned up the black, wet earth. The officer wore riding jodhpurs and polished black boots with spurs. He was stocky, his face round and puffy, a hatchet nose at odds with his baby face.

At that moment the door opened and another officer appeared, this one tall and severe, a pencil-thin mustache seated above narrow lips. His nose had a sharp edge as well, but it fit with the rest of his face. He took our papers from one of the guards and looked through them as the other officer dismounted and handed the reins off to a guard.

"I am Lieutenant Johann Wurz," the sharp-nosed guy said. "What business do you have here?"

"We've come on behalf of Allen Dulles of the American Embassy," I said. "To see Captain Walter Bowman and determine the legal basis of his imprisonment."

"Ah, yes. We received word of *Herr* Dulles and his interest," Wurz said. "We did not expect his delegates to arrive armed." The stocky officer brushed by us. Wurz stood aside and saluted as he entered the building.

"There's a war on, Lieutenant," I said. "The Gestapo tried to kill us in Bern a few days ago, so we armed ourselves out of caution."

"You will be safe enough here, Mr. Boyle and Mr. Kazimierz," he said, reading from our identity papers. "Captain Béguin, our camp commandant, regrets he does not speak English and asked me to attend to you."

"Was that Béguin?" Kaz asked. Wurz nodded. "I speak German as well as French, so we have no need of English."

"No," Wurz said. "Captain Béguin prefers not to meet with you. He dislikes Americans. You will fare better with me. Come inside."

We were brought into an austere room, decorated with a Swiss flag, the white cross set on a bloodred banner. Wurz dropped our papers on a table and took a seat. There weren't any other chairs. A soldier came in and set down the box of food we'd brought for Bowman.

"There's a letter from the embassy," I said. "Asking for information about Captain Bowman's detention."

"Yes, a letter from Dulles," Wurz said. "Who is a spy. All of Switzerland knows this. Who is Captain Bowman to him? And to you?"

"Walter Bowman is an evadee, who was attending a reception at the invitation of Max Huber of the Red Cross. The next morning, he was picked up by the police and sent here. We demand to know why," I said.

"Because obviously he violated the terms of his parole," Wurz said. "That is a matter for courts to decide. We run a penal camp. We do not decide who our guests are. The government is responsible for that."

"Was Captain Bowman brought before a court?" Kaz asked.

"According to the Geneva Convention, there are requirements for charging a prisoner of war with additional punishments. No more than thirty days' confinement for trying to escape, for example."

"We are some distance from Geneva, gentlemen. This is a prison, not a normal prisoner of war camp. Your Captain Bowman is here until a military tribunal can be convened to review the charges against him," Wurz said, lighting a cigarette and smiling as he blew smoke in our faces.

"When will that be?" I asked, working to contain my anger, since he had bayonets on call in the hallway.

"These things take time," he said. "We will notify the American Embassy when arrangements are made. Now, I can take you to see Captain Bowman if you wish. Then, you will leave."

"We brought this food for him," Kaz said, moving to take the box on the table in front of Wurz.

"We will check it for contraband, then it will be distributed. You have my word," Wurz said, placing his hand on the box and drawing it out of Kaz's reach. I believed him, too, since he left out who was going to be on the receiving end of the distribution.

Wurz led us into the compound, two guards trailing our little party. The path between the shabby barracks was thick with muddy ruts. Wood planks set on either side of the lane were already partially submerged, water oozing over our shoes with every step. Wurz gave us a lecture about how this area had been underwater until the lake was drained and the area turned into farmland.

"All this water must be good for crops," Kaz said. "Less so for men to live in."

"I quite agree," Wurz said, flicking his cigarette into a pool of brown water. Prisoners gazed out of windows, dull looks of fatigue and hunger on their faces. "If our American guests would simply stay within their designated areas, they would never need to be sent here. We only house criminals and repeat offenders. Not a pleasant group, take my word for it. Poles, Russians, German deserters, the worst Europe has to offer. I advise you to tell your comrades to stay in their hotels and not try to rejoin their forces. A ski vacation in Davos, what better way to sit out the war?"

"Not everyone likes to ski," I said, leaping from one wood plank to another. "Tell me, why does Captain Béguin dislike Americans?"

"He does not like the English, either. He admires Adolf Hitler and what he has done for Germany. He likes discipline and obedience. It is our experience that Americans practice neither. The English at least act with politeness, but are little better."

All around us, prisoners edged away from Wurz and the guards, taking to their barracks and crowding around open windows. Their clothing was filthy, barely recognizable as the flight suits and khaki uniforms worn as they left on their last mission. The odor of decay hung heavy in the air, as if the wooden barracks were rotting into the ooze.

One prisoner scurried by, his feet bare and caked with mud. He clutched a worn coat to his chest, his head cast down to avoid making eye contact with the guards.

"And you?" Kaz asked, his nose wrinkled against the smell. "Do you admire the Nazis?"

"Here we are, gentlemen," Wurz said, at the second-to-last barracks. "You have ten minutes." He gestured for us to enter, not answering the question except with a sly, superior smile.

We opened the side door, a couple of steps up from the muck surrounding the barracks. The stench was like a fist in the face.

"Billy," a voice gasped from a bunk. Well, not a bunk at all, I saw. Two wooden platforms strewn with straw ran the length of the interior. POWs sat glassy-eyed, staring at us like visions in a dream. "You've got to get me out of here." It was Bowman. Two days in this dump had already changed him. His clothes were caked with mud, his face was bruised, and his eyes wild with desperation.

"We're working on it," I said as he jumped down from the top platform. Then I took notice of where the awful smell came from. The latrines were in the same room, a squat wooden bench paralleling the sleeping area, with holes gaping over the open sewage pit below.

"Work harder," Bowman said. "This place is a hellhole. They beat up on me as soon as I arrived, and dumped me in here. Worst barrack in the place."

"Punishment barrack," another prisoner said. He was sprawled out on the hay, a handkerchief over his nose. "Thing is, Bowman didn't do anything wrong."

"What'd you do to get tossed in here?" I asked the other POW.

"Refused a work detail," he said. "I was sick of them stealing our Red Cross parcels and then sending us out to do heavy labor. They got us digging peat out in the fields every day."

"You've got to do something, Billy. Tell our people at the embassy. I can't believe they know what's going on here," Bowman said, his voice catching in his throat.

"Those pencilpushers have to know," his fellow prisoner said. "They probably think we all landed here on purpose to sit out the war. Me, I tried to escape, going for our lines in Italy. Swiss cops pulled me off a train in Locarno. That's what got me put in this camp in the first place."

"Allen Dulles sent us here," Kaz explained. "He wants a full report, and will pass it on to the embassy. We will tell him everything."

"And we brought a carton of food," I said. "But Wurz confiscated it. Said he was checking for contraband."

"We'll never see it," Bowman said. "Wurz is a sadist. He loves to tell us how good the food in the Red Cross parcels are, not to mention taunting guys with letters from home."

"Do you think Wurz or the commandant can be bribed?" Kaz asked in a low voice, glancing at the door.

"I doubt it," Bowman said. "They're both die-hard Nazis. Béguin even has a German uniform he parades around in. And Wurz has too much fun setting the dogs on prisoners to ease up on anyone. Try to bribe him, and you'll end up in here with us with teeth marks on your ass."

"Get out while you're still in one piece," the other prisoner said. "And tell the world what the Swiss are really up to, okay?"

"We will," I said, hoping that Dulles had the juice to do something about what these guys were enduring. "But right now, we only have a few minutes, and I need to ask you something. You and Maureen Conaty went back to your hotel after the reception. Did you notice anyone following you? Or watching you at the bar?"

"No, but I wasn't watching my six. All my attention was focused on Maureen, you know?"

"Yeah, she has that effect," I said, smiling at the pilot's jargon. Six o'clock is what lies behind you. "We were followed after we left Huber's place. I wanted to know if the SVV boys were tailing you as well. What about when Maureen left?"

"Uh, Billy, that's kind of personal," Bowman said. "Maureen's terrific, and I don't want to tell tales out of school, you know?"

"What are you talking about?" I said. "There's nothing wrong with having a drink or two at the bar. You are an officer and a gentleman, after all."

"That's just it. I'm trying to be a gentleman," Bowman said, leaning in to whisper. "We didn't go to the bar. We went right up to my room. She left around six o'clock. Said the morning light didn't do a girl any favors, and she had to get to work. She's not in trouble, is she?"

"Not at all, don't worry about it," I said, giving Kaz a quick glance. We were the ones who had to worry. Maureen had lied to us.

There wasn't time to think that one through. A guard rapped on the door, and we left promising to do our best for Bowman and the other prisoners. Wurz brought us to his office, dismissing the two goons. He'd made his point, and this time there were even chairs for us to sit in. The absence of bayonets made it almost cozy.

"I don't suppose an official protest from the American Embassy would do any good?" I said.

"None at all," Wurz answered, lighting another cigarette. "The International Red Cross has inspected this facility only recently. I have taken the liberty of providing an English-language digest of their report for you to bring back to *Herr* Dulles."

He withdrew a folder from his drawer and tossed it on the desk. I took it and scanned the sheets, which contained excerpts from the Red Cross inspectors.

If iron discipline is the norm, there is also a certain sense of justice and understanding that helps with the re-education and improvement of the difficult elements sent there.

Camp conditions are satisfactory.

The complaints concerning the treatment of internees at Wauwilermoos are not justified and are exaggerated for the most part. The regime of Wauwilermoos is stricter than an ordinary camp, but this is necessary all the same since this is a penitentiary and disciplinary camp.

The general methods there left me with an excellent impression of this camp. Captain Béguin is a man made to direct a camp of this type.

There is no abuse here, but on the contrary, strict control on the part of the commandant.

And this from an unnamed internee:

The camp is a relaxing place I would happily return to after the war.

"May we speak to the prisoner who made that comment?" I asked.

"No," Wurz said, hardly bothering to pretend the quote was real or not coerced. "But we should talk about Captain Bowman. His adjustment to this camp has not been easy. Things would be much better for him—perhaps even a release could be arranged—if he provided information leading to the return of certain stolen documents."

"Documents stolen from Max Huber, perhaps?" Kaz asked.

"Captain Bowman was on the premises when the theft occurred," Wurz said. "As were you both."

"I thought you didn't know why Bowman was sent here," I said. "You said that was a decision of the courts and the government."

"Here, we are the court and the government. I think you understand me," Wurz said. "Provide what I ask for and Captain Bowman will once again be granted evadee status. If not, he will remain here, subject to our hospitality." He snapped out an order in German, and our two pals were back with their pig stickers. Wurz crushed out his butt and smiled, thin lips stretched across yellow teeth.

Our car had been thoroughly searched, their disappointment at not finding the documents conveniently stashed in the glove box evident in the mess they'd left behind. Papers were strewn on the floor, seats lifted out, and the spare tire on the ground. But our pistols were in the trunk, which I took to mean Wurz and company didn't mean to ambush us anytime soon, having left us with a couple of six-shooters.

Or it meant that they'd come in numbers with superior firepower.

The only good news was that they'd wait until we found Max Huber's stolen documents. And we were no closer to finding them than we were the night Henri was killed. Which was very bad news for Walter Bowman. We drove out the main gate, tires spinning in the thick mud of the prison camp in the swamp of Wauwil.

CHAPTER TWENTY-FOUR

"YOU WERE SMART not to go inside," I said to Lasho as he took over driving.

"Maybe you were not so smart to go in," he said. "Hospitals and prisons, I try to stay away from both. I like being alive and free."

"The Swiss took the food for themselves. We saw Bowman, but all I did was make promises I'm not sure I can keep," I said.

"You promised to help," Lasho said, shaking his head at such foolishness. "They will live on hope for one or two days. Then they will come to hate you."

"Unfortunately, you are likely correct," Kaz said. "But there was little else to do. Dulles wanted a report on the prison, and now we have one for him. Little good that it will do."

"We did learn something," I said, gazing out the window at the flat wetlands, wondering what it meant, if anything.

"Maureen Conaty lied to us about where she spent the night after the reception," Kaz explained. "She said she left Bowman at the hotel bar and went to spend the night with Victor Hyde. Bowman said she stayed with him until six in the morning."

"Men have been known to lie about their experiences with women," Lasho said.

"Captain Bowman was not bragging about a conquest," Kaz said. "He seemed genuine to me."

"Well, we can ask Victor in a few hours," I said. "You all set with the route?"

"Yes," Kaz said. "North of Lucerne, along the lake shore, and then backroads into the mountains. The route is the most straightforward thing about this entire affair."

"Men, women, gold, greed, these are not complex things," Lasho said. "Understanding how they fit together, that is difficult." He rolled down the window, warm air filling the automobile. The road rose into hilly terrain, leafy green trees shading the route and hiding the dank marshland from view.

"Especially when things are not as they seem," I said. "Like the neutral Swiss. Or the Red Cross."

"We attempt to enter the office of the Swiss Red Cross and we are shot at," Kaz said, turning in his seat to face me. "We attend a reception for the International Red Cross, and Henri enlists your aid in the theft of certain documents. Then we are followed. Henri is killed. Victor disappears. Bowman is arrested. We discover the Gestapo has based their search out of the Alusuisse warehouse, another connection to Max Huber. Then we are followed once again, to Doctor Moret's house."

"And then we visit the prison, which recently received a glowing testimony from the Red Cross about their five-star resort," I said, giving Lasho a run-down on the report Wurz had given us.

"Do not forget Georg Hannes," Lasho said. "A Gestapo man wanted by the Gestapo. Not to mention Ernst, who seemed to be a decent sort. I thought the world had gone insane, but I did not think it had turned upside down as well until I came to Switzerland."

"Let us focus on finding Victor, and bringing Henri's killer to justice," Kaz said.

"Swiss justice?" Lasho asked, giving Kaz a sideways glance.

"I had something in mind much less elusive," Kaz said. "But first, we have to determine who is responsible. It would be easy to say the Germans, along with their SVV allies, but there may be more to this case than the obvious. As you say, everything is upside down."

"So we need to start thinking upside down," I said. "Or inside out."

"Does that mean you'll be taking another nap?" Kaz asked with a grin. I could see Lasho smiling in the rearview mirror.

I didn't sleep. I watched the countryside flow by as we drove north of Lucerne, lush fields of farmland dotted green against the hillsides. On one side of the road, the land sloped upward, stands of pine hard against the deep blue sky. Below, a sparkling lake glittered in the distance. I tried to think upside down, going back to the beginning.

Safehaven.

Who wouldn't want it to succeed? Bankers. Swiss politicians. The SVV.

What about the Germans? Safehaven was essentially a postwar operation. Once it got rolling, the Third Reich would be a pile of rubble. I could see the Nazis protecting their looted gold and the laundering mechanism the Swiss banks gave them. But with the war getting closer to their doorstep, I didn't see them worrying about the long term.

Except for those rats deserting a sinking ship.

Georg Hannes was a blackmailer. Henri Moret took papers from Huber's place that he thought would help him take revenge for his uncle's treatment by the Swiss government. So, those who were threatened by the documents would pay well to get them back. Classic job for a blackmailer. Hannes could extort the high and mighty in Swiss society and further fund his nest egg.

Siegfried Krauch and the Gestapo would want to stop the scandal as well, since nothing embarrasses bankers like the bright light of day.

So who roughed up Henri, perhaps killing him inadvertently? And where was the cigarette case? Obviously the Krauts—all the above factions—didn't have it yet. Or the SVV, judging by Wurz's declarations of mercy for Bowman if we handed it over.

And why the hell had Maureen lied about where she spent the night? One guy or the other, what did it matter? She was a big girl, and there was a war on. Aside from the chaplain, who cared? All that was left was to find Victor and see what he knew.

Lasho braked, and I slid forward on the seat. I hadn't been paying attention to the road, but we were stuck in a line of traffic. Trucks and farm vehicles moved slowly ahead of us, an occasional honking horn signaling an impatient driver.

"What could it be out in the country?" Kaz asked. Off to our right, houses and barns with low, sloping roofs sat huddled together on a hillside. "A roadblock?"

"I don't think so," I said. "There's no traffic coming the other way. Maybe an accident."

The traffic inched along, until it came to a dead stop. A train whistle sounded, long and mournful. I got out, walking up the curving road until I could see ahead around the line of vehicles. Other people were doing the same, chatting like strangers do when caught up in a delay. A guy went on in French, complaining to me about something. I shrugged, in the international language of frustrated motorists, which satisfied him.

I got close enough to see what had happened. The locomotive was stationary, its engine releasing bursts of exhaust steam as it sat on the tracks. Snarled in the cowcatcher was the remains of a tractor. Some unlucky farmer had tried to beat the train at the crossing, or had gotten stuck. Either way, it would be a while. I headed back to the car, hoping the farmer's luck hadn't been all bad and that he'd jumped to safety in time.

I filled Kaz and Lasho in, and it wasn't long before the traffic moved along, lurching ahead in fits and stops. As we rounded the curve, I could see cops ahead, pointing to a side road and hollering orders in German and French. The turnoff came just before a stone bridge that arched over a swift-running mountain stream.

"Detour," Lasho said. As we drew closer, I could make out soldiers as well, their rifles slung, standing across the roadway. It seemed like a lot of manpower for a train-versus-tractor accident.

"It may be a trap," Kaz said, picking up on the oddity of this farmland crossing attracting such a crowd of uniforms. "But it does not make sense. They could have stopped us with a simple road-block."

"Drive slowly," I said to Lasho. We lumbered off onto the side road, letting the distance build between us and the truck ahead. I started to worry about soldiers jumping out and surrounding us, but that was only a case of nerves. Kaz was right. We weren't worth all this trouble.

The dirt road was not much more than a wide lane alongside a field planted with crops. The car behind us started to honk its horn, impatient with our pace. I tapped Lasho on the shoulder and pointed to the side of the road. He pulled over, the grassy verge wide enough to let the line of traffic pass us by.

Dust settled as the vehicles passed, the sound of their engines fading. I looked back for any sign of soldiers taking position, but the road was empty.

"We are not being followed," Lasho said, his eyes fixed on the rearview mirror.

"Perhaps it was a military train," Kaz said. "That would explain the soldiers."

"Maybe," I said, stepping out of the car and scanning the terrain. The field was to our right, woods to our left. I caught a sound, a strange murmur coming through the trees. "What's that?"

"There is a river beyond those trees," Lasho said as he and Kaz joined me.

"It does not sound like running water," Kaz said, a hand cupped behind one ear. "Voices?"

Curious, we made our way through the woods, which thinned out as we drew closer to the river. I caught glimpses of the stalled train through the leaves, the small cattle cars similar to the one we hitched a ride on not that many days ago.

"It is voices," Lasho said, stopping dead in his tracks. A low wailing sound lifted itself above the roiling waters, the noise of anguish, sorrow, and grief. We moved slowly, parting branches and skulking low, until we came to the river, where water splashed over rocks, the frothing current a roar that could not drown out hundreds of voices from the cattle cars.

Or maybe thousands.

Across the river, cries rose from the train. Hands appeared at open slats and ventilation holes, the openings covered by barbed wire. Gray-uniformed Swiss soldiers patrolled the tracks, ignoring the pleas from inside the boxcars. We moved back into the underbrush, hiding from the guards.

Or maybe hiding from the people in the cars, ashamed of our freedom.

"Can you understand anything?" I asked Kaz.

"They are speaking in Italian, Yiddish, some Croatian," Kaz said. "They are begging to be let out. They know this is Switzerland."

"Who are they?" Lasho asked, his voice catching in his throat.

"Jews, from Italy, along with those destined for slave labor. Captured partisans are usually sent to be worked to death in Germany. Usually, the Nazis use the Brenner Pass in Austria, but that route has been heavily bombed," Kaz said.

"More Swiss neutrality," I whispered. I felt my revolver pressing against my rib cage. Useless. There had to be twenty armed guards, or more.

"There is a treaty that allows for nonmilitary goods to be transported across Switzerland," Kaz said, as usual a walking encyclopedia. "Through the Gotthard tunnel, north to Germany and south to Italy. Prisoners being sent to their death can hardly be called nonmilitary."

"Someone's looking the other way," I said. "Which may be why they have so many soldiers out guarding the train. To keep people from getting too close."

"Which means they may use their rifles," Lasho said. "We can do nothing here except be killed."

The alternative, running away, felt only marginally better.

"Look," Kaz said, pointing to a passenger car at the end of the train. A window opened, and a figure in a German uniform leaned out, waving his arms and looking angry. "He wants to know when they will be moving." With that, the train whistle blasted two long notes, which back home was the signal that the engineer was releasing the brakes and heading forward. The Kraut retreated inside and the guards

climbed aboard, some of them into the passenger car and others clam-
bering atop the boxcars.

The cries and wails from inside the cars rose one final time, a futile
protest at the forward movement carrying them into the black heart
of the Third Reich. Then, silence, except for the splash of water
breaking over rocks, a cascade of tears flowing to the sea.

CHAPTER TWENTY-FIVE

WE DIDN'T SPEAK for thirty miles.

We were free, doing what we—more or less—loved doing. We had pistols, cash, and half a tank of gas. Compared to the poor souls in those cattle cars, the world was at our feet. The air was fresh and the sun warm. I wished it would rain, wished that thunder would roll over the mountains and lightning crack the sky at the inhumanity of what we witnessed.

But nothing happened. The beautiful Swiss scenery was vivid and the sky achingly blue. It seemed wrong how quickly normal, everyday life washed over the terrors and horrors of war, leaving only a memory to visit again and again in fitful dreams. But that was the kind of war we had here in Switzerland. It erupted occasionally from beneath the placid façade of neutrality, then retreated back behind the curtain.

Nothing to see here, folks, just a stalled train. Move on. Go about your business.

So we did.

We found the signpost for Alpthal and followed a winding mountain road until it straightened out in a narrow valley, the afternoon sun already nearing the top of the peaks ahead of us. We paralleled railroad tracks, pacing a small train for a while, a few cars making the run from one mountain village to another. The kind of thing trains were supposed to do.

A church steeple came into view, its gray slate spire towering over the squat, sloped roofs surrounding it. We crossed the railroad tracks near a train station and spotted the Haupweg turnoff, right where Doctor Moret said it would be. It was a rutted gravel lane, and the car bounced along until we came to the end, opposite the small pine-log chalet with red shutters. No other vehicle was in sight.

"Victor could have taken the train and walked up from the village," Kaz said, scanning the terrain as I had. "Or left his automobile there, if he didn't want to attract attention."

"Let's see if he's home," I said, as we exited the vehicle and began climbing the hill. The chalet was about a hundred yards up a grassy incline. If Victor was up there, he'd have a perfect view of anyone approaching. Over the sights of Moret's rifle.

We waved our arms and called out, wanting Victor to know we were friendly, in case he was in the mood to shoot first and not give a damn about questions. No response. The faintest whiff of wood smoke swirled in the wind. We stopped short of the house, listening. Silence.

We drew our pistols. Something wasn't right. The smoke said he was at home. The silence meant otherwise.

"Out for a hike up the mountain?" Lasho offered.

"Check the back door," I said. "We'll go in the front."

The door wasn't locked. It wasn't even fully closed. I pushed it open with the barrel of my revolver, the creaking hinges startlingly loud. We stepped into a large room. A wood-burning stove was still warm. Comfortable chairs were arranged around it, one with a coffee cup still on a side table, half full. A book lay open on the floor, an old desk scattered with papers, a quilt folded on one chair. The place was lived in. And recently vacated.

Kaz took the stairs up to a loft. I checked the dining room. Nothing.

"In here," Lasho called from the rear of the house. We entered the kitchen, where a long wooden table dominated the room. One of the chairs was pulled out and strands of cut rope were scattered on the floor, covering red splashes. Blood splatter.

"He was tortured," Lasho said, pointing to two carving knives on the table, caked with blood.

"My god," Kaz said, entering the kitchen. "What happened here?"

"Victor was tied to the chair," I said, moving the pieces of rope aside. "And worked on with those knives."

"At least he is not dead," Lasho said. "Or else he would still be in the chair."

"There's not a lot of blood," I said. Of course, if it had been mine, I would've thought it was a river of the stuff. But it was mostly splatter from dripping blood. It was on the arm of the chair and along the legs. Cuts on the hands and arms, maybe a jab in the thigh. Pain, not death, had been the objective.

"There are no other blood stains," Kaz said, checking the kitchen floor. "Why, if he was let go?"

"I don't know. Let's check the rest of the place," I said, testing the blood with my finger. It was thick and tacky to the touch, but as I rubbed the drops, I could feel the wetness. "It hasn't been that long, maybe an hour or so."

"If whoever did this took Victor away, we may have passed them on the road," Kaz said.

"Damn. I figured he'd be safe enough, since he didn't even know himself that he'd be headed here. If he hadn't stopped at Moret's, he'd be somewhere else. So how did anyone know where to find him?" I couldn't make any sense of it.

"Perhaps Doctor Moret told someone he trusted," Lasho said. "And the SVV got to them."

"But that doesn't work," Kaz said. "The Gestapo sent two men to Moret's. We took care of them. They wouldn't have sent others at the same time, or known Moret was going to his brother's."

"Remember, Moret's brother, Henri's father, is a policeman," I said.

"Even if he did tell him, it would have been late last night," Kaz said. "And Moret said Henri's father wasn't political. What motive would he have in turning Victor over to the wolves?"

"Right," I said. "There's gotta be some other explanation. Let's look around. Lasho, check the ground outside for blood. Maybe they cleaned up the tracks in the kitchen."

"A fastidious torturer, who cleans up after himself, except for the blood around the chair?" Kaz said. I was straining to find an answer, trying to twist any theory into a shape that fit the facts. What I needed were better facts.

"Anything upstairs?" I asked as we went through the living room.

"A bedroom, a small bath. Clothes in the drawers, nothing out of order."

"Nothing out of order? Doesn't that strike you as odd?"

"Of course! Why wasn't the place searched? They've been turning rooms upside down looking for the cigarette case," Kaz said.

"Maybe that was the point of the knife work in the kitchen," I said. "Why waste time searching when agony and suffering can do your work for you?" We got to work searching. Kaz went back upstairs, and I started with the dining room. Fancy table, nice view, and a country hutch full of crockery. I went through the piles of plates. Didn't even find dust. Pulled out the hutch and checked the back. Crawled under the table. Clean.

In the main room, I checked the chairs and found a couple of one franc coins and a button. Kaz came downstairs, shaking his head. No joy up there. He went through a few shelves of books, flipping the pages, scoring bookmarks and dog-eared pages. He searched a closet, coming up with a rifle. Probably Moret's, not that it had done Victor any good.

Except for the blood and rope in the kitchen, the place looked completely normal. So what had happened here? I sat at the desk and tried to work it out. Bad guy, or guys, sneak up on Victor. But there's no sign of a struggle. Maybe he was outside. Going for a walk, like Kaz suggested. They drag him in and tie him down. Ask where the documents are. He clams up, they go to work on him.

He talks. Tells them what they want to know. But they still need him for some reason, so they clean him up, apply a few bandages, and take him away.

"No blood outside," Lasho said, coming in the front door. "But there is a rubbish bin out back with a torn and bloody shirt and trousers."

"They needed Victor," I said. "So they bandaged him up and took him along."

"Why?"

"Good question," I said. "Why would they need Victor to get the documents, assuming he told them where they were?"

"Some place only he could get to," Lasho said.

"A bank. A safe deposit box," Kaz said.

"Or someplace simpler," I said. "If Victor was in fear of his life the morning he left Bern, would he have taken the time to wait for the banks to open?"

"I think not," Kaz said, pacing back and forth, tapping his finger to his lips. "Also, how could he trust the bank staff, with Hannes and his connections?"

"I would use the poor man's safe deposit," Lasho said. "The post."

"He mailed it to himself," I said. "Or someone he could trust."

"If it was to someone else, they would not need to keep him alive, except to be certain," Kaz said.

"Maybe he sent it to Dulles," I suggested.

"Henri did not entirely trust Dulles, as you recall. Perhaps Victor felt the same, about whatever this secret is," Kaz said. "If only he had been able to leave some clue."

I drummed my fingers on the desktop, trying to think it through. I searched the cubbyholes in the desk, finding stamps, pencils, paper, the usual debris. A pad set square in front of me. Nice thick paper. A fountain pen laid next to it. Dots of blue were scattered across the paper, where ink had leaked through. I grabbed a pencil and began rubbing the lead over the paper.

"It's a letter, dated today," I said. "Victor pressed down hard to leave impressions, see?"

"Clever man," Lasho said as I finished the page. It was in German.

"It's to the concierge at 20 Alpenstrasse, Victor's apartment," Kaz said, tracing the reverse image. "He instructs him to turn over his mail to a friend, who will pick it up for him. Georg Hannes."

"He mailed it to himself?" Lasho said. "He must not have known his concierge was an informant."

"It seems as if Hannes didn't know either," I said. "Otherwise he wouldn't have needed this letter. We did see him knock on the concierge's door the night of the reception, but it doesn't mean Hannes knew he was being paid by the Gestapo."

"He wouldn't, necessarily," Kaz said. "Krauch is in charge. Hannes has a very specific job in Bern, draining bank accounts. He was probably pressed into service as a lookout and would not have the full picture about every informer on the payroll."

"So right now, Hannes has Victor in tow, heading for Bern, ready to grab the documents," I said.

"But not on behalf of the Gestapo," Lasho said, moving to the window to watch the approach from the road.

"No, for himself," Kaz said. "Probably to sell it back to Max Huber."

"Then we need to talk to Huber," I said. "Big shot or no, he's at the center of this." I tore the paper from the pad, not wanting to leave a clue in case Krauch and his boys came this way. I noticed a small box of matches next to the fountain pen. *Goldener Adler* was printed in ornate script, over a picture of our hotel. The Golden Eagle. Where Victor went to listen to jazz, as he told us at the reception.

Right on top was a single postage stamp.

"Victor is in big trouble," I said, pointing to the matchbox. "He mailed the documents to us, at the hotel. When Hannes strikes out at the apartment, there's going to be hell to pay."

"Victor will be forced to reveal the truth. Which is why Hannes kept him alive, in case he was lying," Kaz said. "Which means Hannes will either give up or come after us."

"I hope he comes after us. I have wanted to kill him from the first," Lasho said. "But why would Victor leave that clue? He would have no reason to think we were coming."

I didn't have an answer for that. I took the crumpled sheet and opened the wood stove to toss it in. Charred, smoky embers were all that remained from the most recent fire. Except for a blackened remnant of flimsy paper with *Schweiz Telegraphen* emblazoned across the top.

"Here," I said. "Moret must have sent a telegram this morning, telling Victor we were coming."

"He may have let his guard down when he heard a car pull up, or a knock at the door," Kaz said.

"Enough. He is waiting for us, and in grave danger," Lasho said, grabbing the rifle and heading out the door. We followed.

CHAPTER TWENTY-SIX

WE STOPPED TO buy petrol, and that was it. The rest of the time Lasho kept it floored, trying to buy time for us to get to Victor's place before Hannes realized he'd been duped. I figured he'd keep Victor alive until he got the documents in his grubby hands, but that didn't mean he wouldn't revisit the knife work.

"If Victor ends up telling Hannes the truth, at least we know where we can find him," I said. "Waiting to ambush us at the hotel."

"Perhaps you should call in reinforcements," Lasho said, downshifting as he took another curve in the winding road.

"Who?" Kaz asked, as he grabbed the hanging strap by the passenger door.

"The Gestapo, of course. They want Hannes. We want Victor," Lasho said. "Remember Ernst told us they gather at the *Altes Keller* in the old quarter? It would not be impossible to make an approach."

"The only problem is, we all want the documents," I said. "I can't see Krauch wanting to team up with us. Besides, we don't have time; we've got to get to Victor's apartment, fast."

Kaz leaned back, his arm across the passenger's seat. "But if they've already been there, their next stop may well be the hotel, where Hannes will wait for us. The *Altes Keller* is only a few blocks away. The sight of his fellow Gestapo agents might send Hannes running."

"And they won't know Hannes has Victor," Lasho said. "They'll go straight for their man, which will allow us to get Victor to safety."

"You guys might be onto something," I said. "Let's see how it plays out." I had a lot of questions, and right now, Victor was the key to answering them. What was so valuable about the document in the cigarette case? What was Victor's involvement, if any, with Henri's death? And why did Maureen lie about who she'd spent the night with? Was she covering for Victor, providing him with an alibi for the night after the reception?

I wanted Hannes held accountable for all the lives he'd ruined, and I liked the thought of him getting a taste of Nazi justice himself, so a temporary alliance with Krauch held a certain appeal. But I had to admit, the image of all those captives in the boarded-up cattle cars was burned into my mind, and the last thing I wanted was to make a deal with any Nazi bastard, no matter what the reward.

As we left the mountains, the ground evened out into rolling meadows, farmland, and stands of greening trees. A misty rain began to fall as the sky went gunmetal gray. Deer darted across the road, scant yards ahead of us, and Lasho swerved on the soaked pavement, recovering control as the beasts leaped a stone wall, their white rumps vanishing into the forest. I envied them, even as rain began to pelt heavily against the windshield. Life was simple if you were a deer: eat, find a mate, run. All we had on them was one out of three, and it didn't involve a dame or doughnuts.

We drove into Bern as night fell. The way Lasho had been driving, I was happy not to be careening around country roads during the blackout. We approached Alpenstrasse, the light from our taped-over headlights barely enough to navigate through the city streets.

We turned the corner and pulled over, not twenty yards from the entrance to the apartment. Lasho killed the engine and we scanned the street, checking for any sign of Hannes before barging in. The area was dark, with only a few pedestrians passing by. I rolled down my window for a clear view, and the smell of dinner cooking wafted in from the buildings, reminding me we hadn't eaten since breakfast.

The entry to Victor's lobby opened, a sliver of light escaping before a figure slammed the door and ran down the steps. Hannes. He turned up his collar against the rain and glanced around the street as he moved away from us and got into a car a few spaces up.

"Wait," I said, as Lasho reached for the key. "Let him get ahead, and no lights right away."

Thin beams of light illuminated raindrops as Hannes pulled out in a Tatra, a Czech car that resembled a streamlined version of the Volkswagen. Bright red, which made it easier to tail, even in the drizzly gray blackout. We followed him to the Nydegg Bridge, crossing the river and heading directly into the old quarter. Hannes showed no sign he knew he had a tail, making straight for the Hotel Golden Eagle. Home sweet home.

Hannes took a left on a side street, opposite the hotel. Lasho drove past it, slowly enough for us to spot the Tatra pulling over into a narrow lane that connected to the next street over. We parked and watched behind us, wondering what move Hannes would make.

"I couldn't tell if anyone else was in the car," Kaz said. "Too dark to tell."

"Victor could be tied up in the backseat, or in the trunk," Lasho said. "Or dead."

"Then what's he waiting for?" I said. "Working up his nerve, or watching for us?"

"Perhaps he is interrogating Victor," Kaz suggested. "Should we take him now?"

"I don't want to spook the bastard," I said. "If he's got a knife at Victor's throat, I don't know what he'll do if we surprise him."

"Hannes does not know me," Lasho said. "I could get close."

"Okay," I said. "Walk around the block and wait at the other end of that alley. If he drives out, stop him."

"You mean shoot him?" Lasho said, grinning as he opened the driver's door.

"That's one way to do it," I said, sitting sideways on the backseat for a better view out the rear window. The rain had lessened, the drumbeat on the roof down to a sprinkling patter.

"How long do we wait?" Kaz asked, as Lasho turned the corner ahead.

"I'm not sure. I'm tempted to go into the hotel and claim our mail. But I don't want Hannes to spot us going in." I waited, watching people on the street, entering and leaving restaurants and shops, unfurling umbrellas, pulling down hat brims. All oblivious to the suffering going on in their country, in the prison camps, and in the railcars traveling north to Germany. I hoped whatever was in the damn cigarette case would shake them out of their complacency.

"There!" Kaz said, spotting Victor being pushed across the road by Hannes, who had one hand on Victor's shoulder and the other in his coat pocket. They stopped, waiting for a car to pass, then walked toward the hotel entrance, Hannes a half-step behind, the bulge in his raincoat pocket in the small of Victor's back.

"Wait a second, then we'll follow," I said. "We'll grab him inside." I laid my hand on the door handle, ready to go.

Victor had other ideas. He twisted away from Hannes and sent a right hook smashing into his captor's jaw. Hannes went down and rolled, scrambling to get back up and in control. Victor kicked at Hannes's arm, trying to keep him from drawing his pistol.

"Go!" I shouted, sprinting from the rear seat. I saw Hannes skitter back on his hands and knees as Victor jumped clear of a car madly tooting its horn. I pulled my revolver as another car nearly sideswiped me, and I danced backward, working to keep my balance.

I looked up. Hannes was on his feet, running. Victor was nowhere in sight, but I could tell by Hannes's gait that he was tracking him. He ran fast, gun down by his side, his eyes fixed on the target as he darted between vehicles and under the covered archways spanning the side-walk. The road curved, and Hannes picked up his pace, not wanting to lose sight of Victor somewhere in the crowd ahead.

I heard someone running behind me and hoped it was Kaz. I holstered my pistol, which made running easier, but was a distinct disadvantage if I got close enough for Hannes to realize I was after him and closing in. A slug to the chest disadvantage.

The old quarter of Bern sits on a spit of land jutting into the River Aare, so it wasn't long before the paving stones led close to the water. The weather wasn't made for strolling along the promenade, so as we

left the shops, bars, and restaurants behind, we had the streets to ourselves. Hannes crossed in front of a church, skidding to a stop for a
moment to check a side street. I slowed, catching a glimpse of Kaz
and signaling him to go around the church, hoping to cut Hannes off.
I slumped against the corner of a building, catching my breath and
watching Hannes, praying he didn't feel my eyes on his back.

I heard the smack of leather on stone, and so did Hannes. He
bolted toward the river, this time with his pistol held up, ready to fire.
I ran after him, but not before I saw a woman with her face pressed
up against a window in the building opposite, the room lit by a faint
light. She drew the curtain quickly, and I wondered at the chances of
her calling the police. Gunmen racing through her quaint streets were
probably a rarity.

I followed Hannes down a set of steep stone steps, leading to a
broad parklike walkway along the river. I caught a glimpse of his face
as he turned, and knew he spotted me. I darted to the cover of a tree,
expecting a shot, but he kept going, probably thinking I was Gestapo.
If he knew that the addressee of the letter he was after was behind
him, he might've tried to get the drop on me.

I kept pumping my arms, trying to keep up with Hannes and not
think about the fact he might turn around at any moment and shoot.
That he'd shortly be disappointed at the loss of his meal ticket was of
no comfort.

I kept my eye on Hannes's flapping raincoat, the fabric billowing
as he ran. In the distance, I thought I spotted Victor, hustling up
another set of stairs, making for the warren of streets again. My lungs
were heaving and my legs felt like lead, but I kept pace with Hannes,
even after he went up the steps, taking them two at a time.

I did the same, pain shooting through my thighs. I had to stop at
the top to listen for footsteps and catch my breath. Ahead of me were
two darkened alleyways. The tread of feet echoed down the alley on
the left. I went right. The left alley was a hard turn, but this one led
straight from the stairs, and I figured Victor wouldn't have slowed
down but gone headlong ahead.

More echoing footsteps, but they sounded like they were coming my way. I skidded to a halt, the wet cobblestones slick beneath my feet. All around me were closed doors and shuttered windows, rainspouts gurgling water and trash cans stuck in narrow gaps between buildings. Water dripped from my forehead, and I rubbed my eyes with my sleeve, trying to focus on what was ahead.

Something moved behind me. A quiet rustle of clothing, and then cold steel was pressed into my neck. The barrel of a pistol.

"Not move," came in a guttural whisper, thick with a Germanic accent. "*Pistole.*" His hand reached around me, relieving me of my pistol as he jabbed his harder under my ear.

"Hannes?" I said, as loudly as I dared, knowing it was him. He must have recognized me and led me into this trap.

"Shhh!" he hissed. "*Papiere. Dokumente, ja?* You have?"

"Yeah, sure, back at the hotel," I said, turning to face him. That got me a smack on the head with the butt of his revolver, hard enough to send a message while keeping me upright.

"*Nein.* You give, to me. Now. *Jetzt!*"

"I don't have it, pal. Take it easy, okay?" I raised my hands to show how cooperative I was, and to get ready to elbow him in the face, which was a great plan except for his finger on the trigger a few inches from my carotid artery. His free hand started patting me down, and I steeled myself to swing around with a fast hit to the jaw and a quick prayer to the Archangel Michael, him being the patron saint for cops and no slouch at fighting the forces of Satan.

Hannes muttered something in German as steps sounded coming up the stairs from the river. He turned, the muzzle now burying itself in my ear, and his hand gripping my shoulder. If it was Kaz or Victor, I needed to alert them, but right now that would result in a warning shot that might be muffled by what brains I had. How did I let him grab me? A rookie would have known better than to stop in dark alley. Hannes pulled me back against the wall, both of us in shadows as he waited for the steps to come our way.

I caught movement out of the corner of my eye, coming from the opposite direction. No sound, just a hurtling shadow that flew into us, sending Hannes and me head over heels and tumbling to the paving stones in a jumble of limbs. I heard Hannes grunt as he hit, then came the gunshot.

Very loud, very close to my ear. I heard the zing of the bullet as it ricocheted off the wall, or maybe that was the ringing inside my head. I tried to pin Hannes down by his gun hand but he squirmed free, his face contorted with rage, one hand grasping his knee as he tried to stand.

"Stop! Halt!" It was Kaz, coming from the stairs. I tried to get up and fell over Victor, who half rose, watching Hannes, his gaze fixed on the pistol.

Hannes grimaced, his gun hand wavering as he held it on us, and then aimed toward Kaz, less than twenty yards away. Kaz stopped, turned sideways to present the smallest target, and held his Webley trained on Hannes. The sound of a police siren drifted across the river. Hannes spat out a curse and took off down the street, running with an uneven gait.

"Halt!" Kaz shouted again, running with his arm extended, revolver tracking Hannes as he weaved and limped down the darkened street.

"Don't shoot, we need him!" Victor said, getting up and sprinting after Hannes. In stocking feet, I noticed, which was why we didn't hear him as he ran toward us. Kaz flew by, getting ahead of Victor and shielding him. I grabbed my pistol, dropped by Hannes when Victor did his freight train impression, and tried to catch up.

Victor and Kaz were in a small plaza overlooking the river, dominated by a church, its thin spire barely visible in the misty gloom.

"He went in there," Kaz said, huddled against a chestnut tree. "We heard the door slam shut."

"He might get away out the back," Victor said, lacing up his shoes, which he must have retrieved along the way.

"Thanks, Victor, I owe you," I said.

"I'd say we're even, given that you tried to find me, and figured out the clues I left," he said. "Now let's go."

"Slow down," I said. "Kaz, you circle around back. I'll go in the main door. Victor, you move down that way, where you should have an angle on the back as well. If you see him come out of either, yell out. And duck."

"Okay," Victor said, jogging off to a low wall that gave him a side view of the church. Kaz and I ran low, splitting up as I mounted the front steps, watching for a pistol to appear in any of the narrow windows on the steeple. I didn't see anything. The police siren faded away. It wasn't for us; some other poor bastard was in trouble.

The door was massive oak, with an iron latch and hinges that clanked and creaked as I opened it. I ducked, hoping to avoid a bullet if Hannes was waiting close by. Nothing. I squeezed in, trying to minimize the noise, but the centuries-old oak door had other ideas and slammed shut, sending a shudder through me and into the empty church. I darted to a corner, which gave me a view of the interior and a door that must've led to the steeple. I listened. No clamber of feet. No shouts from Victor. Now all I had to do was find where Hannes was hiding and not shoot Kaz in the process.

I waited, hoping for my quarry to make the first move.

I thought about what Victor had said. That we needed Hannes. Which was what we'd come up with as well not long ago. But how much did Victor know, and what did he have in mind? It also occurred to me that Hannes could have shot the two of us with a good chance of getting away. But he didn't, which meant we were worth something alive. He wouldn't want to shoot me, or Kaz, since the document had been mailed to us.

One of us, I corrected myself. If Hannes knew which one, he might not have any qualms about plugging the other. And since he'd already held off putting a bullet in me, chances were my name was on that envelope. I hoped.

I strolled down the aisle, about ten paces, enough for Hannes to spot me if he was there. Nothing. A door latch clicked from behind the altar, and seconds later Kaz emerged, looking anything but priestly with his Webley revolver ready for action. I motioned for him to stay put, and that I was going up into the belfry. Not having bats in his, he quickly agreed with a nod and hunkered down behind an ornate pulpit, the perfect spot to observe the entire church.

I pressed the latch on the door to the church tower and pushed the door open, standing back. It creaked in the silence, revealing a spiral metal staircase and a lot of damp, cold stone. I didn't like the idea of stepping into the chamber, since the only reason I could think of for Hannes to have climbed the steps was to shoot whoever came up after him. Maybe he didn't want to kill me, or maybe that was wishful thinking.

Time to find out.

"Hannes!" I yelled, taking a small step. "You want the document? Let's talk. *Sprechen, ja?*"

Silence.

I stepped closer to the staircase and looked up, pistol at the ready. For the second time tonight, I felt cold steel at my neck.

"*Ja, das Dokument,*" Hannes whispered. I glanced to my side and saw where he'd hidden, in the shadows beneath the spiraling staircase.

"Hotel," I said, keeping my words simple. "Mail. The post."

"*Komm mit mir,*" he said, grabbing me by the arm. This was beginning to get tiresome.

"No," came a voice from the foyer. Victor. "*Nicht mehr.*" Yeah, I'd had enough myself. Hannes swiveled around, keeping me between him and Victor, who was quickly joined by Kaz.

"This would be a good time for a convincing talk in his own language," I said, grunting as the barrel of his pistol ground into my neck. "Tell him he has nowhere to go. Tell him about the Gestapo warrant."

"He knows," Victor said. "Ask him." Kaz unleashed a torrent of Teutonic at Hannes, who let out a sigh of warm breath on my neck as he took my revolver. Again.

"Let us speak in English, Baron Kazimierz," Hannes said, his diction as clipped and perfect as any English boarding school boy. "There is no longer a need to disguise my familiarity with the English language. It is a useful tool, at times, to pretend to not understand what people are saying, be it in French or English."

"Sorry, but I can't concentrate on how well you speak English with that Walther pressed against my neck," I said. "Ease up, okay?"

"I will ease up once I have the document in my hands," Hannes said. "Victor tells me it was mailed to you, Mr. Boyle, at your hotel. I want you to fetch it for me and return here promptly. Otherwise, I will shoot these two men, starting with your friend."

"At which point you will shoot all of us anyway," Kaz said, his

Webley still aimed at Hannes. Who was standing behind Mrs. Boyle's oldest son.

"Do not be melodramatic, Baron," Hannes said. "Put your pistol down and slide it to me with your foot. Carefully."

"No," Kaz said. I could feel my eyebrows pop up in surprise. "There is no reason. Let Billy go fetch the document. I will be your hostage, and Victor will hold my pistol. That will help insure our survival after Billy returns."

"Very well," Hannes said. "Give Victor your pistol, then come here." Hannes grabbed Kaz and shoved me aside, taking a seat on the stairs with Kaz standing in front of him. Victor lounged against the wall, forming a bizarre triangle of mistrust and death.

"Tell me this," I said, as I straightened out my rumpled coat. "Did you know about this document all along? What's in it?"

"I have no idea, except that it is very valuable to *Herr* Huber," Hannes said. "Now go."

"You have been diverting withdrawals for your own purposes," Kaz said, looking up at Hannes. "Which is why your former employers are after you. You must be a disappointment to Siegfried Krauch."

"I am simply an old vice detective with a penchant for languages, which is what led me to this assignment. I don't care a fig about the Nazis, and I certainly don't plan to stay until the bitter end. A Gestapo man's life won't be worth a *Reichsmark* once the Russians march under the Brandenburg gate."

"So you killed Lowenberg, and probably others, to cover up your embezzlement," I said.

"They would have died sooner or later, in one of the camps, and they'd never see their money anyway. With me, they got a nice trip and a last meal, almost a kindness. Now, I like to talk about myself as much as the next man, but my leg hurts and I am growing impatient. Go now, come back with the document, and we go our separate ways. Believe me, I have no desire to leave three bodies behind. It would raise too many questions."

I looked at the Walther, now shoved against Kaz's neck. I looked at Hannes, his eyes narrowed and his brow creased. He was a man with his back against the wall, gambling on a big payoff to fund his getaway. He had nothing to lose, everything to gain.

We had everything to lose.

"I'll hurry back, Kaz," I said.

"Hurry there too, Billy," he said, trying for a wry grin. Tough with the business end of a pistol at your throat.

I trotted out to the plaza and cut across until I came to Junkergasse, the main drag where our hotel was. It was near midnight, but there were still people out, navigating the darkened streets, heading home or out for one last drink. Maybe the jazz band was playing tonight at the Golden Eagle. As the hotel came into sight, I slowed to a fast walk. My mind was racing with worry. I was exhausted, hungry, and right now all I cared about was getting Kaz and Victor out of the jam they were in. I looked for Lasho, hoping he'd returned to the hotel, but he was nowhere to be seen. Probably out looking for us who knows where.

I took the steps into the hotel two at a time. The jazz band was in full swing, brassy notes flowing from the bar at the far end of the room. The lobby full of revelers, a waiter circulating and delivering drinks. I weaved through the crowd to the reception desk and decided to register, figuring it would be easier for a current guest to get his mail.

It was simple. I signed the register, showed my identity papers, and in a few minutes I had my key along with a small package wrapped in plain brown paper handed to me with a smile.

"May I have an envelope and paper, please?" I asked. I took everything and sat in the lobby, checking the package. No return address. Henri would have been too careful for that. Secured with tightly knotted string. Canceled stamps, of course. I thought about opening it and replacing the contents, but there wasn't time. I wrote my name and the hotel address on the envelope, stuffed the paper in, and added a folded piece of newspaper from the side table to give it some heft. I hoped Hannes would rip it open to check the contents, which would give us a split second to pounce on him.

It wasn't much of a plan. Hardly even qualified as a plan, really. But it was all I had, all that was standing between Victor and Kaz taking a slug to the head if I didn't hurry.

CHAPTER TWENTY-SEVEN

I LEFT THE hotel walking at a fast clip, too fast to notice a couple of mugs on my tail. By the time the big black Mercedes slammed on its brakes alongside me, they had me by the arms, pushing me toward the rear door. They shoved me in, one of them taking up position outside the rolled-down window, his Walther automatic discreetly aimed at my head.

I should have been upset about being grabbed again, but I got the crazy notion that since I hadn't been shot yet tonight by Hannes, odds were I wouldn't be by this guy either. Then the church bells struck midnight. It was a new day, and the odds were starting all over again.

"We have been wondering where you were, *Herr* Boyle," Siegfried Krauch said, from his seat next to me. The Mercedes was plenty big, the rear seat roomy enough for him to cross his legs and sit up straight, even at six foot plus. His black hair glistened with whatever the Krauts used for Brylcreem, and his five o'clock shadow was working overtime. Of course, he had the usual Walther. Not many people in Bern hadn't pointed one at me tonight.

"I've been looking for Georg Hannes, one of your boys," I said, trying to postpone the inevitable. "Know where I can find him?"

"He is a traitor to the Reich," Krauch said. "Turn him over to me and I will make certain of a reward. More than your life, perhaps."

"You can have him, with my compliments. Now turn me loose and

I'll give you a reward. I'll put in a good word at your trial after the war. Maybe they won't hang you."

"In the Greater Reich, that would be defeatist talk, assuming an Allied victory. You are lucky to be in Switzerland, although we could be across the border in time for breakfast. A trip that we may undertake if you do not hand over that envelope. The one you picked up at the hotel ten minutes ago."

I was unarmed, sitting between two pistols, one aimed at my gut, the other at my head. I handed over the package, the real one. Krauch had plenty of time to check, so there was no reason to foist off the phony envelope on him. He studied the brown paper parcel, holstering his pistol and cutting the string with a pocketknife. He unwrapped the paper and removed Henri's silver cigarette case.

"Very nice," he said, admiring the case. He opened it and unfolded two pieces of paper. Invoices, Henri had said. They looked unremarkable, nothing more than standard business paperwork, although Krauch held them close, not letting me get more than a glance. "Do you know what this is?"

"Something everyone wants. I have no idea why, or what it's all about," I said.

"Good. But even if you did know, it would do you no good. Gossip, nothing more. Now, you may go," Krauch said, motioning for his man outside to step back.

"Just like that?" I said.

"Our business is concluded," Krauch said. "After all, this is Switzerland. A friendly nation, and we don't want to litter the street with corpses. I have what I want and see no need to complicate matters."

"Maybe I'll take you up on that offer of a reward for Hannes," I said. "Where can I get in touch with you?"

"Very amusing, *Herr* Boyle. If you do locate Hannes, the reward is ten percent of the money he has stolen. And I will find you, never worry. Simply mention my name at the Golden Eagle," Krauch said, enjoying himself. "The staff all know me well."

I got out, half expecting a bullet in the back. Then the Mercedes roared off, swallowed up in the darkness. The two gunsels sauntered back to the hotel. I was not enough of a threat to warrant a bullet, or even a good shove. I was almost disappointed.

I started running, worried that being shanghaied by Krauch had eaten into whatever time was left before Hannes got nervous. Interesting about the reward, I thought, as I turned off the main drag and headed to the church. Ten percent of how much, I wondered?

Plenty, if the Gestapo was willing to share. If they could be believed. But my problem right now was getting Hannes to believe in the ersatz envelope in my pocket. Victor had known about it; would he recognize this as a substitute? If so, he might react in time. If not, the gunshots would be echoing inside the granite stone tower pretty damn soon.

I opened the massive oak door to the church and called out. Kaz answered, and I walked into the base of the tower. They were all still there, in place as I'd left them.

"Do you have it?" Hannes demanded.

"Sure, what do you think I've been doing all this time?" I said, drawing the envelope from my pocket. I wanted Victor to get a good look at it before I made my move. "Listen, Hannes, I've been thinking. We deserve something extra for this. Some of that money you've got stashed away."

"Be satisfied with your life," he said. "Now hand it over." He stood up from the staircase, pushing Kaz ahead of him. His right hand held the Walther at Kaz's neck. He extended his left arm, waiting for me to give him the envelope.

"We need a plan," I said, stopping a foot short. "To disengage. How are we going to do it?"

"First I confirm you have what I want," he said, his palm out. "Then we plan how to part company."

"Okay," I said. "Just take it easy, we're almost through this." Victor stepped forward, staying to my side to keep Hannes covered. "It would be a shame for anyone to get hurt at this point."

Hannes shifted a bit, which presented me with a good angle on his left leg, the one he'd hurt when Victor had piled onto us. At least

I hoped it was his left leg. I placed the envelope in his hand and shot a glance toward Victor, who gave the slightest nod of recognition.

Hannes was eager to rip open the envelope. Too eager. He moved it to his right hand, gripping it along with the Walther while he tore at it with his left. As he held the envelope steady, his finger moved off the trigger a bit, and the barrel of the Walther moved away from Kaz's neck by a good couple of inches.

I kicked him in the knee, hard. He howled in pain as I grabbed his gun hand and forced it up. Kaz gave him an elbow in the gut and twisted out from his embrace. Victor rushed forward with his revolver trained on Hannes, who clutched his leg with his free hand, the envelope crumpled in his fingers.

I got both hands on his wrist, keeping the Walther pointed toward the ceiling. Hannes was collapsing, his teeth gritted against the pain in his leg, but he held on to his weapon.

Then it went off.

The shot was loud, a sharp cracking echo inside the stone tower. I heard the *zing* of the ricochet, and everyone flinched for a second, which was all the time I needed to wrench the automatic from his grasp and give him a sharp rap on the forehead with the butt.

He sunk to the ground, his eyelids flickering. Victor said something, but my ears were ringing from the blast of the gunshot in close quarters.

"What?" I said, patting down Hannes. I took his wallet and identification, keys, and a folding knife.

"Where's the real package? The cigarette case?" Victor said, louder than he needed too.

"Krauch has it," I said, loosening Hannes's tie and using it to bind his wrists. Based on his moaning and groaning, he wasn't much of a threat at the moment. "He had the hotel under surveillance. They grabbed me on my way back here."

"They let you go?" Kaz asked, taking the knife from my hand. I almost felt bad for Hannes.

"Yeah, Krauch made a point of letting me know how harmless I was now that he had the document. That, and the fact that he didn't want too many dead bodies in his wake."

"Those are our instructions," Hannes said, gasping as he drew in breath. "No unnecessary killing. It makes things difficult for our friends in the government."

"Why are you still yapping?" I said, holding back on giving him another swat on the noggin. "What are we going to do with him?"

"Trade him to Krauch," Victor said. "For the papers."

"I am not worth it," Hannes said, struggling to sit up. "I mean the papers are worth much, much more."

"Krauch offered ten percent of your loot if we turned you over," I said. Victor whistled.

"Why not take half and let me go?" Hannes said, much more calmly. The quest for survival seemed to dampen his pain.

"Why not kill him now and forget about the money?" Kaz said, snapping open the blade. He flashed a smile, his long scar transforming it into an off-kilter maniacal grimace. He might have been kidding or goading Hannes. Or not.

"No, no, wait, I can help you," Hannes said, raising his bound hands in supplication.

"We don't want your blood money," Victor said, leveling his revolver.

"No, I mean I can help you get the document back," he said, his eyes wide and beseeching.

"How?" I said, suddenly interested.

"First, we go somewhere safe," Hannes said. "Someone may have heard the shot. Then, I tell you."

"We can't go to the hotel, at least not with you in tow. You must have a place somewhere," I said, hefting the keys in my hand. "How close?"

"A small *pensione* on the Rathausgasse, not far. I don't know if I can walk, though."

I went to get the car. I kept to the shadows, avoiding the Golden Eagle and the prying eyes inside. I looked around again for Lasho, but no dice. Maybe he'd given up and gone back to his digs at Dulles's joint. I couldn't waste time looking for him; I had other things to worry about. Like Hannes pulling a fast one. Or, even more dangerous,

Hannes on the level, which meant another encounter with Krauch and company.

The car was gone. I double-checked the street, thinking I'd gotten the spot wrong. I hadn't. The keys had been in the ignition when we'd jumped out to go after Hannes, but I hadn't expected grand theft auto in squeaky-clean Bern. Lasho must've taken it. By now he was safe in bed or out driving the streets, looking for us. Either way, he was in better shape than we were.

There were no taxicabs this time of night, so I hotfooted it back to the church, wondering how we were going to transport Hannes. Now I wished I hadn't kicked him so hard.

As I took a side street leading to the plaza, I heard an engine idling. When I turned the corner and saw the church, there was the Peugeot, with Lasho leaning against the fender.

"Lasho, where have you been?" I said, glancing into the car. Hannes was in the backseat, sandwiched between Kaz and Victor.

"Mostly searching for you," he said. "I found you, but unfortunately at the same time the Germans did."

"So why didn't you pick me up?" I asked.

"Because I thought you would like this back," he said, tossing me the silver cigarette case, still wrapped in brown paper.

"My god, Lasho, how'd you do it?"

"I will explain later. Now, where shall we dump the body?"

"He's not dead, Lasho," I said, opening the passenger door. Although from the look of fear on Hannes's face, he thought the end was near.

"No, not yet," Lasho said, with a sly smile and a glance in the rearview mirror.

"We have an arrangement," Hannes croaked.

"Had," I said, fingering the case. "Now we have a problem." Such as what to do with a useless, crippled Gestapo killer on a dark and rainy night. The river called to me, but I wanted to recover the money Hannes had stolen. We drove to the *pensione* and hustled Hannes to the door, unlocking it with one of the keys on his chain. Lasho untied his hands and clapped an iron grip on one arm. We entered a small parlor, with narrow stairs leading up at the far end. The five of us made a lot of noise, heavy shoes clomping up the stairway. A door down the hall creaked open and a woman in a bathrobe shrieked in surprise, jabbering on in German at this invasion of men. Kaz went up to her, speaking soothingly as he pressed a wad of Swiss francs into her hand. She quieted down immediately.

"I told her our friend had too much to drink and we missed our train, so we need to stay the night," Kaz said. "She is bringing food."

That was the best news of the evening, even counting the return of the cigarette case. We got settled in Hannes's room, which had two twin beds and a couple of chairs around a small table. Lasho put Hannes under the covers, tied his hands again, and told him to play drunk. Before too long our hostess appeared with bottles of beer, sliced meats, and crusty bread.

"Georg?" she said, looking at Hannes as she set her tray down. He groaned, acting his part, as Kaz ushered her out, murmuring assurances.

"So what happened, Lasho?" I asked after the door shut behind her. I opened one of the bottles and took a long drink of the cold brew.

"I saw you walk out of the hotel," he said. "Two men followed, so I slowed down and watched. Then the big car pulled over and they took you. I waited. When they let you go, I knew they had taken the documents. There were too many of them, even for both of us." Very gracious of him to mention that.

"Then?" Kaz prompted.

"I followed the Mercedes. It dropped Krauch off in front of the German embassy. I pulled over as he knocked on the door. I saw an upstairs light go on. I knew I had a minute or less, and there was no one else around. He hadn't seen me, so I ran up with my Luger drawn and demanded his valuables, as if it were a robbery. He handed over his wallet, promising to hunt me down and kill me. Which is not the smartest thing to say to a man robbing you at gunpoint. So I hit him, searched his pockets, and found the package with Billy's name. I kept the wallet, so the Germans would think it the work of a thief."

"You got away okay?" Victor asked.

"Yes, I ran as the door opened. Krauch was holding his head and crying. I laughed as I drove away. I thought it better not to kill him and make trouble. Was that right?"

"No," Hannes said. Probably better to have let him live, but I couldn't bring myself to say it.

"Aren't you going to open it?" Kaz asked, chewing on a mouthful of bread and salami.

"Okay," I said. "Victor, you don't know what's in here, right?"

"Not exactly," Victor said, in a low voice that meant he knew a lot more. "I mailed it for Henri. That's my writing." Hannes gave out a snort of laughter that silenced Victor, for some reason. I folded open the wrapping paper, withdrew the silver case, and opened it.

Two sheets filled with German. A swastika letterhead. Max Huber's name, and his company, *Alusuisse*, the aluminum concern. Numbers. That's all I could figure out. I gave it to Kaz.

"It is an invoice from the SS. The *Wirtschafts und Verwaltungshauptamt* division, to be exact. Translates as the SS Main Economic and Administrative Office. SS-WVHA for short," Kaz said, running his finger down the page.

"Watch out for them, boys," Hannes said, acting like one of the gang. "They're the money men, the most dangerous of the lot."

"Apparently *Alusuisse* purchased materials for their plant in Singen, Germany, from the SS," Kaz went on, flipping to the second page and then back to the first. "It's signed by Max Huber, chairman."

"What did they buy?" I asked. Kaz went back over the invoice, his forehead wrinkling as he translated.

"Ukrainians," Kaz said, his voice hushed in disbelief. "Two hundred Ukrainians. Slave laborers for their aluminum factory."

"The head of the International Red Cross purchased two hundred slaves?" I stammered. "From the Nazis?"

"And at a bargain price," Kaz said. "Not that I know the current market rate for a human being."

"You can bet the real money was all under the table," Hannes said, his eyes wide with excitement. "I knew this was big, but I had no idea. Huber will pay anything to keep this quiet." I could see him counting his take, even with his hands tied.

"Now I see what Henri meant," I said. "He was going to show what hypocrites the Swiss government and bankers are, ruining his uncle for speaking the truth about mass murder, while trading with the SS for slave labor."

"Listen to me," Hannes said, hunching himself upright in bed. "I have already made contact with Huber's people. They will pay well, enough for all of us. Let me go to them, before it is too late." He held out his bound wrists, as if it were a foregone conclusion that we'd make a deal with him.

"Where's your loot?" I asked. "The money you extorted from Lowenberg and the others before him."

"Not here. Do you think I would be so foolish? If we work together, we can wait out the end of the war as wealthy men."

"As long as you do not count your soul among your riches," Kaz said, starting to go through the drawers in the single rickety bureau. We all joined in, ransacking the place quietly, and quickly, since there wasn't much in the shabby room. I doubted he'd keep it in a suitcase under the bed.

"I will leave now," Lasho announced after we'd finished. "I will be safe with Mr. Dulles. I will return with the car in the morning. Do you want me to take him?" Hannes looked frightened at the prospect.

"No," I said. "We don't want him spotted, and we may need him. Be careful." I thought about giving the packet to Lasho to give to Dulles, but decided against it. Who knew if the Swiss cops, SVV, Gestapo, or Huber's own men were out hunting for the documents? It was blackmail material for any number of sides in this supposed bastion of neutrality. Besides, I wasn't at all sure what Dulles would do with the information. Henri had had his reasons for not going to him in the first place. And there was something Victor wasn't being entirely straightforward about.

"Okay, Victor," I said, settling into one of the chairs after Lasho had gone, "how could you have mailed that package? According to Maureen, she was with you all night."

"Ha! Not likely," Hannes said, barking out a nasty laugh.

"Be quiet," Kaz ordered him. "Remember, your money holds little value for me. I would much prefer to rid the world of you right now."

"You must be rich, eh?" Hannes replied, eyeing Kaz. "It takes a rich man to say money doesn't matter. And as for this one, I knew right away. Fifteen years on the vice squad in Berlin, and you can tell."

Pieces started falling into place, but I let Victor explain.

"I was not with Maureen that night. I was with Henri," Victor said, holding his head high and ignoring Hannes. "Maureen is a dear friend. She has covered for us on many occasions."

"You're homosexual," I said, keeping my voice neutral.

"Yes. Henri and I had been . . . involved . . . for some time. Very few people knew. But Hannes found out early on. We'd both been paying blackmail to him for the past year," Victor said, his voice rising in anger as he stared at his blackmailer.

"Really, let me shoot him now," Kaz said, leveling his gaze at Hannes. I held up my hand.

"Listen, Victor, I don't have anything against you personally, but isn't that the chance you take? Everyone knows homosexuals are prone to blackmail. That's why the army or the government won't take them." Victor didn't answer. He sighed, shaking his head.

"Oh, Billy, don't be so boringly bourgeois," Kaz said. "It's not as if it isn't all around you, for heaven's sake."

"Where?"

"Well, I'd say a good part of General Eisenhower's WAC staff for a start. You don't see him getting rid of them, do you?"

"What?" That was news to me. "Sorry, but I didn't work vice long enough to become an expert, like Hannes. I don't know any homosexuals."

"Of course you do," Victor said.

"Present company excluded," I said, not wanting to give offense. Victor had been a stand-up guy so far, and I didn't want to make it any harder on him for being the way he was. He couldn't help it. Could he? I didn't know much about guys who were queer for other guys, and didn't really want to. I knew a lot of cops back in Boston who hated them and seemed to go out of their way to arrest them whenever they could. Me, I didn't even like thinking about it, and I had to wonder about those cops who did.

"No, what I mean is that you do know plenty of homosexuals, men and women. But they must keep it a secret. It's a dangerous world," Victor said.

"That's my point," I said. "You're creating a danger to the OSS and Operation Safehaven. It's bad enough Hannes blackmailed you, but at least that was only for money. What if Krauch knew? He'd want you to betray your country."

"Billy, if a man is going to betray his country, it's not because of who he loves. You're either a traitor or you're not. Look at Hannes. He believes in nothing, and would betray his own brother for enough cold cash," Victor said. "It has nothing to do with who he has sex with."

"And look at Dulles," Kaz said. "The man openly betrays his own wife, making a show of it. Why does no one think him vulnerable to blackmail?"

"When did you get so . . . ?" I was at a loss for what I thought Kaz was.

"Tolerant?" Kaz said, jumping in. "Who are you to judge Victor or Henri? What has either of them done but work for what is right? I wish I had done so years ago, when I watched my friend Lucek get beaten at school because the older boys thought him not masculine enough," Kaz said. "I believed I was too weak and sickly to stand up for him. But I was scared, I must now admit, to my great shame."

"What happened to Lucek?" Victor asked.

"He died," Kaz said. "After we both went to university. He was not one to keep who he was hidden; he had a great joy inside him, but also a great sadness at how the world treated him. The constant taunting, the abuse, and the fear of betrayal, it all became too much of a burden. Perhaps also the loneliness, with no one to speak up and defend him, not even his childhood friend. He took pills. He was so very smart; he would have been a brilliant scientist, if only he'd been left alone to live his life."

"I am sorry," Victor said.

"You never told me about Lucek," I said.

"Billy, you are a very good man, but like many Americans, quite provincial at times. I didn't want to explain Lucek, to justify his existence. He was a real person, a good friend, and so much more than an epithet to be casually tossed out."

"I'm sorry," I said. Then to Victor, realizing that he'd lost someone important. "I'm sorry, Victor. About Henri. He was a brave man to do what he did."

"He fought for what he believed in," Victor said, a tired smile of memory playing on his lips. "Nothing so unusual these days. Some of us fight with different weapons, that's all."

"How much did Hannes take from you?" I asked, in a bit of a hurry to steer the conversation away from Kaz's pain and my own quick judgments.

"In dollars, it came to about ten thousand, total, from both of us," Victor answered. "He'd followed us to the cabin—Dr. Moret's place— and taken photos. Very incriminating photographs. He threatened to mail them to Henri's bank and to Dulles. We both would have been ruined."

"Arrested, as well as ruined," I said.

"Not in Switzerland, anyway," Victor said. "A few years ago they abolished the laws against homosexual acts. Quite forward thinking for such a conservative country. But the scandal would have cost Henri dearly, and would put me at risk back in the States, as well as cost me my job. Dulles is the old-fashioned sort, at least when it comes to the behavior of others."

"You may not think well of me," Hannes piped up, "but this does prove one thing. I did not kill Henri Moret. He was too valuable to me alive. It must have been Krauch, I tell you! He has a vicious temper."

"Shut up," I said, wishing we'd dumped him in the river. But now I wanted to get Victor his money back, not to mention the photographs. It was the right thing to do, no matter how Victor handled his personal life. I knew the Nazis were sending homosexuals to concentration camps, along with all the other groups that didn't fit the Aryan bill. That alone should have been enough for me not to sit in judgment of him and Henri.

"You left before the killer struck?" Kaz said to Victor.

"Yes. I would always get up before dawn and leave by the rear stairs, to avoid suspicion. I left a little after five o'clock that morning. I went back to my place, and then mailed the package. I came back to Henri's apartment. Usually we'd go out for coffee before work. But instead I found him dead." He buried his face in his hands. The room went quiet. Even Hannes.

Then came the pounding at the door.

CHAPTER TWENTY-EIGHT

FISTS HAMMERED AGAINST the downstairs door. I rushed to the window and saw two black cars marked *Polizei* in the street and guys in raincoats banging against the entrance. Kaz was already at the door, checking the hall. He shook his head. No way out.

The knocking stopped, and in seconds the stairway was filled with pounding feet and shouts in German. Hannes leaned back in the bed and held out his bound hands. He didn't seem the least bit surprised.

"The landlady," I said as the cops burst into the room. Hannes nodded, admiring of his own forethought. I raised my hands in surrender.

We were searched as Hannes was untied. A big guy with beefy jowls took my revolver and held it on me, jabbering in German. Kaz was getting the same treatment, and he translated. They wanted the contents of our pockets on the table.

"Keep to the same story," I said, nodding my head as if in answer. I tossed my wallet next to the cigarette case, still on the table. Then they patted us down. One of the uniformed cops gathered up the wallets and the silver case, which brought Hannes to his feet, pointing and claiming the case was his.

Given our situation, there wasn't anything left to say. The cop politely handed it to him.

The three of us were roughly bundled downstairs as one plain-clothes detective stayed with Hannes, doubtless taking a statement.

We passed the landlady in the sitting room, wringing her hands and muttering. I wondered how much Hannes had paid her to call the cops if he ever showed up in trouble. Or maybe she was another loyal SVV auxiliary.

I was stuffed into the rear seat of one their cars, in between a young kid in uniform and an older detective with a florid face and breath smelling of schnapps. The midnight shift was often populated by rookies and cops no one else wanted to work with, and I saw no reason for things to be different in Bern. The detective took a half-smoked cigar out of his pocket and lit up, puffing it to life. I knew an old-timer at the Boston PD who'd do the same thing. He'd knock the glowing ashes off a stogie and stuff it in his pocket for later. His nickname was Pockets since he burned so many holes in his. He worked the late night shift as well.

It was a short ride to police headquarters. This time we didn't go through the front door. The cars drove around back and parked too close to the morgue for my taste, but pretty soon we were hustled through an entrance and down a dank hallway to the holding cells. The three of us were tossed into the same cell, inhabited by a snoring bum and a bucket he'd been sick in.

"Delightful accommodations," Kaz said, looking at the single wooden bench with the sleeping form stretched out on it.

"Keep to the same basic story," I said to Victor. "Hannes is a pal, he got nasty drunk, we tied his hands for his own good and brought him home."

"They didn't seem terribly surprised to find three armed men in his room," Kaz said, leaning against the bars. "Nor do they seem to care that since we are together, we can get our stories straight."

"If Hannes had an arrangement with his landlady, he could have given her a specific name to ask for, an SVV contact, perhaps," Victor said. "Or simply a man he bribed."

"It doesn't matter," I said, grasping the iron bars. "They could let us out in ten minutes, and it wouldn't change the fact that Hannes is out there, with the invoice. And his money."

"We do have one advantage," Kaz said.

"What? We don't even have our own bucket."

"Hannes will make contact with Huber," Victor said, faster on the uptake than I was.

"Right," I said. "And soon. I bet he's nervous after his close call. If I were in his shoes, I'd make a quick sale to Huber, take my loot, and clear out."

"We won't be the only ones thinking that," Kaz said. "If Hannes has contacts with the police, Krauch is also certain to as well. He will find out where Hannes was hiding, and that he has the invoice."

"Hmmm," I said, slipping down to the cold tile floor and slumping against the bars. "Maybe we can work it to our advantage. If we could get Krauch and Hannes in the same place, we might be able to take both of them."

"And get the invoice back, if we time it right," Kaz said, joining me on the floor.

"Not to mention his cash," I said. "If he was in cahoots with his landlady, he might have had it stashed somewhere in her place. But he'd probably move it, now that we know about it."

"Perhaps not," Kaz said. "Where would he hide it? I doubt he'd use a bank. Too many people know him."

"If I were in his shoes, I'd pack up my luggage and check it at the railroad station. Then sell the invoice and skip town on the next train," I said. "Although Krauch may have the station watched." Actually, if I were Hannes, I'd clear out right now. But he was greedy; I knew there'd be no way he'd pass up making a quick profit.

"I know someone on the Red Cross staff," Victor said. "He may be willing to alert us to any contact by Hannes."

"He'd have to be a trusted confidant to have that information," I said. "You sure about this guy?"

"Remember the guy I was looking for at the reception? That's him. Vadim Fournier has Huber's trust and is one of his top money men. But I happen to know he has gambling debts. He's a lot more careful with other people's money than he is with his own. If I suggest we might be able to intercept Hannes without turning over the cash, he may be amenable."

"Meaning he'll expect to pocket the proceeds," I said. "Which is fine, except that we don't plan on turning over the invoice to Huber."

"One problem at a time," Victor said.

"We could also bring in Krauch," Kaz said.

"We grab the invoice, let Krauch take Hannes, and let Victor's pal snatch the cash? Inspired," I said. "Except that lets Krauch off scot-free."

"No, we will figure something out," Victor said, pressing his head against the cold iron bars. "It's Krauch I want, for killing Henri. Then the invoice, to finish the work Henri began. You can have Hannes."

"We'll get them," I said. "I promise. For Henri and all those whose lives Hannes destroyed. And you'll be there, Victor. Count on it."

"I will," he said, moving to the corner of the cell, grasping the bars until his knuckles turned white. He stayed upright, tears falling to the tiles at his feet. We laid our heads on our arms and left him to his grief.

"Wake up, my friends, and follow me." Inspector Emil Escher stood outside the cell, motioning for a guard to unlock the door. I got up stiffly, giving Victor a hand to do the same. Kaz stretched, as if he'd had a good night's sleep. Bloodstains dotted Victor's shirtsleeves, where his bandages had fallen away. He hurriedly put on his jacket, wincing but waving off my offer of help.

The door opened, and we filed out, the original occupant trailing behind us. The guard pushed him back in, but I gave the bum points for trying. Escher led us to his office, where a carafe of coffee awaited. The man knew how to organize a jailbreak.

"No charges are being pressed," Escher said as he poured. "Which means you are free to go."

"Our pistols?" Victor asked.

"My, my, Victor, I thought you were a financial man, not a spy," Escher said. He opened his drawer and set the three weapons on his desk.

"It comes from associating with these two fellows," Victor said, his tone lighthearted. For the first time, I wondered at the price he had to pay to hide his true feelings. Escher was kidding around, but Victor had to play a part to hide what he felt. It would have torn me apart. I can't pretend to fathom what makes a guy want to roll in the hay with another guy, but I did grasp the desire for revenge when a loved one was harmed. More than most, actually, and I suddenly found myself feeling protective of Victor, his secrets, and his great loss.

"You know what's been going on?" I asked Escher. Nice and open-ended, so we didn't give anything away.

"I know everybody wants something. You want some document. So do Krauch and Hannes. I guess you came close last night but Hannes managed to get the police involved," Escher said, dropping a cube of sugar into his coffee.

"Do you know Hannes is wanted by the Gestapo?" I asked. "Krauch is after him. Apparently they tumbled to his scheme to enrich himself. The Nazis like to steal gold, but don't take kindly to one of their own stealing from them."

"No, I did not know that," Escher said. "Although it explains why Hannes is nowhere to be found."

"Your people are searching for him?" Victor asked.

"No, since we have no hard evidence of a crime. The officer who took his statement went back this morning, and Hannes was gone. The woman who runs the *pensione* said he left before dawn with bags packed."

"She was in on it," I said. "He must have paid her to call the police if it looked like he was in trouble."

"Interesting," Escher said. "Do you think he killed Henri Moret?"

"No," Victor said. "I am certain it was not him. Krauch did it. According to Hannes, he easily loses his temper."

"I get the impression you all know much more about this mysterious document," Escher said.

"You may not want to know," Kaz said. "That way no one can pressure you."

"I may already be in trouble for letting you go, not to mention returning your firearms. But I have no need of additional trouble, so please finish your coffee and then Lasho will pick you up out front. I took the liberty of notifying *Herr* Dulles. He was most anxious to speak with you," Escher said, draining the last of his coffee.

"I bet," I said. "But first, a change of clothes and a shave."

"You may want to bathe," Escher said, sniffing the air. "Dulles seemed mad enough already."

Lasho was waiting in the Peugeot out front, which was a big improvement over our arrival at the rear entrance last night. We dropped Victor off at his place, warning him about how it had been tossed. He planned to call his pal at the IRC and gauge his interest in our scheme. He'd meet us at a café near Dulles's office once he got that squared away. At the Golden Eagle, Kaz and I washed up and changed, then grabbed a couple hours' shuteye. Time was tight, but we had to have our wits about us. After more coffee and food, I felt almost human. We walked to Dulles's place, taking the vineyard path to the discreet back door.

As I laid my hand on the latch, the door opened and a tall man with his hat brim pulled down and his coat collar turned up nearly barreled into us.

"Excuse me, gentlemen," Hans Bernd Gisevius said, in his precise German accent. He held open the door for us, his finger to his lips in a gesture of secrecy.

"What is the German vice counsel doing visiting Allen Dulles?" Kaz asked as the door closed behind us. "It was odd that he was so friendly with that Jewish lawyer we met at the reception, and this is odder still."

"Odd is the order of the day in Switzerland," I said, taking the stairs to Dulles's office.

"The prodigal children return at last," Maureen Conaty said from her usual perch on Dulles's desk. She slid off, tapping her cigarette on a cut-glass ashtray. "We were wondering what trouble you'd get into next."

"The quiet kind, I hope," Dulles growled. "Not another Wild West shoot-out. Have a seat and tell me what's happened. The short version."

"First," I said, sitting on the comfortable couch and hoping to stay awake, "we saw Captain Bowman at Wauwilermoos. It's a pit. Americans are treated miserably, and unfortunately there's no chance of a breakout. There are too many guards. It's situated out in the open, on wet marshy land. You can barely walk without sinking in up to your ankles; a tunnel would be impossible, and there's no cover outside the wire for a hundred yards."

"Is anyone doing anything about it?" Kaz asked. Dulles looked like he was unused to being asked such a direct question.

"I'm in touch with the US military attaché at our embassy," he said. "But there's little we can accomplish. The Swiss do have a legal basis for placing escaped internees in a penal camp."

"The commandant is a sadist, and his second-in-command isn't much better. Pro-Nazi to the core," I said.

"I'll do what I can," Dulles said. "I was hoping there was a chance to organize an escape, but that seems ill-advised."

"Why don't you ask your German pal, Gisevius?" I said, watching for a reaction. Dulles gripped his pipe so tightly it quivered between his teeth. Maureen raised her eyebrows and shook her head.

"Don't ever mention that outside this room," he said, pointing at both of us. "If you do, you'll cause a good man great harm."

"Boys, you do realize we run a spy outfit here," Maureen said.

"Okay, sorry," I said, holding up my hand. "It was hard to leave those guys in that camp. The food package we brought never got to them, and you should see the barracks. Open latrines in the same room where they sleep."

"Understood," Dulles said. "Now, catch me up on the rest."

I told him about our visit to Doctor Moret, and the Gestapo agent Ernst, who told us about Krauch's hangout, the *Altes Keller*. I sort of apologized for letting Ernst live, but Dulles was fine with us keeping the body count low. He'd already heard about the Gestapo arrest warrant for Hannes, and I didn't ask how.

I reviewed our trip to *Alpthal* and finding evidence of Victor having been taken prisoner. He asked how Hannes had known about the hideout, and I said someone must have tipped him off. No reason to go into Hannes's previous trip with a camera. I went over spotting Hannes with Victor at the hotel, how Victor had broken free, and the late-night chase in the rain. I was embarrassed to admit how Krauch had gotten the drop on me, but left that topic quickly and described Lasho's snatch and grab.

Dulles had heard the cops brought us in, but didn't know the whole story. I filled him in on Hannes's ruse with his landlady and that Escher had sprung us a few hours ago.

"Do you still have this document everyone's been after?" Dulles said, leaning forward. "What's in it?"

"We don't have it. Hannes does. It was stashed in a silver cigarette case, and he claimed it was his as the cops were dragging us away. They weren't in a mood to listen to us and they let him keep it. Right now he's in the wind, on the run from everyone. But we have an idea how to get it back." A rather vague idea, but he didn't need to know that.

"Damn it, man! What's in the document?" Dulles thundered.

"It is an invoice. For slave labor in the form of two hundred Ukrainians, purchased by *Alusuisse* from the SS. Max Huber, as president, has his name on the invoice," Kaz said. "They were delivered to the *Alusuisse* factory in Singen, southern Germany."

"My god, the head of the International Red Cross, buying slaves from the Nazis," Maureen said, for once at a loss for a snappy comment. "No wonder the Gestapo called in the cavalry."

"And no wonder Henri was murdered for taking it," I said.

"He wasn't happy with the treatment his uncle received," Maureen said, lighting another smoke and admiring her red nail polish as she blew out the match. "This would do nicely as revenge, wouldn't it?" Her eyes were on Dulles, waiting for a reaction.

"Hannes has the invoice and is looking to sell it back to Huber?" Dulles asked, his tone not giving anything away.

"Yes," I said. "We have an idea about how to intercept him. Victor has a friend on Huber's staff who may be able to give us information about when Hannes is going to deliver. We'll be there." I didn't want to go into details, since we didn't have any.

Dulles knocked the dead ash out of his pipe and filled it with fresh tobacco. He lit a match and puffed at it like a locomotive building up a head of steam. After he got it going and released a stream of smoke, he finally fixed his attention on us.

"Don't," he said. "Don't be there. Don't interfere in any manner. That's an order."

"You want Hannes to get away with this?" I asked, not believing what I was hearing.

"I hope Georg Hannes gets hit by a bus, right after he returns that invoice to Huber," Dulles said, leaning across his desk and pointing at us with his pipe. "We're not in the business of embarrassing one of Switzerland's luminaries. We're in the business of winning this war, and right now, Operation Safehaven is a big part of ensuring that the Nazis aren't left with enough resources to start another war in twenty years. Or did you forget why you were sent here?"

"Two days ago, we were worried about the Germans coming after you, like they went for Henri," I said. "Safehaven is one thing, but matters escalated when they killed Henri."

"No, matters escalated when Henri Moret stole that document for personal reasons. Understandably so, but he unleashed this chain of events. Events, I might add, that may conspire against the success of Safehaven." He relaxed back into his chair and motioned for Maureen to jump in and explain the obvious.

"Listen, you two did a great job finding Victor and tracking down Hannes," she said, leaning forward as she crossed her legs, which I guess was meant to take our minds off the bad news she was about to deliver. "But remember, the purpose of Safehaven is to prevent the transfer of Nazi wealth outside of our control, and to ensure those funds are available to help rebuild Europe."

"Sure, but that doesn't mean we have to cover up Huber contracting with the SS for slave labor," I said. As soon as I did, I realized what the hardball answer to that would be. Yes we do. But Maureen was going to deliver it sugar-coated.

"We've been able to secure a certain amount of cooperation from the Swiss banking community," she said. "The fact that the war is going our way doesn't hurt, but some of these bankers are truly concerned about aiding the Nazis and think their banks may have gone too far. And truth be told, Henri's death has garnered some sympathy, since it's been attributed to the SVV."

"Hannes was sure it was Krauch," Kaz put in.

"Perhaps," Maureen said, raising a finger as if to emphasize the point. "That's one reason the Gestapo uses their SVV cronies: to take the blame when necessary, to avoid a diplomatic incident. But the important thing to understand is that we depend a great deal upon the Red Cross. Allied POWs are under their protection, and we can't risk a scandal threatening our only link to all those prisoners. This revelation regarding Max Huber, a revered statesman and humanitarian, would send everyone running for cover. The very people we depend on for the success of Safehaven would have nothing to do with us."

"Which means less money for refugees and rebuilding after the war," Dulles said, pipe firmly in place between clenched teeth. "And more money for the top Nazis who manage to escape justice. That's not what you want, is it?"

"Put like that, what can I say?" I glanced at Kaz. He managed to look nonchalant. There wasn't much else to do when a heavy hitter like Dulles came after you, allied with Maureen and her soft, persuasive murmurs. The fix was in, and like always, the rich and the powerful came up roses. "So what's next?"

"We're putting a plan in place to get you two out of Switzerland," Dulles said. "I'm not saying it's your fault, but things got out of control very quickly as soon as you both came on the scene, and we need to contain the situation. Come back tomorrow morning and we'll brief you. Meanwhile, get some rest and stay out of trouble."

Dulles picked up a file and started leafing through it, a signal that he was done with us. The feeling was mutual.

"I almost forgot," Dulles said, looking up suddenly from his papers and glancing at his wristwatch. "I've got something for Lasho. He should be here shortly, so wait a few minutes if you have time." As if we had other pressing business to attend to now that he'd given us our walking papers.

"Let's have a farewell dinner tonight, boys," Maureen said as we waited, standing around awkwardly as Dulles perused his paperwork. "I'll meet you at your hotel."

"Sure, let's include Victor," I said. "Since you and he are such an item."

"I don't have items, Billy," she said. "I have fun. It's a dangerous world, so why not? But do bring Victor along; he's fun as well."

"I'll tell him. We're meeting him at a café for lunch." A knock sounded at the door, and Lasho entered with another tall, swarthy guy in tow. He looked vaguely familiar. He had dark hair, a prominent nose, bushy eyebrows, and a serious expression as he glanced around the room.

"Have a seat with me, Moe," Maureen cooed, leading him to the couch. Moe. I thought I knew the guy, but I couldn't place him.

"Lasho, I have something for you," Dulles announced, handing over a passport marked *Repubblica Sociale Italiana* and bearing the insignia of Mussolini's fascist party. "It's in your name and perfectly legal."

"Thank you," Lasho said, flipping through the pages and checking the photograph that Maureen had taken of him a few days ago. "Is this good in Switzerland?"

"Absolutely," Maureen said. "It's a valid identification and would also be good in northern Italy, where Mussolini still holds power, as long as the Germans allow, anyway. Not that I'd recommend a visit to Milan or Venice these days."

"It will allow you to stay on and work with us," Dulles said. "If you wish."

"I will stay. It is a fascist passport, but it is better than nothing," Lasho said. "I am in your debt. All of you."

"This was issued by the Italian consulate in Berlin," Kaz said, looking at the document. "These stamps appear quite real."

"They are," Maureen said. "I told you, we're a spy outfit. That's what spies do, isn't it, Allen?"

"Only the great ones," he said, gracing us with a rare smile. Gisevius. German Vice Counsel Hans Bernd Gisevius had probably delivered the passport minutes before. Nice to know Dulles had an inside man. Nice for Lasho, that is. I kept that notion to myself, not wanting to speak up with a stranger in the room.

But was he a stranger? He looked so damn familiar. Moe, Maureen had called him. She was whispering to him, nodding in our direction, probably explaining we were a couple of bums getting the heave-ho, and to pay us no mind. I stared at Moe, hoping to catch a glimpse of recognition, but no dice.

Catch.

I knew exactly who he was.

"You're Moe Berg," I said. "I saw you play at Fenway. Back in '39, I think."

"You're among the few who did," he said, looking up from his murmured conversation with Maureen. "I played fewer than thirty games that season."

"What is Fenway?" Kaz asked. "And what game did you play there?"

I introduced Kaz and myself and started to launch into a description of Boston baseball when Dulles harrumphed and nodded to the exit. We took the hint, telling Moe we'd wait for him in the vineyard.

"A baseball player?" Kaz asked as we sat on a bench under the spreading vines. "Visiting an OSS spymaster's office in neutral Switzerland? How strange."

"Maybe not," I said. "The press called him the brainiest man in baseball. Also the strangest, now that I think about it. He speaks eight or nine languages, went to Princeton, and then earned a law degree. Kind of a Renaissance man."

"Is he as good at baseball as he is at languages?" Kaz asked.

"No, unfortunately. He's a good catcher, not so great at hitting. But don't let on I said that."

"Don't worry, Billy. I am not even sure who hits what in baseball. And please, don't try explaining it to me again. Now, shouldn't we get to the café to meet Victor? I could tell by your instant acquiescence that you have a plan in mind. If so, it has to happen soon."

"You're right. But we'll need Lasho, and it seems Dulles has teamed him up with Moe."

"We may need to convince Lasho," Kaz said. "He may feel loyalty to Dulles now that he's given him that passport. It is life itself within these borders."

"Maybe," I said. "I'll try not to put him in a difficult spot."

"What about Moe?" Kaz asked.

"Good question. If Lasho will help out, all we need is for Moe to keep quiet."

"Are you sure you want to go through with this?" Kaz asked, looking out over the river flowing past the sloped vineyard. "We are about to take our leave of this place, and I shall not miss much about Switzerland."

"I'm sure," I said. "I don't like what these bankers have gotten away with, and I can't stand people like Huber making believe they're something they're not. I sure as hell don't like the Gestapo stealing whatever money their victims managed to put away for their families."

"The victims number in the thousands and thousands," Kaz said. "The crime of theft surely pales against what is being done in the extermination camps. Are you sure it is worth it?"

"I can't imagine how many people are dying in those camps. But I have seen Lowenberg's body, dumped like trash into the river. I've listened to Hannes justify his actions, as if sausage and potatoes were payment enough for all he's taken from the Lowenbergs of the world."

"Do you think Dulles is right? That we may upset some delicate balance and ruin the chances for Safehaven's success?" Kaz asked.

"I don't think that's what this is all about. I say Dulles can't bear the thought of Huber's dirty laundry being aired. After all, they travel in the same circles. They're all part of the rich elite who run things. Sure, if Dulles thought there was anything useful in it, he wouldn't hesitate. But since the truth holds no value for him unless it serves his own purposes, he can't be bothered. The old-boy network rules kick in, and Huber is safe to pocket his profits from slave labor. It's not an applecart they care to upset."

"Billy, I didn't know you were such a firebrand. Count me in," Kaz said, his grin a half grimace where it met his terrible scar. "What do we do?"

"Wait for Lasho and Moe Berg," I said. I needed Lasho's help, and I hoped either he wouldn't be escorting Moe full time, or that the strangest man in baseball would be willing to go along with a strange adventure. Strange and dangerous.

A half hour later they exited from the rear door. Lasho looked serious. Moe, I couldn't read.

"Want to grab a cup of coffee?" I asked as they approached.

"Only if they put brandy in it," Lasho said. Moe smiled, but it was a wistful smile, as if he were remembering another place and time.

"Sure," Moe said. "As long as we can stop for some newspapers."

"I haven't seen any English-language papers," I said as we rose to walk the path up to the main road.

"Not a problem," Moe said. "I could read one in Sanskrit if I had to."

"*Wie war diene Riese?*" Kaz asked. Whatever the question, Moe answered and they were off to the races in several languages by the time we came to a newsstand. Moe grabbed four papers, two in German, one each in French and Italian.

"Impressive," Kaz said as we approached the café. "Where did you study?"

"Princeton and Columbia," Moe said. "Languages come pretty easily to me, I have to admit."

"Like baseball?" Kaz asked. I was pretty sure Kaz didn't even know what a baseball looked like, but he was sounding out the guy. We took an outdoor table, at a corner farthest from the other customers.

"Sanskrit is easy, baseball is hard," Moe said. "But my playing days are over. It's a young man's game, after all. I coached for the Red Sox for a couple of years, then the war came along, which offered a more interesting diversion." He went silent as a waiter came to the table. We ordered coffee, and I kept an eye out for Victor.

"And the war brought you here?" I asked, leaving the question as to what he was doing here hanging in the air like a pop-up fly ball. "Meaning the OSS, right?"

"I have a job to do," was all Moe said, leaning back and opening his jacket slightly. He wore a shoulder holster. Kaz and I did the same, which got a laugh out of him.

"Why bring you in when they have us?" I asked, not mentioning that we were being thrown out by our ears.

"How much do you know about the uncertainty principle in quantum mechanics?" Moe asked, his voice a whisper. I could feel a blank look spread across my face.

"You mean Werner Heisenberg's uncertainty principle?" Kaz asked. Of course Kaz would know. I could see that Moe hadn't expected that.

"Sorry," Moe said, waving one hand as if to erase his question. "I shouldn't have said anything."

"You can trust these men," Lasho said. "I do."

"Dulles wasn't so complimentary," Moe said. "But then again, I can't say I warmed to the man."

"Will one of you explain this uncertainty thing?" I asked. We all were quiet as the waiter delivered the coffee.

"It has to do with the limits to which certain physical properties of an object can be understood. Basically, the more precisely the position of a particle is known, the less precisely its momentum can be determined, and vice versa, of course," Moe said. Of course.

"What Heisenberg stated, back in the twenties, I think," Kaz said, "was that the mere observation of a system in quantum mechanics disturbs the system itself, enough to make it impossible to know everything about the system." As Kaz finished delivering this statement, to which I was nodding as if I'd understood any of it, I saw him set down his coffee cup and stare at Moe. He'd figured something out. I was observing him, but I was pretty uncertain about what was going on.

"Werner Heisenberg," Kaz said, his voice also settling into a whisper. "Head of the Prussian Academy of Sciences. In charge of the German atomic weapons program."

"They can be trusted, you're certain?" Moe said to Lasho.

"I have already said I trust them. With my life, which they saved, and perhaps my soul," he said.

"Do not repeat that name," Moe said, referring to Heisenberg. "The individual in question is traveling to Zurich to lecture at the university there. Dulles has arranged an invitation. It has to be someone who knows enough about quantum theory to pass muster as a scientist or student. That's me."

"The smartest man in baseball," I said.

"I can't stand that moniker," Moe said. "But I fit the bill."

"Are you going to kidnap him?" I asked over the rim of my cup as I sipped the hot joe.

"No. I'll listen to him. If he says anything that leads me to believe they're close to an atom bomb, I shoot him dead," Moe said. "If not, Lasho here drives me back to Bern and I make my report to Dulles, and Heisenberg goes back home."

"What is an atom bomb?" Lasho asked, his forehead furrowed. I was glad there was one other person who knew less about this than I did.

"A single bomb that can destroy an entire city, if it works. No one knows. One scientist worries that a chain reaction will ignite the atmosphere. Everywhere," Moe said. He poured more coffee and added a cube of sugar, as calm as if discussing the chance of rain.

"Then you must shoot him," Lasho said. "Many times."

"If necessary, I will," Moe said. "It's my own uncertainty principle."

"Position and momentum, those are the two factors at work?" Kaz asked.

"Right. The theory states that if you measure one of those values accurately, the less accurately you can know the other. But we're talking about atoms and electrons, not everyday objects."

"It seems to apply to the case we are involved with as well," Kaz said. "We were followed recently by a Gestapo agent. He took a shot at us, right outside the Red Cross office." He raised an eyebrow in my direction, daring me to follow his logic.

"We were busy with momentum, trying to get away from him," I said. "So we didn't pay attention to position. It was the Red Cross office. That's why he shot at us."

"We simply wanted to escape through the back door," Kaz explained. "But the agent must have thought we were after evidence of Huber and his transactions with the SS. He was likely under orders to stop any investigation at all costs."

"Maybe they caught wind of Henri's plan, or at least someone's interest in the invoices," I said.

"Which is why the bank arranged for Henri to deliver the papers to Huber at the reception," Kaz said, warming to the idea. "It would have been more secret, except for the fact that it was Henri himself who was after that information."

"Whoa, fellas," Moe said. "I know seven languages, but I'm not following you at all."

So I gave him the nutshell version. Our route into Switzerland, courtesy of Lasho. Kaz's connections with the banks and our original mission. Lowenberg in the river. The attempt on our lives, followed by the reception, Henri lifting the invoice, the late-night tail, Henri's death and the missing evidence. Hannes and his hidden loot, along with Krauch, who was after him for betraying the thieves of the Third Reich. Our search for Victor, leaving out the prison camp at Wauwilermoos and Victor's private life—for the sake of brevity and tact—finishing up with our version of musical chairs with the *Alusuisse* invoice for slave labor.

"You're a trio of troublemakers, I can see that," Moe said, his dark eyes studying us. "Why is Dulles sending you back?"

"He wants to make nice with the Swiss banks and figures a scandal involving Huber would get in the way. So he gets a free pass," I said.

"I have not known you long, Billy," Lasho said, draining his coffee. "But I do know you cannot give up so easily. And you, Baron, I know you don't want to leave any Gestapo alive. Excepting our friend Ernst, of course." That took a little more explanation.

"Do you have a plan?" Moe asked.

"I hope so," I said. "And here comes our best hope." Victor hurried over to the table, waving away the hovering waiter. I introduced Moe and vouched for him.

"Not the Moe Berg who played for the Washington Senators?" Victor asked. "My dad took me to see you back in—"

"Don't make me feel old, kid," Moe said, holding up a hand to interrupt Victor. "And lay off the soft soap. Tell these boys what you've got. They have their hopes pinned on you."

"Okay," he said, taking a deep breath. "It's on, eight o'clock tonight."

"Hannes?" Kaz asked, glancing around to see if anyone was close.

"Yes. I talked to my pal Vadim this morning. He's on the finance side at *Alusuisse*. He's in worse shape than I thought. His gambling debts are heavy, and from what he alluded to, he may have borrowed money from work."

"In other words, he's willing to cooperate," I said. A guy with his hand in the till is the perfect accomplice when it comes to cash in a briefcase.

"Quite willing, once I outlined our plan," Victor said. "Hannes made contact with the Swiss National Bank, and they communicated with Huber."

"Rich men do not do such work," Lasho said. "This is where your friend comes in?"

"Exactly. Huber turned the job over to his finance department. Fournier was among the select few who knew about the slave labor already, so it's no big risk for Huber to use him," Victor said. "You were right, Billy. Hannes is cashing in cheap. Thirty thousand Swiss francs."

"About six thousand dollars," Moe said. "Pretty good for traveling money."

"I'm pretty sure he does plan on traveling," Victor said. "The meet is set up for eight o'clock tonight. At the University of Bern's Botanical Gardens. But Vadim said one of Huber's bodyguards is going with him."

"Smart. Huber can't afford for Fournier to get mugged on the way to the payoff. And the botanical garden is a good place for a swap, from Hannes's perspective," I said. "Lots of open space for an approach and getaway, plus big plants to hide behind."

"And it's right across the river from the train station," Victor said. "I'd bet Hannes is carrying a key to a luggage locker, like you thought."

"I will help you," Lasho said, his face impassive.

"I can't endanger my mission," Moe said. "And I'll need Lasho to get me there. But if we can help with a good chance of not getting knocked out of commission, then tell us what to do."

"Moe is right," Lasho said. "We must stop the man who will destroy the sky. But tonight, we help you."

"Okay. Are we all in?" I looked to Kaz and Victor.

"All in," Victor said. "For Henri, and all the others." Kaz put his hand on Victor's shoulder and nodded his assent.

"Good. Here's the plan."

CHAPTER TWENTY-NINE

THE *Altes Keller* was on the Postgasse, one of the narrow streets in the old quarter, not far from where Krauch had intercepted me and grabbed the invoice. Before Lasho took it from him and Hannes snatched it back when the cops hauled us off to the clink. The damn thing had a complicated itinerary, which put me and Krauch on the same side in this scavenger hunt. Or at least not on opposite sides, for the moment.

Altes Keller meant "old cellar," according to Kaz, who'd gone off to scout the botanical garden along with the quickest route to the train station. I had another reason for going in alone. I didn't want to tempt Kaz to unload his Webley at this gathering of Nazi goons. A guy who'd lost his entire family to the killing squads of the SS couldn't be expected to keep his finger off the trigger when presented with targets in close proximity.

I had enough of a problem myself.

I spotted the sign for the *Altes Keller* ahead, under the covered archway above the sidewalk. It was a small sign, over a flight of stone steps leading down to a brightly painted red door. As I went in, it took a second for my eyes to adjust to the darkened, musty gloom. Old cellar was a pretty good description. A bar ran along a brick wall, with barely enough room to pass by a few gray-hairs nursing steins of beer.

Past the bar, a room opened up in the back. Rough-hewn wooden tables and chairs made it look almost homey, but the black, red, and white Nazi banner hanging from the ceiling spoiled the effect. For me, but not for the nine men gathered at the tables, eating and drinking their lunch.

Raucous laughter faded into silence as I entered. Daylight filtered in from casement windows, as hanging lights wreathed in cigarette smoke cast the drinkers in a feeble yellow glow. Most of the men leaned back, brushing jackets aside, ready to grab iron. I tried not to startle anyone.

"*Herr* Boyle, what an unexpected pleasure," a familiar voice spoke from a far corner. Krauch. He snapped out an order and I was frisked. Pretty professional, no unnecessary cheap shots, which I appreciated. One goon took my revolver while another patted down my pockets, shaking his head as he came up empty. He shoved me toward Krauch, who lit a cigarette and smoothed back his pomaded hair. He nodded to the guy at his table, who moved off, leaning against the wall, his gaze fixed on me.

"So you do not have the document with you," Krauch said, spitting out a bit of stray tobacco. "Pity. I presume you wish to sell it?"

"I don't have it," I said, taking the vacated seat, a plate smeared with congealed grease before me. "But I know who does. And where he will be tonight."

"Why are you telling me this? And why here, where we could carry you out the rear door, never to be seen again?"

"Because I know the invoice is far more valuable than my life. Or yours," I said, staring hard into his dark eyes.

"You are correct," he said. "But you did not answer my first question. Why come to me?"

"I want Hannes," I said.

"As do I. He is a traitor and must be made an example of."

"He won't be a happy man if I get hold of him, I guarantee you that," I said.

"So you are proposing we work together?" Krauch ground out his cigarette in the remains of his food. "I help you capture Hannes in return for the invoice?"

"Yeah," I said, nodding. I watched Krauch carefully, studying his face, waiting for the next question.

"Why do you want him so badly? For that Jew he killed?"

"No," I said, shaking my head as if a mere Jew would be no concern of mine. "For killing Henri Moret."

His head moved back, slightly. A faint but sharp intake of breath, like a guy drawing to an inside straight. Krauch wouldn't last long in a poker game. He had a double tell, and what it told me was that he'd bought my line.

"The banker, yes," he said, a false frown of sadness passing over his face. "I thought that might have been Hannes. He often carries things to an extreme. But Moret was a homosexual, you know? Perhaps he made an improper advance." The frown turned to a smirk.

As much as he liked placing the blame for Henri's death conveniently on Georg Hannes, he couldn't resist the comment. After all, Jews and homosexuals, among others, were not supermen like Krauch and his crew. You could hardly blame Hannes for losing his temper.

"I know," I said. "It's no matter."

"Oh, are you ... one of those?" Krauch sneered as made a comment in German. His men laughed, like any bunch of sycophants listening to the boss tell a lousy joke.

"Don't worry, Siegfried, you're not that good looking," I said. It occurred to me I was glad Victor wasn't here with his pistol either. Then I realized I was glad they'd taken mine. I never gave much thought to guys who liked guys—other than the occasional wisecrack, to tell the truth—but sitting with this Nazi clown as he made jokes about Henri didn't sit well. Not well at all.

"You are an amusing fellow, Boyle," Krauch said. "But tell me, what is your plan?"

"Do you agree? I get Hannes, you get the invoice. No double-cross," I said.

"You will do well to remember that requirement yourself. Yes, I agree. When we each have what we want, we part company. No trickery, Boyle."

"Agreed," I said, resisting the normal impulse to shake on it.

But then I decided it had to be done, for authenticity's sake. I stuck out my hand and grasped his clammy paw. He thought he'd made the deal of a lifetime. If he had any worries about the local cops tumbling to him as Henri's killer, they were now put to rest. Dollars to doughnuts he'd tell Inspector Escher himself that I'd gone after Hannes to avenge Henri's murder. All the time murmuring his regret that one of the Gestapo's finest had gone bad. Then he'd get a medal for being a good boy and pulling Huber's fat from the fire. It was even better than bringing in Hannes himself; he could count on me to eliminate the chief suspect in Henri's death, leaving him free of suspicion.

Right where I wanted him.

"Where and when?" Krauch said, all business.

"Nine o'clock tonight, the botanical gardens at the university. The entrance is right off the Lorrainebrücke, on the north side of the river," I said.

"I know it," Krauch said. "And now I know why you need our help. There are many exits and entrances to cover. Does *Herr* Dulles not have other men to call on?"

"They're all busy winning the war. We're only the second string," I said. I could see he didn't understand that, but I didn't bother explaining. "There's only three of us. Let's meet at the main entrance an hour before, at eight o'clock. Then we'll get in position."

"Three of you? But who is Hannes there to meet?"

"He thinks he's selling the invoice to Huber. One of Huber's men from *Alusuisse* is meeting him there with thirty thousand Swiss francs. We intercepted the message this morning."

"Who?" Krauch asked. It stood to reason he might know any number of Huber's business cronies.

"No, no," I said, wagging my finger. "We'll get Hannes long before the money man shows. Standard procedure to show up early and watch the meeting place, isn't it?"

"Yes, of course. We will be ready at eight o'clock. A nice, quiet affair is what we need. No gunfire, no local police. You didn't think I would go after the money, did you?"

"Steal money?" I said. "In Switzerland? The thought never crossed my mind."

Krauch translated, and we all enjoyed a good laugh over that one.

I LEFT THE *Altes Keller* with my revolver restored, along with my faith in the gullibility of the criminal class. Which is right where I placed Krauch and his cutthroat Gestapo crew. I'd given him what he wanted, three times over. Hannes, the invoice, and an iron-clad alibi for Henri's murder. He was probably having a good laugh right now, making his plans to grab Hannes and then go running to Huber with the invoice. Or to plug Hannes and lay the blame at my feet. Both of which would be toes up in the botanical garden if he had his way.

I believed him about the money, only because there'd be too many of his men involved to make a split worthwhile. Better to take an under-the-table finder's fee from Huber for saving him the payoff.

As I took a pedestrian bridge across the Aare River, it began to rain. Lightly at first, then turning to a constant patter, the dark gray sky a match for the tumbling water below. I hoofed it along the Uferweg, a gravel path at the river's edge, until I caught sight of the Lorrainebrücke ahead, its solid concrete arches a ghostly white as it spanned the river. Beyond it, I could see another bridge, steel girders nearly invisible in the slanting rain.

I left the Uferweg just before one of the entrances to the botanical garden and found the Café Fleuri where Kaz and I had planned to meet. Inside, I shook the rain off my trench coat and hung it up, joining Kaz in a booth near the fireplace. It was June, but the cold rain made me wish for a crackling fire.

"Did it go well?" Kaz asked.

"Perfectly," I said. "How about you?"

"There are three entrances to the gardens," Kaz said, leaning in across the table. "One you saw on the path by the river. Another is off this road, leading to the university buildings at the edge of the gardens. The other is the main entrance, which descends into the gardens from the road, right after the bridge."

"Is there much cover?"

"Not at the main entrance, no. The approach from either direction is on a sidewalk next to the open road. If he comes across the bridge, he'd be easy to spot. The same for the Uferweg, since it runs along the river. But as you'll see, the entrance off this road is lined with trees, and there are several buildings that give good cover. It is how I would make an approach," Kaz said.

"He's bound to be cautious, if only out of habit and training," I said. "So you're probably right. If he has a car, or takes a taxi, the main entrance would work as well. He could be down those stairs and out of sight in no time."

"Then one of us should be between those two spots," Kaz said. "Victor could watch the main entrance from the bottom of the steps. There's plenty of shrubbery to hide in. I will wait inside the path that leads to the university buildings, with you in between the two of us. The flower gardens in the center are fairly open, and you should be able to spot Hannes from any direction."

"Okay, it's the best we can do. Are Moe and Lasho all set?"

"Yes. They are at Victor's place, resting. He took them through the gardens earlier," Kaz said.

"Well, I guess everything's in place. The only wild card is the bodyguard who's escorting Victor's pal."

"Moe plans to impersonate Hannes," Kaz said. "It is doubtful anyone at *Alusuisse* knows what he looks like. He'll get close enough to deal with the bodyguard. Lasho will be close by, in any case."

"Good. I told Krauch the handoff was at nine. We planned to meet at the main entrance at eight o'clock," I said.

"Which is the actual time of the meeting with Hannes," Kaz said. "You know Krauch will arrive even earlier."

"Yep. As will Hannes, an hour ahead of him. They're both trained in surveillance by the Gestapo, so I imagine their patterns will be the same. The extra hour will let us deal with Hannes," I said. Keeping them an hour apart was the key to dealing with them separately. Divide and conquer.

"And if not?"

"Then plan B, with Moe and Lasho playing the part of bagman and escort. If for some reason Hannes shows up at the appointed hour, we'll still have help in nabbing him."

"I shall hope for plan A," Kaz said. "Since that will leave both Krauch and Hannes dead."

"And the invoice in our hands," I said. I had no idea what we'd do with it, though. Dulles would bury it. Maybe take it out with us and give it to Uncle Ike. Or any one of several newspaper reporters who hung around SHAEF. Plenty of time for that later. Right now we had to get through this night.

The waitress came. Kaz ordered pastries and coffee.

"Was Ernst there?" Kaz asked, staring out the rain-splattered window as the waitress departed.

"No, I'm glad to say. I'd hate to have to shoot him."

"I imagine there are any number of honest policemen in Germany who found themselves reorganized into the Gestapo," Kaz said. "If Ernst is a decent man, as he seemed to be, then his country will need him after the war. But if he is in my way tonight, God help him. I will not."

There are many horrible things about this war; one of them being the necessity to kill a man who might otherwise have been a colleague or friend. I prayed it wouldn't come to that. I already had a heavy enough weight on my soul knowing I fervently hoped to put two men in the ground tonight.

CHAPTER THIRTY

SIX O'CLOCK AND the weather was terrible. It had rained even harder during the late afternoon, and now a thick, misty fog was rising up from the river. Tiny droplets danced in the air, lifted and swirled by cooling gusts of air. The good news was that no one in their right mind would go out for a stroll in the gardens tonight. The bad news was that I couldn't see a damn thing.

I was screened by shrubs at the edge of the flower beds. A greenhouse was at my back, and I could see the steps leading down from the main entrance to my right, the hedge behind which Victor hid, and not much more. To the left, where Kaz stood watch, the path that continued up to the university building was shrouded in shadows and low-hanging branches, their greenery heavy with moisture.

Everything hinged on Hannes arriving early to scout the gardens and lay in wait for a possible double-cross. We'd been here since five o'clock, and I doubted even the most paranoid Gestapo agent would stake out a meet three hours early in the pouring rain. Especially since he had no way of knowing anyone but Huber and his closest associates had any idea this was happening tonight. And Hannes had been smart, asking for only thirty thousand. It was cheap. Cheap enough for Huber to be happy to pay and be done with it.

Unless he knew about Fournier's gambling debts, he'd have no reason to suspect a trap.

Which is the best kind of trap.

Six thirty. Nothing. I had to stand, rising from my kneeling position and massaging my aching legs. Then back down on the soggy ground, listening and watching.

Six forty. Where was Krauch? I knew he'd be here before our agreed-upon eight o'clock hour, but how early, I had no idea.

Seven. Damn.

Seven fifteen. I'd been certain Krauch and crew would be here by now, getting the lay of the land, but it was quiet enough to hear the rain-swollen river flowing swiftly beneath the bridge.

Seven thirty. I stepped out from my cover, half expecting a shot to ring out, half disappointed when it didn't. Nobody was here. I trotted over to Kaz, giving a low whistle as I got close to his hiding place.

"Here," he whispered, stepping out onto the path. "Anything?"

"No, all quiet. I hope Krauch hasn't found Hannes on his own."

"Perhaps the Gestapo does not like being out in the rain and fog. I know I do not," Kaz said.

"Maybe they're more sensible than I gave them credit for. I'll check with Victor, then get back into position."

I made my way quietly to Victor, listening for footsteps or any sign of life. The fog was even thicker now, the evening air dripping with moisture, beads of water dropping from the brim of my hat.

"What's happening, Billy?" he whispered. "No sign of Hannes?"

"Nothing. And we don't have much more time."

A car door slammed. Then another, drawing my ear to the sound of the automobile pulling away. "Damn it! That must be Krauch." I glanced at my watch.

Seven forty.

Christ on a crutch. Twenty minutes until Hannes's scheduled arrival. Plus, Moe and Lasho, if they managed to intercept Fournier and his escort. We were about to have a grand soiree in the garden, with bullet cocktails. Victor scooted back behind the bushes as I drew my revolver, taking the steps two at a time, wishing I could part the fog and see five feet ahead.

As I came to the corner at the top of the stairs I hesitated, my palm damp and slippery on the pistol grip. Footsteps from the sidewalk sounded against the wet pavement until a dark figure stood before me, his pistol nearly barrel to barrel with mine.

"There you are, *Herr* Boyle," Krauch murmured from behind his stooge. He patted him on the arm and the pistol disappeared into the folds of his coat as I stuffed mine into my pocket. "I see you arrived early as well."

"Just checking the exits," I said. "I have one man on each. What about you?"

"Two men in two cars up here," he said, very businesslike. "One car across the bridge, to catch him if he crosses on foot. The other down the road, in case he comes from that direction. One man walking the path along the river, and then Bruno and myself. We will find a spot to hide in the garden."

"Smart plan," I said. It wasn't. He'd wasted five men on perimeter patrol, which would only serve to scare Hannes off. I hadn't taken into account the Gestapo's lack of subtlety. "Everyone knows to let the payoff man and his escort in?"

"Yes, yes, if we don't have Hannes by then, of course. Here, we all have police whistles. Take one," Krauch said, handing me a small brass whistle. "Sound it if you spot Hannes and we will converge. Remember, do not shoot him."

"You want him taken alive?" I asked.

"I do not want the invoice ruined, by bullet holes or blood. Now, let us get into position," Krauch said, stomping down the stairs with Bruno in tow. I was sure Krauch wanted to spare Huber the sight of blood, being such a sensitive guy, but I knew he wanted Hannes in one piece in order to torture him for the location of his stolen loot. I hoped I was right about it being stashed at the railway station; that would allow us to grab it quickly, assuming we found the key on Hannes.

I followed them down slowly, stopping to tie my shoe when I got close to Victor, although with the fog that subterfuge was hardly necessary. As I stood, I realized the fog was not as dense as it had been, and the misty rain had let up.

"Stay put," I said. "If you hear a whistle, four Gestapo are likely to come down those stairs. Fire a few shots and make them think twice about it, then find another spot to hunker down in. Can you do that?"

"With a great deal of pleasure," Victor whispered from his hiding place.

"Keep your fingers crossed," I answered, and ran back to my spot, catching a glimpse of Krauch and Bruno making their way through the flower beds, heading for a line of trees down the slope, close to the river. Maybe they were checking in with their man on the path, or just concealing themselves amid the dark shadows.

Back to waiting.

Eight.

Krauch and his men were still expecting Hannes to arrive an hour from now. That gave me a bit of an edge once I spotted Hannes, hopefully any minute now. They wouldn't be expecting it, and we were ready. I glanced at the stairs, hoping that Lasho and Moe had made out okay pulling a fast one on Huber's men. If not, there'd be another wild card to contend with.

Five after eight.

I got up, moving the shrub in front of me to check on Kaz's position. I strained to see in the darkness.

Then a noise, a dull click.

In the foggy dark, it was hard to tell where the sound came from. I felt adrift in gray-black as I listened for another sound.

A footstep.

I turned around. Hannes was right behind me, his pistol leveled at my head.

His right hand held the gun. His left came to his mouth, a finger raised in the gesture of silence. He didn't need to worry. I had no desire to have him disturb the quiet night with a shot that would blow my brains out.

"The greenhouse," I whispered, in my most hushed voice. He nodded.

"Since three o'clock," he said, grinning at how he'd outsmarted me. "So warm inside on a cold, rainy day. No one around to bother me, either, until that unfortunate guard came along to lock up. Well, too bad for him, but it all worked out. Now, don't tell me the money is not coming. I would be terribly disappointed." He edged closer, his weapon centered on my forehead.

"It's coming," I said. "Anytime now."

"Good," he whispered in my ear, grabbing me by the collar and turning me around. "Because if not—" The cold steel of the barrel ground into my neck. I was beginning to get irritated with this routine. Not to mention the murder of an innocent security guard. What did he mean about it all working out?

"There," I whispered, as footfalls echoed in the stone stairway. Please let it be Lasho and Moe, I prayed, invoking all the saints I'd ignored since the last tight spot I was in.

The shadows drew closer. It looked like them, but it was impossible to tell. Hannes stepped out from behind the bushes, dragging me along. He stuffed the gun into his pocket, probably worried about spooking them. He waved, his left hand still clenching my collar and dragging me along with him.

I had about two seconds. I grabbed the whistle in my pocket and gave it one long ear-piercing blast. Hannes slugged me with his right hand, knocking the brass whistle flying, his other hand still grasping my collar.

Stupid, I thought, as the blow to my jaw sent stars pinwheeling across my clouded vision. He should have shot me. I stumbled and rolled away from Hannes, expecting him to come to the same conclusion. I reached for my revolver as other whistles shrieked and shouts sounded from every direction.

A pistol shot cracked, then another, two flashes in the fog not ten feet from me.

"Victor, stay put!" I yelled, then darted away into the flower beds in case my voice drew a bullet. "Lasho, Moe, hide!" Again I moved, running low, trying to figure Hannes's best hope of escape. I was between him and Krauch; Victor had the stairs covered, and Kaz was at the other entrance.

I ducked behind a rosebush. What that protected me from, I had no idea.

The guard. Hannes had said something about the guard he'd killed. Keys. He would have had keys to the university building up the hill. Keys that would get Hannes in the door and out to the street. Hannes would know we had the exits covered, so that was his best bet to get away.

Shots again, this time from the stone staircase. Victor was firing at the Gestapo, who blew their whistles, the sound carrying as they retreated back up the steps. I ran to Kaz, gasping out a message for him to follow me. We ran up the hill, past the greenhouse, heading for the rear of the building.

"Halt!"

Krauch stepped out, his pistol leveled. Two men stood behind him. Bruno and the guy from the path. It had to be.

"He's going out through the building. He has keys," I said, starting to move.

"I said halt." Krauch's gun was still aimed at my gut. He spoke to Bruno, who vanished, heading toward the building. The other man stepped closer, revealing himself to be Ernst. None of us signaled any recognition.

"What's going on?" I asked, although it was obvious.

"We no longer need you, *Herr* Boyle. I have more men than I claimed, I am afraid. They are securing all exits now. It is a shame the traitor Hannes had to kill you. But not before he executed another worthless Pole," Krauch said, turning to Ernst, waving his pistol in our direction.

Ernst took our revolvers, his mouth set in a thin grimace. He didn't look me in the eye, a bad sign. I glanced around, hoping for anyone to come to our rescue. It didn't seem likely. Victor was at his post, with Lasho and Moe taking cover as I'd told them to.

"*Schiessen,*" Krauch said, snapping out an order that I was pretty sure meant shoot. Krauch walked away, leaving the dirty work to Ernst.

"*Herr Kriminalinspektor,*" Ernst called out, sounding somewhat more formal than the situation called for. Maybe he was going to file a complaint.

"*Ja?*" Krauch said, irritation evident in his tone as he turned back.

Ernst raised my revolver. And shot Krauch twice, in what heart he had.

Before Krauch's body hit the ground, Ernst handed our pistols back to us.

"*Erschiesse mich*," he said. Kaz was the language expert, but it sure sounded like he wanted us to shoot him. "*Bitte.*"

"I get it," I said to Kaz. "Tell him thanks, and I'm sorry." Kaz spoke a few quick words, and Ernst answered, then gave me a grim nod. I raised my revolver enough to shoot him in the meaty part of the thigh. Ernst was a stocky guy, and as long as I missed the bone, he'd be okay. I squeezed the trigger.

He grunted and grabbed his leg, managing not to fall over. It was a through-and-through, leaving neat entrance and exit holes in his now blood-soaked trousers.

"*Danke*," I said, gripping his hand. Ernst smiled through clenched teeth, then said something in German, pushing me away as soon as he finished. We bolted, rushing to find everyone before the whistles sounded again.

"Ernst said we should hide, quickly," Kaz said as we looked for Moe and Lasho. We found them behind a neatly trimmed hedge and we all scurried off to Victor's hiding place.

"What the hell is happening?" he asked as we squeezed in with him.

"No time to explain," I said, turning to Moe. "Everything go okay with Fournier?"

"Yes. We had to tie up his minder. Fournier's waiting at the café where you and Kaz ate."

"Okay. The place is swarming with Gestapo. Hannes is probably in the building. They're surrounding it," I said.

"Krauch?" Victor asked, gripping his pistol.

"Dead. Sorry we couldn't let you do the honors," I said. "But we still have to get out of here alive and find Hannes."

"He's probably going to try for the train station," Kaz said. "If we were right about his plan."

"The Gestapo men have the place surrounded," I said. "We're trapped in here."

Then the whistle sounded. Three long sharp blasts, followed by a short one. The sound came from where we'd left Ernst.

"Ernst," Kaz said. "That's why he said to hide. He's calling the troops to him."

"Who the hell is Ernst?" Victor asked.

"A German," Lasho said. "Gestapo, but a good man. Strange, is it not?"

There wasn't time to discuss the concept of a decent Gestapo agent doing us a good turn, then asking me to shoot him. Heavy feet thundered down the stairs, and I put my hand on Victor's pistol, lowering it as we held our breath while a pack of Krauch's men headed to their dead boss and grievously wounded partner. I hoped Ernst laid it on thick. Maybe he'd get a medal.

"Come on," I said, once the coast was clear. We ran up the steps, making it to the sidewalk and the wide roadway that led to the bridge and the railway station beyond. Automobiles moved slowly, the thin slits in their covered headlights showing little more than pinpricks of lights appearing and disappearing in the gloom. The fog had lifted and I felt the beginnings of a breeze as the raindrops began to solidify, hitting the ground in heavy splats.

"We probably have a minute's start on Hannes before he figures out the team has been pulled away," I said. "Moe and Lasho, go around the gardens and make your way to the path along the river, in case he heads out that way. If nothing happens, head to the café and give Fournier his payoff."

"If we see Hannes?" Moe asked.

"Kill him. Get the invoice and any keys he has in his pockets. We'll meet at the train station. Go," I said.

Without a word, they trotted off, going the long way around the university building. Where Hannes would be making his exit anytime soon. He'd know about the whistles and what the signal meant. It was his only chance. Police sirens sounded from across the river, drawing closer. The gunfire had gotten someone's attention.

"Come on," I said, crouching low and running in the road, keeping the occasional parked car between us and the building. It was three stories tall, the gray granite dark and blurry against the rainy night sky.

"Here," I said as we came to a side entrance. "Kaz. Watch the door." He knelt by the bumper of a car. Victor and I went around to the front, where steps led up to the double-door main entrance. I took up position there and sent Victor to the next corner. I figured Hannes would avoid the side where Kaz was as too obvious, and Victor's side as too far away from the bridge. That left the front door. I was ready.

All the windows were dark. The only light came from the occasional solitary vehicle on the road. The sirens wailed, still sounding far away. If I were Hannes, I'd get a move on.

If I were him. I realized I wouldn't go out any of the doors. Talk about obvious. A window would do just as well. Drop quietly to the ground and take off. I scanned the front of the building, all windows dark and shut up tight. No movement anywhere.

Crack.

A single gunshot. Then another. From Victor's direction.

Tires screeched on the roadway as a driver slammed on the brakes, as if avoiding some maniac darting across the street. A dark form came around the corner, headed my way. I stepped onto the sidewalk, revolver at the ready. I aimed, but held my fire. Whoever it was stumbled, then regained his footing.

It was Victor, one arm bloodied.

"Across the street," he gasped. "He came out a window. I didn't see him."

"Tell Kaz," I yelled, and headed out into the street, straining to catch sight of Hannes making his getaway. Not to mention any cars careening my way.

I angled left, figuring he'd turn the corner and head across the bridge. I came to the main road, squinting and trying to catch a glimpse of him. I headed toward Kaz, finally seeing him and Victor, who was still clutching his pistol in his good hand.

The screeching sound of tires again, behind me. This time it had to be Hannes crossing over. I turned and ran, wondering if I'd been wrong about the railway station. The car beeped its horn as I ran past, and I was disappointed I hadn't heard the thump of a body hitting the pavement. I heard Kaz shout, but couldn't make out what he was saying.

The sirens were closer. I chanced a glance back and saw what Kaz was yelling about. Police lights coming across the bridge, bright and vivid as the wind and rain blew off the fog drifting up from the river. Hannes definitely wasn't going that way.

Not over that bridge, anyway. But there was the rail bridge, not far from the Lorrainebrücke. I'd seen it earlier, the steel lattice-work span a clear contrast with the solid concrete roadway.

I had to find it.

I ran across the lanes of traffic, slipping on the wet pavement, in a hurry to catch Hannes and also avoid the *polizei,* who were probably on the lookout for guys with guns running around their city. I took a side street across from the gardens, hoping it would lead to the other bridge. I passed houses and a restaurant, and then the street curved away, making room for the railroad bridge.

High above me, tall columns held up the elevated bridge. Thirty, maybe forty feet tall. With no way up. I ran along the street, straining to find an access point. There was nothing in sight, just the smooth concrete plinths.

But not where it spanned the river. I ran back, darting between buildings, searching for the riverside path. The curved steel span was anchored on the riverbank, not far from the path. I jumped a fence and slid down a muddy incline, ending up in the backyard of a house tucked right under the bridge.

There he was. Raincoat flapping as he ran, making for the base of the span, where the steel framework gave plenty of handholds for a motivated climber. And Hannes had motivation; the train station was directly across the river. He was up into the understructure quick enough, grasping handholds, feet shuffling carefully along the narrow edge of the truss. I didn't dare shoot, not even a warning shot. If he dropped into the river, the current would take him and all his secrets. I didn't yell his name either, for fear of startling him or letting him take a few potshots at me. I wasn't too crazy about taking a chance with that swift current myself.

So I ran for the base of the span, ditching my trench coat and hat for freedom of movement, hoping that Hannes wouldn't look back. I pulled myself up and instantly slipped on the wet metal girder. I got up again, more carefully this time, and figured the chances of Hannes turning to look back were slim. I was terrified enough two feet off the ground.

Rain pelted my face as I edged along, grabbing beams and pulling myself forward as the span arched upward. There was no way to take a step; I had to adopt the same shuffling motion as Hannes with only about four inches of flat surface jutting out from the massive steel girders. It looked a lot easier from a distance.

I was out over the river now, the water raging beneath me, wind and water buffeting my body and conspiring to tear away my hand-holds and sweep my feet off the slippery steel. Hannes was at the apex of the span, about to start the downward slope to the far shore and safety. When he got there, he was bound to look back.

And see me, a sitting duck.

"Hannes, you bastard!" Victor's harsh scream came from behind, startling me as I pulled my body forward. I froze, grabbing the rough painted metal as tightly as possible. I took a deep breath and saw Hannes slip a bit himself, then turn his head to the riverbank.

A shot, and I heard the ricochet as Victor's bullet went wide and struck steel.

"No!" I shouted, but Victor fired again, another missed shot. It was some distance for an accurate pistol shot, but he might get lucky, and we'd lose everything. Victor was in a rage: from his gunshot wound, from the stress of the chase, from his loss at the hands of the Gestapo, maybe from all the wrongs and secrets he'd endured. Whatever it was, he was out of control, and as he began to climb the girder I knew his anger would not sustain him, not with one bad arm.

"Go back!" I shouted. "You'll kill yourself up here!"

He stopped a few feet up from the riverbank, hesitating as he grasped how difficult, or impossible, it would be with an injured arm. He jumped down and took aim, again. Even through the rain, I could see his face contorted in a snarl of anger as he steadied his aim and pulled the trigger.

Another missed shot as the zing of the ricochet echoed beneath the bridge, and I began to worry about getting hit.

"Stop!" I hollered, then moved on, knowing that Victor wasn't in a mood to think this through. Not that I could blame him. Hannes was moving as well, the wind snapping at his open raincoat, whipping it around his body. I was soaked through, my hands wet and slippery, water pelting my eyes.

Another shot. This time Hannes reacted. He went flat again the girder, slumping slightly, then dragged himself on, one leg nearly folding beneath him. He'd been hit. He was still up, but looked wobbly as he took hold of the latticework and made his way on the downward slope.

Then Hannes slipped. One leg went off the girder and the other nearly did. He hung on and pulled himself up. A dark stain spread down one trouser leg. If only he could make it to the other side, we'd have him, wounded but intact.

He slipped again, and hung on with both hands, the wounded leg near to collapse. I pulled myself up to the apex and moved toward him, close enough to see the panic in his eyes. One hand slipped and caught on the edge, level with my foot. He hung on with the other, his feet flailing over the churning water.

"Tell that fool to stop shooting!" Hannes yelled. With me being this close, I hoped nobody needed to tell Victor that.

"Hang on," I said.

"Help me," Hannes said. "I'll give you the document. That's what you want, yes?" He clung to the lattice, his knuckles white as he held on.

"Sure," I said, inching closer. "Where is it?"

"Next to my heart," Hannes said, giving a sharp laugh that turned to a grimace of pain. "Help me."

I had about three feet to go. There was no way I was going to let him escape, not that he had much of a chance with a bullet through his leg. But he was grasping at straws, which was fine with me if it kept him calm. If he suddenly got realistic about his chances, his best bet would be to grab me and take us both into the river.

"Okay, we have a deal," I said, sliding my foot closer, working at keeping him focused. "You really have it?"

"Yes, yes! Hurry."

Hurrying wasn't going to help either of us. I got a firm grip and let my feet slide down the wet metal, almost to Hannes. I released, going for the next handhold, but the soles of my shoes had a life of their own and kept sliding toward Hannes's hand.

I grabbed a section of steel and stopped my forward momentum a foot short of his hand. I leaned forward, almost kneeling, my left hand stretching until I got Hannes by the wrist, lifting his arm, guiding him to a better grip. He swung his good leg up, desperate to move his center of gravity higher, onto that narrow four-inch strip that he'd traversed so effortlessly only moments before. He didn't make it, missing by an inch.

The bridge began to rattle.

A steam locomotive whistled in the distance, headed for the station. The engine rumbled closer. I held on to Hannes, my legs shaking with the effort of keeping my own balance and holding on to his wrist. The train was directly overhead, slowing but still thunderously loud as car after car rolled by above our heads. Hannes squeezed his eyes shut and tried again.

His foot almost reached the edge, then slid off, sending him swinging, a heavy weight suddenly dangling off my left arm. He grabbed onto the girder with his free hand and swung his leg up again, a mighty effort that only made it worse when he missed and fell back, losing his grip, scrambling to grab hold of something, anything, that would stop his body swaying out over open air.

Every surface he touched was wet and slick. In a panic, he twisted his body, trying to grab onto my arm with both hands. He missed, but I kept my grip on his wrist, feeling the tendons in my arm tremble from the weight. My fingers, tight on the steel strut behind me, felt like they might snap from the pressure.

I tried to lift him, putting everything I had into it, my forearm shaking as Hannes rose a few inches, then almost a foot. He angled his leg up again, but the momentum was too much and instead his wrist slipped through my hand until all I had were his fingers, tight as a claw, gripping my palm, losing strength every second. He let go and clamped a hold on my foot, nearly pulling me down as he thrashed about. I reached for him, grabbing at one shoulder, working my hand under his arm, worrying all the time he would pull me down with him.

He yelled, but I couldn't make out what, or even what language, it was. He arched his head back, eyes wide in terror, heaving himself up almost as if he were climbing on air. I got a firm grip and tried to help, but I couldn't get his body any higher. His fingers slipped off my foot and I made a last attempt to hold on to him, but the scream was already drawn from his throat even before he lost his last tenuous grasp.

He waved his hands futilely, attempting one last time to secure a firm grip. Then the weight I held lessened, as I watched him drop slightly, his face obscured by an upturned collar. The sleeves of his raincoat held him in place for one paralyzing second, then released him as his arms slipped through, the weight of his body pulling him down, out of my grasp, sending him head over heels to disappear beneath the churning foam of the swollen Aare River.

I clutched the sodden raincoat, trying to regain my balance after the sudden shift in weight. I pressed my cheek against the cold steel, closing my eyes for a second, then taking a deep breath. Krauch, dead. Hannes, presumably drowned. The invoice and the treasure Hannes had stolen? Maybe in the raincoat pocket. Maybe not. I didn't care at that moment. All I wanted was to get off that damned bridge.

I jumped from the bridge as soon as I could, falling and rolling in soft, wet grass, the raincoat still tightly held to my chest. I stayed like that longer than I want to admit. Finally, I sat up and went through the pockets.

One key, marked with a brightly painted number. Nice that I was right about something tonight. I was a stone's throw from a storage locker that would match that key, I was certain.

One cigarette case. Henri's case. I held it in my hand, feeling the heavy silver beneath my fingers. Why had Hannes said the invoice was close to his heart? I flipped the case open.

It was filled with cigarettes. Ever the thief, Hannes had seen even this as loot to be taken.

If the invoice was in his shirt pocket, near his heart, then it was a gob of pulp and melted ink by now.

"Damn," I muttered, cursing my sore muscles as I rose and headed up to the station.

Damn.

CHAPTER THIRTY-ONE

A PUDDLE FORMED at my feet as I stood in front of the locker inside the station. I was soaked to the bone, and a chill ran through my body as I waited for Kaz and Victor. We'd come this far together, so I figured I might as well hold off until they arrived. I leaned against the lockers, fighting to stay upright. I was tired. Tired of the Gestapo, tired of Switzerland, tired of duplicity and secrets. Tired of knowing men like Huber slept soundly in expensive houses while using slave labor to make ever greater profits. And tired that they fooled the world doing it.

Footsteps echoed in the empty corridor. I looked up to see Kaz supporting Victor, who wore my trench coat draped over his shoulders. He looked pale.

"Hannes is gone," I said as they drew close.

"We know," Kaz said. "We saw him fall. He never came up."

"Did he have the invoice in his coat?" Victor said, pointing to the sodden heap on the floor.

"No," I said. "He told me it was in his pocket. It went into the river with him. But I did get this." I handed him the cigarette case. He opened it, his face sagging as he saw the smokes, as if he'd hoped I was joking. Not that there was anything funny about tonight.

Then he ran his fingers over the engraved initials. Henri's initials. His face softened and threatened to crumble. I put my hand on his shoulder.

"Thank you," Victor said, clasping the silver case between his hands.

"I'm sorry," I said. Sorry that Henri was dead, sorry for Victor's loss, and sorry that there was less love in the world because of it. With so much hate and sadness surrounding us, loss of love was a tragedy, regardless of who the lovers were. I might not have thought that before, but the grief in Victor's eyes was proof enough of that simple truth.

"This means a lot," Victor said, tucking Henri's cigarette case in his pocket with a wistful smile.

"That's not all," I said, holding up the key. "Something good may come of this yet."

"Right, the key!" Victor said, taking a deep breath and rallying. "Although Krauch being shot dead by one of his own men isn't too shabby either. Let's see what's inside."

I gave him the key. He deserved to do the honors.

He inserted the key in the lock and opened the storage locker. Inside, at about face level, sat one small suitcase. Victor reached in with his good arm and pulled it out. It fell to the floor with a hard *thump*.

"The damned thing's heavy," Victor said, a smile spreading across his face. None of us dared whisper the word.

Gold.

Lasho and Moe picked us up outside the station, and we drove to the hotel. They'd given Fournier his payoff and released his bodyguard. Now everyone was in a hurry to look inside the suitcase, but I wanted to be behind a locked door when we opened it. Kaz urged Victor to get to a doctor, but he wasn't buying it. The bullet had gone through his lower arm, and Kaz had tied a handkerchief around it. That would have to do, until we found a doctor who wouldn't ask questions. There was nothing to connect us to Krauch's shooting or Hannes's free-form dive from the bridge, and I planned on keeping it that way.

We trooped into the hotel lobby, feet squishing in waterlogged shoes. I told myself we didn't look out of place. Too much.

I unlocked the door to our room, stepping aside to let Kaz enter first with the suitcase.

The light was on.

Maureen Conaty sat in the armchair by a small table set with glasses and a bottle of Scotch.

"Come on in, boys, and have a drink. From what I hear, you deserve it." She stuck a Lucky Strike between her ruby red lips and lit up. I was sick and tired of a lot of things in Switzerland, but Maureen wasn't one of them.

"How'd you know?" I asked, shedding my suit jacket.

"Don't you remember our dinner date? When you didn't show, I started asking around. When I heard about a shooting at the botanical garden, I knew you had to be in on it. Bern is usually a very peaceful place."

"Thanks for not calling the police," I said.

"Who do you think called me? Inspector Escher is a good friend, and a smart cookie to boot. He can keep things under a lid until tomorrow. By then you'll be on your way. And poor Victor! You're hurt. Come, sit by me," she said. From a satchel at her feet she pulled out a musette bag with a red cross. She'd thought of everything.

"Does Dulles know?" Moe asked. "I hope this doesn't affect our Zürich plans."

"Do not worry," Lasho said. "Miss Conaty knows what she is doing. Even if Dulles does not."

That summed her up pretty well. She put a proper bandage on Victor's arm, telling him she'd take him to a doctor on the OSS payroll after we were done here. Then we got to the main event.

"Krauch is dead," I said, to get the ball rolling. "Hannes too, we're certain. He may wash up somewhere downstream. He still had the invoice on him. It's probably destroyed."

"There's poetic justice at work there. Anyway, the less I know, the better. I see you didn't come away empty-handed though," she said, eyeing the suitcase.

Kaz lifted it up on the bed and worked the snaps. It was locked. Lasho took over, opening his knife and gently working the blade into the small keyhole. With a faint *click*, it opened.

Even in the meager light of the hotel room, the gold glistened. Rows of kilobars—two-pound flat rectangles marked with the stamps of various Swiss banks—sparkled and gave off the warm glow of wealth. Credit Suisse, SBC, all the big names were there. Hannes had gotten creative with packing material to keep the bars from clanking against each other. Swiss francs, US dollars, British pounds, and Spanish pesetas kept everything in place. Small denominations, good for bribes, pocket money, whatever Hannes needed to make his way to safety.

"It's a goddamn fortune," Moe said.

"Get rid of it," Lasho said. "Neither money nor the devil can remain in peace, my grandfather always said."

"Blood money, all of it," Victor said. "Family fortunes, stolen from the dead."

"What can we do with it?" Kaz asked as we stood around the open suitcase, attracted and repelled by the riches Hannes had extorted. "Even if we knew which accounts they came from, the banks can hardly be trusted to return the money to family members."

"I heard about the bank asking you for a death certificate," Moe said. "I'm sorry."

"It is absurd," Kaz said. "For me, a matter of principle more than anything. But for the few who make it out of the camps alive, it will mean survival. And it will be kept from them, based on what we have seen."

"I wish we could do something about that," Maureen said. She stood and poured six drinks. "Maybe Safehaven will help, at least to stop the Nazis from transferring the looted gold out of Switzerland. Who knows? Right now, let's drink a toast to Henri." She passed the glasses around.

"A courageous man," Kaz said, raising his glass.

"He did what he thought was right, even when it cost his life," Victor said. "There's many in this world who will have much less to offer as an epitaph."

"We are all wanderers on this earth," Lasho said. "Some of us never learn our purpose. Your friend Henri knew his." He downed his drink in one ferocious gulp, and we all followed suit.

"I have an idea about the money," Maureen said, setting down her glass. "Bring it with you tomorrow. Don't mention it to Allen, okay? He's a good man, and there are things I don't want to burden him with."

"What's the idea?" I asked.

"I'll explain tomorrow. Right now I want to get Victor patched up. Say your goodbyes, fellas. You're all going your separate ways, and none too soon," she said.

"So long, Billy," Victor said. "Thanks for finding me, and letting me be part of this."

"Give those Swiss bankers hell, Victor," I said, shaking his good hand. "Make Henri proud."

Kaz and Victor embraced, Kaz planting one of those Polish three-cheek kiss routines on him, the sort of thing that always made me nervous no matter who the other person liked to sleep with.

I wished Moe luck, and pretty much left it at that. If he needed to carry out a hit on a famous German scientist, there was little reason to think he'd make it out alive. Kind of a conversation stopper, so I just told him how much I'd enjoyed watching him catch for the Red Sox, which he accepted with a proud modesty.

"*Latcho drom,*" Lasho said, giving me a bear hug that threatened to crack ribs. He engulfed Kaz, who nearly disappeared in the big Sinti's arms.

"Safe journey to you as well, my friend," Kaz said as he was let loose.

They all filed out, murmuring good nights, leaving Kaz and me with the spoils of war. I closed the suitcase, unable to look at the gold. Gold stolen from nations, gold stolen from the necks and fingers of thousands sent to extermination camps, gold pried from the jaws of the dead. That should have been why I couldn't bear to set eyes on it. But the real reason was the temptation that seemed to call out from the shining gold bars.

As much as I didn't want to admit it, I felt it, felt the lure of the soft golden glow.

I pushed the suitcase under the bed.

CHAPTER THIRTY-TWO

THE NEXT MORNING Kaz and I showed up at Dulles's office as ordered, suitcases in hand. The one Kaz carried was heavier than mine, which contained our spare clothes, but he hefted it as if it held nothing more than dirty laundry. Maureen shot him a sly wink from her spot on the sofa.

"I've heard reports that the Gestapo was involved in a shooting last night," Dulles said as soon as we crossed the threshold. "Siegfried Krauch was killed." He stared us down as we stashed our suitcases by the door and took our seats.

"Always nice to start off the morning with good news," I said. "Maybe he was after Hannes and got bushwhacked."

"I doubt that," Dulles said. "The police pulled Hannes's body from the river an hour ago. You two know anything about that?"

"Not a thing," I said. "We had dinner with Maureen and got a good night's sleep. But good to know about Hannes as well, thanks."

Dulles glowered, then glanced at Maureen, who nodded in verification of what I'd claimed.

"So, how do we take our leave of Switzerland?" Kaz asked, moving the discussion along.

"A Swiss Air flight to Barcelona, later today," Dulles said. "We've arranged passports for you both, and transit visas that will not be scrutinized too carefully. Miss Conaty will take you to the airport and facilitate your boarding."

"I hope the bribes were big enough," I said.

"Bigger than any reward a customs official might expect for spotting forged papers," Maureen said. "No worries there."

"Why Barcelona?" I asked. "Why not Lisbon? We can get a flight to England from there."

"Barcelona is the only stop Swiss Air makes. Outside of Germany, that is," she said. "I didn't think you wanted a flight to Berlin."

"An OSS agent will meet you at the airport there," Dulles said. "You'll be back in London in no time."

"Sounds fine," I said. "We better get a move on."

"Not so fast," Dulles said, holding up a hand. I wondered if he were about to lower the boom. "There's one more thing. I want you to know that I appreciate what you've done, and the work it took to get here. Not to mention bringing Lasho to us. He's a valuable asset."

"And a decent man," I said. "I hope you can work some passport magic for him."

"When the war's over we'll take care of our own, don't worry. But right now, I have something for you, Baron. You might find it helpful."

"Why, thank you, sir," Kaz said, clearly surprised. "But what about Billy?"

"This has to do with your visit to the bank the other day. I thought I might be able to help with that." Dulles gave a nod to Maureen, who left the room and returned seconds later with a familiar guy in tow.

"I believe you've met Hans Bernd Gisevius, the German vice consul," Dulles said. "Both at the reception and outside my door. So you know not to repeat anything of this meeting."

"Of course not," Kaz said, standing as Gisevius came nearer. He was a tall man and towered over both of us. We shook hands, and I wondered what the hell a German, even one working with Dulles, could do for Kaz.

"Baron, Allen has told me of your experience at the Credit Suisse bank. He asked me to determine if it were possible to obtain an official death certificate for your father," Gisevius said.

"That is very kind of you both, but I doubt it would be possible, given the circumstances," Kaz said, somewhat stiffly.

"Yes, I thought so myself. I was prepared to see to a forgery, which would not be terribly difficult. But that was not necessary. Please, Baron, have a seat." Gisevius gestured to the empty chair and leaned against Dulles's desk. Kaz looked warily at Dulles and then sat, curiosity overcoming his studied formality.

"I believe I have news for you. You do know that your family was targeted by the SS, as members of the Polish intelligentsia." Kaz nodded, his hand clenched in a fist. "But what you may not know is that your father succumbed to a heart attack several days after the invasion of Poland but before the capitulation."

"Oh my god," Kaz whispered. His hand went to his face, and then he quickly recovered. "That means my family was left without him when the Germans came." I could see the horror in his face, the image of his mother, younger brothers, and sisters alone and at the mercy of the SS. "I always imagined he would have given them strength."

"Baron, if my pitiful condolences mean anything, you have them. And the promise that I, and others, are working to bring down this monstrous regime," Gisevius said, making his own fist and slamming it against his leg.

"Yes, yes, of course, thank you," Kaz said, still struggling to take in this new information. "But what does this have to do with the bank?"

"I was able to secure this," Gisevius said, withdrawing a document from his pocket. "The death certificate from the hospital where your father died."

Kaz took the certificate, his hand trembling as he read it. He didn't speak. The room went silent as he stared at the paper. Dulles fired up his pipe and looked out the window.

"There is one other thing," Gisevius said, his voice nearly a whisper.

"Dear god, what else?" Kaz said, a sob catching in his throat.

"Your sister Angelika. I cannot say for certain, but she may be alive. At least, she is not on the list of those who were . . . put to death."

"Angelika? She was twelve years old in 1939," Kaz said, jumping up from his chair. "Is it possible? She is alive?"

"The SS keeps meticulous records. No other Kazimierz has been taken into custody since those early days. She may be alive and using

other identity papers. Or with the underground, the Polish Home
Army. I am sorry to awaken all these memories, Baron, but I thought
you would want to know."

"Yes, I do, thank you!" Kaz said, grasping Gisevius by the hand and
pumping it with both of his. No kisses for the German, though. "It
does give me hope, and for that I am in your debt."

After a few minutes more of chitchat, there wasn't much left to
say except farewell. Maureen bundled us out into her car. Kaz sat in
the back, cradling the suitcase and still in a daze.

"Did you know about all that?" I asked her.

"Hans came back from Germany yesterday and told us. Quite a
surprise, eh?"

"Yeah, I'll say. Now what about your idea for the gold?"

"We're headed there now. Remember Dr. Veit Wyler? He was with
Hans at Huber's reception," she said.

"The lawyer," Kaz said. "The chap who used the old law about
military uniforms to give Jewish refugees sanctuary."

"Precisely. He keeps secret bank accounts for Jews who have sent
him money instead of the banks. He'll know what to do."

"How secret are they if you know about them?" I asked.

"Secrets are my business, Billy, dear boy," she said. "Veit will know
what to do."

In half an hour we were seated in Veit Wyler's office, sipping coffee.
The suitcase sat on the floor by his desk, unopened. He'd felt its weight
and had been impressed.

"No record of the accounts that were drained by this Hannes
creature?" Wyler asked.

"None," Maureen said. "He covered his tracks well. And you know
the banking community."

"Ah yes, the famous Swiss sphere of secrecy. Bank records are
sacrosanct. Unless you're a Nazi and the account holder is Jewish," he
said.

"You maintain accounts for many people, I understand. Do you
have any ideas?" Kaz said.

"Miss Conaty told me of your problems at Credit Suisse, Baron,"

Wyler said. "There will be many others after the war, when surviving family members make their way here. Perhaps we could set up a fund for those who have some proof, but not enough for the banks."

"That would be perfect," Kaz said. "We will leave the gold with you, to use as you see fit." Wyler looked at Maureen, who nodded her approval.

"Very well. Thank you for your trust," he said.

"Tell me, why do you do it?" I asked. "For people you don't know."

"I am Jewish myself, so I must help my own people, mustn't I? Also, I believe that where you find a lack of human kindness, you must make up the deficit yourself. So I do what I can. I hold the repository of hope for those who have none. As Miss Conaty knows, here, hidden among my law volumes, are the ledgers of accounts I hold in trust." Behind his desk were rows and rows of legal books, hiding the secrets of the oppressed in plain sight.

I watched Kaz tap his fingers on his knee, a nervous habit I'd seen before. His gaze darted from the law books to Wyler, then back again. The drumming fingers relaxed.

"Dr. Wyler, we do not have much time," Kaz said, withdrawing the death certificate from his jacket pocket. "I would like a power of attorney document drawn up, with you as my agent."

"What do you wish me to do, Baron?" Wyler said, taking a fountain pen and starting to make notes.

"Bring this death certificate to the Credit Suisse bank and establish access to my late father's account there for myself and one other person," Kaz said, placing the paper on Wyler's desk.

"The other person's name?"

"Angelika Kazimierz. My sister, whom I hope is alive, somewhere in occupied Poland."

Hope. Love. The lights that illuminate the darkness of war.

I left Kaz to finish the paperwork with Wyler and walked outside, feeling the sun on my face, breathing the clean, crisp air. I sent up a quick prayer to Saint Jude, the patron saint of lost causes, that one day I'd see Kaz reunited with his sister.

My prayer felt empty. Mere Sunday school words against the

onslaught of this war with all of its mechanized terror and the evil men who served it on the battlefield, in concentration camps, government offices, factories, and even in the quiet marble corridors of Swiss banks.

The devouring was upon us. It sought Lasho, Angelika, and all those who struggled to survive until the war burned itself out. It sought our bodies, killing and maiming with industrial efficiency.

It sought our souls, leaving us killers as we drew breath at the end of the day.

"Let's go, Billy," Kaz said, appearing silently at my side. "I'm finished here."

"That was a good idea, Kaz. Angelika will be well taken care of if she makes it here," I said as we descended the steps.

"Do you think there is a chance she's still alive?" Kaz asked. His voice broke and he halted, turning his face away, feigning a sudden interest in the white clouds drifting across the sky.

"Sure," I said, putting my arm around his shoulders. "She's a Kazimierz, of the Augustus clan. She'll make it."

If the devouring could be kept at bay.

AUTHOR'S NOTE

SWITZERLAND MAINTAINED A stance of armed neutrality during the Second World War, but it was tilted in favor of Nazi Germany. The leader of the nation's armed forces during the war, General Henri Guisan, is revered today by the Swiss for his leadership and determination to resist any foreign invasion.

But Switzerland was far too valuable to Adolph Hitler as a neutral state. An invasion, even if it succeeded militarily, would do far less for Nazi Germany than Switzerland could as a sovereign nation. Swiss banks accepted and laundered looted gold from the capitals of nations the Germans conquered, and turned a blind eye to the other source of gold provided by the SS: gold fillings and jewelry delivered from extermination camps. The triangle system, as described in this book, was a reality of wartime dealings for Swiss banks. Looted gold from Germany was sold to the banks for Swiss francs. The Germans then used that currency to purchase war materials from other nations, and those countries would then use the Swiss francs to buy the gold of uncertain provenance.

The Swiss profited greatly from World War II, having taken in, by Allied estimates, more than seven hundred eighty-one million dollars in Nazi gold, of which five hundred seventy-nine million dollars had been looted from the victims of Nazi aggression.

Switzerland also provided war materials directly to Nazi Germany, which they manufactured on neutral ground safe from Allied bombers.

Railroad traffic through the Swiss Alps was also a much safer means of travel to and from Italy than the routes through Austria. While such transit was supposed to have been limited to nonmilitary supplies, there were a number of witnesses who testified to seeing slave laborers, prisoners of war, and other victims herded into cattle cars and transported through neutral Switzerland, as shown in this narrative.

The aluminum-producing firm *Alusuisse*, which was bought out by the Canadian firm Alcan in 2008, did purchase Ukrainian slave laborers from the SS for their plant in Singen, Germany. Max Huber, president of the International Committee of the Red Cross, was chairman of *Alusuisse* during those years.

The Gestapo did resort to the kind of trickery practiced by the character Georg Hannes, who is based on the real-life Georg Hannes Thomae, a Gestapo agent who was able to penetrate the vaunted "sphere of secrecy" and discover secrets about Germans who illegally maintained Swiss bank accounts. As far as I have been able to determine, Thomae suffered no fate as rewarding as the one meted out to Hannes in these pages.

Operation Safehaven was a real effort by the US Treasury Department and the Office of Strategic Services to contain and control the vast riches built up by the Nazis and deposited in neutral nations. While Safehaven did identify a great deal of looted wealth, it was never able to secure all questionable accounts in Swiss hands. Swiss banks stonewalled efforts to determine the extent of holdings, and the controversy continued for decades.

The description of conditions at the Wauwilermoos prison have been taken from historical records. The treatment of Allied prisoners was much worse than that of German fliers who were downed over Swiss airspace. The sadistic commander of that prison, Captain André Béguin, was finally arrested by Swiss authorities in September 1945. A Swiss military court called Béguin a "crook, embezzler, con-man and inhuman." He was convicted of dishonoring Switzerland and its army, administrative misdemeanors, embezzlement, and abuse of authority. He served three and a half years in prison. The italicized passages in Chapter 23 are taken from an actual report from the

International Committee of the Red Cross following an inspection of the camp.

Moe Berg, "the smartest man in baseball," is a fascinating historical character. His spy career began in 1934, when as part of a baseball team (which included Babe Ruth and Lou Gehrig) on a good-will tour of Japan, he slipped away to film home movies from the top of the tallest building in Tokyo. That film was used by the military in planning the famous Doolittle raid on Japan in 1942.

Berg was assigned to attend the lecture in Switzerland given by Werner Heisenberg in 1944. He was the only OSS spy smart enough, and fluent enough in German, to get away with it. Not only did Berg get into the lecture, he befriended Heisenberg and joined him for dinner that night. After an evening's conversation, Berg let him live, confident that Germany was nowhere near the development of an atom bomb.

The record of Switzerland and refugees during the Second World War cries out for comment. Almost 30,000 Jews were turned back at the border, where they could expect to be sent to concentration camps. About 25,000 were allowed entry. Switzerland levied a tax on their Jewish citizens to help pay for Jewish refugees, a burden not imposed on any other group. In addition, Jews who escaped across the border and were arrested often found themselves charged for transportation back to the border crossing, where they were handed over to the Nazis.

Dr. Rudolph Moret is based on the experiences of Dr. Rudolf Bucher, a Swiss Army medical officer who went on a medical mission to the Eastern Front in 1941–42, and witnessed the atrocities described by the fictional Dr. Moret. Bucher suffered the same fate, stripped of his commission and ostracized for the crime of speaking the truth.

The Roma (Gypsy) genocide during the Second World War, also known as the *Porrajmos*, was part of the plan to exterminate Jews, Gypsies, and other "enemies of the race-based state" by the Nazis. Historians do not agree on the number of Roma killed; estimates range from 220,000 to 1.5 million. Roma were systematically turned away at the Swiss border during the war and left to make their way in German-occupied France.

The character of Maureen Conaty is a stand-in for the real-life Mary Bancroft, who was an OSS spy and one of the many real-life mistresses of Allen Foster Dulles. Maureen Conaty won a character naming at the Murder and Mayhem in Milwaukee mystery conference, and therefore got to play the role of Mary Bancroft. Those were tough high heels to fill.

Bancroft worked closely with Hans Bernd Gisevius, who provided her with information concerning the anti-Nazi July 20 plot to kill Hitler. Bancroft and Gisevius also had an affair, making Bern a hotbed of espionage in more ways than one. Gisevius survived the war, going into hiding after the failed July 20 plot and fleeing to Switzerland in 1945.

Finally, gays and lesbians served and fought in all theaters during the Second World War. Theirs was a secret struggle, even as gay soldiers went into combat with the same fears and bravery as their heterosexual comrades. Their story deserves to be told, even though after decades of hidden secrets, many accounts may be lost forever. For readers wishing a more in-depth look, I heartily recommend *Coming Out Under Fire: The History of Gay Men and Women in World War Two*, by Allan Bérubé.